THE BREAK-UP RETREAT

ALSO BY CAMILLA STEN

The Bachelorette Party
The Lost Village
The Resting Place

THE BREAK-UP RETREAT

A NOVEL

CAMILLA STEN

MINOTAUR BOOKS
NEW YORK

This is a work of fiction. All of the names, characters, organizations, places, and events portrayed in this work are either products of the author's imagination or are used fictitiously.

First published in the United States by Minotaur Books,
an imprint of St. Martin's Publishing Group

EU Representative: Macmillan Publishers Ireland Ltd, 1st Floor, The Liffey Trust Centre,
117–126 Sheriff Street Upper, Dublin 1, D01 YC43

www.minotaurbooks.com

Designed by Steven Seighman

The Library of Congress Cataloging-in-Publication Data is available upon request.

ISBN 978-1-250-86852-7 (hardcover)
ISBN 978-1-250-86853-4 (ebook)

First Edition: 2026

10 9 8 7 6 5 4 3 2 1

To the amazing therapists and psychologists
who have helped me through the years.
You saved my life.

HEARTBREAK DOESN'T HAVE TO BE THE END.

It can be a new beginning. A doorway into your future.

Growing up, we were taught to seek our happy endings in relationships. When you were little, you were told that one day your prince, or princess, would come—and that on that day, all your troubles would disappear.

But no one ever taught you how to pick the right person.

We are often told we have to choose between our heart and our ambition; between romance and self-actualization. But love is part of a full, healthy life.

You should not have to feel ashamed of wanting love. You shouldn't have to feel embarrassed over not having found it.

You just don't have the right set of tools.

But we can help you find them.

Imagine what you could do with all the hours you have spent on the wrong relationships. Imagine the kind of person you could be if you knew how to find, and pick, the right partner.

With our revolutionary approach to attachment therapy,* we here at the Himlafall Clinic believe that you shouldn't have to choose. You can, and deserve to, have everything you want.

Whether you need help discovering and breaking out of bad patterns, soothing your inner child, reprogramming your attachment style, disrupting people-pleasing tendencies, or simply finding peace within, we can help you.

---

*All therapy is performed by licensed psychotherapists, psychologists, or psychiatrists.

At our state-of-the-art facilities, we offer a unique one-week therapeutic inpatient treatment program to help you heal and grow.[†] The program has been designed by our founder, the world-renowned Dr. Martina Hastings.

At the Himlafall Clinic, we don't believe that you need to be fixed. We believe that, given the right set of tools, and the right kind of support, you can create the life you want for yourself.

And we would be honored to accompany you on your journey.

No one can complete you but you.

Welcome to the Himlafall Clinic.[‡]

FURTHER READING ABOUT THE HIMLAFALL CLINIC

Vogue Scandinavia
Psychology Today
Elle Sweden
PopSugar
Cosmopolitan Europe

FURTHER READING ABOUT DR. MARTINA HASTINGS

"Meet the Psychologist Revolutionizing Romance," *The Guardian*, March 11, 2022.
"How Dr. Martina Hastings Turned Her Divorce into a Radical New Movement," *Stockholm Daily*, July 9, 2022.

DO YOU WANT TO BUY DR. MARTINA'S LATEST BOOK?

Freud's Ex-Girlfriend: A Psychologist's Guide to Break-Ups, Amazon Sweden.

[†]Any specific dietary needs should be reported at least one week before arrival at the Himlafall Clinic. The Himlafall Clinic is not legally or financially responsible for any allergic reactions, illnesses, or other negative health conditions that might result as a consequence of failing to do so.

[‡]The Himlafall Clinic is a privately owned and operated medical facility. As such, you need a referral from a doctor in order to apply for treatment at the Himlafall Clinic. The Himlafall Clinic does not accept insurance. Payment expected in full one week before admittance.

Chapter 1

DESPITE BLASTING THE AIR-CONDITIONING, MY HANDS ARE sweaty on the steering wheel. The sun seems brighter up north than I'm used to, the light so harsh and white I'm squinting through the windshield despite my sunglasses.

The car smells like stress sweat, and antiseptic cleaning agent, and pine, courtesy of the jaunty little air freshener hanging from the mirror. It's bright pink and heart-shaped, which makes me think it *should* smell like strawberry, something that irritates me more than it ought to.

The combination of smells reminds me of a hospital room. I wonder if the car rental people thought about that. If there was some other, worse smell here before, and they decided this was preferable.

I've been on the road for over four hours now, the rolling fields of sprouting wheat and rye slowly and steadily being replaced by woods, first sparse and lush, now thick and impenetrable. I've only stopped twice, first to use the bathroom, then to get some terrible burnt roadside coffee.

When my phone rings, I twitch, my hands slipping on the wheel momentarily. For a second, I think it'll be them, somehow. That they're calling to tell me they know that I'm a fraud, that they've reported me to the police, and that I won't be admitted to the clinic.

But then I see the name flashing on the fancy Bluetooth-connected touch screen on the dashboard, and I feel myself relaxing for the first time today.

It takes me a couple of seconds to figure out how to accept the call, but then my best friend's voice fills the car at maximum volume.

"Isobel!" Armin yells at me.

"Holy fuck, that's loud." I struggle to turn the volume down. As I fiddle with the different faux buttons on the touch screen, I once again curse inwardly over my decision to get a shiny modern vehicle at the rental place.

I thought it would help with my cover story. But I won't have any use for a cover story if I end up crashing the rented car into a tree because I can't figure out how to operate it.

"Are you still alive?" Armin asks me as I finally manage to get his voice down to a manageable level.

"More or less," I respond, noticing that I'm using my speakerphone voice but unable to stop myself. Slightly louder and more articulated than normal, as though I'm talking to someone who's hard of hearing.

"Have they murdered you yet?" he continues, not acknowledging what I've said. "Did they tar and feather you? Or put you in a bear costume and burn you in a pagan ritual? Put a cage full of bees on your head?"

"Not yet." I laugh. "But I am still on my way there, so don't give up hope."

Armin sighs.

"All I want is to be interviewed for one of those true crime podcasts," he ponders wistfully. "Like, I want to go on *My Favorite Murder* or *The Witching Hour* and talk about what a wonderful person you were, and how all I want is to see justice served."

"I don't think they are doing *The Witching Hour* anymore," I say, mildly distracted by a sign warning me for potential moose crossings up ahead.

Jesus, I really am in the rural north.

"Also, I think you'd come across better on TV. One of those Netflix originals, you know?"

Armin hums thoughtfully.

"You might have a point there," he says. "I know exactly what I'd wear, too."

"Well, I'll do my very best to get murdered so that your dreams can come true," I tell him, a smile still lingering on my face as my anxiety begins to fade, little by little.

"Seriously, though." Armin's voice grows serious. "How are you feeling? Still feeling good? Pumped?"

I consider lying, but he'd hear it in my voice if I did.

"Nervous, mostly," I respond. "But it's too late to back out now."

A few moments of silence pass by, and then he says, the levity leeched from his voice, "If you want to back out, I'll help you out with it. I can loan you some money, you know."

A pang of something akin to shame hits me, makes my palms prickle and my cheeks grow hot.

"I'd never ask you for that," I say, trying make it sound lighthearted, knowing I'm not successful.

"I know," Armin sighs. "I know that. But I just wanted to offer." He pauses for a moment, and then adds: "Again."

There is a lingering discomfort in the silence that follows, stemming from the talk we had last night.

I can see his face as clearly now as I could fourteen hours ago, sitting in a small, dingy pub—my choice, not his—his sharp, regal features softened by the dim lighting, his eyes full of concern.

It hadn't been a fight. Not really. But it had been as close to a fight as we'd had since we were teenagers.

"All right," he says, clearly making an effort to try and brighten the mood. "I'll quiz you before you get there. How did you hear about the Break-Up Rehab?"

"They won't call it that," I correct him. "Apparently, they're very particular about calling it by its legal name."

Another car passes me, going the opposite direction; it's a sleek, shiny gray BMW. There's a woman in the driver's seat.

For a fleeting second, I wonder if she's coming from the clinic, but then I shake off the thought. There are lots of other reasons she'd be on this road.

Most of the people going to the clinic probably don't drive themselves there, either. Based on the price tag, they probably have a driver take them.

Or a helicopter.

More likely, the woman just lives somewhere around here, in one of the small, quaint, interchangeable towns I've passed in the last hour and a half.

She might not even be aware of the clinic, or the rumors around it, at all.

"Fine," Armin says. "How did you hear about *the Himlafall Clinic*?"

I smirk at the mockery in his voice.

"Well, I first heard about *the Himlafall Clinic*—"

"You can't say it like that," he interrupts me. "They will sus you out. You have to say it like you mean it."

"Fine," I say, taking a deep breath. "I first heard about the Himlafall Clinic a few months ago. An influencer I was following went to the clinic after separating from her partner, and the way she spoke about her experience really made an impact on me."

"Which influencer?" Armin shoots back, lightning quick.

"Lina Lee," I answer immediately. "Suck it," I add.

"I'm on your side, dickhead," Armin mutters, before continuing. "Okay, Lina Lee, very good."

"Do you know who Lina Lee is?" I ask him.

"Yeah. Tanya was obsessed with her. She used to make me look at pictures of Lina Lee and ask me if I thought she was prettier than her."

"Shocker that the relationship didn't work out," I say, my voice dry as a bone.

"Yeah, yeah," Armin says. "Whatever. We're not talking about me. Back to your cover story. So, Isobel, what made you decide to seek out treatment at the clinic?"

I strike a sad, beaten-down tone.

"My boyfriend of four years, Kaveh, broke up with me a month ago," I say, adding a tremor to my voice. "I felt like my whole life fell apart. I couldn't sleep, couldn't work. . . . I lost almost twenty pounds because I couldn't keep any food down."

"Tell me more about this boyfriend," Armin says. "Very handsome, was he? Successful? Grew up with three sisters, which meant he wasn't embarrassed to buy tampons for you?"

I laugh.

"Yeah, he was a real catch. Love of my life." I feel awkward after saying that, and, so as not to let it linger, I add: "Thanks again for agreeing to lend me your pictures for the Instagram, by the way."

"No problem," he says. "I'm honored you asked me to play the role of the scoundrel who broke your heart."

I've been building the fake social media account for about four months at this point. I named it @IsobelAnderssen01, mentioned in the first post that my previous (nonexistent) account had been hacked in order to justify why it didn't go farther back. I started posting pictures of food and cute dogs and, once in a while, Armin, with cutesy couple captions like "Brunch with this one!" and "We scrub up pretty good!" All to build the image of a normal woman in an average over-thirty relationship, someone who was pretty sure she was heading for marriage and two-point-four kids within a couple of years.

And then, a month ago, I let the account go dark.

"Do you really think they are going to look you up?" Armin asks me.

"I don't know," I say. "But based on what I've heard . . . maybe."

The road has started climbing again, and the car climbs along with it. According to the map, I'm getting close. Only five minutes to go.

"Listen," Armin says, and I hear all the things he's not saying in the silent seconds that follow, an echo from last night.

"I'm really not sure this is a good idea, Isobel. It's a lot of money. You might not find anything. And I'm still not convinced this doesn't legally constitute fraud."

"Just . . . take care of yourself, okay?"

I don't know if I imagine his voice wavering.

"You know I will," I say, quietly. "And I won't be alone. Sandra is going to be there. You know she'd never let anything happen to me. She's a mama bear."

"I know. She told me the same thing a couple of days ago when I called her to try to talk her out of it." He sighs. "Call me every day, okay? And don't get angry with me for saying this, but if you change your mind, I can come pick you up. I'll pose as your boyfriend. Say that I decided I couldn't live without you, that I've changed my ways."

"It's going to be fine," I tell him.

Just as I reach the crest of the hill, I see the sign.

It doesn't look like the other road signs. This one has clearly not been put up by the government, which makes me wonder if it's even legal, but with the amount of taxes Himlafall Clinic must be paying, I can't imagine anyone caring.

It's a slim wooden sign, about four feet long, painted a partially transparent white to show the wood underneath, which makes it look like a naked cake.

On the sign is written, in tall, slightly curling letters:

WELCOME TO HIMLAFALL. YOUR NEW LIFE BEGINS TODAY.

. . . with an arrow pointing down a wide, well-kept side road.

"I think I'm here," I tell Armin, breath slightly catching. "I mean, I think *it's* here. I think I've made it."

"Last chance to turn back," Armin says, and I know he's only halfway joking. If that.

"Seriously, it's going to be fine," I laugh, my voice pitched high, my heart thrumming in my chest.

I'm anxious, sure. But I'm also excited.

After so many long hours alone in my room, trying to get people to come forward, setting up my trail of breadcrumbs, taking out a loan I might not be able to pay back . . . I'm finally here.

It's been six months and four days since I stumbled upon the forum post that set me on this path.

If all goes right, I'll be able to take the Himlafall Clinic, and Dr. Martina Hastings, down.

Kick-start the career that has, so far, utterly failed to materialize.

And maybe, just maybe, once and for all, prove to both myself and the world that I am nothing like the man who raised me.

If I pull this off, the sign will have been right. My new life will, indeed, have started today.

r/SelfImprovement
02:13 12/07/2023
i think my sister is in a cult and i don't know what to do
posted by: u/maxwallin (user deleted)

susie, i know you go on this page a lot. if you see this, please just let me know you are okay.

does anyone have any experience with cult deprogramming?

background: my sister has always been v. susceptible to outside influences. shes passionate but not much of a critical thinker. she got really churchy in our teenage years, then after high school she abandoned her softball scholarship to start selling cheap makeup for one of those multilevel marketing things. every time she falls in love its "the one." you probably know the type.

ive never worried too much before bcs i thought she would grow out of it. she met someone a few months ago and they got engaged. i thought maybe she was finally growing up. stupid, maybe, but i had my own life and problems. not making excuses, just saying how it felt.

but then the relationship fell apart. im not sure what happened, but next thing we know she's taken all her savings and all the money she's put aside for the wedding to go to some kind of "break-up rehab"? i thought it seemed insane but our mom thought it might be good for her. i looked it up and it sounded legit.

but then she just cut all of us off. at first she wouldnt take any of our calls, and then it just said that her phone number had been disconnected. i tried going to her apartment but she wouldnt answer the door. or she wasnt there. i texted and called all of her friends, and they said they hadnt heard from her. i got in touch with her gym and the club where she plays tennis and they said she hasnt been around in months. i even tried to get in touch with her ex and just got a short text msg saying "havent seen her, dont contact me again."

im so worried. she went away in september. no one in my family has heard from her in months. i called the so-called treatment facility and they said that she had already left. they wouldnt tell me if anything had happened. i made a report to the police and they said they would look into it but i dont think they even took me seriously. i dont know if they even made a report.

the place is called himlafall clinic. its really fancy. if you look it up online you see all these people talking about what a great experience they had and how it changed their lives. i feel like im going crazy. my mom thinks my sister is just going through something but this isnt like her. it seems like this place is some kind of cult and im worried they brainwashed her or did something to her.

does anyone know if there is something i could say to the police to get them to take me seriously? i dont have a lot of money but if there is someone you can hire to help then i can give them what i have.

im just so scared and worried for her. shes my baby sister. i just want to make sure she is okay.

2 upvotes
1 comment

AutoMod—02:19 12/07/2023

This post has been closed due to not following rule #1 ("Posts must fit the 'self-improvement' mindset").

Your post does not fit the parameters for r/SelfImprovement. Please rewrite your post and resubmit.

Chapter 2

THE FIRST THING I FOUND WHEN I STARTED LOOKING UP THE Himlafall Clinic six months ago was that there were no pictures of the premises anywhere on the internet.

There were plenty of interviews with the founder, Martina Hastings—the so-called revolutionary new actor whose romance-centric vision of psychological treatment is changing the world—but they were all performed in the safety of hotel restaurants; cozy little coffee shops; or, on one occasion, which resulted in a clearly very starstruck reporter, an exclusive private club.

The topic of the lack of images came up in a couple of the interviews I found, and Martina always gave a variation on the same answer.

"I want our clients to come to us without any preconceptions, with a completely clean slate. It's important for the success of our treatment model. We also put a high value on our clients' privacy. Even a faraway picture might give away a client's identity, from a reflection or a silhouette, and the very possibility of that goes against our basic philosophy. All our employees sign NDAs when they start working with us, and our guests do as well."

The reporter had tried to ask a couple of inferred questions about some of the rumored celebrity clients—a famous musician, a well-known Danish director—but Martina had deflected with a laughter the reporter had described as "strangely seductive," while also getting in a quick description of her impressively toned shoulders.

"Some deeply vulnerable things are processed at the Himlafall Clinic, and

that is built on a level of trust that is incredibly precious to me. I want to do my best to honor that."

So when my car rolls up to the gates, I, like all the other patients to have ever arrived at the Himlafall Clinic, am seeing it for the first time.

From a distance, it looks like a farm. Low buildings, close to the ground, half-covered in ivy, all painted white, with small windows and tiled roofs, all in a row on the near side of a small, picturesque pond.

The road is blocked off with a pretty, ornate cast-iron fence. It's low enough that a woman of average height would be able to climb it, as long as her pants were stretchy and she wasn't wearing heels, but I can't drive through the gates. Instead, I have to stop my rental car and get out of the driver's seat.

It's colder than I expected, but the air is pleasantly crisp, as opposed to biting; the pale white sun in the sky holds more warmth than I would have thought.

The aesthetic of the fence is somewhat ruined by the massive, clunky intercom on the left-hand side. There's only one button; I press it and step back as the voice of a young woman comes through, as clear as if she was standing right in front of me.

"Welcome to Himlafall Clinic. How can I help you today?"

For a moment, I wonder if it's Martina Hastings herself, but I quickly reject the notion. Martina is the owner, founder, and face of the operation. Surely she's much too important to man the intercom.

Whoever it is I'm talking to must be one of the employees. Her voice sounds breathy and ethereal. I resist the urge to ask if she has to talk like that, and instead say:

"Hi, yeah, this is Isobel . . . Anderssen." I correct myself at the last minute; my real last name almost slips out. Pure muscle memory.

"I'm supposed to check in today? I think I'm a bit early."

"No problem at all, Isobel," the voice responds, in a tone that suggests she's delighted by my early arrival, and by the sound of my voice, and, indeed, by my very existence. "I'll open the gates. Did you arrive here by car?"

"Yes, I did," I say.

"The parking lot is on your left-hand side. Belinda will come and greet you."

A brief pause, and then she adds, with an extra helping of warmth:

"We're truly so happy you're here, Isobel. I look forward to getting to know you."

The intercom beeps, and after a few short seconds, the gates start opening inward.

I get back into the driver's seat and start up the road.

As I get closer, little details begin to come into view. The wildflowers peeking out through the moss on both sides of the driveway; the blueberry bushes crowded beneath the windowsills of the buildings, little white buds just starting to form on their spiky branches.

I can see three small, neat cabins from over here, and two larger houses on the other side of what looks to be the main building.

If Armin was here with me, he'd make a joke about it. He'd say something like, "*That big one at the end is probably where they do their satanic rituals.*"

I feel a pang in my chest. For a second, I turn back in my seat, but the gates have already closed behind me.

It feels like my chest is constricting.

Don't panic, Isobel. It's going to be fine. You've been planning this for months. You can leave whenever you want.

The road branches off to my left, and, just as described, I see a small parking lot under a corrugated steel roof. There are seven cars parked there, and three spaces still open.

I ease the car into one of the free spaces, terrified of scratching the electric BMW parked next to it; the Toyota Camry is bigger than what I'm used to driving, which would be an electric scooter. I could barely cover the cost of the two weeks for the rental. If I dent someone's luxury car, I'll have to run away in the dark of night and pray they don't try to find me.

Once I manage to ease the car into the space, I try to exhale, but some of the air still feels like it's stuck in there. My ribs hurt, and I try to tell myself it's from the seat belt and the five-hour drive.

I close my eyes, breathe in deep through my nostrils.

Then I force myself to think of every job interview I've been to in the last seven years. Every gray, worn-out-looking elder journalist who's peered at my résumé through bifocals, lines etched around their eyes, stress pulling the corners of their mouths down before they look up to meet my pathetically hopeful gaze.

The sympathy is always the worst part. That, and the explanations.

Hiring freeze right now . . . Really looking for someone with more of an established following . . . Is there any chance you speak German? Or Mandarin? No?

Maybe try to build up your portfolio. Do some more freelance work.

Have you thought about applying for an internship?

I've been in so many of those sad little conference rooms over the years. Borrowed so many ill-fitting nice blazers from friends. Pored over my résumé for hours, trying to find the right wording, attempting to tweak it to perfection. Written and rewritten my work samples, hoping that a single sentence might break through the fog, show someone, anyone, that despite the shitty economy, despite my lack of on-the-job experience, and despite the cratering newspaper industry, I'm worth taking a chance on.

When I started studying journalism, everyone told me not to. My mother cried when I insisted that this was the path I wanted to take.

She told me it was a job without any security, that I'd be better off going into something more stable, something with some promise. Like law, or finance, or computer programming.

She told me I had nothing to prove.

She told me that I was just trying to fix history, and that I would be better served to just move on.

But I insisted, and she let me go.

She wanted me to burn the past and look forward, like she had. She couldn't understand that that was never an option for me.

My fingers go to the pendant resting between my collarbones. I almost left it behind, but just as I've almost thrown it out hundreds of times, I couldn't quite bring myself to do it.

My father gave it to me on my fourteenth birthday. A silver rose, small and exquisite. A little inside joke, since his name was Rosenwald. The name I bore as well.

I could sever myself from the ruined family name. But I couldn't cut off the half of me that had grown in tainted soil.

I can only try to cleanse it. Prove myself different. Show the world, and everyone who doubted me, that they were wrong to do so.

And now I might have a story. I might have the kind of story that's good enough, juicy enough, *important* enough that it'll get syndicated. That it will spread like wildfire through the world and make it clear, once and for all, that I am someone to be counted on.

This is my shot. Himlafall Clinic is my shot.

All I have to do is not fuck it up.

The knock on the window makes me yelp and open my eyes.

A smiling, beautiful face peers in at me. A quick impression of very white, very even teeth and the kind of freckles influencers spend hours trying to fake with liquid bronzer.

"Hi!" the woman says and waves at me through the window, her voice ever so slightly muted by the glass. "You must be Isobel!"

I nod.

"I'm Belinda," she says, still smiling. "If you're all ready to go, I'm here to bring you to Martina."

Chapter 3

As Belinda leads me into the main building, making pleasant chitchat most likely meant to soothe and welcome me, I can feel my mouth growing ever drier. I take in vague snapshots of the pleasant surroundings—the well-groomed graveled path, the white paint still gleaming on the wooden walls, the smooth rocks scattered artfully along the road. When I look closer at them, I see that they have self-help aphorisms written on them.

You contain the world.

The door will open when you are ready.

Dear God.

Belinda opens the door for me when we reach the end of the path and seems to notice my half a second of hesitation.

She leans in and puts her hand on my shoulder, squeezing it reassuringly. The gentle pressure and soft warmth of her palm does calm me down.

I wonder if they have to practice that squeeze. If it's part of the training the employees go through.

"It's okay," Belinda encourages me, with a small, gentle smile on her lips. She's about my height, and she's wearing a white T-shirt tucked into black pants. She doesn't look like a nurse—with her clean-faced good looks and smooth, elegant voice, she might as well have been a mixologist at a molecular cocktail bar too upscale for my empty wallet.

"You've made a really brave decision coming here. I understand it must be scary."

If you only knew.

"What's she like?" I ask her. "Martina?"

Belinda's smile remains fixed on her perfect lips. No part of her face moves.

"Well, I'll let you get your own impression of Dr. Martina," she says. "I don't want to spoil the surprise."

There is a reception right in front of the door, a low, smooth desk in light polished wood. Another woman is sitting behind it; she looks to be in her early thirties, her white-blond locks in a high ponytail, not a hair out of place. There is a small name tag on her white linen shirt that says *Anna*, and she smiles at me before nodding at Belinda.

"Is this Isobel?" she asks Belinda, who turns to me and smiles encouragingly.

I feel like a kindergartner, like my mother is trying to get me to practice introducing myself to new people.

"Uh, yeah," I say. "Hi."

"So lovely to have you here," Anna says to me, all sunshine and sincerity, and then she continues, to Belinda, "Dr. Martina is ready for her."

Belinda turns to me.

"Right this way," she says, leading me to the left, down the hallway.

There is no art on the walls, no photographs, just large potted plants with wide, sharp deep-green leaves standing sturdily on the floor and small, neat signs outside every door.

GROUP THERAPY OFFICE 2

PHYSICAL THERAPY ROOM 1

Belinda stops outside the last door on the left and raises her hand to knock, when something suddenly occurs to me, and I stop her.

"Wait," I blurt out. "I left my bags in my car."

Belinda, her hand still held high, looks at me and says:

"Yes, that's perfectly normal. I will go get them for you and take them to your cabin while you're having your talk with Dr. Martina."

She smiles again, like an afterthought.

"But . . ."

Belinda lowers her hand. She reaches out and clasps my fingers in her own.

"I know you're probably the kind of person who is used to having to take care of everything themselves," she says quietly. "But part of this journey is learning to let yourself be taken care of. Can you trust that, if you let go just a little bit, we will make sure it gets done?"

I keep my face still, hoping my sudden bolt of anxiety isn't showing.

What if they search my bags?

But she must see what I'm thinking, because that sweet serenity cracks, and Belinda lets out a laugh. It's lower and harsher than her speaking voice, and I find I like it significantly better.

"Oh, don't you worry," she says, eyes crinkling at the corners, and, in a conspiratorial whisper, continues, "We're sex positive here. No matter what toys you brought, I guarantee you we won't judge. My Satisfyer got me through my last two break-ups."

I laugh too, partly out of surprise, mostly out of relief.

It's not a vibrator I'm concerned they will find.

"Thank God," I exhale.

Belinda, still laughing a bit, raises her hand and knocks on the door before opening it.

"Dr. Martina?" she says. "Isobel Anderssen is here to see you."

Chapter 4

Dr. Martina Hastings, author of the internationally bestselling self-help book *Freud's Ex-Girlfriend* and founder of the Himlafall Clinic, is shorter in person than she looks on TV.

She's got the kind of polish I associate with the famous and the very dedicated, a white linen button-down that falls just so, tucked into straight-legged jeans so artfully worn in that I assume they cost more than my rent.

Shamefully, I feel a little frisson when I recognize the necklace resting in the hollow of her throat. It's a golden Aum, inherited from her British Indian mother. She wrote about it in *Freud's Ex-Girlfriend*; I've seen it hanging around her neck in the countless TV interviews I've watched on YouTube.

"Hi, Isobel," she says, smiling like we're old friends. Like I've only been gone for a few minutes, ducked out for coffee.

It's oddly disconcerting.

"Hello," I squeak out, just as I hear the door shutting behind me. I look back reflexively and see that Belinda has left.

When I turn back, Martina has come out from behind her desk.

"Please, sit," she says, gesturing to the beautiful chairs standing in front of her desk. They look old, the seat and backrest clad in bottle-green leather, the dark wood polished to a high shine.

"Would you like something to drink? Tea, maybe? I would offer you coffee, but I generally recommend that patients stay away from stimulants for the first few days here. It's up to you, of course, but your nervous system is already in flux. I have a lovely rose tea here. I brought it back from London last time I went to visit my mother. Would you like to try it?"

The steady stream of words makes it feel impossible to argue with her.

I sit down in a chair, which is, not surprisingly, extremely comfortable, and just manage to eke out a:

"Sure. That sounds nice. Thank you."

Martina's office is small but beautiful; there is a matching deep-green couch and armchair by the tall window, separated by a low coffee table, and a bookshelf on the opposite wall right next to the little counter where she is busying herself with a kettle and two stoneware mugs.

I see all three of her books on the top shelf—the first two, *How to Be an Adult: A Survival Guide to Your 20s* and *I'm Thriving, Thanks: A Good Girl's Guide to Avoiding Burnout*, launched her into the public consciousness some eight or nine years ago. But it was the third one, the one staring at me both from the bookshelf and from the framed, shockingly pink book cover blown up on the wall, that turned her into a superstar.

The kettle beeps, and Martina pours two cups of tea, swiftly places one in front of me on the desk, and then sits back down, cupping her mug with both hands and smiling at me.

"You know, I still think that tea was what got me through my divorce," she says. It sounds conversational, off the cuff, but I'd be willing to bet money on her having said the same thing in the exact same way to every single woman who's come through this clinic.

The true mark of a skilled manipulator is the ability to make scripts sound spontaneous, to turn the canned and commonplace into something intimate and special.

I should know.

"Well, Isobel," she continues, tilting her head just so, making her expertly highlighted hair slide gently off her shoulder. Holding my gaze. "Tell me about you."

I open my mouth to get my well-practiced story out and find that it sticks in my chest.

Jesus. How embarrassing. I think I'm actually a little bit starstruck.

It's just strange, finally sitting face-to-face with the woman whose pictures have been staring back at me from the computer screen for months on end. I know her public biography forward and backward. I've read both raving testimonials and hushed anonymous condemnations of her work.

I know as much about her as her most fervent fans.

And now here she is, in the flesh.

She doesn't look dangerous.

But that doesn't mean anything.

Predators are so often pretty to look at.

I can feel a blush creeping up my neck, and reflexively, I put my hand to it.

"I'm sorry," I say. "I don't know what's wrong with me."

I've decided that Isobel Anderssen, my wounded alter ego, is insecure; wilting rather than shy.

"Don't worry," Martina says, smiling in a way that seems designed to be disarming. "You can take your time. You must be exhausted."

I give a nervous little laugh.

"Yeah," I admit. "I haven't slept a full night in weeks."

It's the truth. Just not for the reason she thinks.

Martina presses her lips together, furrows her brow.

"Tell me what happened," she urges me, in a voice that is both a whisper and a command.

Showtime.

"It's just . . . I thought it was all going so well, you know? I thought we were so happy together, and then it all just . . . fell apart. So fast."

"Tell me about him," Dr. Martina encourages me.

"I met Kaveh on Tinder," I start. "I know, not very romantic, but I wanted to meet someone. I felt like I was ready for something real. We didn't really click over text, but I agreed to meet him for drinks anyway, and then when we actually met, it was like . . ." I snap my fingers, and then I hide my face in my hands.

Oh, God. Was that too much? It's very quiet in here. All I can hear is the ticking of the clock on the wall.

I hear something sliding over the surface of the desk.

"Take your time," Martina soothes me. "We're not in a hurry."

When I look up, I see a box of organic tissues. I reach for one despite my dry eyes.

"I just feel so lost ever since he left," I continue. "I thought he was the love of my life. When we met, I felt like . . . like it made it all okay, you know? Like all the mistakes I had made in the past, all the bad people I had picked, were worth it because it had all led me to him. And I thought he felt the same way. I mean, we moved in together after our fifth date." I stop, take a deep breath, before continuing.

"He'd been acting a little weird for a couple of weeks, but I thought . . ." I swallow to make it seem like the words are burning my lips.

"I thought he might have been planning a proposal," I say. "When he said he wanted to break up, I thought he was kidding at first." I close my eyes and shake my head.

"You're embarrassed," Martina says. "You feel humiliated."

I open my eyes.

Martina is resting her elbows on the table, leaning forward, looking at me intently.

"Yes," I say.

"You felt like you had spent so long looking for this thing, thinking it would complete you," she continues. "Trying, over and over again, and getting rejected, again and again. You pretended to be fine, and pretended that it was all okay, but it started to eat away at you. You started to wonder, after a while, why it seemed so easy for other people. Why everyone else seemed to get this thing that you wanted, more than anything, and why you were still there, stuck in place, fighting desperately and getting nowhere, all while having to pretend that you didn't care so that no one would see how much it hurt you."

My mouth has gone dry.

I see flashes of those interviews again. All those sad, resigned faces. My hands trembling with impotent anger under the table.

The faint disappointment in my mother's voice.

The long, dark nights when I couldn't sleep, when it was too late to call my mother, or Armin, or Sandra, or anyone else, when the weight of all my little failures threatened to crush me.

"Something like that." For a moment, it's not Isobel Anderssen speaking. It's me.

Martina smiles, but her eyes are sad.

"You've been working so hard for such a long time," she says. "You must be very tired."

"It's just hard to feel like you have a piece missing," I hear myself say. "I wonder if there's something about me . . . if I'm stuck. If I made the wrong decision, a long time ago, and maybe I'm just too stubborn to let go of it."

I have to stop. Get ahold of myself.

"You're hurt," Martina notes. "That's natural. And you've been hurt so many times, you've learned to cut yourself off from the things that hurt you."

Martina reaches out across the table and touches my hand, ever so softly.

"I really am so glad you are here, Isobel," Martina says. "I think you're going to be shocked to see where you are in just a week's time. I think you are going to be truly surprised at the person you can be once your past is no longer holding you back."

Martina pulls her hand away and then bares every single shining white tooth in an unbearably radiant smile before saying:

"One last thing. Before Anna comes and brings you to your cabin, I just want to make sure that we have your card on file."

I freeze where I'm sitting.

Then I have to hold back a laugh. Of course.

I was almost taken in there for a minute. She's better than I expected; better, I think, than I could have been prepared for.

But I'm not here for me. Not here to heal whatever petty little wounds I might think I'm carrying.

I'm here for the women I've read about. The ones who have sat in this chair before me, feeling hope for the first time in weeks, or months, or years.

The ones who have taken out loans against their homes to fund their stay, hoping, desperately, that this doctor and this clinic might be the thing that can help them finally find the piece they have been convinced they are missing.

The ones who have been convinced to go back to relationships they ought to have left, because Martina Hastings told them to.

And the ones who never came back from Himlafall at all.

"Sure," I say, smiling back at her. "Of course."

"Saddened, but relieved"—Dr. Martina Hastings speaks out about recent investigation
by Greta Ludwigsson
08:24 04/09/2024

The investigation that was initiated by the SPA's Ethics Board against the Himlafall Clinic last fall after anonymous accusations were filed alleging patient abuse has found no evidence of wrongdoing. In conversation with *Stockholm Daily*, founder Dr. Martina Hastings says she is happy but not surprised with the ruling.

The Himlafall Clinic is a privately owned psychological treatment center founded and run by Dr. Martina Hastings, known from her internationally bestselling book *Freud's Ex-Girlfriend* and her work as the on-staff psychologist for *Good Morning, Stockholm*. The Himlafall Clinic opened in June of 2022 and has been operating ever since, treating patients seeking help for problems with romantic relationships.

In October, Dr. Martina spoke out on her Instagram account about the fact that the Swedish Psychologist's Association's Ethics Board had opened an investigation into the clinic after a person who wished to remain anonymous had filed a complaint. According to Dr. Martina's statement, the person had alleged that the clinic was mistreating its patients, providing insufficient support, and neglecting to meet the standard of care set for in-patient treatment centers.

"Basically, they are saying that we are gaslighting and abusing the people who come to us for help, and I have to admit that that hurts my heart," Dr. Martina said in the video, posted on October 19. "But I welcome the investigation. I want our current and future patients to feel completely safe in our care, and I am confident that the SPA will find that they are."

When asked to comment on the conclusion of the investigation, Dr. Martina said that she is happy with how the process has been handled.

"The SPA investigators treated us with the utmost respect, but I have to admit, I'll be glad to put this behind me. As any kind of caregiver will tell you, when you dedicate your life to helping other people, it's painful to have your methods and motivations questioned."

When asked whether they will be changing their procedures following the investigation, Dr. Martina said no.

"Our method has a solid scientific basis, and in the last two years, we have seen truly fantastic results with our patients. I do not believe that a patient of ours was the one to file the complaint. Sadly, many of the women who come through our clinic have been in toxic and sometimes abusive relationships. When I started my work with the Himlafall Clinic, I knew there was a risk of retaliation from jilted ex-lovers. All we can do is keep performing the work, remember the importance of it, and hope that the people who would do something like this will find the strength to seek out the care they need."

Chapter 5

As the other caretaker, Anna, leads me out of the building, the cold, crisp air jolts me back into myself.

I didn't realize just how strange I was feeling in that room, with Martina, until now. My knees feel watery, and there is a strange lump in my throat.

I'm not scared, I tell myself as we walk toward the pond. *She's a fraud, not a monster.*

It would be more soothing if I could make myself believe it.

The sun has begun its slow journey toward the treetops, the light turning from searing white to a softer yellow, the surface of the pond shimmering in the late-afternoon sunshine.

Trying to shake myself from my reverie, I ask Anna:

"Was the pond here when the place was built? Or did Martina have it . . . installed?"

Anna laughs. She's got a slightly different vibe from Belinda, I notice now; less meditative, more energetic. Or maybe it's just the fact that she's taller and has broader shoulders than her colleague.

Armin once told me I was prone to making assumptions about character based on looks, something that deeply offended me, mostly due to the fact that he was completely correct.

"I don't know," she responds, sounding genuinely amused. "But putting a pond here because she thought there should be a pond here feels like a very Dr. Martina–like thing to do."

"Yeah, she seems very . . ." I search for the right word, something to capture the force of her personality without giving away my true feelings. ". . . determined."

"That she is," Anna agrees.

As we pass by the first cabin on the right, I look up at it, taking in the neat red tiles on the pointed roof and the lingonberry bushes crowding the corners.

There is a flash of a shadow behind one of the windows. Someone moving inside.

One of my fellow "patients"? Or a Himlafall employee?

I can't help but wonder what brings someone to a place like this. Despite the idyllic surroundings, the soft, velvety silence hanging over the surface of the pond, the cool, crisp air, there is a quiet whisper in the recesses of my mind. Like a warning.

Is Anna feeling it, too?

"How long have you been working here?" I ask her.

"Just a few weeks," Anna says. "Belinda has been here for a couple of months, I think."

This lines up with what I've been told.

"They can't keep any staff members for longer than a couple of months. People just keep rotating in and out of there. There is no continuity. I think it's by design."

Sandra's voice, echoing in my head.

"And do you like it?" I ask.

Anna looks out over the pond for a few seconds, the glimmering light bouncing off the water reflected in her gray eyes.

Then she smiles, bright and sudden.

"It's intense," she says. "Really intense. But it's good. I think you're going to like it here."

"Well, my experience will probably be a bit different," I say. "I mean, I won't be working."

At this, Anna turns to me, her smile turning into a smirk.

"Trust me," she says. "It's definitely going to feel like work."

A small chill runs up my spine.

"What do you mean?" I ask, light and breezy. Just making conversation.

"Nothing," Anna says. "Just that it's hard work. Becoming the best version of yourself."

Is there a hollow quality to her voice? Did she say that slightly too quickly, as though regretting her initial comment?

For a moment, a name hovers on my lips, a question fueled by the doubt I can almost convince myself I hear in her voice.

But then she adds:

"But I'm sure you are going to love it!"

My resolve dies, and I swallow the question. I remember, once again, what Sandra told me before I left.

"The staff worships her. They are not your friends. Don't trust them. They will tell her immediately, and you'll be out on your ass, and we'll both end up either destitute or in prison."

When we get to the fourth cabin, Anna reaches into her pocket, pulls out a little notebook, checks one of the pages, and then says:

"Here we are! Welcome to your home for the week."

She fishes a key chain out of her pocket and unlocks the door.

As I step in, I notice that, just as I was told, my bags are stacked by the bed. The space is small but impeccable; the walls are covered in cream wallpaper with sage-green leaves hanging off lazily twirling vines, the bed is made up with pristine white sheets, and there is a nightstand next to it, gleaming dark wood with brass detailing.

I do what everyone does when first entering a new room: I walk up to the window and look out. The cabin is slightly raised above the walking path, so that I can see all the way across the pond to the woods on the other side. Even in the soft, dreamy late-spring sunlight, the dark, dense forest looks forbidding. All too easy to get lost in.

"There is a welcome dinner for all the new patients in about an hour and a half," Anna says. "It's in the big house at the other end. There's a map in the nightstand, if you need help getting there, but you should have no problems finding it. Just follow the smell."

"Oh," I say. "That's nice."

"It's mandatory," Anna adds, as a breezy sidenote. "So just make sure to be there on time."

"Huh."

"People usually enjoy it," Anna hurries to assure me. "It's a chance to meet everyone and relax a bit before diving in. Kind of like summer camp."

I think the summer camp comparison is meant to denote fun and lifelong memories, but it doesn't have the desired effect.

Rather than long, lazy days in the sun, I immediately flash to an old slasher film. Camp counselors being picked off, one by one.

I smile.

"That sounds great."

Anna still isn't making any move to leave. I switch my weight to my other foot, feeling a mild twinge in my lower back from the long car ride.

"Is there anything else?" I ask her.

The silence seems to stretch between us, thick and ragged. Anna's smile grows wider.

"Don't want to give it up, huh?" she says.

Her tone implies it's a joke, but her posture contradicts it.

I feel my pulse quickening.

"I'm sorry?" I tilt my head to the side, palms open, signaling confusion, trying to radiate innocence.

A beat passes. Two.

Anna is still staring at me.

She knows.

No. There is no way. How could she know? How could they?

"Your phone," Anna clarifies, and it takes me a second to understand; when I realize what's happening, I start laughing in pure relief.

Anna joins in.

I stick my hand into my back pocket and pull out my cell phone.

"Here you go." I hand the iPhone to Anna, and she tucks it away.

"Any iPads? Computers?" she asks me.

I shake my head.

"Thank you," Anna smiles. "I promise we'll take good care of it."

"How is the reception up here?" I ask her. "I mean, I won't have my phone, so I guess it doesn't matter. I just want to make sure my mom can reach me if she needs me."

Isobel Anderssen has a mother who is very worried about her. The phone number I've given them goes to Armin, who knows that I'm here, as opposed to my actual mom, who has no idea.

"We have a signal booster," Anna assures me. "Best coverage this side of the Baltic."

"Must be nice for you guys," I remark, and she laughs again.

"Don't I know it," she says. "I have to get that *Bridgerton* fix at the end of a long day."

With a quick wave, she turns around and leaves, shutting the door behind her.

I remain standing in place, waiting as I hear her steps winding around the house, and then, sneaking a peek out the window, I see her growing smaller as she walks the path back to the main building.

It's only when she's almost out of sight that I sit down on the floor quietly and unzip my bag.

I push past the rolled-up ball of underwear, the poorly folded T-shirts, and the plastic grocery bag full of toiletries, and finally I find what I'm looking for, hidden inside a knitted sweater.

Two hard rectangles.

My backup phone. And my portable recorder.

I exhale with relief. They didn't search my luggage after all. It was a rookie mistake, packing them in my bag; I should have snuck them into my socks, or the back of my jeans.

I can't afford to make mistakes like that. Not now.

Up until today, it all seemed, still, like a game. Dr. Martina Hastings, the evil, beautiful queen; the Himlafall Clinic, a secret enchanted kingdom, full of dark and dangerous secrets.

But now that I'm actually here, it is all quickly becoming achingly real.

This is not a game. What I do in the next seven days might come to determine the rest of my life. If I pull this off, it could open up the world for me and ensure that no one else is ruined by this place.

But if I don't . . . it won't just be my name and reputation on the line.

After all, I wouldn't be the first person not to return from Himlafall.

Taking one final look out the window, I pull out the recorder, turn it on, and begin speaking quietly into it.

"Arrived at the Himlafall Clinic. First impressions are of a beautiful place, full of beautiful people. Everything is perfectly tailored to set you at ease."

I pause.

"The staff seems small. I've met two so-called caretakers. The information I had going in seems to be accurate in that neither of them have worked here for very long. I can't tell whether they have bought into the premise of the place. If they are true believers, or just here for a paycheck. Do they know about the bankruptcies, the broken marriages? About Susannah Wallin? I can't tell yet."

I bite the inside of my cheek, and I grimace. It's a bad habit, and the skin inside feels raw and tender. I've been doing it too much lately. Gnawing on my cuticles, grinding my teeth, my body manually breaking itself down from the weight of stress and anticipation.

"The doctor . . ." I begin, and then I realize I can't quite find the words.

I can't describe Martina Hastings, even to myself.

"I met Dr. Martina, too." My voice sounds halting, unsure. "She is . . . interesting. A character."

Alone in this room that isn't mine, this hostile place pretending to be home, the words that have been my comfort and my companions all my life are letting me down.

"I hope to find out more about her. I think she is going to be at dinner. My first session with her will be tomorrow."

I turn the recording off, the click of the button too loud in the small space.

A sour taste fills my mouth, and I swallow.

"Welcome to Himlafall," I say softly to no one at all.

Maybe just to hear a familiar voice. To not have to sit in the silence.

To not have to wonder whether that sour taste is the taste of fear.

Chapter 6

I PULL MY SWEATER TIGHTER AROUND MYSELF AS I START walking. I'm the only one on the path; the other cabins are all dark, the windows all reflecting the pond and the woods. It's like walking past a set of mirrors, each containing a slightly hunched, nigh unrecognizable version of me.

The smell does, indeed, reach me before the sound. The tart, crispy notes of fresh tomatoes; the smoky umami of frying meat; the thick, yeasty scent of bread baking.

The larger, barnlike structure at the end is the only one that is lit up. There is a long, low building in between the main house and the dining hall—staff housing, probably.

For a moment, I consider going in there, trying the door, trying to sneak a peek while everyone is at dinner, but I decide against it. It's too early to get caught somewhere I don't belong. If I get kicked out now, all this will have been for nothing.

And I will get access later anyway. If nothing else, I know that much.

As I approach the dining hall, I see that the doors are open, warm light spilling through them into the early evening, and I hear voices. A low murmur, short and halting. Music playing softly, some kind of piano composition.

I stop and draw a deep breath, taste the pine in the air from the nearby trees. I can hear my heart thumping in my chest, feel my pulse in my lips.

I am Isobel Anderssen. I am heartbroken. I am miserable. I am here because I want to heal.

Exhaling, I switch on the recorder hidden deep in my pocket.

Showtime.

When I'm a few steps away from the doors, a figure appears, silhouetted against the light, and I stop, squinting.

"Come on in," Belinda says, putting an arm around my shoulders. "Now that we're all here, we can get going."

She leads me in through the doors, her arm strong and firm around my shoulders. Reminding me that it's too late to back out now.

I blink as we walk in through the doors, my eyes adjusting to the light.

The ceiling is very high, upward of twenty feet, and the interior very bare. There is a long table in the middle of the room, medieval-hall-style, and Martina is standing at the end of it.

"Isobel," she greets me, smiling. "Hi. I'm so glad you could join us."

Funny phrasing, given that I was told it was mandatory.

Martina claps her hands, looking around the table, and her smile grows ever more luminous. Her hair is in a soft, loose braid now, and she's got a shawl over her white button-down.

It makes her look like an off-duty socialite, or maybe a tech CEO, someone who's spent all day trying to figure out how to get away with firing workers in favor of AI and is planning on spending the weekend at a meditation retreat in the mountains.

"Don't worry, I'm not going to make a speech," she says, and the woman next to me laughs, much louder than the joke deserves.

When I look at her through the corner of my eye, I see that she's much younger than anyone I might have expected to see at Himlafall. She's at most in her early twenties, sporting a golden tan and long, luscious peach-pink waves in a high ponytail. When she turns her head to Martina, I see that she's got a tiny star tattooed behind one ear.

"The first night here is always hard," Martina continues, sounding very much like she is, in fact, making a speech.

"You are all in a new place, surrounded by people you have never met before. You have left behind your homes, your jobs, your friends and families in order to come here."

Her eyes seem to glisten with tears for a second, but when she blinks, they are gone. A trick of the light.

"And I am so grateful," she continues, "that you made that decision. Not just for the privilege of meeting all of you. Not just for the journey we are going to go on together. But for yourselves. For the fact that all of you decided to take care of yourselves. To love yourselves enough to do this."

The woman next to me is nodding energetically, her pink ponytail bouncing. When I sneak a glance at the woman sitting opposite me, who appears to be closer to my age, with long, straight black hair falling around her shoulders and a long, thin face, she appears to be listening intently, a small but deep wrinkle between her eyebrows.

"Tomorrow, we are going to start the work. And I am not going to lie to you. I am not going to tell you that this will be easy. Nor will it always be pleasant. Change is painful. Opening up is painful. At the end of this week, you will have discovered things about yourself you had buried deep down within. You will see yourself, and your history, and your context in a very different light than you do right now."

Martina looks around the table once more. Am I imagining it, or does she linger when she looks at me? Is there an intensity there, a sense of connection?

Or is that just her specific brand of charisma?

Maybe we all feel like she's looking directly at us. Talking directly to us.

The skin on my arms prickling, I pull at my sweater.

"But it won't all be painful," Martina says, her voice softer now. "It will be a time of discovery. Of recognition. Right now, you are all strangers to each other. But at the end of this week, these women will be your community. Your family. You might not believe me right now, but I have seen it over and over again.

"There is a reason we focus on group therapy here at Himlafall. Because the issues that have brought you here, the issues that have kept you from finding real, lasting romantic connections, are not just individual. They are systemic. You will find your own experiences mirrored in the stories you hear. You will realize that you are not alone. You will see, together, that you are lovable. That you are deserving of so much more than what you have received up until now.

"And the first people who will show you what you are worth, and how it feels when you are loved, openly and truly, will be the women sitting next to you."

Martina falls silent.

As I look up, I see the faces around me, mirroring the apprehension I'm feeling. Eyes searching warily around the table, making contact, then looking away.

"But that is all ahead of us," Martina announces. "Tonight, we will just have dinner together. We'll get to know each other a little bit, we'll have some good food, and then we will go to bed."

She sits down.

The girl with the pink ponytail starts clapping loudly, and after a few confused seconds, the rest of us join in.

Martina laughs and shakes her head. But I swear that the high blush on her cheeks is one of satisfaction, not embarrassment.

"Well," the girl with the pink ponytail says, her voice loud and clear. "Maybe we should start by introducing ourselves?"

She looks over at Martina immediately for reassurance, and the doctor smiles.

"I'm Clara," she says, leaning forward over the table. "I'm twenty-three. I've grown up a bit all over, but most recently I've spent the last year traveling around Southeast Asia. It was a really wonderful experience. I don't want to sound like a typical white-girl cliché, but I really do feel like I began to find myself there."

She laughs. There is not a trace of self-consciousness in it.

As I take a closer look at her, I notice the various diamond studs making her ears glitter as she turns her head.

Ah. Not a young artistic type, as I'd first assumed, based on the pink hair. No, a would-be bohemian, funded by the bank of Mom and Dad.

Clara opens her mouth to say something else, but just then, the door at the other end of the room opens, and our collective attention is drawn by both the sound and the smell.

A man and a woman enter, both carrying heaping plates of spaghetti and Italian meatballs swimming in thick red tomato sauce. Two more waiters follow behind, and the food is placed in front of each of us with such speed and efficiency that I hardly have time to get a good look at the waiters before they have disappeared again.

"Wow," the woman opposite me mutters, looking down at her plate with a dazed expression on her face.

"Don't worry," Martina says from down at the end of the table. "For those of you who reported food allergies, intolerances, and preferences, they have been taken into account. Yours is vegan, Katarina."

The woman—whose name is apparently Katarina—looks up, surprised, before forming her lips into a smile.

"Thank you," she says.

The older woman sitting next to Katarina lets out a sigh and shakes her head.

"I simply don't know if I will be able to eat this much," she says, seemingly half to herself, half to the rest of us. "This just seems like too much food."

She looks to be in her late fifties or early sixties, with the kind of good looks that speak about healthy living and generous tweakments. Her hair is shoulder-length, an artful mix of golden blond and silver gray, and though her discreet cream cardigan and fitted navy slacks bear no obvious brands, I'm fairly certain the bracelet dangling off her skinny wrist says *Cartier*.

"Don't worry, Pernilla," Martina says. "You don't have to eat any more than you want to."

I hear a snorting laugh from the other side of Clara, and as I stretch my neck to see, I catch sight of the woman between her and the caretaker, Anna.

She's looking at Pernilla with a smirk tugging at the corners of her lips. Her thick black hair is cut short in a classic French pixie, and her dark eyes are sparkling with something that might be amusement, might be anger, might be both.

She picks up her fork, spears a meatball on to it, and then asks Martina:

"Hey, Doc, just a quick question. What if we get hungry between meals? We don't all have the same nutritional needs, you know. It just seems a bit concerning that we're all getting served the same amount of food."

"There is a snack bar available in the main building," Belinda hurries to respond in Martina's place.

"And if there is anything specific you want that you didn't bring, we get grocery deliveries twice a week. If you tell me, or any of the other staff members, we can put in an order for you."

"Great." The woman puts the meatball in her mouth and chews slowly, looking directly at Pernilla. "Fabulous."

As she starts to twirl the fork in the spaghetti, I spot the intricate tattoo sleeve on her left arm, teal and black and burgundy blooming against the backdrop of her brown skin.

Then the older woman, Pernilla, raises her head and looks at Clara.

"I am curious," she says, her voice so sweet and polite it nearly manages to hide the razor-sharp disdain hiding underneath, "as to what would make you come directly to a place like this from traversing the beaches of Thailand?"

Clara laughs a bit and says:

"I think . . . I mean, we are just meant to be getting to know each other tonight. Right? We can go over all of that tomorrow, when we start therapy."

"I'm sorry," Pernilla says, not sounding sorry in the slightest. "I was just curious."

Clara seems thrown; for a moment, she casts her eyes around, and despite the impeccable grooming, she suddenly looks every bit the teenager she was just a few years ago.

Never having had much of a maternal streak, I still feel a pang of protectiveness. Despite my plan to blend into the background as much as possible, I clear my throat.

"I guess we should continue with the introductions, huh?" I say. My voice is a bit hoarse; I've barely spoken at all since Anna left my cabin two hours ago.

"I'm Isobel," I say. "I've lived in Stockholm my whole life. Not much traveling, I'm afraid, but"—I look at Clara—"I would love to see a bit more of the world someday."

The woman across from me, Katarina, pipes up.

"What do you do for a living?" she asks me.

"I'm a technical copywriter," I say. "I guess I run my own business, but

I functionally work full-time for an online kitchenware retailer. It's a lot of SEO, and completely B2B, so not very sexy."

Armin helped me come up with the fake job, and the description. Something that sounded qualified but boring, which would conceivably give me enough disposable income to make my presence at Himlafall make sense but wouldn't invite any follow-up questions.

He told me to make sure to use at least two acronyms. In his experience, he'd said, people stopped listening after two acronyms.

Katarina perks up.

"Oh," she says. "Which company do you work with? I recently handled a copyright case for a big whiteware retailer. I had to learn a lot about marketing. I thought it was really fascinating."

"So, wait, are you a lawyer?" Clara cuts in next to me.

Katarina turns to her.

"Yes," she says. "I mainly work with intellectual property rights. Mostly cases of international copyright disputes."

"Like, with China?" Clara says.

Katarina's face doesn't betray any emotion as she responds.

"No," she says. "It's usually within the EU. I was adopted as a child. I've never been to China. You have probably spent more time in Asia than I have, based on what you said before."

It's hard to tell under the liquid blush, but I think Clara turns red.

"Sorry," she says. "Shit. I shouldn't have assumed."

"It is no problem," Katarina says, her voice as even as ever.

I hear a laugh from the other side of Clara, a low chuckle.

"Easy mistake to make, right, Clara? I'm sure you didn't spend much time with any actual Asian people when you were gallivanting around Thailand and Vietnam, discovering yourself."

Clara clamps her lips together before turning to the woman sitting next to her, the only one whose name I've yet to learn.

"Listen," she says. "I get it. I fucked up. But I think it's between me and Katarina, and she already said that it's okay. I don't understand why you feel the need to make me out to be someone I'm not."

"I'm not trying to make you out to be anyone at all," the tattooed woman says, her eyes dancing.

"Leyla," Martina says.

She doesn't raise her voice. She doesn't need to. We all fall silent.

The tattooed woman raises her chin a smidge as she looks over at Martina.

"That protective instinct you're feeling is a good thing," she says. "But I think you would agree, if you are being truthful, that what you are doing right now isn't coming from an entirely altruistic place. Am I correct?"

Leyla doesn't answer her.

"Let's just move on for now," Martina says. "I'll go tell the kitchen that we are ready for dessert."

She pushes her chair back, stands up, and disappears through the doors in the back.

When she's gone, Belinda appears to decide to take control of the room before it spirals back into conflict. The mood is still tense; Clara has turned her body away from Leyla, Katarina is staring down at her half-empty plate, and Pernilla has her arms crossed so tightly across her torso that it looks like she's locked them in place.

"I think we should introduce ourselves too," Belinda says, just on the verge of too loudly and too cheerfully. "Some of you met me when you arrived, and some of you met Anna. We're the general caretakers here at Himlafall."

Anna does a funny little wave, which makes Belinda smile, the tension leaking out of her shoulders.

"And this is Ellen," she says, referring to the small, compact woman to her right, the one who, so far, hasn't said a single word. She looks young and grim, her fair hair cut close to her scalp and her mouth set in a thin line.

"Ellen is going to be your physical therapist for the next couple of days."

I stiffen in my seat.

"Physical therapist?" I ask before I can stop myself.

Belinda, thankfully, misinterprets my question.

"Yes," she says. "She is going to be working with all of you, leading you in group classes, helping you handle and express your feelings through movement."

Belinda adds:

"And don't worry, it won't be too physically strenuous for those of you who aren't used to heavy exercise."

"Who would you assume isn't used to heavy exercise?" Leyla asks her, raising her eyebrows.

"No one," Belinda stammers. "I—"

"I have a bad knee," Pernilla interjects, her eyes steely, her words crisp. "So I appreciate that, Belinda. Thank you."

I reach for my water glass, barely aware of the conversation taking place around me.

Did I miss something? Did she text me? Did I not see it?

Fuck.

"Like she said, I will only be here for a couple of days," Ellen says. Her voice doesn't match her face; it's high and lilting, nigh on sweet.

"After that, the other physical therapist, Sandra, will be taking over. She would have been here to start off your week, but something came up, so I am covering for her until she gets here."

What could have come up?

Last time we spoke was only a couple of days ago.

The whole plan is contingent on Sandra being here. I'm not sure I can do it without her. She's my inside woman, my access point, my—

I realize I'm squeezing the fork so hard my knuckles have gone white, and I force my hand to relax.

This wouldn't mean anything at all to Isobel Anderssen; she wouldn't care about which physical therapist is working and when.

"I'm just going to go check that everything is going okay in the kitchen," Anna says, standing up from the table and leaving. I'm dimly aware that Belinda is still attempting to make conversation with the others, but I'm having a hard time focusing on it.

It's only when one of the waiters picks up my plate, and I hear my name, that I snap back into focus.

". . . Isobel?"

I look up, and see Clara staring at me, a small, expectant smile on her lips.

"What?" I blurt out. "I'm sorry, I wasn't focusing. I'm tired."

"She asked how you heard about the clinic," Katarina explains.

"I . . ."

The news about Sandra has thrown me off. And I wasn't lying when I said I was tired. I am on the verge of exhausted, actually.

Being off-balance and tired has never done much for my sense of impulse control.

I look straight at Ellen and Belinda, and I say, as casually as I can muster:

"It was recommended to me by a former patient. Susannah Wallin?"

Ellen looks confused. Confused or . . . stricken.

She opens her mouth to speak, but Belinda stops her with a hand on her arm. Whispers something to her.

Ellen turns to Belinda and begins to say:

"What . . . ?"

Just then, Anna comes walking out the doors.

"I'm sorry that took so long, ladies," she says. "Martina has something she needed to take care of, so she won't be able to join us for dessert. But it's on its way now."

Anna beams at us.

"I hope you still have room for brownies!"

The anticlimactic disappointment nearly makes me dizzy. I bite down, not allowing it to show, swallowing my frustration.

It doesn't matter that Anna interrupted. Because I saw it.

Ellen recognized the name. She had heard it before. She was surprised to hear me mention Susannah Wallin.

And of course she was.

Because Susannah disappeared without a trace after her week at the Himlafall Clinic, nine months ago.

Chapter 7

When I make it back to my own cabin, I shut the door behind me and reach to lock it, only to realize there is no key to twist.

I stare at it for a few seconds, as though I've only just missed it, as though it'll appear if I just look for it a little harder.

I remember Anna unlocking the door to the cabin; I just assumed it could be locked from the inside as well.

There is a cold, swirling sensation deep down in my belly. I swallow, again and again, against the rising nausea.

Sandra isn't here. I'm all alone, out here in the woods, with a door I can't lock.

No. I can't let myself panic. I've worked too hard; there is too much on the line.

I walk over to the window and look out.

The stars are twinkling gently outside, thin clouds like gentle brushes of paint over the deep-blue sky. The trees on the other side of the pond are completely still. They hardly look real, the dense darkness erasing any sense of dimension, as though they were nothing but a backdrop to whatever is happening here.

The surface of the pond is still. There is no wind at all. It feels like the woods surrounding us are holding their breath, waiting to exhale.

After a few seconds, I get down on my knees on the floor, dig out the phone from my suitcase, and turn it on. I briefly glance up at the window, and then I crawl behind the chair, sitting with my back to it so that I won't be visible from the window.

The cheap, used iPhone takes almost a minute to turn on. I bought it a few days ago, in a transaction that made me feel very much like I was doing something illicit. I wondered, briefly, in the store, if the cashier thought I was a drug dealer but came to the somewhat depressing conclusion that he probably thought I was too old and uncool to do anything as subversive as sell cocaine.

Once the phone has turned on, I go to the list of contacts. I've programmed in only two numbers—Armin's and Sandra's.

I press one, push the phone against my ear, and wait, teeth gnawing on the chewed-up cuticle on my left thumb. My fingers already look like they've been put through a meat grinder after the anxiety of the last few days.

No response.

Jesus, she probably isn't picking up because she doesn't recognize the number.

I pull the phone away and type:

> This is Isobel. Please call me back right now.

About thirty seconds after I've sent the text, the phone begins to shout out a polyphonic version of "Auld Lang Syne." I answer as quickly as possible, reminding myself to set it to silent.

"Sandra?" I answer the call.

"Hey, Isobel." I hear Sandra's voice from the other end of the line. "I'm sorry I didn't pick up. I thought it was a spam call."

"It's my . . . burner phone," I say, feeling mildly silly.

"Yeah, I got that now." She's speaking in a hushed tone. "What's up?"

"What's up is that I'm at Himlafall, and you're not here," I hiss into the phone.

"I know," Sandra says. "I texted you this afternoon, but I guess they had already taken your phone."

"Yes," I confirm. "They did."

"Look," Sandra says, "Andrea got sick this morning. Martin doesn't get back into town for another two days. I know we had a plan, but she's my kid, Isobel. I'm not going to just leave her here when she's not feeling well."

"I know that." I rub my eyes with two fingers, feeling how dry and tired they are, and I nod, despite the fact that she can't see me. "I'm sorry. I didn't mean to sound like . . . I don't know."

"It'll be fine," Sandra assures me. "I'll be there the day after tomorrow. Wednesday, at the latest. We'll still have time."

I bite the inside of my cheek.

"Of course it will be," I say.

A brief pause. I hear what sounds like Sandra walking in the background, and then her voice, now with an edge to it:

"So you've met the doctor now?"

"I have," I say. "She's . . . interesting."

Sandra sighs, or maybe snorts; the reception, despite the signal booster, isn't great, and it's a harsh, crackling sound.

"Yeah. Interesting," she echoes. "Don't worry, Isobel. I'm with you on this. We're going to take that place down. I'll make sure you get the access you need."

I swallow.

"Thanks, Sandra," I say. "And I hope Andrea feels better soon. What kind of sick is she?"

"It's just a stomach bug," Sandra sighs. "She was at a sleepover yesterday. I'm sure she caught it from one of her friends. She's miserable, of course, but it will pass quickly."

"I'm sorry," I say. "Can't be fun. For either of you."

"I've got to go," Sandra says. "I promised I'd watch some Korean show in bed with her. But just . . . hang on and hang out, okay? Just act like a patient for a couple of days until I get there."

"I will," I say.

"And don't drink the Kool-Aid." I'm sure she means for it to sound like a joke, but there is a sharpness, a concern, in there as well. "Martina is charismatic. Even I fell for it—at first. But she's a hack. She's dangerous."

"I won't," I say. "And they didn't drink Kool-Aid at Jonestown. It was Flavor Aid. It's a common misconception."

"Jesus, you're insufferable." Sandra laughs. "Take care of yourself. Stick to your cover story. I'll be there before you know it."

She hangs up.

I'm left staring at the phone.

I can't be upset with Sandra. She's taking a risk, helping me with this, and I know that. She's putting her own job, and potentially her own safety, on the line, and, unlike me, she's got people to take care of.

The original plan was for this to take place in another six to eight weeks, give Sandra time to get another job lined up.

But when they offered me a spot due to a patient dropping out last minute, she didn't argue. She didn't try to pull out. She went along with it, because it's the right thing to do.

Sandra has always been that way, ever since we were kids, ever since our mothers used to drink cheap red wine in the kitchen and gossip about their colleagues in academia while we watched the Disney Channel in their living room.

She's rough around the edges but deeply kind, and with the rare kind of integrity that has managed to maintain its fervor through all the petty little irritants and trials of adulthood.

And she was the person who first confirmed my suspicions: There was something deeply wrong with the Himlafall Clinic.

Chapter 8

It was six or so months ago that I first approached Sandra about her place of employment, and she saw through me immediately.

"*What have you heard?*" she asked me, that deep groove between her eyebrows showing as she chugged the last of the beer in her glass.

I told her about the Reddit post I'd found, and how the cops had confirmed that someone named Susannah Wallin had been reported missing in November of last year but that they'd refused to show me a police report or a picture.

I'd managed to track down a couple of articles about Susannah Wallin from back in the day that seemed to confirm her existence: one about her achievements as a young rising softball star, with a picture of a beaming, white teenage girl with pigtails and braces, holding a glove in one hand and a trophy in the other, and one about the very same Susannah Wallin six years later as one of the top-performing saleswomen in what was clearly a pyramid scheme. By that point, she'd lost the braces and dyed her hair a deep caramel, her young face caked in products from the MLM she was apparently excelling in.

She looked like any young woman in any random town in Sweden; she could have been anyone or no one. Still, there was a sweetness to her smile, and something else, in both pictures, both articles, like a sort of yearning. A desperation to be seen, recognized. Loved.

I showed Sandra the pictures I'd found, and she shook her head.

"These are too old. This last one is from 2016. Anything more current? Social media?"

I told her there was no social media. No Instagram, no TikTok, no Facebook, no Twitter, no LinkedIn. It was like she'd been wiped from the internet.

Sandra looked troubled.

"I wouldn't put it past them," she said. *"I haven't heard anything about this girl, specifically. But, Christ . . . the way that place is run. What they do to those women. It's haunting. It's like they come out different people. And not in a good way."*

She told me about the patients who had breakdowns and left, midweek, mute and with reddened eyes. She told me about the patients who'd come back, over and over again, convinced that all they needed, more than their jobs, or houses, or children, was just one more week at Himlafall.

And she told me about the patients who'd arrive at the exercise sessions quiet, and sluggish, as though they'd taken something. Or had been given something.

"I've tried talking to the other employees about it. But they won't acknowledge it. Or maybe they just don't stick around long enough to notice, or care. The whole staff has been cycled out twice in the time I've been there, and it's been less than a year."

At the end of the evening, I'd asked her if she'd be willing to help me. Willing to work with me on taking down Himlafall, if I could come up with a referral and enough money to secure a spot.

And she'd said yes.

It was the final piece of the puzzle. The domino that led to me coming here.

Last night, I told Armin that he didn't have to worry about me being here. That I'd have Sandra, and that we'd take care of each other.

The only source of light in the cabin is the small, cold rectangle of the phone screen, and as it goes to sleep, I find myself sitting in the soft, blue dark, the faint smell of pine soap and laundry detergent stinging my nostrils.

I pull out the recorder from my pocket and rewind. It takes me a while to find the right spot on the recording.

I hear my own voice, harsher and more nasally than I would have thought, and I wince slightly at the sound of it:

"It was recommended to me by a former patient. Susannah Wallin?"

Silence.

I hear the sound of fabric shifting, and a hissing, like a whisper. Belinda. Then Anna's voice, yelling about brownies.

I rewind again. Turn the volume all the way up, until I can feel the crackling of the auditory artifacts in my back teeth.

". . . Susannah Wallin?"

A beat. And then I can only just make out:

". . . lying. Or . . . about it."

Belinda's whisper, quick and harsh.

I replay it three more times.

Finally, I'm sure I'm making it out correctly.

"She's lying. Or joking. Don't worry about it."

Sitting there, on the floor, my legs going numb from the cold wooden planks underneath me, I can feel my breath shortening, both in fear and in excitement.

Because how would Belinda know I was lying?

If she didn't know there was no possible way Susannah Wallin could have told me about the clinic?

If she didn't know that Susannah Wallin couldn't have told me anything at all?

FREUD'S EX-GIRLFRIEND: A PSYCHOLOGIST'S GUIDE TO BREAK-UPS

pg. 157

Chapter 16: "So now what?"

You have gone through all the steps, and you have executed on them perfectly. You have deleted all the pictures of the two of you together. You have burned, donated, or simply thrown out all the mementos from your relationship. You have picked up two new hobbies, and gotten quite good at them. You are going out with friends three nights a week, you have started doing Pilates, and you have managed to dodge the compulsion to cut break-up bangs.

(Because, let us be real for a second: If bangs were a good idea, you would already have them. Never make a radical hair decision when you are a fresh singleton.)

But still, you cannot. Stop. Thinking about them. Every night, whether freshly showered from a vigorous session at the gym or slightly tipsy from too many dirty martinis with your friends, they show up, haunting your thoughts in between waking and dreaming. And even worse than that, despite the fact that, on the surface, you look happier than ever, to the point that your friends and family are talking among themselves about how well you are handling everything, you are not.

You are sad. You are lonely. And you feel, somehow, as though you have done something wrong.

You cannot stop thinking about where it all went wrong. You run the same scenarios in your head, over and over, tweaking them slightly every time, hoping for a different outcome.

If only you had made a bigger fuss over their birthday.

If only you had kept in better shape.

If only you had spent more time with their friends.

If only you had initiated sex more.

In her 2001 article in *Linguistic Psychology*, "Ifs and Buts: The Destructive Potential of Potentialities," Dr. Emilie Steinfeld argued that the words "if only" are the single most potent tool for psychological self-flagellation we possess. Dr. Steinfeld described the process of trying to right the past as a computer stuck in a loop; as long as the brain cannot find a solution to a problem, it will keep trying new points of attack, even when the problem is long in the past. This locks us in a vicious cycle of revisiting difficult or traumatic points in our past, both in our minds and in our actions. Functionally speaking, your brain is stuck.

Dr. Steinfeld suggested in her article that the solution to the problem was to replace "if only I had" with "next time, I will," as a way of teaching your brain to differentiate the past from the future. But despite her enduring genius, I have to confess that I disagree with Dr. Steinfeld on this point.

Instead of replacing "if only" with "next time," I suggest shifting the focus.

When you start thinking about all the mistakes you feel you made, and all the areas where you did not measure up, try to instead shift your focus to all the ways your partner failed you. All the ways they did not fulfill you. All the ways they let you down.

It is easy to think back to someone in our past and view them through the rose-colored glasses of nostalgia. But if your ex was the perfect person for you, they would not have hurt you. That is important to remember. The first criteria for "the one" is that they want to be with you, and second is that they want to treat you the way you deserve to be treated.

Would paying more attention to their interests have made them appreciate the uniqueness of you? Would initiating more in bed have made them pay attention to your needs? Would any of it truly have made you happy?

You are the main character in your own life, and your journey is your own. By allowing someone who is no longer in your life to take up space in your mind, you are sidelining yourself, as so many of us so often do.

Do not let sadness and regret force you to question yourself. By rehashing the wounds of the past, over and over, you are preventing yourself from moving on.

What if nothing could have changed? What if nothing *should* have changed?

Or what if—and stay with me, here—you did not do anything wrong?

We are going to discuss the healing power of anger in a few chapters. But for now, I want you to just sit with this idea for a few seconds. Finish reading this chapter, and then put the book (or Kindle) down.

Close your eyes.

Breathe in deep.

Find those thoughts that have been swirling in your mind, late at night, when you are lying in your bed and sleep evades you.

If only, if only, if only.

Focus on them.

And then erase them. And replace them.

I am not responsible for their pain.

I did not do anything wrong.

Their happiness is not, and never was, my responsibility.

Chapter 9

I WAKE FROM A HALF-REMEMBERED DREAM, MY MOUTH VERY dry and my heart pounding in my chest.

At first, I think that the dream was what woke me up. Despite the cool temperature inside the cabin, I'm sweating, and the blankets are half kicked off, twisted between and around my legs.

I sit up in bed, pulling my lank, damp hair back from my forehead. The T-shirt I'm sleeping in, one I stole from a one-night stand's apartment a couple of years ago as revenge for him having scoffed at the idea of getting me off, is sticking to my torso.

I pull the thin, worn cotton fabric away from my skin, trying to find my bearings in the unfamiliar room.

What was it in the dream that woke me up?

The contents of it are slipping between my fingers even as I try to grasp for it. My father was there. So was Martina Hastings, I think. Or maybe it was my mother.

But . . . no.

It wasn't the dream.

It was something else. A light, or a sound.

I look around the cabin. The door is still firmly closed; so is the window. Everything is as I left it.

Still, the creeping feeling under my skin won't leave me alone. Like someone is watching me.

I close my eyes, so hard I see stars, breathing in through my nose and out through my mouth. It happens instinctively, and it's only then that I remember who taught me to do so.

I was five years old and going through a bad bout of nightmares. I can't remember why; maybe I'd heard a scary story or seen something frightening on the news. My dad always argued that no child was too young to understand what was going on in the world. Sometimes he even read me one of his stories before bed, if he was particularly proud of it, and it made me feel very grown-up, chosen, and special, like a big girl, even if the details of it left me stiff and cold with fear once he'd left and the lights were turned out.

I had woken up, several nights in a row, and gone to my parents' room, wanting to sleep in their bed, where I'd be safe and protected. My mom had let me crawl in with her, but my dad had gotten progressively more annoyed with me, so one morning when it was time to get up for school, he'd come into my room and sat down on the edge of the bed, smoothing my unruly morning bed head down with one hand and smiling fondly at me.

"*You're a big girl now, princess,*" he told me. "*And big girls don't sleep in their mom and dad's bed.*"

The night before, I'd tried to get in with them, only for my dad, with his flinty, angry voice, to tell me to be quiet and go back to my own room, stopping my mom with a hand on her shoulder when she tried to get up to comfort me.

I was too ashamed, and too scared, to look at him, so I just sat there, studying the bruises on my knees, the mystery scrape on one shin I'd gotten at some point. It was almost healed over, and I wanted to pick at the scabs, but I knew it would just make him angrier if I did so.

"*I'm sorry,*" I told him.

"*You don't want to bother Mommy and Daddy, do you?*" he asked me, and I knew it was a trap. If I said no, it meant that I knew better but had done the bad thing anyway; if I said yes, it meant I was being bad, on purpose, and that wasn't good either.

I went for the third option.

"*I didn't mean to,*" I said. "*I just got really scared.*"

I still had a slight lisp at the time, so it came out as *fcared.*

Dad sighed, and I tensed up.

I was an expert at managing his moods—being cute, or precocious, or funny, whichever one was needed; taking his side against Mom, or his boss, or the world; praising him, hugging him, telling him he was the best dad in the world, even when he was upsetting me.

Especially when he was upsetting me.

"*Well, princess, if you wake up again tonight, you can't come into our room,*" Dad said. "*I'm going to lock the door, so you can't get in. It doesn't matter if you scream and cry. Do you understand?*"

My lips were quivering, so I pushed them together. He didn't like crying. He didn't care for messes in general; snot and tears were unsightly, and especially so coming from me.

"*Yes,*" I whispered, thinking about the monsters in my nightmares, the dark shadows at the corners of the room, which seemed to shift and whisper horrible things, the odd sounds that would mutate and multiply until I knew in my very bones that there was something very bad in the room, hiding in the dark, waiting to pounce and do painful, twisted things to me, like the things I had seen happen to other kids on the news, the things I had heard about in my father's articles.

"*Good,*" my dad said, and he squished me into his side, a sudden joviality in his voice. "*I'm proud of you, princess.*"

Despite it all, the words felt warm, and provoked a swelling of pride in me.

"*And if you get scared, you can make the scary go away,*" he continued. "*Just breathe in through your nose, and out through your mouth. Close your eyes really tight, and do that until you're not scared anymore.*"

I finally gathered the courage to look up at him. He was happy now, the skin around his pale blue eyes crinkling, and that made me happy.

"*Is that what you do when you're scared?*" I asked him, and when he laughed, it was with genuine amusement.

He leaned over and kissed me on the forehead.

"*I'm never scared, princess,*" he told me.

I believed him then.

It dawns on me that I'm holding my breath, grinding my teeth together, and I let out the air I've been holding in, easing the pain in my chest.

I wonder if it was true, what he said. If he believed it as he said it.

Maybe my father really was never scared, even when he was out there, early in his career, tailing soldiers in Lebanon and Sri Lanka. Maybe he wasn't even scared when he went undercover, gathering information for the in-depth investigative articles that would eventually propel him to fame. Maybe that was the key to his success; someone who never looks inward can't see his own inherent vulnerability, the frailty of the facade.

Maybe that's why he got away with the lies for so long. That lack of fear. The earliest evidence that was brought up in the trial was from 1991, the year I was born; a number thrown out mid-article, exaggerated way beyond what the sources actually said for shock and dramatic value.

"*He was testing the waters*," the prosecutor said at the time. "*And the more he got away with, the more confident he became.*"

And I think she might have been right. At least partially; he probably was testing the waters, the young hotshot journalist, wanting the attention that reporting mere reality could not get him.

Had he been born later, my father probably would have shied away from investigative reporting and pivoted, instead, to the life of a political pundit. No need to stick to the facts there.

But I think she was wrong, too. I don't think my father became more confident over time. I think he was born that way. In the end, he had very little imagination. Enough to exaggerate and embellish, not enough to imagine what might happen the day he was caught.

Imagination is required to be truly afraid.

So maybe that is what really separates me from my father. He never saw monsters in the shadows. He never thought himself the small, frail creature hiding under the blankets.

I swing my feet off the bed, the bare floor strikingly cold against my skin, and stand up. Walk over to the door. The air in the cabin is stuffy, heavy with humidity.

When I'm about to open the door, something at the bottom of it catches my eye. I did not see it from the bed, but here, standing above it, the faint light of the moon through the window bounces off the white paper, creating its own luminescence.

Quietly, slowly, as though I'm still dreaming, hearing nothing but the ticking of my own heartbeat in my ears, I reach down and grasp the paper someone has pushed under the door.

That was what woke me up, I think. *Footsteps by the door.*

It's a neat square of printer paper, folded perfectly in half. I open it.

GO HOME. THERE IS NOTHING FOR YOU HERE.

IT'S TOO LATE.

Chapter 10

I WAKE TO THE SUN RISING SHARP AND JUDGMENTAL AT 5:30, light blaring in through the windows and skewering the gossamer-thin curtains.

The note is resting next to me on the pillow, the very opposite of a comforting companion.

Some part of me had hoped that it was yet another bad dream.

Even as I get out of bed, take a quick cold shower, hoping it will clear my mind; brush my teeth; and pull on the jeans from yesterday, my mind is racing.

Who would have done that?

It seems almost laughable, in a way. Like something out of a bad movie. It would be funny were I not so unsettled.

My first thought was of Martina, but it can't be her. If she wanted me out, she could kick me out. She is owner, CEO, and God-Empress of Himlafall; her word is clearly law. If Dr. Martina had decided, at two in the morning, that she wanted me gone, I'm sure I would have been in my car with my things packed by 2:05.

Is it one of the other patients? But what reason would they have to want me out? I've barely met them so far. Sure, a couple of them seemed hostile, but that hostility seemed more directed at the world at large than at me, specifically.

Maybe one of the other staff members?

I slide down onto the floor and pull out my recorder from under the bed again. Clicking the button, I begin to narrate:

"First morning at Himlafall. Something . . . ridiculous happened last night.

"I woke up last night to footsteps outside my door, and when I went to check, I found an anonymous note under my door. Someone is telling me to leave here, to get out, and saying that it's *too late.* I'm not sure what they are referring to, but, if nothing else, it seems like proof that there really is something going on at the Himlafall Clinic.

"It must have to do with Susannah Wallin. I asked the staff members about her last night, and one of them, the physical therapist, had a visible reaction to her name.

"I thought that Martina Hastings had to be the one to be blamed for Susannah going missing. But if Martina had wanted me gone, I'd be gone. So now I'm left asking myself . . . *Is it possible that she's not involved at all?*

"Is it possible that one of the other staff members was responsible for Susannah's disappearance? That Martina has no idea?

"And how far are they willing to go to stop anyone from finding out?"

Chapter 11

THE GROUP THERAPY ROOM IS LARGE AND PERFECTLY SQUARE, with a circle of chairs arranged in the middle, in a way that reminds me of the fictionalized AA meetings I've seen on TV. Flimsy curtains have been drawn at the windows to prevent others from looking in, or us from looking out, I'm not sure.

There are paintings on the walls, large abstract canvases in soothing blues and greens. The shapes remind me of Rorschach tests, and I wonder if that's intentional, or if, ironically, I'm just projecting my biases onto them.

As we sit down, I take note of the others. Is there any possibility one of them left the note under my door? I don't want to lock into one answer too early; my favorite journalism professor once told me that "*Certainty is tempting, which is why it's dangerous.*"

It's hard to imagine. Clara is looking daisy fresh, pink hair pulled back in a loose braid, her cheeks so smooth and taut the abundance of collagen seems to be taunting me. Leyla looks grumpy but relaxed, which appears to be her standard setting.

Katarina is sitting rigid on her chair, her back straight and her fingers picking nervously at her cuticles. Pernilla folds her arms across her torso as soon as she sits down, eyes pointed at the floor.

If I was to keep an eye on anyone, it would be Pernilla. There is something there, bubbling under the surface. Could it be guilt? Fear?

Rage?

Martina enters the room, and all of our eyes go directly to her. She sits in the one empty chair and crosses her legs at the ankles without saying a word.

Then she smiles, and the room seems just a little bit brighter.

"Welcome." Her voice is hardly louder than a whisper. "Let's begin with a breathing exercise."

She instructs us to close our eyes and start breathing in tandem, feeling the rhythm of the others in our chests.

It makes me a little bit dizzy, and after a while, I decide to open my eyes, instead.

"Imagine you are a tree," Martina instructs us. "You are in the middle of a forest. It is a quiet day. You have been standing on this spot for hundreds of years, and you will stand for hundreds more."

Her voice is a soothing monotone. I can see the others inhaling and exhaling in perfect lockstep. Clara's cheeks are flushed; there is a small wrinkle between Leyla's eyebrows.

"Imagine the sunshine on your branches, and leaves, as you stretch ever higher," Martina continues.

The note flashes before my eyes again.

GO HOME. THERE IS NOTHING FOR YOU HERE.

It was typed, not written by hand, so whoever wrote it had access to a computer and a printer.

It couldn't have been one of the other patients, could it?

Unless they managed to sneak into the office. Unless they asked for a favor from one of the staff members. Unless they, like me, figured out a way around the lax security measures.

Unless, unless, unless.

My palms are sweaty. I tell myself I'm being ridiculous; it was a note, not a threat. I can't let something that small frighten me. I'm a reporter, not a girl detective.

Actually, fuck that. A girl detective would never let a little note scare her. Nancy Drew would spit at a stupid little note.

"Stay there for a few moments," Martina continues. "Feel the light on your branches. Feel the strength you are gathering from the roots. You have no obligations; there is nothing calling for your attention. You are not letting anyone down, and no one is expecting anything from you. You are fulfilling your purpose by doing exactly this. By breathing, and drinking in the light, and existing."

It's a nice mantra. I decide to go with my own instead.

I close my eyes with the others, and I tell myself:

You are exactly where you are supposed to be.

That note means that you were right, and there is something here.

You were right all along.

I let my fingers skim over the comforting weight of the recorder in my pocket, and I exhale.

"When you feel ready, you can stretch, and come back to yourself, and open your eyes."

I open my eyes.

Martina reaches for the cup of tea standing on the table in the middle of the circle. There is a pitcher of water there, too, and a box full of organic tissues.

She smiles at us.

"I like to start the day with a breathing exercise," Martina addresses the circle. "When we first started our work here, we used to begin with an hour of meditation, but everyone hated it." She laughs a little, and Clara immediately laughs with her.

Martina then puts her palm to her chest and lets it rest there, smiling at the rest of us. Lets the silence percolate for a few seconds.

"How did you sleep last night?" she asks us.

I expect Clara to respond, eager to impress as she seems, but Pernilla surprises me by speaking up.

"I couldn't sleep," she admits.

Martina nods, leaning forward a bit.

"Why was that?" she asks.

Pernilla looks around the circle, appears to be weighing her words. She's beautifully put together, looking as pristine today as she did yesterday: in a softly patterned silk blouse, slim-fitting white slacks, her sparse jewelry still flashy enough to signal casual, off-duty wealth. But the concealer can't hide the bags under her eyes, the slight tremor in her hands as she begins to twist the wedding ring around her finger.

"I don't know," she says, and I wonder if she's lying.

"Did anyone else have trouble sleeping?" Martina asks.

Clara shakes her head; Katarina slowly raises her hand.

As does Leyla.

Martina looks at me.

"Not you, Isobel?" she asks me.

I don't like the way she singled me out, but I smile automatically. Isobel Anderssen wouldn't be offended at being called out; she'd be delighted at the attention of her hero.

"I never sleep well," I say. "I've always woken up a lot. I'm a little bit tired all the time."

I laugh, but no one laughs with me.

Martina keeps her eyes locked on me, long enough that I have to force myself not to squirm.

"It's natural for all of you to have trouble sleeping," she says, finally breaking the eye contact. "Sleep is usually one of the first areas to be affected in times of great trauma. Our bodies end up in fight-or-flight. Often, we process emotional distress much in the same way we would process physical distress." She pauses.

"It is, in fact, possible to die from a broken heart. Acute emotion-induced stress can put so much strain on the system that your heart simply gives out. Isn't that fascinating?"

There's something near lascivious about the way she says this, the way her eyes are shining.

"I'm telling you this because we are so often told to hide our pain," Martina continues.

"We are told our emotions are not real. That they are not relevant. That we should *move on, distract ourselves*, and not let our emotions run our lives. But our feelings fulfill important functions. Our bodies work as a system, and feelings are a part of that. If your feelings have been hurt, deeply hurt, it is no less important of a wound than a broken leg would be.

"You wouldn't keep walking on a fractured ankle. You wouldn't try to hide it from the world, pretending like nothing was wrong. Yet, I think you have all been attempting to pretend, to various extents, like these recent break-ups haven't impacted you the way that they have. You have been, in accordance with the metaphor, walking, and running, and jumping, on your broken bones."

She draws a deep breath, and I find myself echoing her movement, filling my lungs with air, as I hear the women around me doing the same.

"So, the first thing we are going to do," Martina says, "is bring those fractures into the light. We are going to practice acknowledging the pain. By sharing our stories, one by one, with each other."

Martina looks at me again.

"Isobel," she says. "You go first."

Chapter 12

"I MET KAVEH ON A DATING APP," I BEGIN. "I DIDN'T THINK IT would turn into anything. I'd been single for a long time. I went on a lot of first dates, and most of the time, it just fizzled out. They just weren't interesting enough, or funny enough, or . . . something."

"But Kaveh was different," Martina says.

"Yeah," I say. "He always makes me . . ." I pretend to correct myself, shaking my head. This is another thing I have practiced: the heartbroken tend to speak in accidental present tense.

"I mean, he *made* me feel safe. But not in a dull way. And he never seemed to judge me. He never pried when I didn't feel like talking about something, but he was always ready to listen when I was ready to talk. It just felt . . . easy. I thought we were it. I thought we were going to get married and spend the rest of our lives together."

"And the sexual connection?" Martina asks.

I keep my face still.

There is a challenge in her voice.

Can she tell there is something just slightly off about my story? Are her psychological Spidey senses tingling?

Or is it a power play?

"I don't think I'm ready to talk about that," I say, casting my eyes down, feigning shyness. "I'm a pretty private person."

"Sex is an important part of romantic relationships," Martina says. "Don't you agree, Isobel?"

She pushes my name, putting the emphasis on the first syllable.

It's funny. None of it is real, and I still feel a pang of real discomfort, the social pressure like a physical sensation.

I can't imagine how I'd feel if it was all real. If I was actually dissecting a recently dissolved relationship.

I clear my throat.

"It was good," I say. "Maybe not as frequent toward the end as it was in the beginning, but it was always . . . good."

"You were attracted to him," Martina says. It's not a question.

When I look up again, she's staring at me.

"Of course I am," I say. "I mean, of course I was."

"How long did you wait to have sex?"

Jesus, I feel like a bug pinned to a table for examination. As though she's forcing my wings apart and peeling my exoskeleton off, studying every detail, looking for irregularities.

"We slept together on the second date," I say.

"And how was it, the first time?" Martina tilts her head to the side.

I didn't prepare much about my fictional sex life for my backstory. I've got Isobel Anderssen's entire work and family history clear to me, but not so much her sex life, other than having decided that she doesn't have any major kinks or fetishes, that she's a solidly vanilla heterosexual who would consider pink handcuffs scandalous.

I thought that would be enough. I was more worried about getting caught on irregularities, years and dates, things that could be memorized and verified. I didn't expect to be questioned in detail like this in the first session.

But maybe I should have been.

Forum posts and anonymous reviews of Himlafall swirl in my head. *Boundary-crossing. Disrespectful. I felt violated.*

Suddenly, I can feel the others staring at me, their undivided attention like an itch. I can't wait too long; I have to say something.

"It was . . ." I search through memories of sex, a hazy vortex of sweaty skin and faces that blend together. Finally, I land on a memory of Poor Linus, the only proper boyfriend I've ever had, and I grasp onto it.

"It was clumsy," I finally say. "We didn't know each other well enough yet. And we were a bit drunk."

"Did you have an orgasm?" Martina asks immediately.

"Jesus Christ," I say, in genuine shock.

"Answer the question, Isobel." The softness has gone from her voice.

I want, so badly, to push back, to show anger; to tell her that she can't talk to me like this, that she's not entitled to this kind of information from me, or from anyone. That these are vulnerable people in this room, people who trust her, and that this is a disgusting way to treat that trust.

But I have to swallow it down. I have to play along. See what comes next, what comes after this.

The memory of Poor Linus rubbing the space between my left labia and my thigh until I faked a satisfied sigh pops in my head.

"No," I respond. "No, okay? I didn't."

"Yet you say your sex life was good," Martina says.

A faint smile is playing on her lips now.

Stress and frustration get the better of me.

"What do you want me to say?" I blurt out.

"How did you feel, when you were having sex?" Martina leans back in her chair.

"I felt . . . powerful," I say, surprising myself.

I didn't mean to say that; I don't know where it came from.

"Because of his attraction to you?" Martina says.

"Yes," I say. "It felt good, to know that I could . . ."

"To know that you could have that effect on another person," Martina finishes my sentence. "And to know that you could be that close to someone and still withhold that part of yourself."

I stare at her, the shock of recognition making my fingertips tingle.

"Yes," I say, feeling oddly breathless. "Exactly."

Martina nods slowly.

"How many of your relationships have functioned that way?" she asks me. "Sexually, that is."

I open my mouth, but no words come out.

"How many of the people you have slept with have you actually been attracted to?" Martina elaborates. "How many of them did you sleep with because you were simply drawn to the fact that they were attracted to you?"

"I don't know," I say. My voice sounds weak and far away.

"I think you do know, Isobel." Martina shakes her head. "I think it's quite clear to everyone in this room."

I can feel the weight of the stares on my face like something physical, like heat, or pressure, both light and utterly unbearable, all at the same time.

I feel dizzy.

I have to pull back, have to regain control.

I'm not supposed to be telling her about myself. I'm not supposed to be talking about Isobel Lindschold. I'm supposed to be talking about Isobel Anderssen, the woman who falls too fast and too easily, the woman who is still dreaming about the ex-boyfriend who left her and blocked her phone number.

"How did you feel when he left you?" Martina asks, snapping me back to attention.

I think the sudden change in direction is meant to disorient me, but this is better. This part, I've practiced.

"Horrible." I draw a deep breath. "I felt lost. I felt . . . like I'd never be whole again. I felt like he'd taken the rest of my life away. All those plans, for our wedding, for our family, just . . . gone. In an instant."

Martina's gaze lingers on me.

Then she smiles and looks over at Pernilla.

"Do you believe her, Pernilla?" she asks. "Do you think she's being truthful?"

"No," Pernilla says. Her voice is higher now than it was, some of the polish having come off it. "She's just saying what you want to hear."

I open my mouth to respond, fake outrage mixing with real anger, but Martina holds up a hand in my direction, stopping me cold.

I feel like a child being scolded, decades-old shame rising to my cheeks.

"Keep going," Martina says.

"You're just saying words," Pernilla spits at me, like she's been waiting for the opportunity. "I don't even think you loved him. How could you have? Look at you. I don't even think you cared about this man. You say you wanted to marry him, but you didn't think about what that would mean. You didn't think about the sacrifices you would have to make. You just wanted to wear a pretty dress, and take some pretty pictures, and this man was nothing but a placeholder. Someone to stand next to you and look pretty. You never cared about him. You *never* cared about him!"

Her voice rises until it's a screech; small, red dots are burning high up on her cheeks. Her hands are closed so tightly her knuckles have gone completely white.

Once she goes quiet, Pernilla is panting, her lips pale and trembling.

Martina stands up from her chair.

"Thank you," she says, sincerity dripping from her words, "for sharing that, Pernilla. Thank you for being *truthful* with us."

Martina throws me a look.

It's only for a second, but it feels longer. Like she can see through not only Isobel Anderssen but Isobel Lindschold as well.

All the way down to the rottenness under the skin.

"I think we should take a little break now," Martina says, and looks away, at the others. "There's tea and snacks in the lounge at the end of the hallway. If you want, please feel free to go outside and walk around for a bit. The fresh air is nice."

I hurry to stand up and begin to walk toward the door, but then I hear Martina's voice:

"Hold on a second."

I start to turn slowly, like in a nightmare, but then I see she's not looking at me. She's looking at Pernilla.

"Pernilla, would you mind staying here with me a little while longer?"

It's only when I get outside, in the hallway, that I realize I've clenched my jaws, my shoulders, my hands; when I force them to release, my muscles are shaking.

I remember what Sandra said, back when this all started.

"I don't know what she tells them in those therapy sessions. But it's not good. She's got some kind of strange hold over them. It's scary.

"You have to see it to believe it."

79.4k likes

doctormartinahastings I've been thinking a lot about change lately. Most people seem to think about winter as a time to hunker down, batten down the hatches, and hold out until spring. But it's also a wonderful time for reflection—for taking stock of your life and trying to figure out whether or not this is what you really want.

I decided to divorce my husband in the winter. I remember the exact moment when I realized it was over. It was 2020, the first year of the pandemic (I know, a covid divorce—such a cliché), a few weeks before Christmas. We had both been working from home for eight months. Henrik took his meetings in the office, and I took mine in the bathroom. We had dinner together every night, and we took turns cooking.

There was nothing especially awful about that evening. From the outside looking in, it would have seemed charming, maybe even perfect. I made stroganoff, and Henrik set the table. He asked me how my new book was coming along. I asked him when he thought the market would begin to recover. We chatted a little about Christmas, and about whether or not it would be worth the risk to have his sister and her two boys over on Christmas Eve.

We were two charming, attractive (it's not cute to pretend like you don't know you're cute), highly accomplished professionals. We still had sex on a regular basis. By all objective metrics, we were doing great.

But I remember looking at him over our beautiful, refurbished dinner table, the one we had gotten from his parents as a wedding present, and feeling my heart sinking. Because I couldn't deny the feelings I had been pushing away for so long anymore.

We were divorced six months later. It was the hardest thing I have ever done. And the best thing. Henrik and I are still friends, and we both agree the divorce was the right decision. One of us just had to be brave enough to speak up.

Times of cold and quiet can be times for reflection as well. It can show us who we really are, when we are removed from the hustle and bustle of everyday life. It can resurface old dreams and desires.

That is what I love most about winter. You look around, and everything seems dormant. But under that layer of snow and ice, rebirth is growing.

If you want to hear more about how I made the decision to divorce my husband, you can sign up for my online course on how to know whether your relationship is really right for you. Link in profile!

1007 comments

mmmmarie001 You're book changed my life <3

ztrongnotzkinny Have you considered collaborating with a dietician? I have a new free e-book out on how gut health affects sexual health and libido and I think you'd find it really interesting!

larsenaxel hot

clarabellavida You are SUCH an inspiration!!! Also, looking fab! Loving the snowflake earrings, where did you buy them?

dianainstilettos merry Christmas! do u celebrate?? i thougt you were hindu

ljhefnhvbjgbvmb You make me sick. People should know what you've done. You've ruined so many lives. You are a fucking fraud.

Chapter 13

Belinda is waiting for us in the lounge. One wall is all tall windows, showing the idyllic landscape outside, the surface of the pond rippling gently in the breeze, a few puffy clouds floating by in the high blue sky, as though dotted there by a wistful painter.

There's a small group of puffy couches and chairs, all in soft shades of sage green, and she's in the process of getting a carton of soy milk out of the refrigerator next to the small sink.

"Hi, ladies," she says, gesturing toward the table in the middle of the couch group. "There's both black and green tea, and we've got an assortment of pastries here for you. Katarina, the muffins in the blue wrappers are vegan."

I walk up to her and ask, voice lowered:

"Is there any coffee? Or . . . whiskey?"

Belinda studies me for a few seconds, and then, matching my tone, she asks:

"You were first on the chopping block, then?"

The way she says it is not unkind.

I give a shaky little half sigh, half laugh.

"Yeah," I say. "Something like that. I could just really use some caffeine."

Belinda's finely arched eyebrows knit together in concern.

"Coffee really isn't going to help with the adrenaline, you know," she says, now in a near whisper. "I would strongly recommend the green tea. If you're feeling very stressed, we can go outside, and I can guide you through a quick breathing exercise."

I draw a quick, harsh breath before shaking my head.

"No, thank you," I say. "And thank you so much for offering. It's really very nice of you. But I would really, really like some coffee."

Belinda presses her lips together, and a phrase I remember from one of Martina's books pops into my head.

"It's conditioning," I say. "You know, like one of those, uh, schemas. I always have coffee in the morning, before work. It calms me down, because I usually drink it when I'm calm."

I see the corners of Belinda's mouth twitching upward.

I'm not sure if she's amused by my clumsy attempt at therapy speak, or if she's just decided to throw me a bone, because she leans in and whispers:

"We have some in the staff lounge. I'll go and make you a cup. Just don't tell on me to the doctor, all right?"

I exhale.

"Thank you," I say. "You're an angel."

Belinda turns to the group and says:

"I'll be right back. I just have to run and get something for a second. Please, help yourselves!"

Once she's gone, I wander up to the table, considering the assortment of sweets. There are mini-Danishes, perfect globules of red jam glistening in the middle; tiny cinnamon rolls, exquisitely braided and drizzled with frosting; and a couple of slightly larger blueberry muffins on a plate, off to the side, excommunicated from the pastry community on account of the unforgivable crime of being vegan.

"You can take one of the muffins, if you want," Katarina's shy voice tells me from my left-hand side. When I look up, she holds one up sheepishly, as though showing it to me. "I'm not going to eat all of them."

Truth be told, I'd much rather have one of the nonvegan treats, but given her kind smile and the fact that she's choosing to share with me, I grab one from the plate and sit down next to her. Sharing builds trust, after all, and if I'm going to get some of the others to agree to participate in the article, I'm going to need all the camaraderie I can get.

"Thank you," I say, taking a bite.

It's better than I would have expected, slightly tart from the blueberries and lemon zest and not overly sweet.

Clara takes a seat next to me, reaches out, and grabs a cinnamon roll before turning to me and asking:

"How are you feeling?" Her eyes are shining, and there's greed in the set of her mouth.

"Fine, I guess," I say. "I mean—"

Clara interrupts me.

"Seriously, that was so intense." Turning to Katarina, she adds, "Didn't you think that was just so intense?"

"It wasn't . . . quite what I expected." Katarina is frowning.

Clara shakes her head, her smile growing.

"She's just amazing," she says. "Watching her work is just, like, seeing a master craftsman. It's like she's psychic, or something."

"I just don't know if I'll feel comfortable . . ." Katarina says in a hushed voice, looking my way. "I mean, you didn't seem comfortable. But I don't know. Were you? I'm sorry. I feel like I'm overstepping."

"No, it's okay," I say. "I mean, I wasn't."

Katarina's frown deepens, the little groove between her eyebrows turning into a canyon.

"Have you guys heard anything about anyone else who's been here?" I ask them. "Do you think this is . . . normal?"

"No one knows exactly what the method is before they get here," Clara insists, with all the fervor of a true acolyte. "That's what's so amazing about Dr. Martina. It's, like, proprietary psychology."

A short, barking laugh cuts into the conversation.

"*Proprietary psychology?*" Leyla says.

She's standing in the doorway, leaning oh so casually against it, her eyebrows raised.

Clara reddens, but she pushes her shoulders back.

"Yeah," she says. "Basically. Sorry if I don't know the exact legal terminology."

"Don't you think that sounds a little bit strange?" Leyla asks. In the golden light from the window, she looks like a figure from a Renaissance painting, all strong curves and soft features.

"I don't know what would be strange about that," Clara says, crossing her arms across her chest and raising her chin.

"I'm just saying," Leyla says, "if she's made such a major, revolutionary breakthrough in the field of psychology, wouldn't she want everyone to have access to it? Wouldn't she have wanted to test it in a clinical environment and published a peer-reviewed paper or two on it?"

"The world of academia is old-fashioned and elitist," Clara says, with all the confidence of someone who has recently learned the word *elitist*.

"That may be so," Leyla says. "But I still think it's a bit strange to claim to have developed a radical new treatment protocol and to decide to keep it a secret. Seems a bit greedy to keep that information to yourself is all."

"If you're such a skeptic, then why are you here?" Clara asks, cocking her head to the side, smiling in name only.

Leyla shoots the exact same slim non-smile back at her.

"My mom wanted me to come," she says. "And I love my mom. It's only a week out of my life. So I'm here."

"So you just took a spot that could have gone to someone who would have really needed it?" Clara asks, dangerously close to a sneer. "That was really nice of you."

Leyla rolls her eyes.

"Trust me," she says. "Nobody needs this. Least of all you, princess."

Clara draws a sharp breath, her chest and throat reddening, and I open my mouth to try to break it up, but just then, the door swings open.

"Everyone enjoying the break?" Belinda asks, a bright smile on her face, which falters rapidly as she picks up on the humming tension in the room.

Leyla grins at her.

"I'm having a great time," she says.

Belinda looks over to me, and all I can do is shrug.

"Um," Belinda says, and then, seeming to decide to focus on something less heavily loaded: "I got your tea, Isobel."

"Thank you," I say, taking the cup from her and gulping down half the weak black coffee in two sips.

I burn my tongue, and when I begin to cough, Katarina moves toward me and slaps me on the back with surprising strength.

"Thank you," I manage to choke out.

Katarina looks down at my cup, then up at Belinda.

"That smells like coffee," she says.

"Well, that's it for the break!" Belinda chirps. "Please, if you can all follow me back to the group therapy room."

When we all file back into the room, like unusually obedient children, I notice that Pernilla is sitting back in her chair.

Her eyes are reddened, her lips slack.

Martina is standing by the window, looking out.

And when I look toward Pernilla's finger, she's no longer wearing the heavy diamond ring I saw her twisting less than half an hour ago.

Chapter 14

THE REST OF THE GROUP THERAPY SESSION IS LESS INTENSE than the first hour; Martina pivots away from having us talk about our past relationships, and instead has us play word association games, come up with examples of strategies for moving on from past relationships, and lectures us about the neurobiology of break-ups. For the last half hour, she even brings out a whiteboard.

I keep sneaking looks at Pernilla, who barely seems like she is there at all. Martina doesn't ask her any questions, either; she just sits there, occasionally attempting to twist the ring that is no longer there.

At the end of the session, when we all pile out for lunch, Pernilla doesn't follow.

Once lunch is over, when the waiters are clearing away the plates, I lean over the table and ask Anna, as casually as I can muster:

"Hey, do you know why Pernilla isn't here?"

Anna shakes her head.

"Maybe she just wasn't hungry," she says. "People have different circadian rhythms. She might just not be someone who eats lunch."

"I bet she doesn't," I hear Leyla mutter, but I ignore it.

"Is she okay, though? She looked upset."

Not just upset. She looked devastated. And that ring . . . I think about the way Pernilla was moving when she left the group therapy room. Slowly and with great effort. The way she didn't engage with what was said during the second half of the therapy session.

She almost looked like she'd been drugged.

"It's sweet of you to worry," Anna says, smiling. "But I'm sure she's fine."

I stare at Anna long enough for her smile to begin to falter; only then do I realize that I'm acting weird, and I shake my head, force a laugh.

"Sorry," I say. "Yeah, of course she is. And either way, we're in a safe place. You guys have medical training, right?"

I smile.

"We're trained in therapeutic caretaking," Anna responds. "We're perfectly capable of handling anything that might come up with any of our patients. Don't you worry."

Leyla clears her throat.

"But you don't have any medical training?" she asks Anna. "Like, say one of us had an accident. How long would it take for an ambulance to reach us?"

"I don't know why you would even be thinking about that," Clara butts in. "How would you even get hurt in a place like this?"

Leyla slowly raises her eyebrows.

"There are lots of ways to get hurt," she suggests. "It's only realistic to be prepared for it."

"Jesus," Clara mutters.

"Seriously." Leyla turns back to Anna. "If someone was to get hurt, how long would it take for an ambulance to get here? Or a police car?"

Anna sputters.

"I . . . well, I don't—not very long, I'm sure."

"Stop bullying her!" Clara bursts out. "What does it matter? No one is going to get hurt!"

Leyla makes eye contact with me and smirks for a moment.

I feel a tugging sensation under my ribs, and I force myself to swallow, look relaxed, like nothing about this conversation is out of the ordinary. Just a spat between two fellow "patients."

There are lots of ways to get hurt.

What did she mean by that?

Leyla relents and shrugs at Anna and Clara.

"I'm just saying. Doesn't seem very safe."

Anna's eyebrows twitch for a second; I see her take a deep breath before plastering the now-familiar Himlafall smile on her face.

It's funny; in a way, we're not so different, the Himlafall staff and I.

We're all acting.

The only difference is that they're putting on a face in order to maintain the illusion, and I'm putting one on hoping to shatter it.

"Well," Anna says, "if we're done worrying about that, I have your schedules for the afternoon. You've all got individual therapy, and physical therapy as a group. Other than that, it's free time until dinner."

She clears her throat.

"We recommend you use that time to take a walk, or journal, or simply process. Together or apart."

She collects a stack of papers from the tote bag next to her chair and reaches over the table to give them to me.

"Take one and pass them on," she says.

I grab the top page and hand the rest of them to Leyla.

02:00 p.m.—Leyla Demir, Individual Counseling
03:00 p.m.—Clara af Sperling, Individual Counseling
04:00 p.m.—Isobel Anderssen, Individual Counseling
04:00 p.m.—All, Physical Therapy
05:00 p.m.—Pernilla Boman, Individual Counseling
06:00 p.m.—Katarina Karlsson, Individual Counseling
07:00 p.m.—Dinner

"Well, looks like I better get a move on," Leyla says, pushing her chair away from the table and standing up. "I guess I'll see you all in physical therapy."

"Have fun," Clara chirps. "Enjoy getting healthier and happier." She shoots Leyla a poisonous glance.

Leyla grins at her. "I will." Her voice is sugary sweet. "Thank you so much for wishing me well."

I look closer at the schedule.

"Anna." I look at her. "Why is my therapy at the same time as the exercise?"

Anna blinks.

"You've been exempt from the physical therapy," she responds. "Because of your injury."

"What injury?" I ask.

"The doctor told me you had problems with your knees," she says. "So when we were making the schedule, we put you as exempt."

Wa-wait, n-no, I—I don't . . ." I stutter.

"Do I need to be exempt, too?" Katarina asks. "I have an old ankle thing from a marathon."

"Ellen has been informed of your limitations, and she's altered some of the exercises for you," Anna hurries to reassure her.

"No, wait. I don't have problems with my knees." My voice is too high, too pitchy, but the surprise has thrown me for a loop.

Anna raises her eyebrows.

"But . . ." Her eyes are wide. "But it was in your file?"

"I don't know why it was in my file, but it's not true," I insist. "I want physical therapy. For . . . the full experience of the treatment. It says in the materials that it's important. I don't want to miss out on part of the journey."

I can't miss physical therapy. I need to speak to Ellen, need to ask her about Susannah Wallin—look her in the eyes as I'm doing it—for any clues to what she might know. Whether or not she was the one who slid that note under my door.

I haven't seen her at either breakfast or lunch; haven't seen her since last night, in fact.

It's enough to make me think she's avoiding me on purpose.

"Gosh, I'm really sorry, Isobel." Anna looks bereft. "There must have been some mistake. Is there any way you accidentally checked the box in your application?"

"No," I start to say, but even as I'm speaking, I begin to question myself.

There were so many fucking boxes to check and uncheck in that application form. Pages and pages of probing questions. Is it possible I ticked a box, tired and trigger-happy and just wanting to be done with all the paperwork?

"Either way, I really want to participate," I insist.

Anna bites her cheek and frowns.

"Ellen said she couldn't take responsibility for such a severe injury," she says. "She was worried about the potential of making it worse."

"But there is no injury." I'm having a hard time keeping the frustration from distorting my voice.

"I don't know if anything can be done today." Anna frowns, biting her lip. "But if you talk to the doctor about it, I'm sure your file can be adjusted so that it'll all be taken care of by tomorrow. Is that okay?"

I swallow hard, twice, and then I nod.

"Yeah." I twist my lips into a smile. "That's fine."

Anna exhales.

"Again, I'm so sorry," she says. "Try not to let it ruin your day. We can't dwell on anger and resentment. The world is full of little accidents. Most of them turn out to be happy if you wait long enough."

"Oh," Clara interrupts, "that's from Martina's book, isn't it?"

Anna smiles. "Yes. From her second one. Chapter six."

Katarina puts her hand on my arm as they start talking about the genius of Martina Hastings.

"I'm going for a run after lunch, if you want to come with me." She smiles, all sympathy. "I get it. I lose my mind when I don't get to work out."

I return her smile. "Thanks," I say. "I might take you up on that."

I already know that I won't.

One thing Anna said stood out to me.

"Ellen said she couldn't take responsibility for such a severe injury."

Ellen is a physical therapist. So is Sandra. I've heard Sandra talk about her job enough to know that that is bullshit.

Was there really a mistake in my file? Or did Ellen make that up, knowing no one would check, so that I wouldn't be able to ask her any more questions?

I'm not going to go running. I'm going to go to the staff quarters and ask Ellen about Susannah Wallin.

Chapter 15

I WAIT UNTIL THE OTHERS HAVE LEFT THE DINING HALL BEFORE starting toward the staff quarters.

Sandra told me that the quarters are nice enough, that they are offered as a perk since the job is on-site. I should have asked her if they are locked during the day, if it's possible to access them, but I didn't, because the plan was for her to be here with me from the start.

I curse internally, bright sunshine beating down from above, making my eyes sting. I feel exposed; this would feel more appropriate under the cover of darkness.

When I come around the corner, I see that the curtains have been drawn at every window. The lingonberry bushes by the wall are beginning to bloom, small, green buds clustering, still hard and skeptical, yet unconvinced of the coming spring.

I stop, hesitating.

The sudden, creeping fear prickling along my scalp feels incongruent with the beautiful surroundings. The sky so high and blue, the gentle rippling of the pond.

No one knows I'm here. No one knows I've gone to speak to Ellen.

If she did leave that note—if she did, in fact, do something to Susannah Wallin, for whatever reason—how far might she be willing to go to keep that secret?

My feet feel rooted to the ground.

Should I tell someone?

No. I can't. I knew this would be risky; this is my chosen profession. I heard so many stories growing up about my father, undercover in risky situations, and I idolized him.

Though knowing what I know now, that so many of those stories were lies—knowing, in the end, when it mattered, he was a coward—doesn't inspire much confidence.

I draw a deep breath.

I am not my father. I am better than that.

I walk up to the door, but just as I'm about to grab the door handle, the door swings inward, and I take a step back, surprised.

Belinda is standing in the doorway, blinking at me.

"Isobel!" she says, smile sliding into place, seemingly without effort. "What are you doing here?"

"I . . ."

Belinda cocks her head.

"Is everything all right?" she asks.

She's got such a symmetrical face. It's strangely mesmerizing. Every freckle seems perfectly dotted into place, every eyebrow hair growing at the exact right angle.

"Yes," I say. "I was looking for Ellen. The physical therapist?"

"Why?" Belinda asks, frowning while still smiling.

The effect is disconcerting.

"I wanted to talk to her about . . . my knees," I say. "Apparently there was a mistake with my intake form. I want to partake in the physical therapy."

Belinda steps out onto the small porch and closes the door decisively behind her. The clicking of the mechanism falling into place sounds like a gunshot.

Belinda steps up to me and puts both her hands on my upper arms. She looks into my eyes, her gaze ever so worried.

"What's going on, Isobel?" she asks me.

"Nothing." The weight of her hands on my arms makes me feel uneasy. "I just wanted to clear up the misunderstanding."

"You know patients aren't allowed in the staff quarters." It's not a question, yet Belinda adds: "Right, Isobel?"

"It just . . . seemed like the quickest way to take care of the problem," I say. "I only need to speak to her for a couple of minutes."

Belinda nods slowly and thoughtfully.

Then she says:

"Take a deep breath with me, Isobel."

I want to protest, but she's still gripping both my shoulders, and when she pantomimes a big, deep inhale, I do the same.

"Do you feel better?" she asks me.

"I . . . sure." I nod. "Yes, I feel great."

It makes me feel small and unmoored, having to insist like I'm not upset, that I'm fine. Like an overtired child, up past their bedtime.

"Isobel." Belinda smiles as she says my name. "Do you feel lonely?"

"What?"

It's not what I was expecting her to say.

"I know that the absence of a person in the wake of a relationship can be crushing," she says. "Sometimes that can lead us to reach out to people in ways that aren't healthy."

"I'm not trying to reach out," I protest, but she keeps talking over me.

Her face is very close to mine, her fingers very strong.

"Sometimes we can even tell ourselves we have close bonds to people we don't know very well," Belinda continues. "We can even make things up in order to feel seen and heard."

"I'm not making things up," I manage to protest. "I really don't have a knee injury."

She's squeezing harder now. It's starting to hurt.

"It's okay," she says. "You're safe here. We're all with you."

She looks deep into my eyes, and for a moment I think I see a feeling in there. A glimpse of distaste.

Or disgust.

Then she lets go of me, and the relief is such that I take a step back before I can stop myself.

"You don't have to make things up for us to care about you." Belinda smiles. "Okay? If you want us to spend time with you, you can just ask. That's what Anna and I are here for."

"It's not about that." I look over her shoulder, toward the staff quarters. "I just want—"

Belinda steps closer to me, again, and I flinch.

"It's okay," she whispers. "We're here for you. We're all here with you in this. There is no need to be embarrassed. You just have to be truthful. Otherwise, what's the point? If you can't tell the truth, there's nothing for you here."

Nothing for you here. That is exactly what the note said.

It's very quiet around us. I can no longer hear the laughter in the distance, the wind sweeping through the treetops. It feels like the world is holding its breath.

"Tell me the truth, Isobel."

I stare at her.

"Did you—" I begin, but she interrupts me.

"You were going to sneak in to try to get your phone." Belinda tilts her head. "Weren't you?"

For a few seconds, my brain refuses to interpret what she's saying, turn the syllables into meaning.

"Wh-what?" I sputter.

"It's not the first time someone has tried to do that," Belinda says. "It's hard to handle being in the silence with your thoughts. The first couple of days are the hardest."

"I wasn't . . ." I begin to say, but Belinda shakes her head, and then smiles sadly, a touch condescendingly.

"It's okay, Isobel," she says. "Especially after the first therapy session. This is a tough process. You are functionally detoxing right now. I'm sure you usually spend hours every day stalking his Instagram page, or listening to old voicemails, or looking at pictures of the two of you together. Am I right?"

I feel like I can't think.

Is she fucking with me? Is this some game to her? Did she leave that note and use that phrase just now to test me, to see what I'd do?

Or was it just a coincidence? Is this all part of the twisted therapeutic protocol of Himlafall?

I can't tell. Not yet.

So I smile, as ruefully as I can muster, and say:

"Yeah, you're right."

I slump my shoulders in a show of contrition.

"It's normal," she says. "You have become addicted to the dopamine rush. It's unhealthy, but your brain can't differentiate positive dopamine from negative dopamine. It's going to be really tough for a couple of days, but once you get through that, you are going to be free from it. And from him. I know it's hard to imagine right now, but I promise you it's worth it."

My pulse is still racing, my heart fluttering like hummingbird wings.

"Your individual therapy session is at four, right?" she says, sliding her arm around my shoulders and beginning to walk. "I'll stay with you until then. I'll help distract you. We can walk around the pond a few times. We'll walk slowly so we don't strain your knees. You'll see. It's funny how little exercise you really need to feel better."

"That's okay," I try to tell her, but Belinda stops and looks at me, smiles with bright white teeth.

"Don't worry, Isobel," she says as she walks me away from the staff quarters. Away from Ellen.

"I won't leave your side."

Chapter 16

"THANK YOU, BELINDA," MARTINA SAYS.

Belinda smiles, and then leans down behind me, whispering in my ear, her breath warm on the sensitive skin on my neck.

"Good luck," she whispers, like an omen.

Then she walks off.

True to her word, Belinda hasn't left my side in the hour and a half that has gone by. She's kept up a steady stream of small talk the whole time, talking about music and film and literature, never leaving any space for any questions or pauses.

She steered me expertly, until it was time to hand me over to Martina for my individual therapy session. And now that time has come.

I hear the door closing.

Martina looks down at her notepad on her lap. Then up at me.

"So," she says, drawing the syllable out. "Isobel."

It sounds like she's tasting my name.

We're sitting by the window. I'm on the green couch, Martina in the armchair. There are two cups of tea on the table, and I reach out and grab the one nearest me, just to have something to do with my hands.

She's crossed her legs at the ankles; her shoes, I notice, are white patent leather loafers, and completely spotless.

"Yes," I say. "Hello."

"How nice of Belinda to keep you company this afternoon." Martina looks bemused.

"Very," I agree. "She's very nice. You've all been very nice."

"I'm glad you think so," Martina says.

I take a sip from the tea. It tastes like cardamom and citrus; it's lukewarm, and very good, with just a hint of sweetness.

Martina looks down at her notepad again, tapping the end of her pen against it a few times. The silence feels purposeful, like she's waiting for me to fill it. But I want to see what she will do if I remain quiet.

When she looks up, she asks me:

"Tell me, Isobel, what is it that you want to get out of your experience here at Himlafall?"

"Healing, I guess." An Isobel Anderssen answer. "I want to be happy. I want to find someone."

Martina presses her lips together, studying me closely.

Then she turns the notepad upside down and puts it down on the table, leans back in her chair.

"You know," she begins. Her tone is chatty, like we're two girlfriends sharing casual secrets. "I had a therapist, during my marriage. I saw her twice a week for two years."

"Oh?" I say.

"Yes." Martina nods. "Her name was Mika. She was Finnish. Lovely woman. She was very sweet. Very kind. She had this soft, lilting voice. I found it incredibly soothing."

"Okay," I say, wondering where she is going with this.

"The whole time I was seeing her, I was incredibly unhappy," Martina says. "But I didn't want anyone to know about that, so I didn't tell her about it. I'd let some of it slip occasionally, and then Mika would give me little exercises, and I would come back the next session, telling her I'd done them and that they had helped, and then we were both happy, at least for a little while. She was happy, because she thought she was helping me. And I was happy, because I felt like I had pleased her. I felt like I was being a good patient, and a good psychologist, and a good wife, because I was carrying all my burdens by myself. I wasn't forcing anyone else to have to deal with them."

Martina falls silent. Her amber eyes bore into me without blinking.

After another sip of tea, I put the cup back on the table.

"You're wondering if I'm telling the truth." Martina chuckles. "Aren't you? You're thinking I'm making this up, in order to make a point."

"I . . . no." The surprise makes my voice hollow.

"Yes, you are," Martina says immediately. "But yes, I'm being truthful."

That word again.

Truthful.

As though being truthful is the highest good; as though I'm a liar, and she knows it, and I know it.

Do they repeat that with all the patients?

Or can she tell there is something off about me? Can she tell what I'm hiding?

"I didn't think you were lying."

Martina ignores me.

"I want you to tell me why I told you that story." Martina raises an eyebrow. "Take a guess. Humor me."

"Probably in order to . . . find a parallel in what you're telling me. Right? Like it says in your book. All stories are the same stories."

I surprise myself with the quote. I read all her books cover to cover in preparation for this story, but I didn't know it was going to pop out of my mouth.

Martina leans forward in her chair and rests her chin in her hands, her elbows resting on her knees.

It makes her look like a schoolgirl at a sleepover: conspiratorial, as though about to share a morsel of gossip. Like we are whispering to each other in the dead of night, fragile threads of trust weaving back and forth until the web is stronger than any of the individual fibers could be on their own.

"You think you're too smart for therapy."

"No," I say, but she shakes her head.

"You're lying," she says, a singsongy twist to her words. "You do. You think you can see through all this shit. You think you're too complicated and too intelligent for therapy to work on you. It's a superiority complex. You hold it up as a shield against the world, thinking it will keep you safe, and despite the fact that it keeps failing, despite the fact that the only thing it's doing is keeping you lonely, you keep holding on to it, because you're too scared to try anything else."

I feel my cheeks burning.

In my mind, I flash back to a memory. An old one.

Standing in the kitchen, having broken a plate, panicked tears pooling in my eyes. One of the good ones my mother had inherited from her own grandmother: true bone china, with gold trim and intricate seashell-green patterns.

My dad's hand on my shoulder.

"It will be our secret. You and I, we don't care about silly things like plates. We know they don't matter."

And then, later, when she found out, and she was telling me off, hurt and disappointment radiating from her like waves, repeating his words back at her:

"I don't care about your silly plates. They don't matter at all."

The shock on her face. The strength I found in it, the glorious feeling of being above it all, of not having to admit to a mistake because I was better than that, better than caring about breaking things that were precious to other people.

"I'm here, aren't I?" I shoot back, rattled, and Martina smiles.

"Yes, you are," she says. "Because at the end of the day, you don't want to keep living like this. You're torn between wanting to change and finding that you can't."

She straightens back up, leaning back, and looks at me like she's sizing me up.

"I'm going to tell you something you're not going to like," Martina says. "It's going to make you angry, and it's going to make you want to leave, or hurt my feelings, or shut down. But I think you need to hear it."

"Okay. Hit me." It's not Isobel Anderssen speaking anymore. There is only me.

"You're not as special, or as different, as you think you are," Martina says. "I've seen hundreds of patients like you. This thing you keep doing, this facade you keep putting up? It's not working nearly as well as you think it is."

"That doesn't upset me." I smile, small and tight.

"Sure it doesn't." Martina laughs.

Fuck you lingers on my tongue, but I swallow the words.

It doesn't matter what she thinks she's seeing. It doesn't even matter if she's right. She can't tell me who I am.

I grasp for my role, for the comfort of Isobel Anderssen, but I can't figure out how she'd react in this situation. Isobel Anderssen the character doesn't isolate herself, shut herself off; she seeks out any means of understanding and comfort. If Isobel Anderssen was real, if she was here, Martina Hastings would never have spoken to her like this.

"I don't know why you are trying to make me uncomfortable," I finally manage.

"I'm not trying to do that," Martina says. "That is not my goal. But it's interesting that you're perceiving it that way."

"That is what you said," I insist. "That I would feel attacked."

"Do you feel attacked?"

"I feel like . . ." I search for something to say, something that won't give me away. "I feel like you don't like me."

I don't like the bitter taste the words leave on my tongue.

Like chalk. Like failure.

Is there a part of me that wants her to like me? That wants to be seen, heard, appreciated by this woman, despite what she's done, despite what she is?

I don't want to know the answer to that.

"I don't dislike you, Isobel," Martina says, softer now. "Hey. Look at me."

It's not a question; it's a command.

"I like you very much," Martina says. "I think you are a very intelligent, very compassionate, very interesting woman. I've seen how much care you've tried to take with the other patients, even though you only just met them yesterday. I see how hard you're working to keep it together, to keep your emotions in check so as to not burden other people with them."

She reaches out over the table and puts her hand over mine, squeezing it carefully.

"You're right in that I told you that story because I was hoping you would recognize something in it. I hope it's not too much of a cliché, but I see quite a bit of myself in you."

A shaky laugh tears out of my throat.

"I don't think so."

"You can't see yourself the way others see you," she says. "The way I see you, Isobel. And I want you to trust me enough to open up to me. Because I don't want you to make the mistakes I've made. I don't want you to choose the wrong partner because it feels safer to be loved than to love. I don't want you to get stuck in something that feels just good enough because you are too scared to be vulnerable. You are suffocating yourself slowly, little by little, because it feels easier to hurt yourself than to risk letting others hurt you."

"I'm not," I say, but my voice doesn't sound like my own; it sounds small and scared.

I have to ground myself. I can't let myself be sucked in.

I don't even realize that I've reached for the pendant until she says:

"It's pretty. Your necklace, I mean."

I tug my hand away. Much too quickly to be inconspicuous.

"Does it make you feel safe?" she asks.

"It's just a necklace," I say. Too fast, and too high-pitched.

"A gift?" Martina says. It's not really a question.

I flash back to when my father gave it to me.

My fourteenth birthday party. High, squealing laughter, the taste of chocolate and strawberries in my mouth; candles twinkling on the table, the cheap, sparkly nail polish I had sloppily applied glittering whenever I moved my hands.

My mother had spent weeks putting that party together. Inviting my friends, ordering the cake. She didn't bake, wasn't that kind of mom, but she still wanted me to have a good cake.

And yet, the moment my dad brought the box out of his pocket, all that ceased to matter.

My mom had bought me presents. Of course she had. An iPod, in exactly the teal color I'd coveted, a fuzzy sweater like the one I'd seen on TV.

But the necklace was a different kind of gift. It was a grown-up gift. Real jewelry, made from real white gold, and a rose, meant to tie me to my father. A reference to the last name we both shared, that my mother didn't.

It was meant to make me feel special while shutting my mother out. As always.

And it worked. Of course, it worked. I idolized my father; I thought he hung the moon and the stars. I wanted to be just like him. A truly great journalist. A truth teller and trailblazer.

Until the day he was arrested.

I clear my throat.

"Yes," I say. "It was a birthday present."

"Do you want to tell me about it?" Martina asks.

When I look at her, I get the strong feeling that she's offering me an opportunity. Yet another gift, this time from her to me.

Somehow, it feels like she already knows who gave me the necklace, the combined weight and relief of wearing it.

"My dad gave it to me," I admit, and it doesn't quite feel like I'm the one talking. It feels like she's pulling the words out of me effortlessly.

"On my fourteenth birthday."

"Before he left," Martina says, barely louder than a whisper, and I nod, like I'm in a trance.

"So now you do the leaving," she continues.

I feel trapped by the eye contact. I couldn't look away, even if I wanted to.

And I think I do.

I must.

"Now you do the leaving, and it makes you feel powerful," she continues. "You make sure never to love anyone the way you loved when you were a child, because you know, in your heart, that loving someone that way always leads to being left behind. It's inevitable. Every relationship has a winner, and you are determined to win, every time. To make sure it never happens again."

"Yes."

I have to get out of here. This is some trick she is playing on me.

"Don't let yourself get sucked in," Sandra told me before I left. *"Promise me."*

I promised, and I laughed, thinking I would never get sucked in, never be vulnerable to something or someone like this.

"You must have felt so very, very small." Martina's voice has grown very quiet. "You must have felt so little, and so scared. The person who was supposed to take care of you, the person you looked up to. Gone. And no matter what you did, no matter how hard you tried, you couldn't bring him back. You could never be good enough for him to come back."

I press my eyelids together in a feeble attempt at shutting down, hiding.

"I don't want to . . ." I don't know how to finish the sentence. "May I go, please?"

I hear the sound of Martina standing up from her chair and then feel the shifting of the couch under me as she sits down next to me. The solid weight of her arm around my shoulders.

"I'm not going anywhere, Isobel," her voice says in the dark, and I draw a deep, shuddering breath.

"But you have to trust me. You have to trust that all I do is because I care about you. Because I want you to get better. Because I want you to know that you deserve to never, ever get left behind, ever again. Can you do that? Can you listen to me? Can you trust me, the way you trusted back before you had ever been hurt?"

Yes.

I hate myself for thinking it.

But Martina pulls my head down on her shoulder, like a mother, and I let her, only for a second.

r/MomForAMinute

mom, I need some support

posted by: u/throwawayduckling123

04:56 05/12/2023

I just found this subreddit. I don't really use reddit that much, but my partner does. I hope I'm not breaking any rules by posting this. I've removed any identifying details in case they read this.

My mom passed away a few years ago, and I have really been missing her lately. I never knew my dad, as he left my mom before I was born. She died from cancer. I feel really guilty, because sometimes I'm still angry with her for not being here. I feel like she has abandoned me, even though I know it's not true. I'm sorry. I know that makes me a bad person. I was a better person when she was still around.

I've always struggled with interacting with other people. I was good at school growing up, but it was a stupid kind of smart, if that makes sense. I was good at memorizing things, and understand things like math and physics and grammar, but I couldn't really understand why people did the things they did. It led to me being bullied, but I was naive. A lot of times I didn't even understand that I was being teased or taken advantage of. (And before you ask, I am not neurodivergent. My mother had the doctors do a full work-up. I have some anxiety, but other than that, I'm fully neurotypical. I'm just . . . dumb, I guess. Like a stupid person masquerading as a smart person.)

Anyway, my mom was always the person who helped me make sense of the world. Even after I moved out, I would go visit her a couple of times a week, and she would help me feel better. Once she died, I felt completely lost. I had friends, and hobbies, and a good job that made me a lot of money, but it felt like I was constantly playing a part. My mom was the only person who accepted me the way I was. At least I felt that way, until I met my partner.

It was so good in the beginning. She made me feel so safe and seen. It was almost like having a little part of my mom back in my life, in a way. (Not like I wanted my partner to be my mom. I'm not very good at expressing myself. I'm sorry. I hope it makes sense.)

But in the last few months, everything I do seems like it's the wrong thing. I can't stop making mistakes. I can't stop upsetting her. This is the person I love most in the world, the person I want to spend the rest of my life with, and I'm hurting her, all the time, without meaning to. Sometimes I think about leaving, just so that she won't have to put up with me anymore, but I'm so scared to be alone again. I don't think I will ever find anyone else who will love me. And I know that it's selfish, but it hurts.

Can someone please tell me what to do? Can someone tell me how to stop? I just need my mom. I need a mom to tell me how to fix this. Or how to fix myself.

16 upvotes
6 comments

u/MrsButterworthsBaby—05:11 05/12/2023
Oh, honey. Reading this hurt my heart. You are so very hard on yourself. I wish I could give you a big hug. I hope you can feel that.

u/TeaWithIceIsNotIceTea—05:46 05/12/2023
Sweetheart, I'm not so sure you're doing anything wrong at all. You keep writing that you are stupid, and apologizing, but you have clearly managed to get good grades, and a very good job. You are self-sustaining and successful. Your mother would be very, very proud of you, and so am I.

I'm worried that your partner is abusing you, or grooming you for abuse. Does your partner tell you that you are stupid a lot? When you say that you upset them, do you mean that they scream at you and lose their temper? Have they /told/ you that no one else would ever love you if you left?

> **u/throwawayduckling123—05:48 05/12/2023**
> Would it be okay if I dm'ed you? I would like to keep talking about this, if that is okay and if you have the time. If not, I apologize.
>
> **u/TeaWithIceIsNotIceTea—06:21 05/12/2023**
> Of course you can!

Chapter 17

DINNER SEEMS TO TAKE FOREVER. THROUGHOUT THE MEAL, I find that I can barely choke down a bite, or focus much on what's going on around the table. At one point, my ears prick up as I hear Clara complaining:

"I hope that other physical therapist is better. What was her name? Sanna?"

"Sandra," Leyla corrects her, mouth half full of food.

"Whatever." Clara sighs and massages her neck. "I didn't like those exercises she had us do. I feel like they left me all unbalanced. I think they released some toxins or something."

There is a churning nausea in the pit of my stomach, and a faint buzzing sound in my ears. It feels like I've slipped away from myself, half exited my body; as though I'm watching my hands pick up the fork and spear a piece of chicken, just to put it back down, my own disconnected voice narrating the actions dispassionately.

I can't believe I fell for her act. Can't believe I let her in like that.

When I would ask my father about being undercover, when I was little and still thought of him as some untouchable, golden ideal I could never live up to, he always told me that the most important thing was to *never lose sight of yourself.*

"You have to always hold on to that little core of belief, princess. That belief that what you are doing is right, and important, and that the truth matters above all."

What a joke. What a fucking joke. At the end of the day, that was a lie, just like everything else he said; just like the lies he printed, the lies he told us, and his colleagues, and the court, until it all came crashing down in the biggest libel case of the century. Until our family name was a smear in the same papers he'd used to smear others.

Poetic justice, I guess.

And still. After all that. Still I wonder what strength he might have had that I apparently lack.

I failed. I let go of myself, for a moment, and now everything feels raw and wrong.

It's only when I'm back in the cabin, night having fallen outside, the last dying embers of the sunset flickering through the looming trees on the other side of the pond, that I manage to exhale.

I sit down on the floor by the bed, not wanting to be seen through the window, and bury my head in my hands.

"*Fuck*," I whisper, to the ears of no one.

I need a familiar face. I need to talk to someone who knows me.

Reaching in under the bed, I pull out my phone and go to the Wi-Fi settings. I don't care about getting caught having a device on me, not right now.

Three networks show up: HimlafallStaff, HimlafallOffice, and HimlafallGuest.

The last one isn't password-protected.

I click it, sweat beading on my temples despite the chilly air as I see the shitty, used-up phone working overtime to try to connect.

And then, like a miracle from the heavens, it connects.

With shaking hands, I select Armin's name and click on the FaceTime icon.

He answers within a few seconds.

"Thank fucking God," he says, his voice loud and searing and so very, very comforting in the small space of the cabin.

I hasten to lower the volume, despite not quite wanting to; I'd like to raise it instead, until the voice of my best friend fills the whole place, and chases all the ghosts away.

Armin is sweaty; I can see the screen lighting up his face as he walks up the stairs to his apartment. His purple T-shirt is stained dark around the collar, and a dark lock of hair is clinging to his forehead.

There's an angry little red zit right next to his nose, like a beauty mark; he always gets a pimple there when he's stressed. After he broke up with his last girlfriend, it lingered for months, like a little reminder of heartache.

"I was about to send the cops your way," he continues, and I hear very real anger in his voice, barely hidden below his joking tone. "And the fucking army, and maybe a SWAT team. I cannot *believe* you didn't call me yesterday."

"I'm sorry," I say, pulling my knees up to my chest and resting the arm holding the phone on them, so that I can see him properly.

"You promised, Isobel," Armin says. "You promised you would call every day."

"I didn't think yesterday counted," I say. "We talked in the car on the way up here."

"Don't play dumb with me," Armin says. "It didn't work when you pretended to have not stolen all my vodka in tenth grade, and it won't work now."

I laugh. It's weak, but it feels soothing, like the first blast of cold air from an air conditioner on a brutally hot day.

"I didn't take your vodka," I say. "I've told you so many times, man. That was your sister. I was innocent."

"Tara was thirteen," Armin says. "And she wasn't the one who puked all over the driveway."

He comes to a stop, looks down and away from the phone; I hear the jingling of keys.

"Were you out for a run?" I ask him.

"One sec," Armin says, and the phone shifts, pointing away over his shoulder, so I only see one-third of his face. A second later, I hear the clicking of a lock, the opening of a door.

Then he reappears, his face lit yellow by the hallway lamp, the triangular one from the '70s that came with the apartment.

I know that light well, and just the blurry sight of the front door behind him as he walks instills a sharp ache in my gut, shocking in its strength.

Armin's place is as much home to me as my own apartment, or the house I grew up in. More, probably; it's where I go when I'm sad, or when I'm happy, or when I'm lonely.

"Yeah, well, something like a run," he says as he walks into the living room. "More like a slow, sad jog. A lady in her seventies managed to lap me twice."

"She must have been extremely fast," I say; for the first time today, my smile is genuine.

Armin laughs. "Sure she was," he says. "Thanks for being so supportive."

"Anytime," I say.

I press my hand to the side of my throat, feeling the slowing beat of my heart.

Armin sits down on his couch. The worn millennial-gray fabric hovers in the background, right behind his shoulder.

"Gross," I say. "You're not going to take a shower?"

"Later," he says. "You know what my dad always says. You've got to wait until you stop sweating, otherwise you're just wasting water."

"Of course," I respond. "Very wise man, your father."

"In his own way," Armin agrees.

His face grows still, his eyebrows knitting together.

"Are you okay?" he asks. "You look pale."

I shake my head, leaning my chin on the arm I've hooked around my knees.

"I'm fine," I say.

Such a well-worn untruth that it flies easily from my lips. I know, as I say it, that he won't believe it, and there is such a comfort in that.

"What happened?" he asks. "How is it? The place, I mean."

His breathing is still fast from the run. I know what he would smell like if I was sitting there on the couch with him. The fresh eucalyptus scent from his detergent, the softer, herbal undertones from his deodorant, and then the reassuring smell of sweat, of human, something physical and distinct and reliable.

"It's weird," I say, shaking my head, letting out a little laugh that isn't quite a laugh. "It's . . . yeah. It's really, really weird, Armin."

I pause. I don't want to tell him the truth, but, then again, I clearly do. Why would I have called him, otherwise?

"Don't say I told you so." I raise my eyebrows at him, and he holds up two fingers like the Pope. "I feel like . . . I don't know. I don't want to say it, but I feel like I might have gotten in over my head here."

"Okay." Armin's voice is soft. Nonjudgmental.

"It's all just really fucked-up." I run my fingers on my free hand through my hair; I get caught on a knot, tugging at it, and the slight pain makes me wince.

"It's Martina Hastings," I finally admit. "She got in my head today."

"In what way?"

"It was almost like . . ." I smack my lips, and then I laugh, suddenly self-conscious. "Fuck, I'm going to sound crazy here. I know none of it is real. She's just really good at making people feel like she knows them. That's how she manages to get people to spend their life's savings on this retreat."

"But?" Armin encourages me.

". . . but it really felt like she knew things today," I admit. "Things she couldn't possibly know."

Armin hums. "You know," he says, "just because she might be a fraud and maybe a pseudo cult leader doesn't mean she can't be good at her job."

I bark out a laugh.

"Sure. Psychologist of the year."

"Well, I have been telling you to go to therapy." Armin grins. "Maybe this could be a two birds kind of deal."

"Fuck off."

He laughs.

It makes me feel ever so slightly more like a person. Like myself.

"Sorry about the whining. It's just been a very weird twenty-four hours. Sandra's not here, and I got this note, and—"

His voice pitches higher. "Hold on," Armin interrupts me. "Sandra's not there?"

I waver, feel the want to keep it from him, to not have him worry, not ask for help, not ask for anything but a few moments of his attention and his smile.

But he needs to know. He needs to know in case things go bad.

As they very well could.

"Andrea got sick," I admit to him. "She'll be here soon. Tomorrow. Or the day after, at the latest."

"Isobel." His voice is a warning.

"It's fine," I try to reassure him. "I just need to stick it out on my own for a few more days."

"It's not fine!" Armin rubs his face, and I see him taking a deep breath, visibly trying to calm down. "Isobel, it's not fine at all. You could get killed."

"I won't . . ." I go quiet, then shake my head. "I'm being careful, is my point."

"You've been there for a day," Armin reminds me, "and you say this woman—Martina—has already started to get to you. Who's to say it won't get worse? You were supposed to have Sandra with you. She was supposed to have your back. Keep you sane."

"I'm not going to go insane without Sandra here," I protest, feeling my hackles rising.

"I'm not saying that," Armin says, and I bite back:

"That was exactly what you said."

A moment of silence. Shorter than a breath, longer than it should be.

"I'm sorry." Armin looks sorry, though not quite sorry enough for my taste.

"I know you don't like this." I don't want to argue, because I know he didn't mean anything by what he said, and because I'm fairly certain I won't win.

"I know you think I'm taking a big risk, and I am. But I'm here, and I'm calling you to tell you, and I'm making progress. There really is something here. There is so much more going on here than just Sandra not having shown up."

"Like what?" Armin asks.

"I put Susannah's name out there, as a feeler," I begin. "Last night. And one of the employees clearly recognized the name."

"Really?" Curiosity always gets the better of him.

"Yeah." I nod for emphasis. "The other physical therapist had a big reaction. And I haven't been able to get ahold of her yet. I think she's avoiding me on purpose. And then, last night . . ."

I hesitate. I don't want to freak him out worse than I already have, but equal parts fear over what happened and excitement over my findings win out.

"Someone slid a note under my door. Telling me that it's too late and I should go home."

"They what?" Armin's face freezes.

"I know, it's weird." I sound too enthusiastic; I need to pull back. "But that proves there really is something here. I was right, Armin. Something happened here. Or is still happening. And I must be onto it, or whoever left that note wouldn't have felt the need to do so."

He is very still on the screen. For a moment, I think I've lost the signal.

"Armin?"

"I'm still here." His voice is quiet. Too quiet. He's not a quiet man; he wasn't a quiet boy, either.

"Listen—" I begin, but he shakes his head.

"Please, just hear me out, Isobel," he pleads with me. The tenor of his words, the set of his mouth, it all makes my stomach clench.

"Just . . . please be careful, all right? I know you want to expose this place. I know you want to build a name for yourself. I know this is important to you, and I know how much work you've put into it. I'm not going to ask you to come home, but can you promise me that you'll be safe? That you'll leave if things get more dangerous? Because I'm trying to be supportive, I really am, but all this, it just makes me feel like . . ." I can see him swallowing, the muscles in his throat working.

"It makes me feel like," he continues, his voice gravelly, "I can see the worst coming, on the horizon, and I can't do anything to stop it. There are no barricades I can build and no evacuation procedures I can follow and no good advice I can give. And frankly, that scares the shit out of me."

I close my eyes. And I nod.

"I promise," I say. "Thank you. For doing this. For picking up."

"I'll always pick up when you call," he assures me, and it should make me feel safer, but somehow it just makes me feel worse.

"I just . . . being here, seeing what they are doing, it makes me feel even more strongly about it," I attempt to explain. "I wish you could meet some of the other patients here, Armin. They're . . . vibrant, and smart, and successful. And Martina has convinced them that if they just pay her enough money, if they just give into her teachings, they will find this thing they are missing. An easy five-minute fix to all of their problems and they will have their happy ending. And because they want it so bad, she can break them down so that she can take from them. Money, and time, and trust. And no one is stopping her. It's . . . it's not right."

I draw a deep, shuddering breath.

"Isobel," Armin begins to say, but his voice is all wrong, confusion cut with fear, like ice melting in a strong drink. "There is someone behind you."

"What?"

"There is someone in the window, Isobel!"

I look up from his face on the phone screen to the little square showing mine. My shiny, tired visage; my stringy, air-dried hair; my red-rimmed eyes.

And the window behind me. A little rectangle of blue.

A shadowy outline of a person, standing outside, looking in. Looking at me.

Chapter 18

I DROP THE PHONE AND SPRING TO MY FEET, TURNING AS I GO and almost falling over. I catch myself on the bed and straighten up, only to look out the window and see nothing. Only the deep blue of the night sky staring back at me, reflected in the pond.

But there was someone there. I saw them. Armin saw them. And I can feel it still. Creeping over my skin.

Someone was here. Someone was watching me.

I turn around, running toward the door. I don't stop to put my shoes on. The ground outside is icy cold against my bare feet. The nighttime dew has fallen, and the gravel is slippery. But I run around the cabin, down to the walking path, the pond.

I'm half-blind in the dark, my eyes not yet adjusted to the low light outside. When I turn to face the main building, the staff quarters and the dining hall, they are all dark and abandoned. No light shining in the windows.

Just me, and the water, and the trees.

But I'm not alone. Not really.

There was someone here.

I turn around to look at my cabin again. It's higher than the walking path. You would have had to walk up there on purpose.

Walk up there, still and quiet, so I would not hear the footsteps on the gravel.

My heartbeat thundering in my ears, I hear my own ragged breathing, feel the chill already seeping in under my insufficient clothes, the soles of my feet growing numb.

I turn slowly, looking around me. The air feels sharp in my throat, as though the damp cold is cutting me.

"Hello?" I say.

The word is swallowed up by the night.

I take another few steps down, until I'm standing at the edge of the water. And I try to listen.

Whoever it was must be nearby. But it's entirely quiet. From where I am standing, I would hear the faintest footstep, even coming from the other side of the pond.

So either they managed to get away, quicker than any person should be able to move . . .

Or . . .

Or they are standing somewhere close by. Not moving.

Still watching.

Still waiting.

I can feel my breath tightening in my chest. The adrenaline swirling in my veins.

It's not only the cold making me shiver.

I feel very small. Reduced to my true form. A trembling little animal, with no fur or claws to protect me.

The sky is so much bigger up here. The dark so much deeper. Despite the cozy little cottages, despite the electricity and the Wi-Fi and the catering, we are in the wild. So very far away from anyone who might be able to help.

There is a splash in the pond behind me, and my whole body jerks violently as I spin around and stare out over the water.

Rings are moving lazily from a point about ten feet out, rippling the perfect mirror of the black sky.

Is there someone in the water? Hiding right under the surface? Waiting to burst out and pull me under?

I can see it so vividly. A body bursting forth with sudden violence. Gripping my shoulders with icy strength and pushing me down, until the last image I'd see would be the same thing I saw through the window.

A silhouette. An anonymous shadow.

I can't stay here in the open. But I can't go back, either. The goddamned doors don't lock from the inside.

I refuse to sit there, waiting for them to come back. Waiting for them to find me.

We are in the middle of nowhere. The figure in the window could have been anyone. Ellen, or Belinda, or one of the other patients.

Or someone else entirely.

Someone who has been waiting in the woods, lying still and low and quiet, biding their time until the right moment to pounce and prey on the women staying in these small, unprotected cabins, sleeping and relaxed in their beds, lulled into a false sense of security by flashy marketing.

Here, in the night, alone by the edge of the water, with no company but the deafening silence and the crushing feeling of unseen eyes creeping over my skin, I feel it rolling over me, choking me. The mammalian whisper, far back in my mind, screaming at me to go. To get out.

A droplet of sweat runs down my scalp, ticking the back of my neck, and I choke back hysterical laughter.

And then I freeze.

There. A sound.

Gravel crunching. Right behind one of the cabins. The one on the left.

Weight shifting. Preparing to attack.

I have to run. Have to hide. But there is nowhere to go.

The main house.

Anna told me yesterday that there is always someone there. On the night shift.

Someone who is awake. Someone who can help.

I make a split-second decision. And I take off running.

The rocks are cutting into my feet, but I barely notice. I can hear footsteps behind me, but I don't turn back. They're far away at first, but advancing.

Isobel.

My name. Like a whisper.

Is someone calling for me? Or is it only in my mind?

My vision grows blurry. If it's from fear, or from the icy cold wind in my face, I don't know.

The main house is getting closer. But not fast enough. The steps are advancing. It feels like a nightmare. My chest constricting, the stabbing pain under my ribs. Can't get enough air. Can't run fast enough.

I thought I was brave enough. Thought I was strong enough. I should have known better.

The small, weak child inside of me was never going to outrun the thing in the dark.

A sharp, cutting pain in my foot, and I shriek, almost fall. Sheer will forces me to keep going. I'm almost there.

I see the faint light from the door on the other side.

Safety.

I need someone to see. Someone to protect me.

Someone. Anyone.

A wisp of a feeling. Like outstretched fingers, grazing my hair.

Reaching out.

To grab, to hold.

To crush.

To silence.

With one last push of adrenaline, my muscles screaming, and maybe I'm screaming with them, maybe I'm trying, but no sound will come, because I'm out of breath, I run.

I run, and I grab at the door, and swing it open.

Fall into the light. Fall into safety.

"Isobel?"

Chapter 19

BELINDA STANDS UP BEHIND THE DESK.

I've fallen to my knees, and I hear myself babbling:

". . . the door, you have to barricade the door, they were right behind me, you have to lock it or something, have to—"

"Hey, hey," Belinda says, jogging out from behind the counter and up to me.

"Calm down," she says, but I grab ahold of her arm and look her in the eyes.

"Please," I say. "There was someone behind me. You have to lock the door. Now."

Belinda stares at me. Then she nods, a short, quick movement.

"Okay," she says. "I'll do that, then."

I hear her walking behind me. Hear the clicking of a lock, the slick sound of steel sliding against steel.

It should ease the tension in my body, should allow me to exhale. But I'm still shaking.

There are too many windows. Too many weak points. Too many places where someone could enter, if they wanted to, if they had decided to.

It's all so fragile, after all. Walls and doors and windows. Held up by no more than a mutual unspoken agreement.

A false sense of safety. A duvet against the monster under the bed.

"All right," Belinda says, and she sits down on the floor, opposite me.

Her legs fold neatly underneath her, and she puts her hands together on top of her thighs.

"What happened?" she asks me.

I just shake my head.

"Okay," Belinda says. "Try to breathe. Here, do it like this." She puts her hand at the bottom of her ribs.

"Put your fingers here," she says. "And then breathe in until you can feel your chest moving with your hand, and then breathe out again. In through your nose, out through your mouth."

I copy her movement, only now realizing that my hands are so cold my fingers hurt; I can barely feel anything at all.

But nevertheless, I do as I'm told.

I fill my lungs with air, then push it out through my lips.

Belinda does it a few more times, and I feel sensation beginning to flood back into my body. The immediate, horrifyingly pinpointed clarity of adrenaline begins to ebb away, and I start to notice little details.

Belinda isn't wearing jeans anymore; she's in a knitted dove-gray cashmere set. She's taken off her makeup, her cheeks red and her eyelashes pale, and her hair is in a loose bun at the nape of her neck.

"Better?" she asks, and I nod, let my hand fall back onto my lap.

"Good," she says. "It's okay. Do you know where you are?"

"Yes," I say, somewhat confused. "I'm in the reception. At the main building."

"What is the last thing you remember?" Belinda asks me.

"What . . . from when?"

"From before you fell asleep," Belinda says.

I stare at her.

"I wasn't sleeping," I say.

Belinda smiles.

"Is this the first time you've ever had a sleepwalking episode?" she asks.

"I wasn't sleepwalking," I protest.

Belinda frowns. Her forehead doesn't move, but her eyebrows twitch, and her eyes grow slimmer.

"Of course you were," she insists, her voice soothing, as though talking to an overtired toddler. "Your brain might have made up an explanation for what happened, but that's quite common. Especially in a new environment. You'd be surprised at how often it happens. About a month ago, we found a patient walking out of the woods in the morning. It scared the ever-living crap out of everyone, if you'll excuse my language."

"No." I shake my head.

"Isobel." She is patience personified. "Look at you. Why would you be running around this late, in the dark, with no jacket and no shoes?"

She leans over to take a look at my feet and flinches.

"My goodness!" she exclaims. "Your feet. They're all cut up. I can't believe that didn't wake you. I'm so sorry. Let me go get the first aid kit."

She begins to rise to her feet, but I reach out and grab her arm.

"Wait," I say. "No. I wasn't sleepwalking. There was someone there. Someone was staring in through my window. I went out to see who it was, but they were hiding. I heard them, and I decided to come here, and they were following me. Chasing me." I swallow hard, the iron taste of fear still lingering in the back of my throat.

Belinda blinks.

"What?" she asks.

"I know it sounds crazy. But there was someone there. It felt like they wanted to . . . like they were going to hurt me." I wish I could explain it to her in a way she could understand; wish I could convince her I'm not lying, neither desperate for attention nor sleepwalking.

"We can make up a lot of things in our minds when we're tired." Belinda shakes her head, but her voice is wavering, just slightly. Something in my face or my voice must have gotten to her.

"I didn't make it up," I tell her. "I saw someone. There was someone there."

"It might have been one of the other patients," Belinda says. "We always recommend taking a walk if you have a hard time sleeping."

"But what possible cause could they have had to just stare in through my window like that?" I try to reason. "Someone might have come through the woods. There are no fences in that direction."

For a moment, I see something in her eyes. A flicker.

Not fear. But, perhaps, doubt. Doubt in what she, herself, is saying.

But then it's gone.

"How about this," Belinda says, rising into standing and holding out her hand. "I'll go and have a look out the door, okay? And if there's someone there, we'll call the police."

"No," I protest, but she's already up and walking, and I scramble to get to my feet. "Don't do that—"

With a swift, efficient click, Belinda has unlocked the door and swung it open.

For a second, I'm so convinced that someone, the terror from my nightmares, will come swinging in through the door that I actually see it. I see something huge and dark and monstrous, bursting in with the cold wind.

But I blink, and it's gone.

Belinda takes a couple of steps out on the first step of the low stairs and looks around. I see her shoulders falling, her spine straightening.

When she turns around, her eyes are mild, her tone secure, but I swear there's something like relief in her posture.

"Come on, Isobel," she urges me. "Come out here and take a look."

I don't want to. But I get up, my feet stinging so badly I hiss, and limp on over to the door.

I lean out.

It's calm and silent. I can see the parking lot from where we are standing, the gates like thin, metallic saplings in the distance.

"There's no one here, Isobel," Belinda assures me. "It was a nightmare. That was all."

She walks back in and shuts the door again.

"It's okay," she says. "Like I said, it happens all the time."

When she smiles, teeth exposed and eyes flat, I want to tell her that she's wrong. I want to tell her that there was someone there, that I wasn't the only person who saw them.

But I can't.

Because in order to do that, I would have to tell her that Armin saw them, too. I'd have to tell her about the phone. And the note left under my door.

And as Belinda keeps smiling at me with what must surely be feigned gentle patience, another thought worms its way out through my mind.

Her cheeks have reddened. As though through exertion. Or cold.

And she is wearing shoes. Soft, sturdy sneakers. They aren't making a sound against the floor.

Maybe no one was chasing me after all. Maybe that part was all in my mind.

Maybe the person standing outside the window, watching me talk to Armin, instead snuck back to the main building on the other side, and waited there until I arrived, as though she had been there the whole time.

I won't leave your side.

A different kind of chill floods my body.

"Come on," Belinda says. "Let's get some Band-Aids on those feet, huh? I have some wound cleaner in the first aid kit. We don't want you getting an infection."

I follow her, wordlessly, into the lounge, let her clean my bleeding scrapes without making a sound, as I watch her calm, steady hands bandage up my feet. She gets me a pair of shoes from the lost and found, two sizes too big, so that I can get back to my cabin without hurting my feet any worse than I already have, and I thank her, eyes downcast, mouth set in a firm line, as though ashamed.

Better to let her think she's convinced me. Better to let her think I've accepted the party line.

On the way out, Belinda once more takes her place behind the reception, and she waves cheerfully at me, a little smile on her lips, like we've just shared a joke.

The printer is sitting right behind her.

When I get back to the cabin, my door is still hanging slightly open. I draw a deep breath and push; it swings inward without a sound, hinges perfectly oiled.

Everything is as I left it. The little lamp on the bedside table still casting its warm glow over the bed, the blanket half on the floor. My shoes are where I kicked them off in the corner.

Still, I go into the bathroom, pull the curtain all the way back, inspect the shower. I get down on my hands and knees and look under the bed.

Nothing.

It's only when I turn around and survey the floor that I realize what is missing.

My illicit iPhone, the one I dropped on the rug, is nowhere to be found.

Chapter 20

I BLINK MYSELF AWAKE, HARSH SUNLIGHT STREAMING IN through the window. My eyes feel filled with sand, dry and painful, and my spine seems to have rearranged itself at some point during the night. Thirty-something backs don't like sleeping upright against a wooden door, no matter how much the brain in charge wants to make sure no one can get in and catch it unaware.

I groan, rubbing my eyes until little sparks of light seem to set off behind my eyelids. For a few seconds, exhaustion lets me stay blissfully ignorant of what happened last night, but then, when I try to get up from the floor, the soles of my feet remind me, and it all comes flooding back.

My phone. My one connection to the outside world.

For a second, it feels as though I'm about to puke.

I rush into the bathroom, spitting into the sink, and then I rest my forehead against the cool mirror, drawing a deep breath. I try to trick myself into being calm and collected; maybe, if I tell myself that I'm not freaking out, that I haven't gotten myself into something I'm not sure I can handle, I'll believe it.

Well, what did you think was going to happen?

Not this.

Armin's worried face from the last night before I left comes back to me. Softly lit by the hundred-year-old lamps of the pub where I work Mondays through Thursdays, his fingers worrying away at a coaster, tearing it into tiny little pieces.

I'm just scared that you're treating this like it's some kind of game. It's not a game. It's serious.

God, I thought he was being so condescending. I thought I had it all figured out. It was in my blood, after all.

When I was a kid, and my dad would tell his stories, I found them exciting, never frightening. He always came back no worse for the wear. When he told me about being held at gunpoint, or having to hide from bombs, it never seemed scary; he was my dad, invincible through the sheer forces of charm and destiny. Nothing could touch him, and therefore, he was never in any real danger.

Later, when he was in prison, after the judge gave him the harshest sentence ever doled out in a libel case in Swedish history, I found out along with the rest of the world that some of those stories had never happened. He'd never even been to some of the places he had written about, and if he had, he'd been holed up in a hotel, working off nuggets of information given to him by real journalists, the ones who had actually put themselves in harm's way. Some of whom had never come home to their families the way he always came home to ours.

And I told myself that I would be different. I would not be like my father. I would be like the other journalists, the real journalists, the ones who put the truth above themselves.

But for the first time—and it is vaguely nauseating to realize this—I understand why my father did what he did.

Not all of it.

But being here, cut off from those who might try to help me, knowing now that something is going on, that it's not all in my mind, I understand why he might have stayed in those hotel rooms rather than going out and facing the dangers of the world.

Because I'm frightened. Because I want to go home. Because I'm not sure I'm up for it. Not now that it's all real.

But if I do . . . I'm just like him.

I straighten up and look in the mirror. My short dark hair is tangled in the back, flattened where I have leaned my head against the door. My lips are dry and cracked.

The rose pendant hangs heavy against my chest.

This is what makes us different, Dad, I think as my features seem to morph in the mirror until I'm looking at my father.

We always did look so very alike.

I don't run away when things get hard.

Chapter 21

THE AIR SEEMS TO HAVE SHIFTED DURING THE NIGHT; DESPITE the high, clear skies, there is a heavy sense of anticipation, a pressure that seems to charge the air with something to come.

Before breakfast, I stop by the reception area. Belinda has been replaced by Anna, which makes me feel a little bit calmer.

Anna doesn't seem to be in quite as deep as Belinda is. At least not yet. Though maybe I'm just fooling myself.

"Good morning," she says, swinging her feet down from the desk; she's been sitting with her shoes up, leaning back in the rolling chair and reading a book.

She looks so immaculate it almost hurts to look at her, a fresh white T-shirt tucked into white jeans, blond hair pulled back into a perfect, perky ponytail. It's as though she's advertising something. Toothpaste, maybe. Or probiotic yogurt.

"Did you sleep okay?" she asks.

"Not great," I respond.

"Yeah, you look a bit tired," Anna says.

I don't think she's being bitchy; she's just making an observation.

"What are you reading?" I ask her.

She holds up the book so that I can see the title. The bright orange cover says *Steal My Sunshine: How to Rid Your Life of Energy Vampires and other Ghouls.*

"Huh," I say. "Is it good?"

"It's really interesting," Anna says. "The writing isn't great, but there are some good pointers in there. My ex was really toxic, always trying to put me down, so I'm trying to redirect my romantic energy." She turns a couple of pages back, and starts to read out loud:

"An energy vampire will try to put you down in order to feel better about themselves. When confronted, they will deny this and tell you that you are being insensitive, taking up too much space, or not listening to their needs. In order to free yourself from the limitations others are trying to put on you, you must harden yourself against this oppressive negative feedback. Weaponized feedback is the tool of the cruel."

She looks up at me, eyebrows raised.

"Right?"

"Sure." I hesitate. "I mean, that sounds a little bit sketchy, though. Right? You have to be open to hearing *some* bad things about yourself."

Anna nods energetically.

"Yeah, yeah, of course," she agrees. "But you can tell when it's not sincere. Like, my ex was always trying to fuck with my head. Sometimes I felt like I was going crazy. Like, just affirm my sense of reality, you know? I'm just trying to live here!"

"Totally," I say. "Of course."

Anna closes the book and makes a little face. "I mean, it's not great literature or anything," she admits. "But at least it's better than Dr. Martina's books."

I feel myself snapping to attention; were I a cat, my pupils would have grown to the size of coins.

"What do you mean?" I ask her.

Anna looks down the hallway, then back to me as she lowers her voice.

"Don't tell on me, but I just don't think her stuff is very good," she whispers. "I mean, she doesn't exactly live the way she preaches. Sometimes I think that she's just trying to peddle this *crap* in order to—" Her voice grows frustrated, but then her mouth snaps shut as her eyes move to something behind me, and she sits up at attention.

"Belinda, hey!" she chirps.

I turn around, and Belinda is standing in the doorway with a big cup of something hot in her hand.

"Oh, Isobel." She smiles. "Good morning. I hope you got some sleep last night after you got back? And how are your feet?"

"They're fine." I'm lying. My feet actually hurt quite badly. It's like having a thousand little paper cuts. I peeled the gauze off in the shower, groaning through my teeth with pain as they had stuck to the dried blood.

"Did something happen last night?" Anna asks behind me.

I linger, looking at Belinda, before I turn to Anna and slap on a smile.

"No," I say. "I just had a . . . sleepwalking incident."

"Huh." Anna scrunches up her forehead. "Weird. I've never met anyone here who has sleepwalked. Must be scary, with all these woods and water around."

I look over at Belinda. Her face is still entirely smooth, not a trace of feeling in her eyes.

"You were sleepwalking. It happens all the time."

Not that often, apparently.

"Did you want something, Isobel? They just started serving breakfast," Belinda says, walking past me and behind the counter.

"I wouldn't want you to miss out on it," she says, pure maternal care in her words as she puts the green tea down in front of Anna. "Not after the night you've had."

"Thank you for telling me." I show as many teeth as I can, hoping the very width of my smile will convince her of my lack of suspicion.

"I actually just wanted to ask if it would be possible for you all to place a call to my emergency contact?"

Belinda cocks her head to the side. "Is something wrong?"

The smile is making my cheeks ache.

"Not at all," I respond. "I just promised I'd get in touch after a couple of days. Let my family know that everything is okay and going well. And since I don't have any means of doing that myself . . ."

I let the words trail off, making direct eye contact with Belinda.

"That is so sweet," Anna cuts in. "Don't worry, I'll take care of that for you."

"Thank you so much," I say, and as I turn to leave, I hear Belinda call out, behind my back:

"Don't you worry, Isobel. We'll talk to them for you."

When I look over my shoulder, she's still smiling. The corners of her mouth stretched wide, her eyes perfectly dull, like pebbles polished smooth by the sea.

51.7k likes

doctormartinahastings I did an interview today (with the lovely @karaolsenjournalist—it will run in the Friday edition of @stockholmdaily, keep an eye out for it!) and was asked what the most common question I get asked by patients is.

Some of you might assume that it's "How do I move on?" Others might think it's "How do I find the love of my life?"

It's neither of those.

The question I get asked most often is "How do I get them back?"

Loss is difficult. It's difficult for all the reasons you would assume—loneliness, and regret, and longing. But a break-up also reactivates old feelings.

As children, we learn shame through interrupted attempts at intimacy. We reach out—for a hug, or for a kiss, or for validation—and get rebuffed. It creates a holistic, full-body response in us, a voice that says: I am not wanted. The affection I have to give is bothersome. My love is a nuisance.

When my patients, or my followers, ask me how to get someone back, I always ask them why they want to get back together with that person. The first response is always some variation on the same theme: "I love them," "I miss them," "I thought they were the one."

But when you dig deeper, you might find that the first response you give is not necessarily the truth.

You are not the one screaming out for the boyfriend, girlfriend, or significant other to come back to you. If you listen to that voice, you might find that it is the voice of a child. A small, wounded child who thinks that by fixing this one broken relationship, they can fix all the things that have shattered in the past.

That is not to say that relationships cannot be healed. But first, you need to heal yourself.

When I feel the pull from the past, I always make sure to treat myself in the way I like to be treated. Today, that is through taking control of my gut health. @bloatinggirlies probiotics have really helped me get more energy—15% discount for the first 500 people to use the code #DoctorMartina! Link in my description :)

799 comments

bloatinggirlies We love you!!

clarabellavida ive written you a few times, would love to chat with you if you have time :) you are SUCH an inspiration!!!!!!

micc44444 u look old nd used up

karaolsenjournalist loved our chat today! you look fab!

> **ljhefnhvbjgbvmb** @karaolsenjournalist i have some information about “doctor” martina if you want to know the real story. i’ve dmed you.

Chapter 22

The only person in the dining hall is Pernilla.

She is sitting at the table, staring at a cup of steaming green tea.

At the sight of her, I'm struck by a ridiculous urge to sit farther down the table, keep to myself. It's not because I don't want to sit with her; it's more that her icy perfection reminds me of some of my mom's friends, the way they would scrutinize me as a teenager after my dad went away and my mom retreated into herself in order to keep everything running.

Looking back, I know now that they saved us. They would come over after my mom came home from work, clad in light, gauzy shawls and with their heavy glasses perched at the tips of their noses, always carrying some takeout that they had "just happened" to pick up so that both I and my mom would get fed. Sometimes, they would pour her a glass of wine, if she seemed like she needed it; other times, they would discreetly dispose of the bottle, if they judged that she had had enough.

In their own ways, they were deeply, deeply kind. They cared so much for my mother. They kept her going.

But they didn't know how to care for me in the same way. And I wasn't easy to care for at the time. A small, furious ball of teenage confusion, hacking away at my hair and piercing my nose in the bathroom just to have some way of expressing how lost I felt.

So they would criticize me instead.

Isobel, you look absolutely horrendous.

Isobel, how come you haven't cleaned up around here?

Isobel, please, leave your mother alone. Don't you think she has got enough to deal with?

I still have a hard time with well-put-together women in their fifties and sixties. They make me want to shrink, grow up smaller, take up less space.

They also make me want to throw things, scream at the top of my lungs, burst into tears.

But I'm not sixteen anymore. I'm an adult and, nominally, a fellow patient. And I have questions for Pernilla.

So I sit down opposite Pernilla and clear my throat before saying:

"Good morning."

She looks up.

I don't think I'm imagining the fact that she's scrutinizing me.

"Good morning," she says, her own face quite inscrutable.

It's tempting to just not talk, but I decide to go big instead. Pernilla already doesn't seem to like me, or, well, to be fair, she doesn't seem to like anyone. So I can't possibly make her esteem of me any lower.

"I can't believe how nice you look so early in the morning." I gesture toward her neat cardigan, held together by one big button, the discreet row of pearls around her neck, the impeccably applied makeup.

"I could barely get myself to shower this morning, I was so tired. But you look so . . . well-groomed."

Pernilla raises her eyebrows for a second, and I think that she's going to cut me down with some incredibly elegant, scathing remark, but then she says:

"Thank you. I feel better when I feel like I'm presenting myself well."

"I get that." I smile tentatively.

The lightning-quick once-over I get from her indicates that she doesn't think that I get that at all, actually, but she lets it go.

"It's not so much work, really, once you get it down to a routine," she offers, picking her cup up before appearing to change her mind and putting it down again on the table.

When she meets my eyes, I swear it looks like she's softening.

"It's nice, when you're in a place like this," she continues, shooting a look of disgust down at her green tea.

I lean forward over the table and lower my voice. Something about it being just the two of us in the large, echoing room makes it feel oddly intimate.

"Wouldn't you just kill for a cup of coffee?" I ask her.

She pushes her lips together.

And then she rolls her eyes.

"Lord, would I ever," she whispers back. "I can't stand this herbal nonsense. I don't understand how being given a proper breakfast would interfere with our so-called treatment."

I laugh, delighted, and Pernilla gives me a begrudging smile.

"Yes," I agree with her. "It seems strange, doesn't it? But this whole place seems a little bit strange to me."

"What do you mean?" Pernilla asks.

She has pulled back a bit, and I waver; I don't want to risk the faint connection we have built.

But the memory of yesterday, of how Martina held her back when the rest of us were taking a break, makes me push on.

"I just mean that the methods seem a little bit . . . extreme to me," I say. "And there is something about this place. Isn't there?"

Pernilla knits her hands together in her lap and looks down at them. I can see the indentation where her ring used to be, a faint line of soft skin at the base of her ring finger. She is stroking it with her thumb.

"I hope you don't mind me asking." I lower my voice even further. "I noticed you're not wearing your wedding ring anymore."

Pernilla whips up her head.

She pushes her lips together. I see the muscles working in her achingly thin neck as she swallows.

"Is that so?" Her voice has gone sharp.

"Where did it go?" I ask her.

Pernilla straightens up fully in her chair.

"I don't think what jewelry I wear is any of your business," she says, with all the ironclad confidence a lifetime of condescension can bring.

But I know I'm onto something. I can feel it, almost touch it.

"Did you give it to Martina?" I ask her. "Did she get you to give it to her? Did she talk you into it?"

I can feel her wavering.

She opens her mouth.

But then the doors at the far end fly open, and Leyla comes walking in, followed by Clara.

"Oh, good, I was worried I was late!" Clara says, before waving at us. "Good morning!"

I see something behind Pernilla's eyes locking shut.

She stands up from her chair, pushing it back sharply.

"I have just realized I am not very hungry," she announces to the room, not even giving me a glance as she leaves through the same doors the others have just come in through.

I slump back in my chair, disappointment nailing me to the wooden chair.

A gentle wisp of steam is still rising from her cup of green tea.

"Do you think there is any chance of getting some orange juice?" Leyla asks, taking a seat next to me. "I don't think I can choke down another cup of tea."

The frustration is making me want to snap, but it's not her fault she decided to arrive at breakfast at an inopportune time. Nor is it her fault I decided to try to make a breakthrough with Pernilla in the dining hall.

Clara sits down opposite me.

"Hey, are you okay?" Leyla asks, nudging me with her elbow. "You look tired."

"I didn't sleep great," I mutter.

Clara moves the cup of tea out of her way, so quickly the hot liquid splashes over onto the table.

"I have some green-coffee eye masks you can try," she offers. "They will get rid of those horrible dark circles in a jiffy."

She puts her fingers to her cheeks and pulls upward. "They might actually help with those bags, too," she adds.

"Yeah, and heal her relationship with her parents and grow back her hymen, right?" Leyla asks her, smirking.

Clara flicks her pink braid over her shoulder and stares at Leyla. She's wearing her hair like Martina, I realize, and her clothes look like the good doctor's, too, the same kind of white linen button-down, tucked into the same kind of light-wash straight-legged jeans.

"The hymen is a myth," she points out, with an icy bite to her words. "You of all people should really know that."

Leyla snorts.

Just then, the doors open to the kitchen, and one of the waiters comes out carrying a plate of whole-wheat toast, cottage cheese, and fruit salad.

She stops when she sees us.

"Where did Mrs. Boman go?" she asks.

"Pernilla realized she wasn't hungry," I explain, as Leyla remarks:

"Wait, she asked you to call her Mrs. Boman? That is ridiculous."

"I'll take it!" Clara chimes in. "I'm absolutely starving. I barely slept a wink. I need to refill my energy deposits."

Leyla groans. "Just say you need to eat, like a normal person."

I decide that Pernilla's choice was a good one; I, too, can't take having breakfast with Leyla and Clara today.

I stand up from the table.

Leyla looks up at me. "What's up?" she asks.

"I'm not feeling so good," I tell her, putting my hand on my stomach for effect. "Cramps."

"You poor thing," Clara says. "I have a visualization exercise for menstrual pains that's really good. It's all about picturing how your body is ridding itself of toxicity, and—"

"Or I've got some paracetamol, if you want some," Leyla cuts in.

"No, I'm good, I'm just going to go lay down for a second," I say.

"See you in therapy!" Clara says, and I wave at her before going outside.

The sunlight is too sharp; it feels as though it's actually cutting into my skull through my eyes, worsening the burgeoning headache I can feel pounding behind my eyebrows.

But as I walk out of the dining hall, I stop in my tracks.

There is a beaten-up green Prius parked next to my flashy rental.

A car I know well.

Sandra is finally here.

Chapter 23

"SANDRA!"

I run up to her and throw my arms around her, tilting her momentarily off-balance.

She smells like herself, like mint, and cheap soap, and aggressive deodorant; I have never recognized what a comforting mix of scents that is before.

Sandra wiggles out of my grip almost immediately.

"Jesus, Isobel," she hisses at me. "Not here."

She tosses a glance over at the main building.

"Sorry." I take a step back. "I'm just . . . I'm really happy to see you."

Sandra's short golden-blond hair is pulled back into a bristly ponytail at the nape of her neck, and she is wearing an Adidas tracksuit that pulls over her broad shoulders; it looks as though she might have taken Andrea's by mistake. Andrea takes after her mom more than her dad, with the same short stature and sturdy, muscular build, but she doesn't have Sandra's thirty-plus years of athletic pursuits to fill out her frame yet.

Sandra is still looking around, a haunted expression in her eyes.

"What's wrong?" I ask her.

"Not here, seriously," Sandra mutters. "Come on, get in the passenger seat. Before anyone sees you."

Wordlessly, I follow her instructions, climbing into the car and shutting the door behind me. There is a crumpled-up McDonald's bag on the floor, and a half-empty off-brand sports drink in the cup holder; the radio is still softly playing the maudlin old Swedish classics Sandra always denies liking, despite all the evidence to the contrary.

Sandra pulls the door shut behind her.

"Is everything okay?" I ask her. "Is Andrea all right?"

"Yeah, yeah, of course." Sandra waves me off. "She's with her dad, she's doing fine. I think she just wanted me around for a few days longer, to tell the truth."

"Of course she did," I say. "You're her mom."

Sandra rolls her eyes. "Thanks. More mom guilt is exactly what I needed right now."

"Sorry," I respond, instantly humbled.

Sandra locks the doors before turning to me.

"We can't talk for long. I don't want them seeing us together."

"No, I get that," I say. "I'm sorry. I didn't mean to be an idiot about it."

Sandra drums her fingers on the steering wheel. Her eyes are locked on the trees beyond the fence.

"Listen," she says. "I'll keep this quick, before anyone catches us. I reached out to someone who used to work here. The other psychologist who got let go last year. I was thinking she might be up for being quoted in your article."

"I thought you said no one would be willing to talk?" The surprise makes my voice hitch and climb.

"Listen, Isobel." Sandra draws a deep breath.

I recognize that tone of voice; I've heard it so many times before. The slight lowering, the downcast eyes.

Bad news.

"I don't want to freak you out," she begins. "I'm trying not to freak out, myself. But I almost . . . I nearly called and just quit yesterday. I wasn't sure I could come back."

When she turns to look at me, I notice the fine red veins spiderwebbing across the whites of her eyes, the lack of color in her cheeks.

As long as I've known her, Sandra has always been spiky and energetic. A fundamentally *content* person in a way that has always confused me.

"*Full of piss and vinegar, that one*" was the way my dad would describe her when we were kids, with a note to his voice I would only later come to recognize as dislike. He never did like people with a strong sense of self, my father; they were less likely to be swayed to his sense of reality.

"What happened?" I ask her.

"I got ahold of Dr. Nina," she says. "I thought about it, and I figured that out of all the people who've come through this place, she was the one most likely to talk."

"Who is Dr. Nina?" I've never heard the name before.

"She was the other psychologist here. You know, the one who took over when Martina was down in Stockholm doing press and living it up. Like how Ellen and I trade off every two weeks, or how the caretakers cycle in and out. I didn't think about her before, because we never worked together all that much, but she popped into my head a few weeks ago. I had a hard time getting ahold of her. I only managed to find her a couple of days ago."

"But she doesn't work here anymore?" I try to clarify.

Sandra shakes her head. "No. She left about eight months ago."

I can feel my heart give a near-painful *thump*.

"So around the time Susannah Wallin disappeared." My mouth suddenly feels very dry.

Sandra nods.

"Exactly."

"Do you think it might be connected?" I ask.

"Maybe. I asked around a bit. Apparently, Drs. Nina and Martina got in some huge fight about one of the patients Dr. Nina had treated in Martina's absence. I don't know what the fight was about, but I do know Martina fired her on the spot. Didn't even have a replacement lined up. She still hasn't found anyone." Sandra looks out the window again, seemingly reflexively.

Making sure we're not seen.

"You think that patient might have been Susannah?" I ask her.

Sandra sighs. "I don't know, Isobel. I honestly don't know. I looked at those pictures you sent me again, tried to see if I could recognize them. But I can't remember. There are so many people passing through here, and half of them look like those photos. Smiling blond women somewhere between twenty-five and forty-five."

"I mentioned Susannah's name to Ellen," I say. "It seemed like she recognized it."

"Ellen did?" Sandra raises her eyebrows. "Maybe. Yeah. She's been here almost as long as I have. I mean, I can't even be sure I was here the week Susannah Wallin was a patient."

"Can you ask her?" I ask. "Can you trust her?"

"I don't know." Sandra's shoulders slump. "I don't know if there is anyone who can be trusted in this place."

For a moment, she looks frightened. Defeated. And it scares me.

I've never seen Sandra look terrified before.

"What happened with Dr. Nina, Sandra?" I ask her quietly.

Sandra sighs again. "Once I managed to get ahold of her, she told me . . . she told me she couldn't talk about Himlafall. She seemed scared. She kept hanging up on me. Finally, she texted me. Told me she's been getting threats. Bad ones. Ever since she left."

A frisson runs up my spine. Like someone tracing it lightly with a cold, sharp fingernail. A soft tickle of a warning.

"What kind of threats?" I ask.

"I'm not sure. She seemed to imply it was notes, or letters. But whatever was in them must have been bad, because she's in the process of going underground. That's why I've had such a hard time finding her. She's taken her website down, changed her phone number. She said she's about to move and told me not to contact her again. It's got to be . . ." Sandra goes silent.

"And you think it's . . . ?"

I don't want to say Martina's name. It feels like we are suspended in a little bubble, here in the car. Like saying her name will call her here, break the spell, let her hear the whispered secrets we are trading.

"I don't know what I think," Sandra says. "But I wouldn't put it past her."

She turns in her seat, so that she's facing me.

"You've seen it, right?" she asks. "Now that you've met her. She likes toying with people. Like a cat with a mouse. She's fine as long as you play along with her rules, but if you piss her off, or get on her bad side . . ." She stops, and then says:

"The hold she has on people, it's fucking scary, Isobel. It's like she hypnotizes them."

"Yeah," I agree, mouth dry. "I've seen it."

I've felt it.

"You know, when you first brought up that patient, Susannah, I thought there might not have been much to it," Sandra admits haltingly. "I wanted you to write an exposé on this place, tell the world what a fucked-up circus it is, but I thought that this Susannah might just have been someone who needed more care than she could get here. Someone with greater needs than the clowns at this so-called clinic could meet. But now, knowing what Dr. Nina has been through . . . I don't know."

Sandra's hands are balled up in her lap.

"I can't help but wonder," she adds, like an afterthought.

"Wonder what?" I ask her.

Sandra looks out the windshield.

"Lot of woods, out here," she says. "Miles and miles of them. Plenty of room for someone to disappear."

I give a shaky laugh. Then I stop, just as abruptly.

I say the only thing I can.

"Fuck."

"Yeah," Sandra mutters. "You can say that again."

"Do you think it's . . . I mean, do you think she is capable of something like this? Martina?"

"I don't know." Sandra doesn't look me in the eyes. "I can't say yes. But I can't say no, either. And I've got to be honest, that freaks me out."

She sighs, and then turns to me, eyes steely, mouth set in a grim line.

"Have you gotten anything yet? Anything concrete?"

"I've been recording the therapy sessions," I say. "I haven't had time to go over them yet, but it's at least proof that they are using some potentially harmful techniques. Nothing overtly illegal yet, but I'm sure it's just a matter of time."

"We should look into the records, too." Sandra is chewing on her thumbnail. "Patient records. They are an absolute mess, the recordkeeping here is garbage, but we might be able to dig up Susannah's file if it's still there."

"There was something weird about my file, too, apparently," I tell her. "I'd like to have a look at it."

"I have a meeting with Martina tonight at seven," Sandra says. "I'll ask her to have the meeting in the staff quarters, in the conference room. That way you can sneak into her office. Don't take anything, I don't want her to notice—but take pictures. You still have the phone, right?"

An echo of fright makes my fingertips tingle, the shadowy memory of last night pressing in on me.

"No, I—"

I'm interrupted by a knock on the window.

Chapter 24

Sandra jumps. I yelp at the sight of the familiar face through the window.

"Hey!" Clara's voice is distorted by the glass. "Is this your friend, Isobel?"

Sandra has gone stark white. I open the door and swing my legs out, stand up so quickly I get dizzy, tiny black spots dancing at the edges of my vision, taunting me.

"Hey, Clara." I steady myself with an arm on the roof of the car. It's gritty with dust and pollen from the drive.

Sandra gets out on the other side, and she thrusts her hand out at Clara.

"Hi!" Her voice is different, slightly lower in pitch, though still chipper. It must be her work voice. I realize I've never heard it before.

"I'm Sandra. I'm the new physical therapist. I'm taking over for Ellen."

"What happened to Ellen?" Clara frowns, looking from Sandra to me, as though we've done something to Ellen. Gotten rid of her.

"Her shift up here is over." I hear Sandra smiling politely, though I can't see her face.

The sunlight is stinging my eyes, and I blink rapidly as I close the car door and walk around the hood to Clara.

"Wait." Clara looks from Sandra to me. "So you guys are friends?"

"No." Sandra is too quick to deny it. "No, we're not."

She's never been a very good liar. Her shoulders pulled up to her ears, her arms crossed in front of her chest, she looks exactly like what she is: spiky, guilty, and defensive.

"Clara." I keep my voice low, and I grimace as I lean into the younger woman. "Sandra kind of broke a rule for me. It was really nice of her, but I don't want to get her in trouble. Would you mind keeping this between us?"

Clara's eyes glimmer with interest.

"What rule?"

She's lowered her voice, too; that feels like a good sign.

"I almost passed out on the way back from breakfast," I say. "Period cramps. Real bad ones. Sandra had just pulled in, and she let me sit in her car and rest until I felt better."

Her eyebrows climb higher.

"That's it?"

"And staff aren't supposed to let any patients into staff quarters," I add hastily. "Their personal cars are included in that. She was just doing a nice thing. I don't want her getting punished for that."

"Well." Clara seems to weigh her options. "The rules *are* there to be followed."

"Come on, Clara," I urge her. "We're supposed to take care of each other, right? Have each other's backs? That's what the, uh, Himlafall philosophy is all about."

Clara looks at me. There is a shift in her face, a twitch in her lips, almost like a sneer, but then it's gone, and she looks sweet as summer again.

"Of course." Clara turns to Sandra. "Just make sure not to push me too hard in physical therapy, all right? Quid pro quo?"

She laughs, and Sandra laughs with her, forced to the point of sounding painful.

"You better get a move on, though," Clara says. "Group therapy starts in a little bit. I don't think you get to skip it just because you've got cramps."

"Sure," I agree.

Clara gives a little wave.

"Your secret is safe with me," she tells us, and again, that whisper of a smile seems to flit across her face, like she's amused at some private joke, before she turns and leaves.

Sandra and I remain standing there, completely quiet, until Clara has rounded the corner of the main building and disappeared behind it.

"Jesus *fuck*," Sandra curses, and when I turn to her she's pinched her eyes closed.

"She won't say anything," I attempt to reassure her, but she shakes her head.

"We're idiots." Her voice sounds pained. "I shouldn't have let you in the car. I kept saying how important it was to be discreet, and—"

"It's fine," I interrupt her. "Okay? It was a reasonable story. Just repeat it if anyone asks."

"What about when the article comes out, Isobel?" Sandra sounds like she wants to be shouting, her voice forced into a growl. "What then? They were never supposed to know we had any connection. Your name will be in the byline, Isobel. It won't be that difficult putting two and two together."

"Martina doesn't know yet," I tell Sandra. "None of the staff members know. Don't lose your cool. The moment you let yourself be scared, you've already lost."

Sandra stiffens; then she surprises me by letting out a small laugh.

"Is that one of your dad's sayings?" she asks me.

I feel myself redden.

"Maybe," I admit.

"Yeah," Sandra snorts. "That line of thinking worked out so well for him."

She sighs, and some of the tension seems to drain out of her.

"Okay. Okay. You're right. We'll proceed. I'll take that meeting with the doctor tonight, and you sneak in and check out the files. Then, once they've all gone to bed, you meet me in the woods and we'll debrief."

". . . the woods?" I swallow. "Don't you think that's going a bit far? Can't you just come to my cabin?"

"Still freaked out by nature, are you?" Sandra smirks.

"I'm not *freaked out* by nature." I can't quite keep the sour note out of my voice.

"It's fine." Sandra is clearly amused. "I know you're a big city girl. But there's nothing out there that will hurt you. Just walk to the other side of the pond and in through the trees at the split pine, until you get to the big rock. I'll wait for you there. Ten o'clock."

"There are bears here, you know," I say.

"Trust me, I'd rather tussle with a bear than with Martina Hastings." She grows serious again. "And besides that, we've already been seen together. If I go to your cabin, or if they see you stalking around the staff quarters, that'll be it. I know the woods are mighty dark and deep, but it's safer that way. Nice and quiet, too. No one will hear us."

Chapter 25

MARTINA IS STARTING US OFF WITH A LECTURE ON ATTRACTION, today. She has drawn a diagram on the whiteboard, and she is gesturing with the pen as she talks.

". . . we are told that attraction is something innate, and primal." She stabs the air with her pen. "But when we view attraction as something outside of our control, it leads us to making bad decisions. When we let attraction reside in the subconscious, it gives us an excuse to let ourselves be run by our impulses, as opposed to taking control of the process."

I notice, offhandedly, that she has buttoned her shirt wrong. One side of her collar is higher than the other. And her hair isn't its usual smooth, shiny self; the braid looks hastily pulled together. A little tuft of hair is sticking out the middle of it.

Martina stops and lowers the pen for a second.

"This is important, ladies," she snaps. "So please pay attention."

I see Clara jumping at the harshness of her tone; Leyla seems to sink deeper into her chair in a mild show of teenage-style defiance.

"The world tells us that we have no power." A little bit of spittle has gathered at the corner of her mouth.

"It tells us that we are supposed to wait to be chosen. That to be chosen is an honor, and we should be grateful for any attention, sexual or romantic, that we get. But we have to reframe ourselves as the ones who do the choosing. When we're not thoughtful and proactive in how we go about engaging with potential partners, we fall back on stereotypes. We end up picking who we think we *should* be with, rather than those we might actually be able to build a happy life with."

She looks around the room, fixating on each of us for a few seconds, letting the intensity of her stare do the work.

She's agitated, I realize, my pulse quickening ever so slightly.

Something has happened. Something has changed.

But what?

When Martina lands on me, she smiles. It is not a kind smile.

"Let's take you, Isobel." She taps the pen against the palm of her hand. It's a harsh, meaty sound.

"What about me?" I ask her, my voice climbing half an octave in surprise.

"We established yesterday that you pick sexual partners because you like the attention, correct? And not because of an innate sense of animal attraction."

"I don't—" I start to say, but she raises her voice and begins to talk over me.

"Being chosen made you feel powerful." It's not a question. "Engaging with partners who were attracted to you made you feel like you were the one in a position of strength. But you never actually made use of that strength, did you?"

"What do—what do you mean?" I stammer.

Martina stops tapping her palm.

"Let's open this up to the group." Martina smiles. "How do you think Isobel used her power?"

She looks around the room.

The silence that follows is a terrible, oppressive thing. The pressure to say something, anything, is overwhelming; I feel as though my ears are about to pop.

"You're not helping Isobel by staying quiet, you know." The disappointment in her voice is scalding. "*You* are supposed to be her companions through this process. You are supposed to help nurture her, just as she is supposed to help nurture you."

She throws me another glance, cruel and quick.

"And challenging the harmful ideas she is carrying around is part of that process."

"She didn't use that power," Clara pipes up. "Because it wasn't real."

She leans forward in her chair, eyes locked on me.

"The sense of power was fake," she says. "It was just a comforting story you told yourself so that you wouldn't have to do the work of choosing yourself. As long as you could keep telling yourself you were in charge, you could blind yourself to the fact that you kept giving up your true power to mediocre men who meant nothing to you."

She smiles at me. I don't know if I imagine the slight challenge in her eyes. As though daring me to speak up, defend myself.

Martina nods to her, and says, with a cool, clear voice:

"Very good, Clara."

Then her head snaps around, and she's looking at me again.

"Do you recognize that, Isobel? Does that sound familiar?"

I want to protest, want to give in to the boiling anger that tastes like bitter coal on my tongue, but I swallow it down.

I refuse to end up today like I did yesterday. Yesterday, I wasn't prepared for the intensity of all of this, how quickly it would get under my skin.

But now, the stakes have become clearer than ever. I have Sandra here with me again, and we're about to get things moving. If everything goes as it should, we'll have actual proof by tonight.

All I have to do until then is be Isobel Anderssen.

I let my head hang down, and I draw a deep, theatrical breath.

"Yes." If I give in to it, they might move on.

"So tell us," Martina says.

When I look up, I see that she has walked into the circle, that she has crouched down on the floor in front of me.

"Tell you what?"

"Tell us that you allowed yourself to be taken advantage of," Martina purrs. "Tell us that you let yourself play into a false narrative in order to not have to make yourself vulnerable."

Martina has lowered her voice until it's almost a whisper, like a twisted form of intimacy.

"Don't tell me because you think it's what I want to hear," she says. "I need to see that you understand that it's true. I need to see that you believe it. That is the only way you can change."

"This is a bit much." Leyla has sat up in her chair.

Martina rises to her feet with admirable quickness and dexterity; she's got at least ten years on me, but my knees would have sounded like Pop Rocks if I'd tried the same move.

"What do you mean, Leyla?"

She doesn't sound angry. She sounds curious.

But I can feel the sudden charge in the room all the same; I think we all can.

"You're putting words in her mouth," Leyla shoots back. "That's not how therapy is supposed to work."

She looks over at Clara.

"I know we're supposed to help each other progress, or whatever, but right now it just feels like you're getting us to gang up on Isobel," she continues, now aimed at Clara. "That didn't feel like support. It just felt like bullying."

"That's ridiculous." Clara's voice becomes a squeak. "I wasn't—I wouldn't—"

She turns to Martina.

"She's disrupting the process!" Clara exclaims, pointing at Leyla.

"Now, wait." Martina puts her hand on Clara's shoulder to soothe her, like a mother shushing her child.

"I want to hear what Leyla has to say."

She smiles at Leyla.

"Go on," she says. "This is a safe space."

"It doesn't feel like a safe space. It feels more like you're encouraging us to gang up on each other. This doesn't feel like therapy, it feels like you're trying to get us to break down and cry so that we will feel like we've had some major breakthrough. It's manipulative." Leyla crosses her arms across her chest and looks steadily at Martina.

"Okay." Martina says, removing her hand from Clara's shoulder and nodding slowly. "So what does therapy feel like, then?"

"I mean, in my experience, therapy usually means recounting your experiences and then having the therapist help you untangle them." Leyla raises her eyebrows. "Give some perspective. But you're just telling us what to say and then expecting us to agree with you. That's not therapy, that's a . . . sermon."

Martina stops in front of Leyla and clasps her hands in front of her.

"You've done therapy before, I take it." Martina smiles at Leyla.

Looking from one to the other, I'm struck by an urge to warn Leyla.

Stop. It's a trap.

"Yes," Leyla responds. "Of course I have. That's basically a requirement to be a functional adult."

"And how has that worked out for you?" Martina immediately asks, quick as a flash. Like a snake, striking faster than the eye can see.

Leyla wavers.

"Well," she begins slowly. "It let me work through some stuff. Made me healthy and functional and able to deal with life."

"And yet, you're here," Martina says.

"Because my mom wanted me to," Leyla shoots back, pouncing on the opportunity.

"And why did your mom want you to come here?" Martina's voice is soft and slippery as silk.

"She's worries about me." Leyla looks away.

"Because it didn't work, did it?" Martina continues. "I'm sorry. You're right. I shouldn't be, as you said, putting words in your mouth. How have your relationships gone, Leyla?"

Leyla shakes her head, muttering something to herself.

"What was that?" Martina raises her eyebrows.

"I don't have to take this from you." Leyla stands up from her chair.

She turns to the door, and Martina raises her voice, just a little bit.

"If you leave now, you can leave Himlafall," she says. There's no edge to her words, no open anger; there doesn't need to be.

"You can stay here, and participate, or you can go. It's up to you."

Leyla is standing very still, her back turned to us.

There is a part of me that wants to stand up with her, take her arm. And just go. Leave and not look back.

Go, a voice inside me whispers, urging her on. *Go on, leave. Get out of here.*

"I won't force you to do anything." Martina is sweeter now. Concerned.

It's masterful, really.

"But I want you to ask yourself if you're just repeating the same pattern again."

Leyla isn't moving.

The sinking feeling in my belly gets deeper and darker.

"This is exactly like what happened with Alexia, isn't it?" Martina delivers the name like a gift, and I see Leyla flinching, see her every breath growing shorter.

"She asked you to open up, and you wouldn't. So you walked away. Like you always do. And now you're trying to walk away again."

Leyla turns around slowly. Her lips are gray; her eyes suspiciously shiny.

"I told you that in confidence," she says.

"Because you trusted me," Martina responds. "And I'm asking you to trust me again."

She walks up to Leyla and takes her hands, ever so gently, between her own.

"Do you really want to end up like your mother, Leyla?" she asks, barely more than a breath, yet every syllable rings out in the room.

Leyla draws a quick, sharp inhale.

I see the moment she gives herself over.

"No," she says.

Martina embraces her.

"I know," Martina murmurs, rubbing her back in soft circles, as Leyla begins to cry. "I know."

Clara is covering her mouth with her hand, her eyes wide and shining with admiration. Pernilla is gritting her teeth, a vein jumping in her temple.

When I look at Martina, I see, for but a second, a triumphant gleam in her eyes.

And she's looking directly at me.

to: ethicsboard@swedishpsychologistsassociation.se
fr: anoncomplaint123456@hotmail.com
05:11 09/27/2023

Subject: Filing a complaint against Dr. Martina Hastings

Hello,

I am writing to you with the intention of filing a complaint against Dr. Martina Hastings, as well as the treatment center she founded and now runs, the Himlafall Clinic. I believe she is a danger to her patients, that her license needs to be taken away, and the clinic in question needs to be shut down.

I was a patient at the Himlafall Clinic. My experiences there were very traumatic, and I wish to remain anonymous, so I will not reveal my name or the dates of my stay there, but I urge you to take this complaint seriously and launch an investigation.

The Himlafall Clinic was described to me as a place where patients could go to receive help with their romantic lives. The fee for a stay is very steep, and I paid all my savings in order to secure a spot there. But once there, I found myself in an incredibly toxic environment.

Rather than support and uplift her clients, Dr. Martina Hastings and her colleagues engaged in a targeted brainwashing campaign against me. They attempted to convince me I was a horrible person, and tried to gaslight me into thinking I was irreversibly broken. They refused to listen to what I said, instead pushing their own narrative.

I got the impression that the psychologist who treated me, Dr. Nina, had taken a negative view of me immediately, and was trying to break me down on purpose. I was in an incredibly vulnerable position, and if I had had a weaker sense of self, I am sure I would have given in to their narrative.

The Himlafall Clinic is dangerous. Dr. Martina Hastings preys on the weak, and causes horrible, lasting damage. She is completely unfit to be a psychologist. I suspect she might herself be an undiagnosed narcissist, and that she was drawn to the profession because she was lured by the prospect of being in power over those weaker than herself.

Dr. Martina Hastings should have her license taken away. She should, quite honestly, be in prison for the harm she has caused.

If you have any care or concern for those in her care, please do something about it.

Best regards,
XXX

Chapter 26

Leyla is still there when we get back from the break, sitting in her chair, her eyes puffy and red. I feel a bit of the tension in my shoulders releasing when I see her.

I take the seat next to Leyla, sinking into the chair and leaning over, whispering to her:

"Are you okay?"

"Yeah." Leyla's voice is faint. "I'm fine."

"Do you want to get out of here?" I ask, my lips barely moving. "I can go with you. Say you're sick, or something. I'll walk you to the cabin."

Leyla doesn't move, at first.

But then she slowly shakes her head.

"No. I'll stick around."

"Are you sure?" I ask her.

She raises her face and finally looks me in the eyes.

I think I see something there, shifting: a glimpse of awareness. Of struggle.

"Seriously," I say, trying to make sure no one else can hear. "I can get you out of here. I'll make up a story."

"Hey, I was sitting there," Clara pipes up behind me.

I turn; Clara is standing right behind our chairs, the corners of her mouth turned up but her eyes hard and flinty.

"I don't think there are assigned seats," I begin to argue, but Leyla surprises me by putting her hand on my arm.

"It's fine, Isobel," she says, her voice slightly stronger now. "Just . . . go back to your seat."

I look back to her, searching for something to say, some way to break through to her. But I find nothing.

So I get up, and I sit back down, one seat over, as Clara happily sinks into the now vacated chair.

A surge of irritation rushes through me, and I breathe out hard through my nostrils, trying to contain it.

The room feels smaller now than it did, the walls pushing in. Like this clean, bright environment is a cover for something.

Something with teeth, trying to eat us whole.

"I hope you all had a nice break," Martina greets us as she steps through the door.

There are high, bright spots of color on her cheeks that weren't there before, and a cup of tea in her hands as she makes her way back into the circle.

She pushes the whiteboard out of the way and sits down.

"I want you all to know," Martina begins, slowly stirring her tea, "that it's okay to ask questions. It's okay to question the methodology. And it's okay to say no. Like Leyla just did."

She smiles at Leyla, as though at some private little joke.

"I want to check in with all of you," she continues. "I want to make sure that you all feel good with what's happening in here. That you feel safe. With me, and with each other."

"Of course," Clara hurries to say. "This is amazing."

"I'm glad to hear you feel that way, Clara," Martina soothes her. "But I want to hear from everyone."

She turns to me.

"Isobel?" She folds one long leg over the other. "Do you have anything you'd like to say? You look upset."

Before I came here, I would have thought myself the kind of person who would speak up in this kind of environment. The kind of person who would speak out in defense of others, or myself.

I can blame wanting to keep my cover. But it wouldn't be the whole truth. The weight of expectation feels crushing over my chest.

Despite my suspicions, despite what I've heard, some part of me wants desperately to . . . *please* her.

Wants her to be proud of me.

"I don't even understand why you're here," a voice breaks the silence.

I jerk in my seat and look around.

Pernilla's cut-glass syllables seem to still be ringing through the air.

I open my mouth to defend myself, but then I realize she's not talking to me.

She's looking at Clara.

"What is your problem?" Clara asks, shock coloring her face nearly as pink as her hair. "I have every right to be here."

Pernilla rolls her eyes, making an extravagant show of it.

"Puh-lea-se," she says, making a three-syllable meal out of the one-syllable word. "You've never even been in a serious relationship. You've come to this clinic without even the most baseline need for the help it offers. The seat your parents paid for could have gone to someone who actually needed it. But instead, it's taken up by you."

Clara looks over at Martina, ostensibly searching for help, but Martina remains quiet, still stirring her cup of tea.

"Is that true?" Katarina asks Clara.

"I mean, yeah." Clara is immediately defensive. "But I'm trying to be proactive. I want to fix my attachment style and everything before it becomes a problem. I want to be a life coach. I can't do that if I'm making a bunch of mistakes in my own personal life. I need to learn from the ground up."

"But how did you even get a referral to come here if you haven't gone through a recent break-up?" Katarina has an inquisitive little frown on her face, trying to understand, trying to figure it out.

Pernilla cackles.

"Come now," she sneers. "She went to her parents' private doctor and asked for one. Anything is possible as long as you have money. Or access to your father's credit card."

"I don't know why she seems to have a problem with me," Clara says, addressing it to Martina, her voice shaking with barely held-back anger.

"But this isn't fair. I don't know why I'm being accused of anything. I'm just trying to take care of myself and my health."

"I have a problem with you," Pernilla announces, raising her voice further, "because you are a spoiled child, and you are playacting at feeling things you have never experienced."

"You're just attacking me because you're angry you fucked up your life, and you're mad I'm here to try to make sure I don't end up like you!" Clara yells.

Pernilla smiles, and it is a terrible thing to behold.

"You're a tourist." Pernilla speaks slowly, letting each word linger. "You're here to dig around in other people's pain so you can convince yourself you are more interesting and more intricate than you really are."

Clara looks around, her eyes locking with mine, and I clear my throat, beginning to speak:

"I don't know if that's really—"

Martina holds up her hand at me.

"Isobel, let them speak," she orders me. "This is important."

"How is this important?" It flies out of me.

Martina turns to me.

"I'm going to need you to be quiet and let Clara and Pernilla see their conflict through." Every syllable is a warning.

I bite down, hard enough to hurt, and an iron taste spreads in my mouth.

Be Isobel Anderssen. Isobel Anderssen wouldn't argue with Martina. Isobel Anderssen wouldn't try to defend any of her fellow patients. Isobel Anderssen wouldn't question the method.

But it's hard, so hard, because on a pure, mammalian level, I want to defend them, want to stand up for them, want to protect them. Want to scream out that this is all wrong.

"But . . ." Clara begins to speak, her voice thin and reedy, and Martina lowers her hand.

"Go on, Pernilla," she encourages the older woman, not even acknowledging Clara.

"No." Pernilla, suddenly clamming up. "I shouldn't. This is neither the time nor the place."

"I'm telling you," Martina says, with more force, "that it is. Remember what we talked about yesterday?"

Something seems to pass between the two of them.

"Go on." Martina sounds oddly breathless. "Tell her what you really think."

Pernilla swallows. I see the tendons in her slim neck tensing, her pulse fluttering in the vein winding around her temple.

Then she whips her head around and stares at Clara.

"You disgust me," she hisses. "You really do. You think of yourself as deep, but you're shallow, and vapid, and you are deluding yourself. You treat other people and their lives like set dressing. Like they are characters you're viewing on your phone screen. You throw all these words around as though you know what they mean, and it's *laughable* how you think your life has any meaning or any importance."

"Hey." Katarina tries to speak up, but Clara cuts her off, her voice now shaking with rage.

"I don't know what the fuck happened to you in your life to make you this way, but just because you're a bitter, dried-up old *bitch* who's never been happy or sexually satisfied in your life doesn't mean you have any right to judge me!" she screeches.

"Of course." Pernilla is laughing now, with terrible joy. "Even your insults lack imagination."

"Fuck you," Clara spits out.

"No, fuck *you*," Pernilla responds, making the curse sound like an elegant condemnation. "Fuck you for being so stupid. Fuck you for seeing the world through such a narrow lens you can't even conceive of how conceited you really are. Fuck you for being a hollow shell of a person. Fuck you for being so *blind* to the things you're doing, and for not seeing things the way they really are, and for not—for not—" Her voice grows rougher for every word, and finally she's left gasping for air, appearing to choke on her own venom.

"I've never done anything to you." Clara is shrinking back into herself, tears running down her cheeks.

"No." Pernilla shakes her head. "You've never done anything to anyone, have you? There is nothing there. You are not really a person. You have never worked for anything, or achieved anything. You never had to. You have always just been a daughter, and that has been enough, but now it might not be anymore, and you think, deep down, that you might have nothing else to give. That there might be nothing behind the curtain. No magic trick waiting to happen.

"And you're scared of that, terrified, and so you are going to keep running from it. You are going to marry some man, just because being a wife is better than being nothing at all, and you are going to have a couple of children, and you are going to tell yourself it makes you happy, even as what little promise you had once is rotting away inside of you. And then, once he's gone, then what are you going to be? *Who* are you going to be?" She's panting, red flames reaching up the sides of her neck.

"No one." Pernilla's voice grows faint. "You are no one."

Clara is wiping tears away, mascara smearing prettily under her eyelashes. Martina gets up from her chair and hands her a tissue, which Clara accepts, her hands shaking.

Then Martina turns to Pernilla.

"How old were you, when you got married?" she asks Pernilla.

"Young," Pernilla says, a hollow echo of the righteous fury from just a few seconds ago. "Too young."

"And how long were you married?" Martina asks.

Pernilla draws a shaky breath.

"Thirty-eight years," she answers. "And four months."

"He left you," Martina says.

Pernilla nods.

"How many of those years did you spend wanting to leave?"

Pernilla is staring down at her hands. I'm not sure, but I think she is looking at the thin white skin at the base of her ring finger.

"I couldn't leave." Her words come out thick and unwieldy.

Clara is still crying next to me; I reach out, trying to comfort her silently, but she turns away from me.

"Why not?" Martina asks. "You told me you didn't love him. Not anymore. Maybe not ever."

Pernilla remains quiet.

"You told me you used to lie awake at night, fantasizing about putting a pillow over his sleeping face and pushing down until he became quiet. You said you would lie there, your eyes dry as ash, for hours, imagining selling the house after the funeral, and buying a little place of your own with the inheritance, just so you might sleep in a bed you had picked out yourself."

Pernilla's lips are bone white.

"But you wouldn't leave." Martina makes it sound like an accusation.

"I couldn't," Pernilla manages to push out, her mouth stiff and dry.

"No," Martina says, sharply. "You *wouldn't*. And when he left, you hated him for it. Why?"

Pernilla shakes her head.

"Tell us, Pernilla." Martina's voice is climbing. "Tell us, or walk away. Go back to that life. Go back to that empty bed, and lie there, every night, for the rest of your life, clinging to the wreckage, because you're too much of a coward to tell the truth."

Pernilla flinches, as though struck.

"Because I was too weak," she tries.

"No," Martina rebuffs her. "Try again."

"Because . . ." Pernilla swallows, over and over again, her hand climbing up to her neck, like she is physically trying to hold the words back.

"Because I . . ."

Pernilla looks over at Clara, the corners of her mouth turned down, eyes blazing with hatred, or shame, or some swirling concoction of them both.

"Because *I* didn't leave," she finally manages to say, and it sounds like the very words are choking her. "In those fantasies, I was at least . . . I did something. I earned it. But then he left, and he took that away from me, too. He took that dream away. That maybe I would leave. That maybe I would be capable of leaving. One day. But he took it away from me. Just like he has taken everything else. And I just let him. Again, and again, and again. I let him take everything away. Until there was nothing left."

Her face twists, and she begins to cry, in great, gulping sobs. The sobs of a small child, left alone in the dark, the harsh words still ringing in her ears, with no power to escape.

Martina looks over at Clara.

"Go to her," she tells Clara.

"What?" Clara's voice is harsh and cloudy from the crying.

"Go to her. Comfort her."

Clara begins to shake her head, but Martina stares her down.

"You are the same," she says. "You can heal yourself by healing her. Pernilla hates in you what she hates in herself. You need to forgive her."

I see Clara straining against it, the hurt boiling under the surface of her skin, but as Pernilla's crying continues, and Martina's stare refuses to break, Clara rises to her feet, walks over to Pernilla, and puts her arm around the other woman.

"I forgive you," I hear Clara saying, as Pernilla clings to her. "I forgive you."

"See?" Martina says, soft as the breeze. "Control is what is holding you back. Control, and shame, and anger."

Her amber eyes seem to glow as she looks at me.

"Only by giving up control," she says, "can you become a version of yourself that is free from pain."

Chapter 27

I CLOSE THE CABIN DOOR BEHIND ME.

After lunch, I asked Katarina to tell someone for me that I wasn't feeling well, that my cramps had gotten worse and that I needed to go lie down. Katarina assured me she'd take care of it, and so I slunk away.

The room is still in disarray from last night, the clothes pulled out from the suitcase in piles on the floor. I tore the place apart looking for the missing phone, hoping, in vain, that I might find it somewhere, that I had just misplaced it, only to be left with the sinking realization that it was gone.

I sit down on the bed and pull my recorder out of my pocket. It has run out of battery, and I curse softly to myself, pull the charger out of my bag and go to plug it in next to the bathroom mirror, in the socket meant for a hair dryer.

I stare at myself in the mirror.

The hollows under my eyes look more pronounced, my lips void of color. My hair is lying flat against my skull. I look like the ghost of the person who left my shitty little secondhand rental a few days ago.

And yet, as I look at the shadow staring back at me, she smiles.

I didn't catch it the first time the good doctor did it, with Leyla. I was stuck in the moment, much too focused on what was happening in the room. But with Pernilla, it struck me.

"You told me you used to lie awake at night."

Pernilla never said that in group therapy. Just like Leyla never told us the name of her ex-girlfriend, Alexia.

They both shared that in their individual therapy. And Martina told the rest of us. She shared those buried, hidden intimacies with us like it was nothing, in order to break Leyla and Pernilla. In order to bend them to her will.

This goes against at least two different privacy laws. Secrets shared in therapy count as medical information. And I've got Martina doing it on tape.

I won't be able to use it directly, won't be able to quote it in the article, for fear of violating Leyla's and Pernilla's privacy all over again. But it's proof. It's real, tangible proof. I can already feel the text beginning to unspool in my mind, paragraphs drafting themselves, weaving the web that will eventually ensnare both Martina and Himlafall and put an end to all of this.

You've seen the ads for the Himlafall Clinic. Smiling influencers with perfect skin telling you how the Hastings Method changed their life. Maybe it appeared on your phone screen late at night, in between swiping endlessly on the apps and staring at the TV; or maybe a friend sent it to you, joking that you should both go, take charge of your love lives once and for all.

You probably never did end up going for that stay at the Himlafall Clinic. The vast majority of the population would never be able to afford it. Maybe you felt jealous of the women who could, the ones who secured their spot and set off on a weeklong journey to psychological health and future romantic bliss, a dream come true.

But for the women who actually checked in at the Himlafall Clinic, that dream would turn out to be a nightmare.

In the mirror, I see my own smile begin to fade.

I can still see their faces. Leyla, dull and listless; Clara, crying quietly, like a broken child; Pernilla, with decades and decades of desiccated rage painted on her face and neck in violent red splotches.

I wasn't supposed to care about them. The other patients. They were supposed to be sources, nothing more, the subjects of interviews and the anonymized stories that would make my case for the article.

My dad always told me not to get close to anyone while on a story.

"You have to think of them as characters, princess, not people. The moment they become people, you lose objectivity."

But how can I think of them as anything but people, now that I'm one of them? Until the end of the week, we are stuck in this twisted fun house together. And none of this is theoretical to them.

I wish I could tell them. I wish I could trust them.

But all I can do is hope that this works out. That whatever evidence I got today, and whatever evidence I might find tonight, is going to be enough.

I push my hair back from my face, and I reach for the recorder. Turning it on, I peer down at the tiny little screen and use my thumb to switch it over to the file with the voice notes.

I bring it to my mouth, and I start talking.

"This is my third day at Himlafall," I say. "Things have gotten worse. Last night, I saw someone watching me through the window, and after trying to find who the culprit was, they chased me down. When I came back, my phone had gone missing. I can only conclude that someone here doesn't want me to be in contact with the outside world."

I stop, trying to gather my thoughts.

"I went through the second group therapy session this morning," I continue. "And it . . ."

I don't know how to express what happened in that room. The sheer overwhelming pressure in it. The feeling that we were seconds away from disaster. Like microscopic fractures spreading through glass, invisible to the naked eye.

"It looks like the doctor is . . . breaking the other patients," I try. "Breaking them down on purpose. Finding their pressure points and then digging in, until they are pliable, and desperate, and willing to give up their autonomy. Today, she broke medical privacy twice, revealing the personal information of two of the patients and revealing their sensitive information to the group as a whole. I can't be sure what the end goal is. But—"

There is a knock on the door.

I drop the recorder, the clattering of it hitting the floor making me jump. I hold my breath, hoping I imagined it.

"Isobel?" A muffled voice through the wood. "Are you in there?"

Chapter 28

I TAKE TWO QUICK STEPS OUT OF THE BATHROOM AND TOSS the recorder under the bed as I yell out:

"Yeah, I'm here, one second!"

When I open the door, the caretaker, Anna, is standing outside.

"I hope I didn't wake you up?" She frowns, a look of concern on her face.

"No, of course not." I shake my head and, remembering my lie from earlier, put my hand over my lower stomach. "I've just been doing breathing exercises. Trying to work through the pain."

"Can I come in?" Anna asks.

She's holding a small white paper bag and a bottle of water. Her white-blond hair is down, pulled out of its usual ponytail, the blunt edges of it brushing against her linen-clad shoulders.

"Sure." I step back from the door.

"Are you sure you weren't asleep?" Anna asks, walking into the cabin and looking around. "I thought I heard you talking. I figured you were dreaming."

She turns around, staring at me.

"I was just, uh . . ." I go for an embarrassed smile. "I was talking to myself. It's stupid, I know. I do it sometimes, when I'm alone."

Anna shakes her head.

"No, it's not stupid at all!" she exclaims. "I do it too. Last year, I was on my own for, like, months, and I kept talking to myself just to keep myself company. I think it was just because I was so used to having someone around, you know? After my ex left me, it got really lonely. I was so used to having someone to talk to, so I just started talking to myself instead."

"Yeah, exactly." I exhale.

"I was just . . . I'm sorry, I hope you don't take this the wrong way, but I was worried you had someone in here." Anna smiles, not un-sheepishly.

"What? Why?" I'm bemused.

She makes a face.

"Well, you know, it's stupid, but there are rules against fraternizing. Sexually, I mean."

"*Oh*." I finally understand what she's getting at. "No, no one is here. Just me."

"Well, I wouldn't tell." She winks at me. "It's a silly rule, really. I mean, this place is supposed to be all about love, right? Who's to say when you meet the right person?"

"Well, not to worry. The clientele doesn't exactly swing in the direction of my orientation." I shrug.

Anna smiles.

"Well, Katarina told me you weren't feeling well, you poor thing," she says. "I thought I'd come by and give you some painkillers."

She holds up the white bag.

"Belinda put a little goody bag together for you," she continues. "A couple of paracetamol, and a sleeping pill, if you want to take a nap. I told the doctor you won't be able to make your individual therapy session this afternoon."

I reach out and accept the bag, opening it and looking in. Just as she told me, there're two 500-milligram pills of paracetamol in there, still in the packaging, and a small, round pill which, when I pick it up, says *zolpidem*.

"Zolpidem?" I read out loud. "I've never heard of this."

"It's like Ambien," Anna says. "Fast acting. It should get you a few hours of decent sleep. I usually try to nap through my cramps."

I look up at her.

"Don't you need a prescription for this?"

"I don't think so." Anna shrugs. "Martina has a stash in her office. For patients who can't sleep. Like you. I'm surprised Belinda didn't offer you any last night."

"Me too." I look at the pill again.

"Well, I'll leave you to it." Anna turns to go. "Sweet dreams, and so on. I hope you feel better."

"Wait, hold on a second." I drop the pill back into the bag and look up.

Anna stops.

"What's up?" she asks me.

"Are you ever . . ." I try my best to sound calm, cool, and collected. "Okay, I hope I'm not offending you here, but you don't seem like you're . . . all in on Martina's practices."

Anna grimaces. It's small, and seemingly involuntary, barely more than a twitch.

"I know you've only been here for a few weeks," I say. "But have you heard anything about patients . . . getting hurt? Or . . . going missing?"

"Going missing?" Anna becomes very still. "What do you mean by that?"

"I . . . well, I heard about someone coming here for treatment and not coming back." I choose my words as carefully as possible. "I was just wondering if you might have heard anything about her."

"What was her name?" Anna's voice sounds different, in some way I can't put my finger on.

"Susannah," I say. "Susannah Wallin."

A beat. She stares at me.

Hope flares in my stomach.

Then she shakes her head.

"Never heard of her." Anna makes a face. "Sorry."

"Yeah, I figured as much." I do my best not to show my disappointment. "But you haven't heard anything else? About anyone else getting hurt, or . . . leaving?"

"No."

I'm not sure if I imagine the hesitation in her voice.

"Don't take this the wrong way." Anna is looking at me like I'm a puzzle, and she can't find any of the corner pieces. "But why would you come here, if you'd heard that people had gone missing? That seems like a very strange thing to do."

I need to backpedal, and fast. I got overexcited, took too big of a risk; I have to laugh it off now, make it seem like nothing, or she might bring it up with Belinda, or Martina, and whichever one of them left that note might decide that a note wasn't enough of a deterrent.

"God, I'm sorry." I laugh, going for embarrassment. "It's the hormones. I get really weird when I'm hormonal with the cramps and the exhaustion and everything . . . yeah. I mean, I figured it was just a weird story. I guess the intensity of group therapy today just really got to me."

I silently apologize to my foremothers for blaming my idiocy on my period.

"Just . . . would it be okay to keep this between us?" I ask her. "I feel really stupid for even asking. I don't want Martina thinking I'm running around seeing ghosts."

"Don't worry." Anna holds out her pinkie, and I grasp it with my own, finding it oddly charming. I haven't done a pinkie swear since I was a kid.

"Your secret is safe with me," she adds, and winks.

As she goes, closing the door behind her, I sit back down on the bed, dropping the paper bag onto the floor.

That's the second time today I've messed up.

It's so much harder than I expected to find the right balance, to ask questions without raising suspicion, to gather information without getting caught.

I reach in under the bed for the recorder, but my attention is caught by the paper bag.

It looks innocent, crumpled up on the floor. But when I pick it up and open it again, the pill seems to be staring at me.

Zolpidem.

"It's like Ambien."

I'm no expert, but I know enough—you definitely need a prescription for Ambien. In a flash, I see Pernilla's sluggish movement yesterday, Leyla's empty, drowsy face after the break.

And I think of all those endless cups of tea, strewn all over the clinic.

We're offered tea with breakfast, during therapy, after lunch; always herbal mixtures, always with a slightly strange flavor and a chalky residue left in the bottom of the cup.

I think about my own strange feelings during therapy. The way I've felt dizzy, and powerless, and suggestible.

Maybe Martina decided that the force of her sheer personality wasn't enough.

Maybe, at some point, she decided to give us all a little chemical help on our way toward our "better selves."

r/ActuallyLesbian

How to know if you are in an abusive relationship?

posted by: u/throwawayduckling123

22:16 07/02/2023

I'm 29F, in a relationship with 28F since a few months back.

I thought we were really happy. We had what I guess they call a "whirlwind romance." I've never really been in a relationship before, and it just felt intoxicating to be with someone who seemed to like me so much.

I've felt really lonely since my mom died. I don't know if that's relevant or not. I don't have a lot of friends, or any, really, and no family. I guess I always felt kind of . . . broken. And when I met my girlfriend, it made me feel whole.

But in the last few months, it feels like everything has been going wrong. She keeps getting really upset with everything I do and saying that I'm doing it on purpose to hurt her. I'm not very smart, and I know I'm bad with people, so I've been trying to be better, but nothing I do seems to work.

I posted in another subreddit a couple of months ago, trying to get advice on how to get better and be a better partner, and there they told me I was being abused. I didn't see it at all, and I thought it was just that they couldn't see the whole picture, and couldn't see how hard I am to live with.

But then yesterday, we had a fight, and my girlfriend grabbed me really hard. I got scared. It was only for a second, and then she let go.

She left bruises. I saw them this morning.

My mom always told me to never stay with a man who hit me. That I should always leave the first time it happened, no matter what. But I don't know if that applies here. If I was with a man, he could really hurt me, because he would be stronger than me. I feel like it's different with a woman. I said maybe we should take some time apart, but she said she wouldn't be able to live without me, and I got scared. I don't want her to get hurt, or to hurt herself.

I don't know if I'm just overreacting. I know I do that a lot.

She has good qualities, too. So many. And I think she's genuinely trying to help me, and trying to make this work. She's really into psychology. She even suggested we go to this therapy clinic together. Maybe I should just go? Maybe if we went together, the psychologist could help us work it out? It's out in the woods. If I could get some time off work, maybe it would help. Maybe it could be just what we need.

I don't know. I'm just so confused. I feel bad even writing this, like I'm telling on her. If she could read this, there are so many things she could tell you that I've done. She thinks I might be a narcissist. Maybe she's right.

7 upvotes
4 comments

u/SapphosRoommate—23:11 07/02/2023
First of all, abuse can absolutely happen in relationships of any gender. It doesn't matter whether she's physically stronger than you—women can abuse men, too. It's about power, and it does sound like you are being abused. I am so sorry.

Second of all, absolutely do not go to therapy with your girlfriend. Abusers can manipulate psychologists to their advantage.

Thirdly, she threatened suicide when you implied you wanted to leave. A threat of violence against herself is still a threat of violence. I don't think you are safe with this person.

Sadly, the best thing you can do for yourself is to leave.

u/PapadomBaby—23:31 07/02/2023

seconding what Sappho said above (love your username btw). i was in an abusive relationship in college, huge age difference and power differential, and when i waned to break up she insisted we see a counselor together. it was horrible. it just gave her all these new tools to punish me. whenever i tried to stand up for myself, she would call me toxic, or say that i was retraumatizing her, and i would end up staying and comforting her. look up darvo.

u/SapphosRoommate—23:47 07/02/2023

I'm so sorry that happened to you. And yes, OP, please look up "DARVO." It stands for Deny, Attack, and Reverse Victim & Offender. See if it sounds familiar. Based on what you wrote about your girlfriend calling you a narcissist, it sounds like she might be doing exactly that.

u/MedusaInChains—23:21 07/02/2023

Is no one else worried about this retreat??? Do not go anywhere with her. It could be ANYTHING. Who knows if you'd even come back?? It's literally in the woods. What kind of therapy happens in the woods? This sounds like a horror movie.

Chapter 29

I SEE CLARA LEAVING HER CABIN RIGHT BEFORE SEVEN, HEADING to the dining hall; Katarina follows behind her, and then Leyla, and Pernilla. They turn from women into silhouettes, painted golden by the sinking sun, and then finally into shadows who disappear into the dining hall, one by one.

The doors close behind them, and then all is still.

I wait a few more minutes before slinking out the door.

I decided to wear relaxed clothes, fit for exercise; I figure that if I get caught going to or coming from the main building, I can say I've gone for a walk, to try to ease the pain.

Still, my heart is fluttering in my chest. The cold, brisk air feels good against my face. The feelings from the group therapy session linger in my body, stretching lazily under my skin like tentacles.

Again, I wonder if feelings are all they are. Or if it's something more. Drugs building in my brain, to make me pliable, to render me vulnerable.

The thought lights a small, burning ember of anger under my ribs.

Well, if that's the game she's playing, I'm about to find out.

The main building is dark and looks abandoned. I've prepared a story, just in case someone stayed behind in the reception; I'm almost certain everyone should be at dinner except for Sandra and Martina, but if someone decided to stay behind, I'm going to tell them I feel anxious. That I need someone to talk to.

When I glance over at the staff quarters, I see one of the rooms lit up, the outline of a person moving, and I have to fight the urge to duck.

My father once told me to *"never give in to the urge to hide. People recognize hiding; it looks suspicious. If you pretend like you have every right to do what you're doing, they won't even take notice of you."*

I guess he'd know.

So instead, I stroll, slowly but purposefully, up to the door to the main building, and I open it already posed to ask Anna or Belinda if they have time.

But they are not there.

The reception is, indeed, empty.

I step inside and close the door, tasting the small thrill of being somewhere I'm not supposed to be. The lights are still on, the air humming with silence.

Still, I call out:

"Hello? Is anybody here?"

Loud enough to be heard through the corridor but quiet enough so that it won't be noticed from outside. I hope.

It feels different, being here on my own, walking down the corridor without someone shadowing me. Without the soft voices of staff whispering in my ear, the beautiful, shiny surface suddenly seems to dissipate.

No longer a luxurious, curated space designed for healing, no. Now the plants look placed at random, and the wear and tear of the floor looks obvious. It looks like an office building, or a government facility.

It's like the spell has worn off.

I stop outside of Martina's office. The sign by the door catches my eye.

Dr. Martina Hastings, PhD

"You don't need to say you're a doctor twice," I mutter to myself, and then I push the door handle down and step in.

The office is dusky, lit only by the dying light from the window. It takes me a moment to orient myself; I look around, catching the eyes of the two-dimensional Martina looking at me from a book cover, her flat eyes seeming to follow me around the room.

When I turn away from the bookshelf, I see the cabinet hiding behind the desk. It's low to the ground, dark, polished wood, with two deep drawers.

I consider saying *Bingo* to myself but decide it's too much of a cliché, and so instead I say nothing. I just get down on my knees by the cabinet, pull my recorder out of my pocket, turn it on, and pull the first drawer out.

It's full to bursting with cheap blue paper folders, all marked with little stick-on labels. Names have been written on them with slightly sloppy handwriting. I'm guessing it's Martina's.

Here they are. The patient files.

"I'm in Dr. Martina Hastings's office," I breathe into the recorder as I look down at the box of files. "I'm looking at past patient files. The goal is to find the file of Susannah Wallin, if it's still here." I pause, and then I add:

"I will of course avoid looking at any of the other patient files, in order to preserve patient privacy."

I start rifling through the files, looking for the *W*s, but it soon becomes apparent they are in no particular order. They look shoved in haphazardly; there are bits of paper sticking out of some of them, bent corners from the drawers being opened and shut. Some of the files are sliver-thin, some thicker, and I see names passing by—*Lina, Emilia, Carina, Matilda, Anya, Robin*—until the letters begin to blur.

So many names. But no Susannah.

"Shit," I mutter to myself, before remembering I'm recording.

I clear my throat; the sound seems to echo in the empty room.

"The records are poorly kept," I note. "There doesn't seem to be a system to them. I question whether a former client's healthcare provider would be able to contact Himlafall and get any useful information about their patient. This, again, reinforces the lack of care that the staff take with their—"

I stop talking.

Upon opening the second drawer, I see a stack of files that have been pushed in at the end. The one closest to the handle says *CLARA AF SPERLING*.

I rifle through the next few files until I see my own first name staring back at me.

ISOBEL ANDERSSEN

"I've found my own file."

Pulling it out gingerly, I lay it flat on the floor and open it up.

That's my intake form, all right. But there, at the very top, is a bright blue Post-it note.

FORGOT TO MENTION KNEE INJURY NOT COVERED ON INTAKE FORM. EXEMPT FROM PHYSICAL THERAPY.

I stare at it.

"So, I . . ." I search for the words. "It seems like someone added a note to my file. I was told I had crossed off the wrong box on the intake form, giving the staff the impression that I had an injury that would prevent me from doing any exercise, but it seems like . . . someone added a note in later."

I lean in closer, pull the Post-it off the page, and hold it up. I look from the note to the folders still in the drawer.

The handwriting doesn't match.

"I don't know who wrote this." I keep talking automatically. Anna was right after all: There is something comforting about talking to myself.

"But whoever added the note seems like they were trying to keep me away from the physical therapist, Ellen. The one who recognized the name Susannah Wallin." I pause, and then I say:

"Maybe it was her, all along. Maybe she was the one who added the note. If it was, she has already left, and I might not be able to get any more information about her on location. It's possible my"—I almost say Sandra's name before correcting myself. I can't leave any trail that might give her away—"contact might be able to find out more."

I turn the pages in the folder, until I get to Martina's notes, and then I stop, slightly mesmerized.

There is something so fascinating about reading about yourself, seeing yourself through someone else's eyes. I'm here as a journalist, sure, but I'm only human.

My eyes skim over the words.

First impressions . . . avoidant attachment . . . possible secondary reasons for coming . . .

I turn the page again.

There, at the top of the next page, are the words:

Problems with lying. Makes up connections. May present a problem. Keep away from Anna as much as possible.

I blink.

"I, uh . . ." I don't know how to describe what I'm seeing. "There is an instruction here in my folder calling me a liar and saying to keep me away from a specific member of the staff." I try to gather my thoughts.

"I don't know why Martina thinks I should be kept away from this staff member," I say, halting, then continuing. "I have gotten the impression that the staff member in question might be less dedicated to the clinic than others who work here."

Are they worried I might get to her, somehow? Worried I might convince her to spill any secrets?

"I don't know if—" I begin to say, but I go instantly quiet when I hear something.

The front door. Opening and closing.

I feel my stomach dropping.

Shit.

If I'm lucky . . . no, there is no good scenario here. There is only bad and worse.

Bad would be Anna or Belinda coming back from dinner to take up their shift at reception.

Worse would be Martina, back from her meeting with Sandra, heading for her office.

I put my file back in the drawer, close it as quietly as possible, turn the recorder off, and stuff it down my pocket again.

There are no steps coming this way. That's good; that means it's most likely Anna or Belinda.

I'm still sitting on the floor, my knees beginning to ache. I cast a glance up toward the window, wondering if there is any way I can crawl out of it.

Maybe. But if I do that, they might hear me climbing out, see me running away; and, besides, I will have no way of closing it properly behind me again. It will be obvious someone was in here, and given what I just read, I bet I'll be at the top of their list of suspects.

My breathing is fast and shallow, my eyes skidding from one side of the room to the other. There has to be a good way out of here, something I haven't thought about.

I can try waiting here, hoping for a window.

But what happens if I linger for half an hour, and Martina then decides to pop by, do some late-night work? She insists on her Instagram that she doesn't need more than five hours of sleep per night, after all.

And I'm supposed to meet Sandra in the woods in less than two hours.

No. I have to get out now.

I get up, standing silently behind the desk for a second.

Then I walk as quietly as I can toward the door.

Just as I am about to open it, I freeze.

Footsteps. Down the hall. Coming closer.

Potential explanations run through my head at lightning speed, some way to get out of this, some way to explain my presence. I'm sleepwalking again. I'm looking for some evening therapy. I went for a walk and developed spontaneous agoraphobia, taking shelter in the closest possible room.

But the footsteps don't reach me.

I hear a door opening, closing. The clicking of a lock.

The bathroom.

Maybe guardian angels really do exist. If so, mine is working overtime tonight.

I slip out of the door, walking as quickly and as quietly as I can down the hallway, heart pounding, palms clammy, and then I wait by the front door, unmoving.

The seconds seem to stretch into years.

And then—sweet mercy—the sound of flushing.

I push the door open, praying the sound will be covered by the rushing water through the pipes, and now I can no longer stop myself from running; despite the pain in my feet, I jog all the way back to my cabin, not stopping until, out of breath and sweating, I close the door behind me and sink to the floor in front of it.

I sit there for a few seconds before raising my eyes to the analog clock on the bedside table.

It reads 8:27. A little more than an hour and a half to go.

"Well, Sandra," I whisper, "at least I'll have something to tell you."

Chapter 30

The wind begins to pick up around nine. At first, I hear it as a staccato of short, sharp bursts; then, it gets stronger, forcing its way through the wooden planks in the walls, a high-pitched whine like tortured, distant wailing.

I haven't dared take any notes, in case someone might find them; so instead, I've been sitting on the bed, going over everything in my head. What I saw, what I've heard, what I need to ask Sandra about.

The note under my door. The Post-it in my file. The warning about keeping me away from Anna. The zolpidem, and the possibility that the staff might be giving the patients more than just herbal tea.

My thoughts are spinning. My eyes feel dry, the skin over my forehead stretched too tight. I try to massage my own scalp but find that it's much less satisfying doing it yourself than having someone do it to you. Like so many other things.

The hands on the clock on the bedside table are showing twenty minutes to ten. The smell of cheap vanilla shampoo from the shower I took to pass the time is still lingering in the air, my hair hanging damp around my ears.

God, I wish I still had my phone. I wish I could talk to Armin.

Though I know what he would say.

Opening my mouth, I try to imitate his voice, lowering my own.

"Don't go, Isobel. This has all gotten too fucking weird. This isn't a game. Just go to bed, and then, tomorrow morning, get in your car and drive home."

The attempt at imitating my best friend's voice dies out, and toward the end, I'm just speaking to myself, as myself.

I swallow hard.

It's dark outside. Darker than it was last night. Clouds must have rolled in after sunset. Sitting here, it's almost like I can smell it in the air: distant rain, coming closer by the second.

I read somewhere once that humans are better at smelling rain than sharks are at smelling blood. I wonder if it's true.

The whining in the walls increases. If I was superstitious, I'd think the cabin was haunted. That the voice of Susannah Wallin was ringing out from the beyond, trying to warn me.

Get out.

Jesus. I've got goose bumps. I have to stop thinking about this. I'm just getting myself worked up for no reason.

I bury my head in my hands, draw a deep breath, forcing the air down as low as I can. I tell myself I'm not actually scared. That it's nothing but leftover adrenaline from almost getting caught, and the tension of the last few days.

All I want is to crawl under the blankets and sleep for sixteen hours. And hopefully, miraculously, wake up in my own bed, with the coffee stains on the mattress and the mild smell of mildew wafting in from the bathroom.

But I can't. I have to go and meet Sandra. Wind or no wind. Ghost or no ghost.

I throw a glance over at the clock again. A quarter to ten.

It's almost time.

I scoot over to the edge of the bed, reach down and grab for the sweater on the floor. While bent over, I glimpse the recorder, hidden once more under the bed, and I pull it out.

Looking at the black rectangle in my hand, I feel slightly silly for a second. But the tension in my shoulders, the weight over my chest, is enough to make me hold in the button.

I bring it close to my mouth and say:

"My name is Isobel Lindschold. I'm a journalist. I am here at Himlafall undercover as a patient."

I pause, swallow, and continue.

"I am about to go meet my . . . contact in the woods, in order to talk and come up with a plan for the next few days. But . . . if you're listening to this . . . then you've heard the other things I've listed. The things that have been happening."

I close my eyes, breathing out hard through my nose.

"I'm worried I'm not going to come back," I say, words rattling out rapidly. No time to hesitate. "If you find this, please let people know. It's ten minutes to ten, April sixteenth. The year is 2024."

I release the button.

What is this going to do? Who would find it?

The cleaning crew, most likely. And they would just hand it over to Martina.

But it's something.

It's all I can do, for now.

I push the recorder under my pillow, and I pull the sweater over my long-sleeved T-shirt. The sleeves bunch uncomfortably under the thick woolen knit of the sweater.

It's time.

The wind almost throws the door back as I open it. The temperature has dropped significantly in only a couple of hours; the outside is pitch-black, the cold cutting the inside of my throat as I close the door behind me and take a deep, shocking breath.

For a second, I consider going back in and grabbing my jacket. But it's a stark white; it would be visible from the windows, were anyone to look out at the pond.

I'll have to chance it. I won't freeze to death as long as it's above freezing. At least I don't think I will.

"We couldn't just have met in your car again, Sandra?" I mutter to myself, threading my arms around my torso as I start down toward the pond.

My vision is beginning to adjust, and I throw a glance upward. I can see the silhouettes of dark, heavy clouds crowding above. The gusts of wind are harsh and sudden; when I reach the pond, one of them catches me unaware, cutting through my sweater and chilling me to my core.

The surface of the water is rippling, with small waves biting at the shoreline. The pond is black and looks viscous, more like oil than water.

I glance across it.

Right across the pond. Go halfway around, then walk in through the trees at the split pine.

It's too dark to see any split pine on the other side. I will have to trust that it's there.

As I walk, crouched down against the force of the wind, my heart is pounding in my chest. My mouth tastes like metal.

What is it I'm scared of? Is it the weather? The darkness?

The potential, though unlikely, bears in the woods?

No.

It's the thought of someone waiting in the night. The same dark shadow that was standing outside my window last night, looking in. That waited for me outside, chased me to the main building, and then, once I was in there, went back to my cabin and took my phone, cutting me off from the outside world entirely.

When I picture them, the face is shifting. One second, it's Belinda, or Anna. The next, Martina, or Ellen, who maybe never left at all, who could still be here, watching and waiting. And then someone else, someone I've never met, some stranger, who might have been stalking these grounds for days or weeks, lurking and luring until one of us would be alone.

Are they waiting for me, out here, tonight?

When I pass by the last cabin, I see, to my surprise, that the windows are lit. The curtains are drawn, but I see someone moving in there. I force myself to keep walking straight, though all I want is to crouch and sneak. My body feels unwieldy, my limbs moving neither as swiftly nor as discreetly as I want. The crunching of the gravel under my shoes sounds like thunder, as though it might alert whoever is in there immediately.

I stumble over one of the rocks, the ones with the pithy little sayings on them, and curse softly to myself. It's too dark for me to see what's written on them, but it's easy to imagine. Something like "All you need is already yours" or "To be known is to be loved, and to be loved is to be known."

God, I hope no one heard me.

It's just a walk. I'm perfectly allowed to go for a late-night walk, no matter the weather.

Now, with only trees to one side of me and water to the other, I try to laugh, to trick myself into relaxing.

It doesn't work.

Only a little bit farther to go. It's funny how far it feels. Just a small, most likely man-made pond, put there to inspire feelings of peace and tranquility.

It's the same walking trail that looks so idyllic in the daylight.

So how come it looks twisted and frightening now? In the washed-out colors of the night, it seems haunted. Old stories from my childhood begin to appear, my father's voice echoing in my brain.

"Ghouls, and goblins, and creatures that hide in the dark, waiting to snatch children away. They can look like anything they want, you know. Even me or you.

"Everyone in Sweden used to believe in them. Some people in rural areas still think they are out there."

"Not very appropriate stories to tell kids, you fucking asshole," I whisper to myself.

As I creep along the walking trail, the branches on the trees shaking from the wind, I find myself once more thinking about my dad.

Some of the stories he told were true. Never all of them; the most interesting parts were all found to be lies. Lies that, on occasion, got people convicted of crimes they never committed.

But he really did spend time with some dangerous people. Especially in the beginning of his career.

Did he ever feel like this? Like he was on the verge of passing over some invisible line, crossing into an existence he had never imagined for himself?

Did he ever find himself looking over his shoulder, sure someone was staring at him? Did he ever feel invisible eyes on his skin, crawling like sluggish insects, warm blood rushing under cold skin?

I suddenly, absurdly wish I could ask him about it.

Even knowing that I never will.

He never wrote us after he got out of prison, after all. Eighteen months served, and then he was on the next plane out of Sweden. My mother had to divorce him in absentia.

I don't even know if he's still alive.

Maybe that's the ghost haunting me. Maybe there was never anyone there, outside my window, in the first place.

Maybe it was the shadow of my father, staring at me, screaming silently from the void.

For what?

Forgiveness?

Remembrance?

Or could he have been screaming at me to turn back, before it's too late? To not make the mistakes he made?

When I look over my shoulder, the cabins have turned into vague shapes on the other side of the water. I can see a light turned on in the staff quarters, but as I look at it, it blinks out, plunging the building into darkness.

A fresh gust of wind threatens to push me into the water, and I stagger a bit, then continue walking, somewhat faster, now. It's taking longer than I expected. Sandra is probably already out there, waiting for me in between the trees.

I know I'll feel better when I see her. She's so steady, so secure; she will chase the ghosts away.

I'm almost on the other side of the pond. None of the pine trees look split; they all rise tall and proud from the soil, their roots digging deep into the earth, their branches stretching toward the sky.

I can hear the crowns rustling far above my head, and it sounds like whispering, hoarse and distant and horrifically amused. Like old gods, laughing at the very smallness of me.

For one long moment, in the space between heartbeats, I almost turn around and go back. Everything inside me is screaming that this is wrong. Pure primal instinct, warning me away from the dark and lonely night, back toward the false safety of the familiar.

But . . . there.

I see it.

I take a few steps closer, and there, just as she said: a pine tree, slightly hidden by the sturdier trunk of another, split near down the middle. It's twisted, the bark curling from the wound of whatever cleaved it. A lightning strike, most probably; when I look up, I think I can see the blackened, burned branches, bare of needles.

"Thanks, Sandra, that's not ominous at all," I say to myself, trying to make a joke out of it.

I know what she'll tell me, in just a few seconds.

You're so superstitious. It doesn't mean anything.

I'm not, though. Not usually.

But it's difficult to be a skeptic in the dark.

I walk in through the trees, the cold, wet scent of pine and burnt wood fully enveloping me. The shrubbery on the ground is low, dense, and tough, and there is no easily walkable path.

These are old woods. Not the well-trimmed greenery I'm used to from farther south. No, these are woods that have been here since before the land was overtaken by people. These trees have stood since before I was born and will keep standing long after I'm gone.

A shiver runs through me.

"Sandra?" I call out, but my voice is swallowed by the wind.

I take another few cautionary steps, ducking under a low-hanging branch.

The shadows between the pines are pure black, ink drinking whatever little light there is. There is only so much my eyes can adjust.

The animal in me rears its head, cautioning me, some ancient instinct, screaming for light and warmth and the safety of the pack.

My mouth feels very dry. My fingers have gone numb from the cold. In here, between the trees, the sound of the wind is different, the force of it split up. Some of it catches my hair, tossing it around, like some unseen thing is tugging at it, taunting me.

"Sandra, are you here?" I call out. Louder, this time, but my voice is hardly more than a squeak.

When I turn around, I can barely see the break in the tree line. The pond and the cabins are a distant memory.

I swallow hard, flexing my fingers, trying to get some warmth back in them. Breathing in through my nose, I push the air out through my mouth, trying to calm myself.

I walk in yet a little farther, stepping around a gigantic tree with branches as thick as my waist. Logically, I know that I'm not far from the pond, but it feels as though I'm just one wrong step away from getting lost.

I just have to keep walking in a straight line, I tell myself. *That way, I'll find my way back.*

And Sandra will help me. Sandra knows her way around the wild. She takes Andrea camping all the time.

"Sandra, where are you?" I raise my voice properly this time. "Can you see me?"

My words echo out through the woods.

I stop, breathing hard. My sweater feels thin as paper, my ears hurt from the cold, and the still-damp strands of hair feel sharp when they hit my neck, as though on the verge of freezing.

I do a half turn, straining to see through the shadows.

"Sandra," I say again, trying to sound like I'm joking. Like I'm finding this all funny.

"If you don't come out, I'm going to head back."

Nothing.

Only silence.

Where is she? Did something happen? Did she change her mind?

A disconcerting thought strikes me.

Maybe Clara told after all. Maybe Martina and Belinda are staring her down, right now, questioning her about how she knows me.

But no. If that was the case, surely they would have brought me in, too, to try to get to the bottom of it.

"Come on, Sandra," I whisper to myself, sneaking my arms around my chest, pretending that it's to warm myself up and not because I'm scared.

"Where the hell are you?"

I look around.

There. A crunching sound, like a boot stepping on dead shrubbery.

It's far away, but it's clear.

"Sandra!" I call out, relief flooding through me. "I'm over here!"

I stand still, waiting for her to find me. She's probably brought a flashlight. Sandra is always well prepared; she's the kind of person to have a portable first aid kit in her car, something I know because she told me she does.

Nothing.

"Over here!" I call out again. "Sandra!"

I look in the direction of the sound, seeking for the light I'm sure I will see. But there is nothing.

Only the dark. Only the trees.

The image assaults me again. The figure by the window. The amorphous, faceless shadow.

"Sandra?" I say, and my voice is smaller now.

It's not a question. It's a prayer.

Even the wind seems to have died down, for a second. The silence is deafening. In the emptiness, I can hear my own breathing, short and shallow and strangled, feel the silvery thread of hope that Sandra will suddenly answer and that all my fears will have been for naught.

It's so real I can hear it, clear as day. Hear her voice calling out: *Isobel!*

She'll apologize. She'll have some very good excuse for why she was late. And I'll be angry with her, angry that she wasn't here on time, and she'll ask if I was scared, and I'll deny it.

But it never comes.

The ringing emptiness is all there is.

The wind starts up again, the stillness just a temporary refuge, and the whistling through the treetops is louder than before, bringing with it the scent of rain and electricity: a warning.

I can't stay here.

"Sandra, I'm going," I say, testing out the thought.

I can't stay out here. I'll find her tomorrow, and we'll talk then. But I can't be out here, on my own, in the woods at night.

Animals are not the only danger that might be lurking out here.

"I'm going," I call out, seemingly to no one, and I begin to turn.

Just then, there's a sound.

Voices, in the distance. A murmur, near drowning in the sound of the wind.

But then, rising above it, is something else.

A crack.

And a scream, short and piercing, ringing out all around me.

And I swear that I hear in it, my name.

"Isobel!"

Chapter 31

HANDS SHAKING, HEART POUNDING, I STAND PERFECTLY STILL. I hold my breath, listening.

But the woods around me have gone quiet.

I don't know where the scream came from. But it was short. Sharp and violent.

It was Sandra. I'm sure.

Opening my mouth, I try to call for my friend. To find out where she is. So I can help.

But her name dies on my lips.

I have frozen in place. I can't move. I can't speak.

I need to be as small as possible. And still.

Someone hurt Sandra. Someone hurt her, and they're out here, and so are you.

Small and unprotected.

You can't see them. You can't hear them.

You have to hide. You have to make sure they don't see you.

Be small and still and silent.

I'm shaking. I can smell the scent of my own fear, rising from my skin. Harsh and metallic.

If I can smell it, does that mean they can too? That other in the woods?

Can they see me?

They got Sandra. They're going to get me, too.

Are they already creeping closer? Rock or knife or something else in hand?

I look to the left, to the right. It's all the same. It's all just gray on blue on black, shadows layered over shadows.

If I don't move, I'll end up a heap of forgotten bones on the forest floor, rotting under the twisted roots.

A drop of cold water hits my scalp, and I flinch away from the tree, taking one long step and landing on a fallen branch. It cracks with a sound as loud as a gunshot, and I freeze again, holding my breath.

I have to get out of here. I have to get out and tell someone. I have to get back to the light, back to safety.

I just want to go home. I don't want to do this, anymore.

The woods sound like they're breathing around me. Some ancient, thousand-fingered monster, buried in the earth, slowly waking.

A whisper, traveling on the coming storm. Just a few steps away. Something shifting, in the dark, separating itself from the dozens and hundreds of stark black trees, moving closer on light feet.

"Isobel."

I turn, and start to run.

My feet hurt, equal parts cutting pain and cold. My chest is aching. The taste of adrenaline floods my mouth, dizzying.

I can no longer remember where I came from; everywhere around me is forest. I can't see where the light is.

A branch catches me in the face, and I cry out, but I don't stop.

Have to get away. Have to get to safety.

Where is safety? I don't know. All I know is the animal instinct. Life, light, warmth, people.

Protect me from what resides in the dark.

My foot catches, my ankle twisting; a lightning bolt of pain running up my leg. I fall, trying to catch myself, banging my head, biting my tongue, mouth filling with blood.

Have to get up. Have to get to my feet. Have to keep running.

My father's voice, words long since worn thin and old, echoing.

"You can't show that you're scared. You'll give away the game. That's the important thing. As long as you keep playing, you're safe."

I gave away the game.

Did they get Sandra? Or did she tell them? Did they scare her into complacency? Did she trade herself for me?

I will never leave these woods. Will never leave this place.

As I lie there, on the harsh, prickly floor of the forest, I turn my head, pulse drumming in my ears, and I see it.

A glimpse of unnatural light.

A lamp, through a window.

It's just a few feet away. One of the cabins.

I've run around, parallel to the tree line.

The wind calms, for just a few moments, and I hear it again. Steps. No more than ten, twenty yards away. And breathing, heavy, labored.

This time, there's no denying it. I might have imagined the person by the pond last night. Might have told myself I was frightening myself.

But this is real. There's someone out here with me. And it's not Sandra.

I lie very, very still.

The steps quiet down. They're standing still. They can't see me.

One of the hard, thorny little bushes is stinging my face, digging into the soft skin on my cheek. It hurts, but I dare not move.

The cold damp of the softly rotting fallen pines and moss underneath me is seeping into the fabric of my pants, my shirt. Something runs down my cheek. If it's blood or sweat or rain, I can't say.

My breathing is short and shallow, coming in explosive little bursts. I press my lips together, trying to stay quiet.

"Don't be scared."

It's a whisper. No more. The voice sounds familiar. I can't place it. I don't know if I'm imagining the recognition. My very thoughts have gotten small, become naught more than basal instincts. More commands than cognition.

I am prey, hiding quietly, praying to go unnoticed. To live another day.

Another few steps. Slow, but not hesitant. Moving closer.

And there's a smell, too. Wafting over.

Heavy, and metallic, and instantly recognizable. Had I never smelled it before, I would still know it in my very bones.

It's blood.

"I'm not going to hurt you."

Such a sweet promise.

I know it for a lie the way the rabbit knows the wolf.

Staring at the light, I silently fill my lungs with air, until it feels like they might burst. I blink until my vision unblurs, until I see that taunting light beyond the trees with more clarity than I have ever seen anything before.

There's a strange calm inside me. One I've never felt before.

One chance.

This is not a game anymore. There's no room for mistakes.

Another step. This one can't be more than seven or eight yards away. Even in the night, they'll be able to see me soon. Or sense me. Feel the difference in the air near the trembling mass of me.

I tense my arms.

"Can we talk?"

The whisper harsher now. More urgent. The smell of blood growing stronger.

I push myself to my feet, and I run.

The pain in my feet is gone. I can't feel the cold. I know only that I need to get to that light.

The trees part before me, the light growing closer. The wind is tearing at me, threatening to throw me down, but I won't let it.

For a few seconds, I am flying.

And then I stumble out from the woods, back onto the neatly trimmed lawn, the cabins stretching out before me.

I want to turn around. But I can't let myself.

I can't remember who is where. I can't even remember which one is mine. They all look the same, in the night: small, and forbidding, and anonymous. Like they could hide anything and protect nothing.

Running over to the next nearest cabin, I almost trip, again, over one of those stupid fucking inspirational rocks. Stopping for a second, I reach down to pick it up. Maybe I can use it to defend myself.

"Isobel?"

I stop, and I straighten, rock held firmly in hand.

Clara is standing a about twelve feet away from me.

When she smiles, I see that her lip is bleeding.

"What's wrong?"

Chapter 32

I CLENCH THE ROCK IN MY HAND, MY FINGERS ACHING, THE slick stone surface icy cold against my skin.

"Back away," I tell Clara, and I barely recognize my own voice. It's a scratchy growl, more fit for an animal than a person.

"Jesus, what is going on with you?" Clara asks in a low hush.

Her usually immaculate hair is hanging in stringy ropes around her shoulders, and in the light from the cabin, I can see that her face is shiny with sweat.

"What did you do?" I ask her. "Where is Sandra?"

"What the *fuck* are you talking about?" Clara asks in a harsh whispered shout. "You look insane. Why are you bleeding?"

She takes a step toward me, stretching out her hand.

I back up, raising the rock.

"Have you lost it?" Clara stops. "Is this a psychotic break or something? Fuck." She shakes her head.

"Don't pretend like you weren't out there!" I'm nearly shouting.

"Lower your *voice*," Clara hisses at me. "Someone will hear you, you idiot."

Her face is twisted, her usual lilting way of speaking sliding off her words to give way to a slightly deeper, more obviously upper-class accent.

"What were you doing out there?" I ask her. "What did you do?"

"I don't know what you're talking about, you lunatic!" Clara exclaims. "Now put the rock down. What are you going to do, brain me with that thing?"

She looks at my hand with disgust. The wind catches her hair, throwing the pink strands around her face, some of them sticking to the blood at the corner of her mouth.

"No." I grip it harder. "So, what, are you saying you weren't out in the woods just now?"

"Why would I have been in the woods?" Clara asks, trying to free her face from the tangles of hair. "What, were you out there?" She stops, and stares at me.

A beat passes. Two.

I look over at the trees. Strain my eyes to try to see in between them.

The adrenaline has begun to recede. All that's left behind is shaking muscles, and the sudden, stinging pain from the long, sharp slash along my cheek, the aching in the soles of my feet, the tension in my jaw.

My mouth fills with saliva. I feel as though I'm about to throw up.

I turn to the side, and spit.

"What the fuck?" Clara exclaims with disgust.

"Tell me you weren't just out there." My voice is shaking. "Tell me you didn't chase me in there."

"Why would I have chased you in there?" Clara eyes me with suspicion. "Seriously, are you crazy? Or is it drugs? Did you go into the woods and take something?"

"No." I shake my head, lowering my hand. The rock suddenly feels like it weighs hundreds of pounds. My shoulder aches; I must have torn something when I threw myself off the ground.

"There is something seriously wrong with you," Clara says, voice full of disgust. "Whatever. I'm going to bed."

"Wait," I say.

"No." Clara holds her hands up. "Whatever you're doing, I don't want any part in it. You look super fucked-up. This is so not my vibe."

"No," I say, sharper now, raising my voice, and she stops.

"What are you doing out here, then?" I ask her. "If you weren't in the woods, why aren't you in your cabin?"

Clara is standing very still.

"And why are you sweating? It's cold outside. There is a storm coming."

As if to remind us why, there is a groaning rustle from the trees on our right, straining against the wind.

Clara whips the hair out of her face.

"I don't think that's any of your business." She is trying for cold and haughty, and falling short.

I take a step toward her.

"Clara," I urge her, "I'm not kidding around. This is serious. Why were you out here? Just tell me."

Clara shakes her head, hair falling in front of her face. She makes an odd little sound, like a snort, or a hiccup.

When she looks up at me again, she's smiling. But it's a different kind of smile.

"Listen, Isobel." She closes the distance between us. "I haven't said anything about your little journalistic mission yet, because I didn't think it mattered."

The rock clatters to the ground.

My mouth falls open.

"What . . ."

"Yeah, I heard you the other night." Clara's nostrils flare. "Should have thought about the neighbors. Sneaking in a phone? That was really cute."

When she smiles, I see the crusted blood in the corner of her mouth breaking up and flaking, her teeth colored a ghoulish pink, turned near gray in the faint light.

"But I'm over it now." Clara crosses her arms and stretches to her full height. "So how about you stay out of my business, and I'll stay out of yours. All right? Otherwise I might as well go directly to Dr. Martina and tell her how cozy you and the new physical therapist looked."

"Clara," I stammer. "What are you—"

"No," Clara spits at me. "Go wash your fucking face, Isobel."

She turns and walks away.

I'm left standing for a few seconds, mouth dry and heart still pounding.

But when I look over to the trees, I'm reminded that I'm still not alone.

For a second, I consider going to one of the other cabins. Knocking on the door. Asking if I can sleep in there, just to have someone there. Just to be able to tell someone.

But I can't know if one of them might have been the one who was out there with me.

So instead, I half run, half walk back to my own cabin instead.

When I open the door, it all looks like it did when I left. Clothes bundled on the floor, blanket bunched up at the end of the bed.

I close the door behind me, walk over to the desk, and pull it with a loud screeching across the floor until it's firmly planted against the door. I don't know if it will hold, but it's heavy enough to at least give me a warning.

Then I pull the curtains in front of the window and walk into the bathroom.

The light in there is a harsh and unforgiving white. The cut across my cheek has stopped bleeding; it's long and thin, crusted over with blood and dirt.

I reach down over the sink and wash the cut until all the dirt is gone, until it has opened up and started bleeding again. Then I grab one of the pristine, white hand towels and push it against my cheek, grasping onto the stinging feeling as an anchor as the blood soaks through the white cotton.

It's only when I look back in the mirror that I see my necklace is gone. That impossibly heavy little pendant that's been haunting me for nearly twenty years, torn off somewhere in the woods.

A throaty laugh tears its way out of my mouth, and as I watch the woman in the mirror laughing, she looks like someone else.

Well, I think. I guess I'm on my own now, Dad.

Memorandum re: patient safety and well-being
09/02/2023
Dr. Nina Sundin

Dr. Hastings,

I would like to report some concerns regarding the methodology currently being employed in treating certain patients admitted to the Himlafall Clinic.

Having worked at the Himlafall Clinic for four months now (starting date 04/24/2023), I have made some concerning observations regarding a subset of the patients. This memorandum should not be considered a criticism of the philosophy of the clinic as a whole but rather a reflection of the limitations of that methodology and how it is being applied.

I have reported my concerns in passing, but it is my hope that putting them to paper in an official manner might provoke a deeper reflection as to how we might proceed.

I have on at least three occasions (regarding patients ML, KR, and SW) observed how the Hastings Method has had a less than desirable outcome.

KR came to us after a long, drawn-out divorce, and it became clear rather quickly that not only had the seventeen-year marriage been abusive, but that KR had a long history of emotionally abusive relationships, likely in part stemming from undiagnosed C-PTSD. KR had sought out the Hastings Method in an attempt to find a new partner, and rejected the idea of conventional long-form therapy, something which left me deeply concerned for their well-being. The group therapy setting seemed to aggravate KR's symptoms rather than help them gain clarity or perspective, and at the end of the week I found myself deeply concerned that they might, upon leaving, once again seek out their former abuser.

ML came to us with what they considered a "failure" to find a partner. It became apparent that ML had a long history of cultural and religious trauma, and, furthermore, that these deep-seated beliefs were causing ML enormous psychological pain as they were conflicting with ML's sexual orientation. In a more conventional therapeutic setting, ML would have had the opportunity to process their past experiences and explore their sexual orientation at a speed that felt comfortable, but as a result of the heightened pace of the Hastings Method, ML became re-traumatized by the rapid resurgence of painful memories, and left in what I considered to be a worse state than they arrived in.

SW came to us after a recent break-up, seeking assistance re-establishing the relationship in question. SW presented a narrative that fell apart upon examination, and when I attempted to push back, refused to listen and attempted—with some success—to turn the other patients against me. I grew worried enough that I deviated from the protocol and attempted to challenge the beliefs directly, resulting in what I would classify as a violent emotional outburst.

It is my belief that the Hastings Method, though rooted in sound science and having produced positive results for many of the patients who have undergone treatment, is not suited to all patients, especially not those who might have gone through abusive relationships, either as the abused or the abuser.

I believe that the patients should be screened before admittance to rule out any patients with Cluster B personality disorders, as the Hastings Method is at risk of worsening their destructive and self-destructive tendencies. Patients who fail the screening should, depending on severity, be referred to either outpatient or inpatient treatment options more in line with their specific needs.

I further believe that the relationship between patients and therapists needs to be better delineated. In two cases (patients ML and SW), patients appeared to both have developed strong parasocial bonds to you personally, with SW describing you as "the only person who could save her" (quoted from memory). Both ML and SW displayed significant anger at being treated by another psychologist, and described themselves as feeling alternatively "abandoned" and "cast aside" by you, despite never having previously met or interacted with you. It is my belief that this was not only harmful to the patients, but could potentially become dangerous in the future.

I take from this and other observations that the necessary boundaries are not in place to ensure proper emotional compartmentalization. This is always a challenge in an intimate treatment environment. I propose a strict rule of no contact between the primary psychologist and patients outside of therapeutic sessions, and I would further recommend that the Hastings Method and the Himlafall Clinic not be discussed on your or any other social media, as the parasocial relationships between the aforementioned patients and yourself all seem to have been rooted in interactions with your social media profiles. I believe the potential marketing value lost is a reasonable price to pay for the health and safety of our patients.

Furthermore, communication needs to be improved between caregivers. Written records need to be kept, organized, and cross-referenced. Three weeks ago (08/07–08/13) I received a patient (CL) and only discovered halfway through the week that this patient had already gone through the Himlafall treatment program, something which should have been communicated to me at the start of her treatment. Upon requesting her patient file, I found the file had been misplaced, which was why I had not been informed that CL had already gone through the program, something which greatly impacted my ability to evaluate the patient's needs and design a treatment plan. I further discovered that one of the carers on staff had gone through the program at the same time as CL, resulting in more of the kind of blurring of boundaries described above. As such, I further propose a general ban on hiring former patients as staff members.

I believe the Hastings Method has great potential in treating a certain subset of patients, but the way it is currently being applied risks being harmful not only to the patients, but potentially to the caregivers as well. In order for the Himlafall Clinic to survive long-term, stringent protocols need to be put in place. Otherwise, I fear the consequences might be dire.

Dr. Nina Sundin

Chapter 33

I WAKE TO THE SOUND OF RAIN PITTERING AGAINST THE ROOF. The hollow, thrumming sound seems to be reverberating through the cabin, as though the lack of insulation in the walls is creating a drum for the heavens to play.

When I sit up, I feel my shoulder aching; and as I grimace, the cut on my cheek makes itself known.

I give a grim little laugh.

"Don't think you're supposed to get beaten up this badly at a psychological treatment clinic," I mutter to myself as I survey the room.

The floor is clean, my suitcase all zippered up and ready to go. I packed last night, everything but my toothbrush, before passing out from sheer exhaustion around four in the morning, too tired to keep jumping at every sound from the outside.

There is a relief, I have discovered, in giving up.

I can't do this anymore. It has all just gotten too real, too dangerous, too fast. People spying in the dark, breaking into my cabin to take my phone, skulking in the woods.

Hunting me.

I wanted to find Susannah Wallin. I wanted to get justice for the people who've gotten scammed and broken by Martina Hastings. I wanted to make a name for myself.

All of that is still true. But I'm not willing to pay the price. I always knew there was a risk in coming here, knew that there were whispers and rumors, that at least one person had gotten hurt badly enough, physically or emotionally, to disappear.

I thought I was prepared enough. I thought I was smart enough. I thought I could handle it.

But something has gone wrong. Wrong enough to tell me I have to get out of here.

Some of the fear from last night has subsided with the warmth and light of being indoors and at least nominally safe; enough for my head to clear up, for me to begin to question some of my assumptions.

I don't know what it was I heard last night. Or who. But that conviction that Sandra was out there with me, that she got hurt—that's gone. The fear took over.

Sandra didn't show. Most likely because she got spooked. Someone saw her leaving her room, and she was already freaked out, with no way to leave me a message. Maybe she tried sending me a text, informing me. I never did have time to tell her about the fact that someone got my phone.

It doesn't matter anymore. I need to go and find Sandra, and then we both need to leave. What I have might be enough to hand over to someone, the ethics board or the police, and let them investigate. It might be enough to get the place shut down, maybe even to get the cops to look into Susannah's disappearance again.

I'll have something to show for it. Even if it's not the glorious start to my career that I wanted.

Armin will be happy, at least. Hopefully, happy enough to let me crash on his couch for a couple of months, given that I won't have enough money to pay my rent.

I get up from the bed, pull my hair back into a short ponytail, and, grabbing my jacket, push the desk out of the way from the door so that I can go outside.

It's pouring rain out there, the path turned half into a river, pebbles dancing in the water streaming down the hill to the pond. When I chance a look up at the sky, it's iron gray, clouds so heavy with water they seem near to touch the treetops. The wind is still coming in strong, insistent bursts, throwing the rain droplets in the air and spraying my face.

The air smells of cold, and water, and electricity. It won't be a fun drive. For the first time since I left for this now-failed venture, I find that I'm happy I got the more expensive car.

At least that's something, I guess.

I pull my hood down, lower my chin to my chest, and set off for the staff quarters. The cloud coverage is thick enough that it looks more like twilight than morning, the light gray and muddled.

When I get to the staff quarters, I hesitate by the door. For a second, I think to myself that it doesn't matter; I'm getting out of here anyway.

But then, half a heartbeat later, I remember. It might not matter to me, but it matters to Sandra.

Already soaked to the bone, I curse softly to myself.

Then I creep up to the first window, get up on my toes among the low blueberry bushes, and look in.

It's empty. A neatly made bed, two books stacked on the desk by the window. A duffel bag with the words VALLENTUNA TENNIS CLUB printed on it on the floor next to the bed.

Definitely not Sandra's room. She's never played tennis in her life.

The next window shows a small kitchen. It's messy, the sink full of dirty cups and a full garbage bag on the floor next to the trash can. I can see flies circling the bag, even from outside the window, and despite the circumstances it gives me a small thrill, seeing this thing I'm not supposed to be seeing. The pristine employees of the esteemed Himlafall Clinic; not so perfectly neat behind closed doors, it seems.

My mother once suggested that I wanted to be a journalist not to show up my father but because I wanted to be professionally nosy without getting called out on it. I remember laughing when she said that, even though I was pretty sure she wasn't joking, at all. She never did like how interested I was in the affairs of other people; after what happened with my father, I think she disliked everything about me that reminded her of him.

I move on to the next window. This one is a bedroom, and a messy one; a lamp has been knocked over, and no one has picked it up. There is a small picture on the desk that I can just barely make out. Sandra and Andrea, laughing at the camera.

When I strain to stand taller and twist my neck, I can only just make out the figure of Sandra sleeping in the bed. She has her back to me, the blankets pulled up all the way over her head, so that I only see a little bit of short blond hair sticking out.

I raise my hand to knock.

"Isobel, what are you doing?"

I thunk down back onto my heels and turn around.

Belinda is standing on the stairs. She's got a light-gray rain jacket on, hood pulled over her head, and her usual white sneakers exchanged for low rubber boots.

"I—" I start, mind completely blank.

She walks up to me. "Well?"

I'm out of good explanations. Out of stories, out of energy. I can't get myself to care enough to make it sound believable.

On the other hand . . . that note in my file made me out to be an attention-seeking liar. No matter why that was in there, it can only work in my favor.

"I wanted to talk to Martina," I say.

"Dr. Martina?" Belinda asks.

I clear my throat.

"The very same." I smile. "I went to the main building, and she wasn't there, so I thought . . . well, I figured I'd go to her room and see if she was there."

Belinda stares at me, unblinking.

"It's urgent." I don't have to fake the way my voice is shaking.

"Well, first of all, that is not okay, Isobel," Belinda chides me. "Patients are not allowed in staff quarters."

"I'm not in staff quarters," I point out. "Technically, I'm outside staff quarters."

This earns me a sour little smile.

"Very cute." Belinda does not appear to find this cute. "But that's not even Dr. Martina's room. That's Sandra's room. You would've woken her up if I hadn't stopped you."

She takes me by the elbow, her grip firm, and leads me away from the window, toward the main building. The rain is still falling all around us.

"She's still sleeping?" I ask, trying for innocence. Or stupidity. Whichever works. "Isn't she going to miss breakfast?"

"She's sick," Belinda says, voice short and clipped. "I think she's got a stomach bug, so we don't want anyone to bother her."

"Oh," I say.

That explains it.

Andrea had a stomach bug. That's why Sandra was late to show up. She must have caught it from her daughter, gotten symptoms last night.

Belinda stops, turning to me, her grip tightening. The hood and shoulders of her rain jacket are glistening in the rain, and as the wind blows all around us, it catches a strand of her hair escaped from the hood, making it dance across her face, which is tightened up in suspicion.

Up close, I see that she's got a small brown spot on one iris. A freckle. It makes it look like she's got two pupils in one eye, like there are two people in there, staring out at me.

"Isobel," she says, her voice low. "Tell me the truth. What is going on with you? What are you after?"

"Nothing." I'm too quick to respond; I sound, accurately, like I've got something to hide.

Belinda's mouth twists, for just a second, and I feel like I'm seeing a glimpse of the person behind the picture-perfect mask for the first time. An actual human emotion, as opposed to pure blissful serenity.

"It was you, wasn't it?" She brings her face closer to mine, her grip on my elbow tightening.

"What was me?" I ask, with genuine surprise.

Belinda stares at me. For one second. Two.

Whatever she sees in my face, it's enough to make her let me go.

"Never mind." She turns away, but I swear there was . . . something, in her eyes. "Come on. I'll bring you to Martina."

Belinda walks me over to the main building. The reception area is empty, the lamp in the ceiling giving off a slight electric buzzing I can feel in my teeth.

As we walk in, she pulls her hood down, shaking her hair out.

For a moment, the frustration and irritation still naked on her face, with raindrops running down the surface of her jacket and her dirty rubber boots, I think she looks like someone who could have been my friend, under other circumstances.

"She's in her office." Belinda's voice is clipped. "Just go over there. If she doesn't have time, she'll tell you."

"Thank you," I say, and Belinda waves me off as she sits down behind the desk.

I hesitate.

"Is everything okay?" My curiosity still winning out.

She looks up. There are dark circles under her eyes, and in the artificial light, she looks washed out, like all the colors have leached out of her.

But then, as though on reflex, she plasters on that by now familiar wide, bright smile.

"It's fine, Isobel." That smooth, friendly voice. "Absolutely nothing to worry about. You go talk to the doctor."

I linger for yet a few more seconds, but Belinda has turned to her computer, her well-kept square fingernails tapping away at the keyboard.

After a few seconds, I turn and walk down the hallway.

The door to Martina's office is closed. I don't knock; I just swing it open.

Martina looks up in surprise as I step in.

"Hi," I say, smiling. "I'd like to go home."

Chapter 34

MARTINA, TO HER CREDIT, APPEARS UNRUFFLED BY MY STATEMENT.

Instead, she leans back in her chair, gesturing to the chair on the other side of the desk.

"Take a seat, Isobel," she instructs me.

I close the door behind me and sit down. I look around, mentally comparing the state of the office to what I saw last night.

Strangely, it looks no less menacing in the daylight.

"I'd like my car keys and my cell phone." After a second, I add: "Please."

Martina just smiles.

"Do you want to take off your jacket?" she asks, as though it's a question and not a command, adding: "It's wet. I wouldn't want you to catch a cold."

I can't find a reason not to, so I shrug out of my jacket, leaving it hanging over the back of the chair. One sleeve begins to drip onto the floor, a dull, rhythmic sound that ties into the drumming of the rain on the roof.

"So," Martina says, "how are you feeling?"

I shake my head.

"Thank you for asking. But we don't need to talk about my feelings today. I just want to go home."

Martina's eyes narrow, ever so slightly, her smile remaining, slim and closed, on her lips.

"Why is that?" she asks me.

"Does it matter?" I shoot back.

Dr. Martina sighs. It's not the frustrated sigh of one who hasn't received an answer to a question; it's the disappointed sigh of a parent whose child is misbehaving.

"Of course it matters, Isobel." She's playing at being the ever-patient parental figure again. "I was expecting something like this, to be honest."

"You were expecting for me to want to leave?" I ask.

Martina leans forward over her desk, resting her elbow on the leather-clad surface, her hands clasped together as though in soft prayer.

Everything about her, I see now, is designed to seem soft: the casual, though immaculate clothing, the toned-down makeup. But behind it all, there is something sharp, a razor without a handle.

"You know, Isobel," she begins, "our lives are just repeating patterns. We learn them from an early age, and then we keep doing the same dance, over and over again, trying to figure out where we are going wrong, never wondering if the dance itself might be the problem."

"I'm not here for therapy," I say, and Martina laughs.

"Oh." She tilts her head. "But of course you are. Do you know why therapy works?"

I try to protest, but she keeps talking over me until her voice drowns mine out and swallows it.

"Therapy works because you keep repeating the same patterns with your therapist that you do in your other relationships," Martina tells me. "And so of course you've decided you want to leave now."

"This is not about patterns."

"Yes, it is." Martina's lips stretch in what's not quite a smile. "You're doing what you always do. You let me and your fellow patients in, let us peek behind the curtain, and now you have decided to cut and run. That's your pattern, isn't it? You thought this was going to be some cute little retreat where you wouldn't be challenged, and instead you found that it's hard, and painful, and risky, and now you want to run, instead of seeing it through."

"I'm not leaving because of that." I keep my voice steady. This is not an argument; I am not open to being convinced otherwise. There is nothing she can say that will change my mind, because I am not Isobel Anderssen, and I am ready to go back to being myself.

"So tell me," Martina encourages me sweetly, "why do you want to leave?"

"It doesn't matter." I refuse to play. "I want to go, so I am going. Today."

"You're right." Martina nods, as though we are agreeing with each other. "It doesn't. It doesn't matter what you're telling yourself is the reason. We both know it wouldn't be the truth. You're lying to yourself, because you don't want to admit what you are doing."

I stare at her. "I'm—"

She interrupts me. It's as though I haven't said anything at all.

"Every single relationship"—Martina leans forward over the table—"every single time someone gets close, you have to push them away. Just run away, and never let anyone see you for who you really are. Where does it end, Isobel? Aren't you tired of being alone? Don't you want to get to relax into something? Don't you want to let go? Wouldn't it feel good to take your walls down, to trust someone, to trust that they want the best for you? Don't you want to get to be *soft*, for once? *Yielding?*"

Her mouth stretches against the last words, lingering on the last syllable.

"I am not running away." I can feel the agitation taking hold, just like it did when I was a child; that feeling of not being heard, not being treated like my own person.

She's doing it on purpose.

"Of course you do, Isobel. You've been running ever since you were a child. Because if you stop, you're frightened of what might catch you. Isn't that right?"

Her teeth glimmer white in the soft light from the Tiffany lamp on the desk. Straight and sharp.

For a moment, last night flashes before my eyes.

Running through the trees in the night. Hearing someone whispering my name.

A familiar voice I couldn't quite place. A scent on the wind.

Could it have been her? Could it have been Martina?

Could she have seen me, going to meet Sandra, and followed me out there?

"I'm sure you're telling yourself some story about why you have to go," Martina says. "Maybe you think this isn't for you. Maybe you think you don't want to be away from home. Maybe you think you can figure it out on your own."

She shakes her head slowly.

"Remember when you promised to trust me?" she asks. "Is that really a promise you want to break?"

"It's not—" I start to say, but she interrupts me yet again.

"Believe in me," she urges me. "Believe in yourself. I know you can do this."

"If I say I still want to go," I ask, voice sweetened, "what would you say?"

Martina sighs, smile never leaving her lips. It's quite a trick.

"Well, Isobel, I'd say that you are signed into what is, technically, an inpatient treatment facility for a weeklong stay." Her tone is deep and rich. "So as the psychologist responsible for your care, I would highly recommend you stay for the full duration."

"And if I still want to go?" I push.

My mind has gone still, my thoughts sharp. Something pulsates between us, turning the air thick.

"I'd advise you against it," Martina says.

Still smiling. Never not smiling.

She's not going to let me leave.

She is not going to give me my car keys. Or my phone. This is not a discussion; it's a hostage negotiation, with me as the hostage, and I've already lost.

What will happen if I keep pushing?

I don't want to find out.

"I guess I don't have a choice, then." It's a question, not a statement. One we both already know the answer to.

"Isobel." Martina laughs, as if I've made a funny little joke. "Of course you have a choice."

She reaches over the table and grasps my hand, her skin hot and feverish against my cold fingers. When she squeezes it, my fingers crush against each other hard enough to hurt.

"But sometimes, someone has to encourage you to choose the right option," she says. "So that you don't hurt yourself. Or someone else."

She's still squeezing my fingers.

"We don't want anyone to get hurt," she sighs. "Least of all you, Isobel. You're a very special person. And I'm so delighted that you've decided to stay."

I smile at her, lips stretched, jaw rigid, eyes locked on hers.

Might as well play along. It could buy me some time.

Because I'm getting out of here, whether she is willing to let me go or not.

Chapter 35

"ISOBEL, HEY!" KATARINA CALLS OUT WHEN I WALK INTO THE dining hall. I'm in enough of a daze that I barely hear her, but I take the open chair next to her and sit down.

"It's nice with some rain, isn't it?" she adds. "I really liked the sound of the wind last night, it was like having a white noise machine in the room."

The sound is quieter in here, muffled by the sturdier build of the dining hall; but I can still hear it, like the muted sound of someone tapping on the door, begging to get in. It's colder in here than before, too, enough to make my skin break out in goose pimples. A shiver runs through me.

"Delighted you've decided to stay."

"You're a very special person, Isobel."

"We don't want anyone to get hurt."

What have I gotten myself into? I should have seen it earlier. Should have listened to Sandra and Armin, as they both told me, each in their own way, that I should leave.

It all added up slowly enough that I could talk myself into thinking I still had the situation under control. Up until the point when it became all too clear that I was never in control, that I have, the whole time, been the proverbial frog in the proverbial pot.

Worse, actually. The famous saying is a lie; a frog would have gotten out long before I tried to.

Now the water is boiling all around me, and I'm scratching frantically at the walls, trying and failing to climb out.

But there is a way. There has to be a way.

"Isobel, are you okay?" Leyla is looking at me from across the table. Her hair has frizzed up in the humidity. It makes her look younger, less hardened by life.

For a moment, the words linger on my lips. Wild ideas flit through my head.

Maybe, if we all went to Martina, she'd let us go. Maybe if we staged some kind of revolt. Surely she couldn't hold us all back, if we decided we wanted to leave, if we demanded it.

But as I look into Leyla's eyes, I remember the scene from yesterday; I remember Martina embracing her, and Leyla crying in her arms.

She's already gotten to them, broken down their defenses. Why would I think they would take my side?

Sandra is the only person I can rely on. Sick or not, I have to get to her.

She's surely got the key, or combination to the gate. We can take her car. I don't care about the rental anymore. All I care about is getting out.

"I'm fine." I pull the corners of my mouth up manually, as though piloting a marionette. "Just tired. I had a hard time sleeping through the storm."

The doors open, and I twitch, stiffen in my seat when I see Clara walking in. Her hair is in a high ponytail, her face dotted with rain, all fresh and lovely.

I can barely see the cut on her lip anymore. But I remember her face from last night vividly.

The blood caught between her teeth. The threat, delivered in a low growl.

"Good morning, gang," Clara greets us, sitting down next to Leyla. She doesn't look directly at me.

Instead, she takes stock of the surprisingly empty table, with nothing on it but a couple of yogurts and four untoasted slices of bread stacked on a plate, and asks:

"What happened to the breakfast?"

The doors to the kitchen opens up, and Anna comes walking out with a pot of tea.

"Hey, Clara. Isobel." She puts the pot down in the middle of the table. I catch a whiff of lavender and raspberry, and my stomach turns.

Anna looks at me and asks:

"Are you feeling better today, honey? Did you sleep okay?"

It takes me a moment to remember what she's talking about.

"Much better. The cramps are almost gone."

Clara holds up a finger to get Anna's attention.

"Sorry, but what happened to the breakfast? Is the kitchen out of those overnight oats? It's been really good for balancing my hormones."

"It's the rain." Anna takes a seat next to Katarina, shaking her head. Her hair is damp, I notice now, the icy blond somewhat muted.

"The kitchen staff doesn't stay on location. They called this morning. Apparently, the road isn't safe. Something about a flood warning. So we're on our own in the kitchen today." She grimaces. "We'll do our best, but I'm afraid it won't be up to the usual standard. Sorry."

"A flood warning?" I repeat.

Anna nods, and, reaching out, she grabs one of the tired-looking pieces of bread and takes a big bite out of it.

"The head chef sounded really upset about it on the phone." Her words turn muddled by the chewing. "I told him not to worry. We've got enough food out here to last us for weeks."

Fuck.

Sandra's car isn't sturdy enough to drive through flooded streets. My rental might be, but the keys are somewhere in the main building.

Panic has started bubbling in my stomach, low and sharp, a tart taste filling my mouth. My head is spinning.

There is no way out of here.

Maybe there is no flood warning at all. Maybe Martina made it up to keep me here. Maybe I've been sitting in a rattrap this whole time, thinking I'm a cat, while the doors shut all around me and the glue started working its quiet deadly magic.

No. I have to calm down. I can't let myself get paranoid, not now. Fear will not serve me, only make me feel small and helpless; and if I stop believing I can get out, I will already be lost.

I can sneak into Martina's office. I did it last night, and I can do it again. I'll find the keys to the rental, and get Sandra, and we'll get out of here. We might not even have to drive through the flood. We just have to get far away enough that we can call for help.

"I've never heard of a flood warning in this part of the country," Leyla comments. "I'd have thought the elevation would make it unlikely," she adds.

Anna shrugs. "Climate change, I guess," she says.

"Are we at risk?" Katarina's voice is tinged with worry. "With the pond, and everything."

"I don't think so." Anna smiles, teeth glinting white in the gray light. "The warning concerned the area down the road, not up here. You're all perfectly safe."

"Yeah, guys." Clara raises her voice. "It'll be really cozy. Like camp. We can stay up and tell ghost stories tonight."

I catch her eyes as she says:

"As long as we all do as we're told, I'm sure we're going to be just fine."

Chapter 36

As the others begin to walk over to the main building for the morning session of group therapy, their jackets and sweaters pulled up over their heads, I wait a couple of seconds to let them get a head start before turning instead to the staff quarters.

The clouds have only gotten thicker and darker, the raindrops heavy enough for the sound outside to be deafening. The pond looks like a ballet in the abstract, droplets dancing over the iron-gray surface.

I only need a few minutes. Wake Sandra up, borrow her phone, call for help. One call to Armin, one to the police. I'll tell them someone is being held here against their will, that they need to send a car, or a helicopter, or even a goddamned horse.

That'll be enough.

"Isobel?"

I stop midstep, cursing my luck, cursing the weather. Cursing Himlafall.

Turning, I see Anna, standing there with a frown on her beautiful face, her light hair covered by the hood of a pretty pink rain jacket

"Where are you going?"

"I was just going to go and get a dry sweater," I hasten to say. "Don't worry, I'll be along in just a minute."

Anna bites her lip. "I'd really rather you stick with the others right now. With this weather, we don't want any accidents."

"I'm not going to have an accident. I'll be careful, and it's such a short walk." Even as I'm speaking, the wind picks up, nearly knocking me over, as if nature itself is contradicting me.

"Please, just get back to the group, Isobel." Anna smiles, but there is tension in her lips, in the line of her jaw.

I notice now, what I didn't see in the dining hall: There are circles under her eyes, a small muscle twitching by her jaw.

Keep away from Anna.

Why did they want me to be kept away from her?

Maybe it's not that she knows anything about the secrets of Himlafall. Maybe it's the fact that she's not as dedicated to Martina as the rest.

Maybe she would help me, if I asked.

I decide to chance it.

"Anna, why don't you want me walking around? It can't just be the weather."

She shakes her head empathetically.

"Of course not," she says, but her smile is sliding, becoming lopsided.

My eyes are drawn, as though without my consent, to the woods. The branches hang heavy with moisture, the trees groaning in the wind.

"Did they tell you to keep an eye on me?" I turn back to her. I want to whisper, but the wind demands I almost scream to be heard.

"Did they tell you not to let me leave?"

She seems to falter, on the verge of speaking.

"You can tell me," I say. "Am I in danger?"

Wrong word. Wrong choice. Wrong something.

"No, no, of course not," she says, snapping to attention, polite mask sliding back into place. "You're perfectly safe. Everything is fine. Everything is going to *be* fine."

For a long, quivering moment, we just stand there, looking at each other, the space between us taut as a piano wire, ready to snap from tension.

"Let me go to my cabin." I'm not asking. "I will go to therapy after that. I promise."

She's wavering.

"Where else would I go?" Hysterical laughter threatens to tear from my throat, and I bite down on my tongue to keep it from slipping out.

"Fine," Anna finally says. "But don't go anywhere else. And don't go in the staff quarters, Isobel. It's for your own good. Please. Just listen to me. Promise me."

Her eyes look suspiciously shiny, like she's about to cry, something like fear making her lips and cheeks grow pale, the shadows under her eyes deeper.

I don't object, don't pretend not to know what she is talking about. Somehow, it feels like we're past that.

"Okay. Straight to the cabin."

Anna appears to hesitate, but then she surprises me by pulling me in for a desperate, sudden hug.

She smells like rainwater and organic shampoo, and I feel her body shaking under the pink rain jacket.

To my own surprise, I hug her back.

Then, just as suddenly, she lets go of me, turns around, and walks up to the staff quarters, disappearing through the door.

I'm left there, alone and shivering in the rain, the sinking feeling in my stomach ever stronger.

Maybe I'm not the only one stuck in this trap.

The difference is that I think there is still time to get out.

Anna seems to have accepted whatever fate may be waiting for us.

I can only hope that she is wrong. Even though my instincts tell me otherwise.

Chapter 37

Back in my cabin, I hurry to collect the things I need. I can't carry my suitcase with me to therapy without giving away the game. These aren't normal circumstances; I can live with leaving behind my clothes, my books, my things.

What I really need is my proof. And decent enough clothes and shoes to get out. If worst comes to worst, if I can't get to Sandra in time and have to make a run for it, I can jump the fence and try to hike to the nearest town. There was a gas station about twenty-five minutes from here; I might be able to flag down a car, too, if I can make it to the highway.

I layer on several sweaters, pull my jeans off to get thermal leggings on under them. Two pairs of socks will have to do, or I won't be able to fit my boots over them.

Once I'm done, I'm overheated, sweaty, and nearly ready.

I hope it won't come to hiking. Sandra was right: I've never been one for the outdoors. The idea of walking along that road, the rain thundering down from above, the wind threatening to throw me down to the ground, all in the hopes that I won't get too cold or too tired, praying they won't come after me, makes my heart sink.

But it might be my only option. And if it is, I'll take it.

I look around the cabin. I've once again made a mess of it. I consider cleaning up but decide against it. If it looks like I left all my stuff, they may assume I haven't left. It'll buy me some time.

Now all I need is my recorder.

I get down on my knees by the bag, reach into it for the recorder. The black rectangle with its silly little screen has become the closest thing to comfort I've got.

It gives me something the necklace never could. Certainty.

I try to turn it on but find that it's out of battery, and I frown. I charged it just last night, while I was waiting for Sandra; it shouldn't have run out already.

Quickly, I tug out the cord to the lamp on the bedside table and plug in the charger instead. The recorder beeps to life after only a couple of seconds, and it only takes me a moment to see why it's run out.

I forgot to turn it off last night. After leaving my "last message."

It all seems so trite and pointless now.

The recording is six hours long. It lay here, dutifully documenting the sound of the oncoming storm until the battery ran out.

When I click on it, and it shows the track, I see, to my surprise, that there are three major peaks on the recording. The first one is clearly the message I left; after that, there are ten or so minutes of low-level sound from the rain, and a small blip. Finally, there is a big chunk about an hour or so in.

When I fast-forward to the final burst, I'm greeted by muffled voices. It takes me a little while to recognize them.

". . . you lunatic!"

It's Clara. Me and Clara, arguing last night.

I don't need to listen to it back. I remember it well enough.

Instead, I go back to the little blip, about ten minutes after I left. It's short, voices rising and falling over the sound of the rain. Even at a strain, I'm having a hard time making them out; whoever it is, they must have been right outside my cabin, but the sound of the wind is drowning out the voices.

I raise the volume, rewind again, and try once more. It's easier to make out the tone than it is the words themselves. First, a short burst, like a greeting; then, a period of only rain . . . and then, sounding closer, slightly louder, something I can almost make out. There is a strong vowel sound, a *U*, and then what sounds like *rear*.

I go back, listen to it three more times.

I'm almost, almost certain they are saying "*. . . you here?*"

Finally, a few seconds later, are the only three words I'm sure of. It's not a full sentence; the first one is spoken by a different voice than the last two, and in the middle are sounds too muffled to interpret.

". . . Isobel . . . about Susannah."

I recognize the first voice. Recognize the way it says my name.

It's the same voice I heard in the woods last night. Whispering for me in the dark.

I turn the recorder back off. Slowly slide it into my pocket. I try to get to my feet, but my legs won't cooperate.

That voice in the woods was real. They went out there to find me. They knew I'd be out there, and they knew about Susannah.

And they weren't alone.

A sentence from the Himlafall brochure pops into my head, and I begin to laugh, pressing the back of my hand to my mouth, trying to swallow the sound back down.

There are no secrets at Himlafall. Here, you are never alone.

Clearly, I should have read that literally.

The door opens behind my back. There is no knock, no warning.

I turn my head, and I see Belinda standing in the doorway, softly backlit in ominous gray, the hood of her rain jacket making her look like some ancient monk, come to make me repent for my sins.

"Isobel. You're late for group therapy."

Chapter 38

THE OTHERS ARE ALREADY SITTING IN THE CIRCLE: CLARA, straight-backed and perky, rigid grin on her lips, Leyla inspecting her nails, Katarina picking at the ends of her ponytail, and Pernilla, folded up and closed off.

I take my seat.

The rain is whipping against the windows, the patter stronger in here than it was in the hallway. Martina smacks the light switch on the wall, bathing the room in artificial light.

"Well, aren't we all so cozy in here." She makes it sound like a threat.

Martina slowly sits down in the one empty chair, looking around the circle.

"You know, weather like this can actually be helpful to bring emotions to the surface," Martina begins. "I know it might feel a little bit scary, but whether we like it or not, our feelings are influenced by the world around us. A storm can be a chance to let loose. Let our feelings fly free."

She leans forward in her chair, tilting her head so that her braid slides sensually down the side of her neck. Her necklace is dangling freely over her clasped hands, glinting in the light.

"Who would like to start?" she asks.

At first, no one speaks.

All that can be heard is the sound of the rain, and the wind.

For a second, I'm struck, absurdly, by the thought that this is all the set of a play. That we are performing for her pleasure. It feels like we've been gathered in here, neatly cordoned off, pushed together in a tight space with our emotions running high so that it might culminate in an explosion.

It all feels inevitable, somehow. Like I'm being cut off at every exit, neatly and on purpose.

I'm never going to leave this place.

My hair is standing on end. I tell myself I'm overreacting, that it's all going to be fine.

Tomorrow, I'm going to wake up in my shitty apartment, sore and tired from the drive, and this is all going to feel like a dream I had long ago, a failed endeavor that exhausted and frightened me but doesn't anymore, because I'll be safe.

But that idea is hard to trust, at this point.

Somehow, some part of me believes that I was always meant to end up here.

"Katarina." Martina speaks her name like a command, and Katarina sits up in her chair, her hands folded neatly on her lap.

"Yes?" Her voice is bright. Too chipper to sound real.

"How are you feeling right now?"

"I feel good." Katarina pulls her mouth into a tentative smile, but her eyes flicker toward the windows.

"I slept well," she adds.

Martina looks at her without speaking, and Katarina continues, voice faltering slightly.

"And, well, of course I'm excited to start talking about . . . well, about my issues."

She looks around the circle.

"I look forward to hearing what you think I should do. I like getting feedback. It's so easy to get stuck in your own head otherwise."

"Stop that," Martina snaps, and Katarina flinches.

"Stop . . . stop what?" Katarina is hunched over, as though trying to make herself as small as possible.

"Stop trying to please me," Martina orders her. "Stop acting the way you think I want you to act."

"I'm not," Katarina whispers.

Martina laughs. It's not a kind laugh; it's the laugh of a delighted child pushing a pin through a still-wriggling butterfly.

"I don't know what you want me to say." Katarina sounds helpless, and I feel it echoing in me.

Stuck. We're all stuck here. There is nothing we can do.

"That's your problem," Martina says. There is no feigned softness left now; the facade has fallen.

She turns, and says:

"Clara," with sudden warmth.

"Yes?" Clara snaps to attention.

"How are you feeling right now?"

"About Katarina?" Clara asks.

Martina smirks.

"No," she says. "Not yet. About everything. About the weather. About the breakfast."

"Bad," Clara answers immediately. "It's cold. I'm uncomfortable. I barely slept last night. I'm worried about the storm. And I'm irritated with Katarina."

Martins turns to Katarina, eyebrows ever so slightly raised.

"See? Clara is frustrated. She is uncomfortable. I think everyone is. You had to eat a cold, stale breakfast. It's damp, and rainy, and dark. Of course you're unhappy with it. So why can't you just say so?"

Katarina is visibly shrinking in her chair. "I'm sorry," she says.

"No!" Martina explodes, her voice bouncing of the walls and seeming to multiply. "No, don't apologize! *Stop* apologizing! Have you ever stood up for yourself in your life?"

"Yes." Katarina's lower lip is quivering. "No, I mean."

Martina slowly leans back in her chair, crossing her arms over her chest. All the while, she's staring at Katarina.

"Tell me how you feel right now." She makes it sound like a test. Like a challenge.

As though this is her final chance, and there will be a price to pay if she gives the wrong answer.

"I feel . . ." Katarina whispers. "I feel . . . sad."

"Sad?" Martina repeats. "Really?"

Katarina is staring down at her lap.

"No," Martina snaps. "You feel angry. At me. For doing this to you. For putting you on the spot."

"I'm not mad at you." Katarina is speaking very quietly. "You're trying to help me."

"Like your parents tried to help you?" Martina raises her eyebrows.

Katarina looks up. There is a flash of some intensely felt emotion in her eyes but only for a fraction of a second.

"I'm sad," she repeats, voice slightly stronger now.

Martina looks around.

"Do we think she's sad?"

"No," Clara jumps in again, hungry and eager. "She's angry. She just doesn't want to admit it."

"Why do you think that is?" Martina asks Clara.

"She's worried we won't like her." There is something sharp and raw in Clara's face. Excitement, tinged with fear. Like she's smelling blood.

Yesterday, she was the prey; today, she gets to be the predator.

This is all wrong. Someone has to put a stop to this.

"She wants to be liked so *badly*." Clara says the last word so forcefully I see spit flying from her lips. "She wants us to think she's all sweet, and nice, and caring—and she's scared of being anything else, or saying anything that might offend someone, so instead she just does nothing. She never acts. She only reacts."

"No, I don't," Katarina protests.

Clara draws a deep breath, as if to keep going, but then, out of the corner of my eye, I see Leyla putting her hand on Clara's arm and shaking her head, and Clara deflates.

Martina doesn't catch it. She's turned back to Katarina.

"Now how do you feel?" she asks.

"I don't know," Katarina mumbles.

"Really?" Martina asks. "How do you feel about Clara? About what she just said?"

Katarina chances a glance up at Clara.

"I guess she's just saying how . . . she feels." She swallows audibly. "What she thinks. That doesn't make it true. But maybe it feels true to her."

Martina is sitting very, very still. Her back is straight, her hands clamped down at the sides of the chair.

The lamp in the corner is casting her shadow to the left, long and spindly, climbing up the wall. It's quivering in the light, as though it might start moving of its own accord.

"Okay," she finally says, nodding slowly. "Okay."

She turns away from Katarina, looking at the rest of us.

"Katarina's parents told her she should be grateful to have a bed when she was eight years old," she says. "Isn't that funny?"

No one moves.

Martina gives a high, pearly laugh. The kind of laugh that belongs at a cotillion, or a polo match; rich and distant.

"See, when Katarina was a little girl, and when she was bad," Dr. Martina begins, her voice now low, conspiratorial, as though she's sharing a juicy piece of gossip, "her parents would make her sleep on the floor. They told her that she shouldn't take anything for granted. Not even a bed. So when she didn't do her homework, or when she didn't complete her chores, she had to sleep on the floor. Not even on the rug. Can you imagine?"

Martina laughs again. She slaps her knee.

"Isn't that the funniest thing you've ever heard?"

Katarina is looking at Martina. Her eyes are open so wide I can see all around her iris.

Something in me snaps. It feels like I've suddenly woken up.

"That's not fucking funny," I say. Somehow, my voice sounds calm and controlled, even though that is the last thing I feel.

Martina turns to me.

"Well, of course it's funny, Isobel," she coos. "Just picture it. Little Katarina, curled up on the floor, *crying* because she was cold. All she had to do was not talk back so much! It's all just so *silly*."

"*Stop it*!" I raise my voice, but she's still talking, now turning to Pernilla, who looks on in equal parts horror and fascination.

"When she was a teenager, Katarina's mom and dad would do weekly weigh-ins for her," Martina keeps going, in a hushed tone. "And if she had gained weight, they wouldn't let her have dinner until the next week. Once . . ." She leans in even farther.

"Once, Katarina snuck down and ate the leftovers out of the trash. She was crying into the garbage, she was so scared of getting caught. Isn't that absolutely mad?" Her eyes are sparkling.

"Don't *tell* them about that." Katarina's voice has turned into a low growl.

"Stop it, Martina!" I'm nearly yelling now, but Martina just keeps going, raising her voice until it's louder than the rain, louder than anything, until it's the only thing that exists in the world.

"Katarina still has dinner with her parents once a week. And about a month ago, they decided to send her here to have her fixed. They're upset, you see, that Katarina isn't married yet. So they sent her here to have her taken care of, like she's a broken toy. Isn't that just the funniest thing you've ever heard?"

Martina throws her head back and laughs, and Katarina catapults out of her chair.

"SHUT UP!" she screams at the top of her lungs. "JUST SHUT THE FUCK UP!"

Martina's laugh cuts off, as though someone's pushed a button.

Katarina is standing over her, panting, her cheeks red, her chest working like bellows, and she has one hand raised, shaking, in the air.

I don't know if she's straining to hit Martina, or straining not to.

"There," Martina says softly. "There it is."

Katarina is crying soundlessly, swallowing in giant gulps of air.

"You're angry," Martina states plainly. "Say it. Say that you are angry."

There's hunger in her eyes, in her grasping hands, a sort of horrible anticipation.

"You hate me," she breathes. "Come on. Admit it."

Katarina slowly lowers her hand.

And then she shakes her head.

"No," she says. "I don't."

For a long, vibrating moment, Martina looks at Katarina. Something passes between them.

Then Martina sighs.

"Okay." She stands up, disgust radiating from her. "Fine."

Katarina flinches, but Martina just walks right past her, to the door.

"I think we'll be skipping the break today," she tosses out over her shoulder. "I'll go tell Anna and Belinda to bring us some tea and treats."

She closes the door behind her with a bang.

Chapter 39

I SPRING FROM MY CHAIR THE MOMENT THE DOOR CLOSES, and I put my arm around Katarina. She's shaking, the muscles in her thin shoulders tense like springs, as though she's about to fall apart. Or explode.

"Are you okay?" I ask her.

Leyla has joined up at the other side of her, and I see, to my surprise, that Pernilla has stood up as well, wringing her hands, her face white and drawn.

Katarina shakes her head.

"I shouldn't have done that," she murmurs. "I shouldn't have . . . I shouldn't . . ."

"You didn't do anything wrong." Leyla grasps Katarina's hand lightly in her own.

Katarina looks over at Leyla, and the sight of Leyla's calm, steady gaze seems to soothe her.

"You don't mean that," Katarina says.

"I do," Leyla says. "What she did was horrible. There's no excuse for it."

When Pernilla speaks up, we all start in surprise; her voice is low and, for the first time I've heard it, unsure.

"Surely she shouldn't be . . . doing that," Pernilla says, hesitating, seeking reassurance and landing on Leyla.

"Telling the rest of us what we've shared in private. That can't possibly be how it's done?"

"It's not." I stand up. "It's not how it's done. It's illegal. And immoral. It's wrong on every level."

"When she . . . well, I thought she was helping." Pernilla's eyes are drawn to Clara, the only one still sitting.

"It felt . . . good in the moment." Pernilla is speaking slowly, seeming to feel her way through. "But after, I felt . . . well, it felt horrible. Dragging everything I'd said out like that, without asking me first. And making me . . . or, rather, encouraging me. To say those things to you." This last part she addresses to Clara, who's looking at her without speaking.

"I shouldn't have done that. I'm sorry." The apology is choked but sounds sincere.

Clara's lips pinch together for a moment. But then she says:

"No. Don't be. It's the Hastings Method. You were doing it to foster growth."

Leyla raises her eyebrows, and I say:

"Come on, Clara, you can't actually believe that. Not still." I gesture to Katarina. "I mean, look at her," I say, and then I direct a quick "Sorry" to Katarina.

"Don't worry," Katarina says.

"Does this seem right to you?" I ask Clara. "Does this seem like the actions of someone who is trying to help anyone? Leyla is right. This isn't what therapy is supposed to be like. Whatever is going on here isn't healing or helping anyone."

Clara shakes her head, crossing her arms, much like Martina crossed her arms earlier. "You guys just aren't committed enough," she says. "Growth isn't always pleasant. It's not easy. You have to do the work."

"Fuck *the work*," Leyla exclaims. "This isn't work, this is torture."

Clara rolls her eyes. "Please," she says. "If you knew how much research had gone into the method, you wouldn't be questioning it. You're all just scared."

"I don't think you're supposed to be scared in therapy." Katarina is speaking very quietly but loud enough to be heard.

"Listen, I'm sorry if I hurt your feelings." There is just a hint of remorse in the tilt of Clara's head, in the pause before she continues.

"I didn't mean to say anything that would offend you, or anything. But the Hastings Method requires radical honesty between peers."

"But we're *not* peers," Pernilla chimes in.

"Well, of course *you* would say that." Clara rolls her eyes. "You think you're so much better than the rest of us."

"I didn't mean it like that," Pernilla says, and she actually sounds wounded. "I just meant . . . Dr. Martina isn't treating us like we're peers. She goes on about how we are supposedly in the same boat, saying that we all have something to learn from each other, but she's pitting us against each other."

"Some of us haven't made it much of a challenge for her," Leyla mutters, and Clara's eyes widen; she stares at Leyla, radiating hurt feelings.

"I can't believe you'd say that to me," Clara says. "After—"

"Well, it's the truth." Leyla shuts her down.

"Yeah, it's always the truth with you." Clara stands up, spreading her arms wide. "What, like you're not doing what you always do? Don't you see? You're all just repeating old patterns! You're doing exactly what she said you'd do!"

"Wait." I hold up my hand. "Did you tell Martina? About me?"

"Yeah." Clara's laugh is tinted with hysteria. "Because *everything* is about you, Isobel. You're the most important person in the world, right?"

"No," I snap. "Stop pretending. *Repeating old patterns.* Are you working with them? With her? Is that why you were out last night?"

"You're fucking crazy." Clara shakes her head. "You're a mess."

"Sure," I agree. "But answer my question. Are you in on it? Whatever it is that they're doing here?"

"What are you two *talking* about?" Pernilla exclaims, throwing her hands wide.

"I don't know!" Clara says.

I turn to the others.

"There is something really wrong with Himlafall," I start. "With the Hastings Method, and with the staff, and with Martina. It's not just what she's doing to us in here. Weird stuff has been happening the whole time we've been here. A patient went missing from here nine months ago, and

I think they covered it up. I think something happened to her here. And it might be happening again. Stuff has disappeared from my cabin. Someone's gone through my stuff. And I got chased by someone last night in the woods. They followed me out there, and I heard them talking about the last woman who went missing."

"Wait, why were you in the woods?" Leyla crosses her arms. "What were you doing out there?"

"It's a long story," I say. "But I had my reasons. And I wasn't the only one out there."

I turn my head, looking at Clara.

"Clara was out there, too."

Clara smiles, small and tight. She looks around at the rest of us.

"I don't know why she's trying to freak you all out like this," she says, "but I think there's something you should know."

"Clara—" Leyla starts, a warning note in her voice, but Clara just keeps talking over her.

"Isobel isn't who she says she is. She's a journalist. She's been here this whole time, lying about who she is, listening to all your secrets for a fucking *article* she wants to write."

The others turn and stare at me. I put my hands up.

"Listen," I begin.

"What the—?" Pernilla draws up, every syllable clipped and furious.

The door swings open and hits the opposite wall. Martina is standing there, holding a tray of cookies, Anna right behind her with a teapot and a stack of mugs.

"Ready to continue?" Martina asks, as the wind makes the windows shake in their frames.

198k likes

doctormartinahastings A year of planning, countless hours of sweat, blood (sometimes literal!), and tears, and now I finally get to say what I've been dreaming of saying for almost eighteen months: The Himlafall Clinic is finally open.

I'm not ashamed to tell you all that I cried when the contractor called (shoutout to @mikkelrasmussen for helping me make my dreams come true!) to tell me that everything was, finally, ready to go.

When I started this project, I wanted to create something that had never been done before. I wanted to fuse my years of research, of practice, of psychology and philosophy and spirituality, into something completely new. A place where women could go to heal their inner children, to learn how to love themselves and love others, and to value their own inner voices.

In short: I wanted to create a place where we would treat our patients so well, they would never settle for anything less than what they deserve ever again.

And now it's here. It's reality. I still can't believe it. (I actually woke up last night from a nightmare where I dreamed that they had found snakes in the pond . . . how very Freudian of me.)

In just a couple of weeks, we will open our doors to our first batch of patients. We already have a monthslong waiting list, and I am so honored by that fact. Your belief, your trust, and your patience got us here. Together, we are going to change the world.

Together, we are going to mend each other.

If you are interested in starting your healing journey with us at the Himlafall Clinic, you can go to the link in my profile to sign up for the waiting list. The criteria for admittance are all listed in the form, and we are open to anyone who identifies as a woman and has a broken heart.

If you want to follow along on our journey, or learn more about the Hastings Method, you can sign up for my newsletter, Musings with Dr. Martina (link in profile), where we discuss everything from the healing power of rage to how to tackle dating with an intentional mindset. Please, come join our community of over 20,000 like-minded women, where we grow and evolve together.

Tonight, I will be celebrating the culmination of all our hard work with a special bottle of champagne, delivered to me by @weekly-wines! Every bottle at Weekly Wines is organic and handpicked by their award-winning sommeliers, and right now, you get 15% off when you sign up for their weekly delivery service and use code "DoctorMartina." Whether you're celebrating a win or drowning your sorrows, wine is there to help.

4189 comments

mmmmarie001 you are amazing!!! I wish I could go but sadly im still married, haha!!

larsenaxel ur pretty hot for someone whose so old

clarabellavida Are you hiring? I don't have a degree in psychology but I've read a lot about it and I am so passionate about helping people!! I would love to work with you. I've read all your books twice and I really look up to you.

susiew oh my god!! congratulations! i signed up for the waitlist, i didn't get a spot yet but i can wait.

> **mickewallin** haha yes @doctormartinahastings she's your biggest fan!!
>
> **susiew** oh my god STOPPP!! remove the tag right now, you're so embarrassing!!

Chapter 40

ANNA PULLS OVER A TABLE FROM THE CORNER BEFORE POURING everyone cups of tea, while Martina grabs a cookie from the plate and takes a big bite, the crunch so loud I flinch.

I put my mug back down on the table as the others sip from theirs. I don't want to touch anything they would serve me.

"Doctor, do you want me to go get you a cup of rose hip tea from your office?" Anna is still pale, and I see, when she picks up the now-empty teapot, that her hand is shaking slightly. She grabs her wrist with her other hand, stilling it, and plasters on a smile.

"No, Anna, that's all right." Martina shoots her a thin smile. "I'm not very thirsty. Thank you, though."

Anna exits the room, and Martina says, as though in casual conversation: "Isn't that nice of her? She knows I don't care for lavender."

No one responds. The silence hangs in the air, cold and oppressive, like a miniature version of the rainstorm outside, about to erupt.

Martina directs her attention back to Katarina.

"How are you feeling now, Kat?"

"I don't like to be called that." Katarina's words are sharp and clear.

Martina smiles.

"Good," she says. "That's a good start."

"No," Katarina says. "Not a start. Talk to someone else. I don't want to anymore."

A hint of surprise flitters in Martina's eyes. Gone again in an instant.

"All right." Martina recovers. "Let's take a beat so that you can gather your thoughts, Katarina. How about we go back to Isobel?"

Her head swivels.

"How are you feeling? You look stressed," Martina observes.

Clara mutters something under her breath, and Martina looks over at her. It's clear she expects Clara to speak up, but to my surprise, she clamps her mouth shut instead.

"Is there anything I should know?" Martina asks, clearing her throat.

She's lost control of the room. She doesn't like it.

The lights in the ceiling flicker.

"What the—" Leyla exclaims, but then they stabilize.

"You told us the electricity wouldn't go out." Pernilla's face is pinched.

"It's all okay." Martina tries to calm us down, but she looks visibly distressed. "Even if the electricity did go, we have a backup generator. It will all be fine."

"It doesn't feel fine," Leyla mutters.

"*Anyway,*" Martina says. "Isobel, let's get back to you. I'd like to know how you feel now about this morning. About wanting to leave Himlafall."

It's clear she expects the others to have a big reaction to this, but no one responds.

"I feel fine." I smile, showing as many teeth as I can muster. "Happy as a clam."

Martina's hands clench. Once, twice.

"You all seem unsettled," she manages, looking around the room, turning the full force of her gaze on us. "Are there any questions I can answer for you? To help soothe your nerves?"

"Actually, Doctor"—Leyla raises her voice—"I do have a question."

"About what?" Martina smiles.

"Is it true that someone has been going through our stuff?" Leyla asks.

Martina looks genuinely taken aback by this.

"Of—of course not," she stammers. "Why would we do that?"

Her surprise looks real; none of the overly smooth, closed-off smugness I've come to expect from her. It startles me.

Leyla raises her eyebrows at me, wordlessly urging me on.

"Something was taken," I admit. Martina is the last person in the world I feel like sharing this with, considering I'm fairly convinced she was involved, but if I want the others to see what I have seen I have to. "From my cabin. A couple of days ago."

Martina visibly pales. The slight rouge on her cheeks attempts to conceal it, but I can see the color disappearing from her lips.

"Well." She wets her lips with her tongue. "Maybe you misplaced it?"

I don't know what to think.

Either she's a better actress than I thought, or she's . . . scared.

"I didn't," I say. "I'm sure."

Dr. Martina opens her mouth, stays like that for a couple of seconds. It looks like she's actually lost for words.

The rain is hammering against the roof, the walls, the windows; it feels like an intentional assault, like we're under attack. Like the woods and the skies have decided to rid themselves of this unnatural intrusion into their domain and use wind and water to tear it all down to the foundations, until the forest can take it all back, until there is no trace that any of us were ever here.

"I . . . wish you would have told a staff member, Isobel. We might have been able to help you look for what it was you lost."

"I thought you had taken it." I watch her closely, to see her reacting, but there is nothing: no guilt, no anger, no recognition.

She didn't do it.

"Why would you think that?" Martina sounds baffled.

"Because it was a cell phone," I say. "One I wasn't supposed to have."

Martina just shakes her head, gives a slight, gulping laugh, so very different from her usual pearly peals.

"You think you're the first patient to take a phone in here? For fuck's sake, Isobel, half our guests keep an iPad or a laptop. We don't go through your bags. We're not cops."

She stares at me, her chest moving in short, shallow bursts.

"You didn't take it." I repeat it for confirmation.

"No one working here would ever violate your space like that," Martina insists. "Himlafall is founded on the principle of trust."

"*Principle of trust*?" Pernilla exclaims sharply. "Like how you tell everyone the personal things we've told you in private?"

Martina stands up from her seat and runs her hand over her face.

"Listen to me," she says. "I understand that you're all feeling unmoored and upset right now, but these accusations are ridiculous. This is a very strenuous process, but you all knew that when you came here.

"You came to Himlafall for a one-week therapy intensive. You are all getting the benefits of months and months of rigorous psychological treatment in seven days. That is going to be a somewhat painful experience!" Her voice cracks, and I hear a door being slammed shut in another part of the building; Martina jumps, and her eyes are drawn to the windows.

"No," I say. "You're not telling us everything."

Martina looks to me, and now I see the fear writ large on her face.

"There's someone here, isn't there?" I get up on my feet. "Someone who isn't supposed to be."

Martina is silent. Her eyes flick from me, to Leyla, to Pernilla.

"The running of this clinic is none of your concern, and—"

"No," Leyla interrupts her, standing up too. "It's too late for that. You've got to tell us, Doc. What the hell is going on?"

Martina swallows, over and over again. I can see the muscles in her slim neck working compulsively.

"Nothing." As though she can make it true by saying it. "Nothing at all. Now, I think that this has gone far enough. Clearly, you are all—"

"If we're not safe here, we have a right to know," Pernilla says. "So tell us."

She is clutching her hands together rigidly, her posture absolutely perfect, and I can feel every ounce of social privilege working in her favor, pressuring an answer out of the doctor; it's intense enough that I feel the urge to answer her myself.

Martina shakes her head, her hand flying up to her neck, to the little pendant hanging there, and for one long second, I feel a strange pang of kinship with her.

"Some things have gone missing," she admits. "Patient files. But it's nothing to worry about. None of your files are gone. I think one of the staff members working in the kitchen might have gotten into them, or maybe the cleaning crew. To sell to the press, perhaps."

"Are you sure you didn't take them, Isobel?" Clara raises her eyebrows. Her nostrils are flared, her pupils the size of coins; she's trying to be mean, but her voice is high and frightened.

She wants it to be me, I realize. *Because at least then she doesn't have to be scared.*

"Why would she have done that?" Martina's confusion is turning back into anger.

I decide to get ahead of Clara and do my own dirty work.

"Because I'm a journalist," I confess. "I came here to write an article about the Himlafall Clinic. And yes, I've looked at my own file. But I didn't take any of them."

Martina stares at me.

A beat passes. Two.

Then all hell breaks loose.

"I can't *believe* you would come in here under false pretenses, violating the sanctity of—" Martina yells, her face twisting, as Leyla says:

"Guys, can we just—"

The lights go out, plunging us into darkness.

And then the screaming begins.

r/ActuallyLesbian

My ex is coming by to pick up her stuff and I'm scared

posted by: u/throwawayduckling123

18:16 09/17/2023

I don't even really know what I'm asking, but I feel like I need help. Or maybe just emotional support. You've all been very kind to me before, and I don't have anyone to talk to about this, so I came back here.

If you look through my old posts, you'll see that I was in an abusive relationship. I didn't realize it at the time. It was only when

I sought help on here that people started to point out that the way my girlfriend was treating me wasn't normal, or okay.

I wish I could say that I left when I realized what was going on, but it was so hard. It was so, so hard. It was like my ex noticed me pulling away, and then she started showering me with affection. Suddenly, it was like everything was back on track. I'm ashamed to say that I thought that maybe I could stay with her. She even proposed to me, and I said yes. I know it was stupid. I'm so stupid.

But after a while, it started getting bad again, and one night something in me just . . . snapped. I don't know what happened. We were sitting on the couch, and she was braiding my hair, and she commented that my scalp was dry. She started talking about how I didn't wash my hair often enough, and that it was embarrassing. She said I smelled bad, and that other people could tell, too, and that they just weren't telling me because they didn't want to upset me, but that it was gross. She said I was gross.

It was such a small thing, compared to everything else. And it might sound ridiculous, but . . . I know I don't smell bad. I'm very hygienic. I shower every evening before bed, and I floss twice a day, and I wash my hair with shampoo every two days. It became so very clear to me in that moment that nothing had changed, and that she was just saying that to hurt me, and to make me feel insecure.

My mom (who has passed away) used to braid my hair for me when I was little. It was just the two of us, and she worked two, sometimes three jobs, so there were days when I would only see her in the morning when she braided my hair. And in that moment, I thought about how safe and happy I used to feel when I was little, when my mom was doing that, and how scared and small and disgusting I felt now. And I just realized I couldn't do it anymore.

So we broke up. I broke off the engagement. It got very ugly. I don't really want to go into detail, but at least I didn't have to go to the hospital.

My ex has been trying to talk to me ever since then. I had to change my phone number because she wouldn't stop calling. For a while, she came over every day, just pounding on the door for hours. I work from home, and I was terrified that my boss would hear and that I would get fired. I thought about calling the police, but I was scared they wouldn't take me seriously. Or that they would believe her over me. She's very pretty, and very charming. I know I can come off as strange. I was scared that the police wouldn't believe me if I said that she was harassing me, or that she had hurt me in the past. Luckily, I didn't have to, because she finally stopped.

Yesterday, she left a note in my mailbox. When I recognized her handwriting, I thought my heart would stop. But in the note, she apologized for everything, and she asked if she could come over at seven tonight to pick up the things she left and say sorry in person. She wrote that I don't have to open the door for her, but that she loves me and that she just wants to end things on good terms.

She's supposed to come over in forty minutes. My heart is racing, and I don't know what to do. Please, don't call me dumb for this, because I know I am, but a big part of me misses her. Despite everything. I think it would maybe be good for me to hear her say that she's sorry.

Things went so wrong between us, but she's been through a lot. I know she doesn't mean to be like this, she's just in pain. I know she loves me, and I hurt her. Do I maybe owe it to her to say goodbye, now that she's calmed down?

4 upvotes
6 comments

u/MedusaInChains—18:16 09/17/2023
Do NOT open the door, and dont let her in. Is this the same girl who wanted to take you out into the woods??? Seriously, if she comes by, you should call the cops. They might not listen to you but they will probably scare her off!!!

u/BigBuxomButchBabe—18:19 09/17/2023
Sweetheart, trust someone who is speaking from experience: do not let this woman back in your life. You are not stupid for missing her, but she does not mean you well. This is just another manipulation tactic.

Reading between the lines, it sounds like your ex was not "only" emotionally abusive, but physically as well. I don't think I'm exaggerating when I say she sounds dangerous.

Your instincts were very good when they told you to leave her. Your mom would be so, so proud of you. Make her proud again, and take care of yourself, and keep that door locked. You owe her nothing. Pain does not make someone abusive, nor does it excuse abuse.

u/HappyologyMaster—21:01 09/17/2023
OP, can u update us? i hope im not overstepping but i think i speak for all of us when i say were worried about u

u/BigBuxomButchBabe—07:39 09/18/2023
Second that, OP. No matter what happened, please tell us how it went last night. We're here for you. You can DM me if you don't feel comfortable discussing it in a public forum.

u/HappyologyMaster—16:20 09/26/2023
did she ever write to u? ive been checking this post every day for an update but i havent seen anything

u/BigBuxomButchBabe—19:03 09/26/2023
No. I haven't heard anything. I'm telling myself that she maybe just didn't feel like talking about it on reddit anymore, but I have to confess I'm horribly worried. I wish there was some way we could contact her. I have a really, really bad feeling about this.

Chapter 41

THE SCREAMING IS HIGH-PITCHED AND SEARING, AND I HEAR someone shouting:

"Stop it, stop! It's fine!"

It's not pitch-black in here; a little light is escaping through the gauzy curtains, making it look like I'm surrounded by ghosts, shapes in the dark.

One of them moves over to the window, and then Martina pulls the curtains aside, letting in what little light is out there.

The storm has gotten worse in the short time we've been in here; the rain outside looks like a solid entity, the water thundering down from above, the clouds iron gray and furious.

Martina turns back to us. In the faint light, her lips look black as she says:

"It's all going to be fine. It's nothing. The generator will come back online any second now."

"Why did it go out?" Katarina asks. "You said it wouldn't."

"I'm a psychologist, not an electrician," Martina snaps. "I don't know. The storm might have brought something down."

"The generator hasn't come on yet," Leyla observes. She's standing by Clara, still holding her hand; she must have grabbed it when the lights went out.

Martina wavers.

"I'll go check on it," she finally says. "Might be that it's not on. We've never actually needed it before."

"That's reassuring," Leyla mutters.

"I don't feel so good," Clara says. When I take a closer look at her, she does look pale, but I don't know if that's just the low light.

Leyla looks from Clara to me.

"I think we should . . . go," she says. "Isobel is right."

Martina erupts.

"None of you can go!" she shouts, and the room freezes.

"You can't exactly keep us here against our will," Clara protests.

Martina, looking at Clara, draws a deep, shuddering breath, briefly touching her palm to her sternum.

"None of you can go," she repeats, somewhat calmer, "because there is flooding farther down. It's simply not safe. The storm will pass. We'll have electricity back in just a few minutes, I guarantee it."

Leyla looks over at Clara, and whatever she sees makes her push Clara gently down in a chair, muttering:

"You okay?"

"I don't like this." Katarina is biting her lip, her arms wrapped around her torso.

"I think we should do a breathing exercise," Martina says. "Help everyone calm down a bit and reassess the situation."

I burst out laughing.

"A breathing exercise?" I say. "Are you kidding?"

The door opens, drawing another little shriek from Katarina.

I take a step back; for a moment, all I see in the door is a dark, drenched silhouette, and the image from the window flashes through my mind, as stark and strong as it was the other day. The shadow, watching me.

But then she takes a step inside, and it's Anna, pulling her pink hood off her head, water dripping onto the floor.

"Everyone okay?" she asks. "I heard screaming."

She scans the room, and, her gaze falling on Clara, who is now swaying lightly where she's sitting, she says:

"Christ, you must have had a bad shock."

She sits down on the floor in front of Clara and picks up her mug.

"Here, sweetheart, drink some of this." She pushes the mug into Clara's hands. "There's some honey in there. It should make you feel better."

"Do you know why the generator hasn't turned on?" Martina asks Anna sharply, who shakes her head.

"No idea." Her voice is apologetic. "I can ask Belinda to go and check on it, if you want."

"No," Martina says between gritted teeth, "I'll do it myself."

"Should I bring the girls back to their cabins?" Anna asks. "It looks like some of them need to lie down."

"Yes, I think that might be a good idea," Martina says.

"Alone?" Katarina looks over at me.

"Yes, everyone back to their own cabins." Martina is struggling to get back to her usual soothing voice. "Get cozy. Read a book. Journal. Just . . . relax."

I meet Katarina's eyes. "Pull something in front of the door," I tell her, speaking slowly. "So that no one can get in."

"For God's sake!" Martina cries out. "There's nothing to worry about!"

I turn to Anna. "You'll walk them there?" I hope that whatever connection I might have made with her is enough. "Make sure nothing happens?"

Anna nods solemnly.

"I will," she promises. "All the way to the door."

"Good," I say.

Martina smiles, tight and unhappy.

"You don't work for her," she scoffs, before catching onto what I said and asking me, "Wait, what do you mean by *them*?"

I smile, taut and painful.

"I'm coming with you."

Chapter 42

I CAN SEE THE OTHERS LEAVING THROUGH THE WINDOW NEXT to the door, in a small caravan, tiny figures against the roaring sheets of rain, led by the small pink dot that is Anna in the front.

Martina is busy winding a scarf around her neck, pulling on heavy, shiny lace-up boots that look more expensive than they do waterproof. She's not saying a word to me.

I'm vibrating with tension, skin crackling with what feels like electricity. The storm has a smell to it, one that has made its way into the building; the scent of icy cold water, and pressure, and something else, something primal and dangerous.

When she's finally done, she straightens up to her full height, so that she can look down on me, and says:

"I will have you out of here as soon as the roads open up again. I want you out of my clinic. And you will be hearing from my lawyers."

"Yeah, yeah," I say. "Generator."

Martina opens the door, and it nearly rips out of her fingers, flung wide by a gust of wind that sprays us both with water.

"Fuck." I hear her faint exclamation, before she tucks her chin to her chest and walks outside.

It doesn't matter how much I try to pull my jacket closed, keep my face down; the rain is going sideways, and it makes its way under my clothes quicker than I would have thought possible. The gravel under my shoes is slippery, swimming in the runnels of water, and I see Martina about to fall over; I catch her elbow, and she tears herself loose from my grip.

Only a few yards left to go. The windows are all dark, the staff quarters utterly abandoned.

Martina throws herself in under the porch roof and pulls the door open, stumbling in. I follow quickly behind her and shut the door.

It's not until we're inside that I realize I'm panting. Be it from adrenaline or exhaustion, I don't know.

"Goddammit." Martina throws the hood of her jacket back. Her thick hair is plastered against her scalp, despite the protection, and her eyelashes are wet, black mascara slightly smudged. In the dusky dark, it makes her look slightly inhuman.

An apparition. A drowned woman from the pond, come to haunt us.

"Yeah," I agree. "It's a bad one."

Martina lingers on me. "Why are you even here?" Her lips twitch in disdain. "Who were you going to sell your article to? A celebrity rag?"

"No, of course not," I insist.

"So—what, then?" Her lips curdle into a non-smile. "An exposé? Who did you talk to? All the employees here have NDAs, you know. It doesn't matter what you paid them, it'll pale in comparison to what they will end up paying in court. They will pull their quotes the moment I tell them to."

"I didn't talk to anyone." My heart is hammering away painfully in my chest.

Sandra is sleeping only a few rooms away. If she makes the connection now . . .

"What was your plan, then?" Martina crosses her arms and takes a step toward me.

"We don't have time for this," I protest, refusing to back away. "We need to check on the generator now. Turn it on. And then you need to let us all leave, before you end up with a much bigger problem than a freelance journalist trying to write a story."

Martina shakes her head. "No. Not until you tell me what your objective is."

I'm sick of being scared of her. I'm tired of falling under her spell.

Maybe she could bully me when I wasn't prepared; when her alternating between soulful looks, and understanding, and good old-fashioned cold reading took me by surprise.

But this is not a game anymore.

There are worse things than Dr. Martina Hastings to be scared of.

"It was to be an undercover article about you mistreating your patients. About the fact that people have gone broke after coming to Himlafall. How they've had marriages and families fall apart. How women have gone *missing* after coming here."

Martina looks stricken. "That's ridiculous," she attempts to argue.

"No," I say, making my voice as hard as I can. "It's not. I've seen it. I've seen how you pressure and belittle your patients. This may not be a cult, like some think, but it's not much better."

"You have no idea what you are—" Martina begins to say, and I interrupt her, near yelling:

"Can we *please*, for the love of all that is holy, get to the *goddamned generator and turn the lights back on*?"

Martina opens her mouth.

Then she deflates.

"Fine."

She begins walking out of the small, cramped foyer, where a mess of shoes is stacked against one wall and a mop and a bucket of dark, muddy water are leaning against the other. I think I hear her muttering something that sounds suspiciously like *bitch*.

The hallway is entirely laid in darkness. No natural light and fresh, verdant plants for the workers, apparently; there are doors on both sides, all of them closed, and one at the end.

"Christ, what is that smell?" I ask inadvertently as we're halfway down.

It's strange, thick and heavy enough to cut through the metallic scent of the storm, with an odd sweetness to it; like spoiled meat, mixed with something else.

"I know." Martina sounds just as disgusted as I feel.

She sounds less like Dr. Martina Hastings now. More like a person.

"Sandra must have absolutely destroyed the bathroom last night. We might have to get the whole place sterilized. I don't know what she ate, but it can't have been good."

I almost say something—*Her daughter had stomach flu*—but I bite my tongue at the last second.

Martina stops at the last door, putting her hand on the doorknob.

"Just to be clear," she says, without looking at me. "You might not like my methods. You might think they are too harsh, or too extreme. You might think this place is cultish. But I have never, ever tried to do anything but help my patients. And I have helped them. Many of them. Trust me. I have a desk full of letters from people who say I saved their lives."

She lingers for a second, and then shakes her head.

"Every single time a woman tries to do something," she mutters, before opening the door.

She steps into the dark little room.

There's a small window, high up on the wall; hardly any light is coming through it, water running so thick down the glass that the outside looks distorted.

The place looks like a storage space; I see the outline of shelves full of extra blankets and pillows, some boxes stacked on top of each other in the corner.

Martina turns around, looking this way and that way, and then she mutters:

"I can't see for shit," pulls a cell phone out of her pocket, and turns on the flashlight.

At first, the light is blinding. I raise my hand to cover my eyes, blink a couple of times to let them adjust, before lowering it.

Martina is standing, utterly motionless, a couple of steps away from me. The cold, harsh light from her phone is shining onto the floor and the wall on the short side of the small room.

What remains of the generator looks like it used to be a metal box. Orange and dark gray. An ugly industrial thing, rendered almost beautiful by its own destruction.

There are bits and pieces of it scattered around the box. The cord that used to run into the wall has been severed violently, leaving a deep wound in the cheap wooden flooring underneath.

There are deep, ragged cuts on what used to be the generator, delivered with seeming randomness, malforming and misshaping it, filling the air with the smell of crushed metal.

"I don't understand." Martina's voice is full of something in between horror and wonder.

I crouch down in front of the generator, looking closer, heart hammering in my chest, my mouth so dry I can taste my own teeth.

Gently, ever so gently, I touch the edges of one of the cuts. The metal is thick and sharp; despite my light touch, it cuts me.

"I don't understand," Martina repeats. "What happened?"

I stand back up. I don't bother to brush the dust off my knees.

"Someone destroyed it." My voice sounds like it's coming from far away.

"No." Martina begins to shake her head. "That's ridiculous. Something must have fallen on it. There is too much stuff in here. I told them not to put so much stuff in here, but—"

"Someone *destroyed it,* Martina!" I raise my voice. "On purpose. Someone wanted us lost in the dark."

"You're insane."

I can hear the strain in her voice. She needs to be right. She needs it to be untrue.

"How would they even have done that? It was an accident. Maybe some of the wiring went, or—"

"*Martina.*" I grab her by the shoulders, and I can feel that she's shaking.

"Someone killed your backup generator." I have to spell it out for her. "It wasn't an accident. They destroyed it. They chopped it to pieces. And it looks like they did it with an . . ." My voice hitches. But I have to say it. I have to allow it to be true.

"With an axe."

Chapter 43

"No." Martina is looking around as if to find someone, anyone but me, who can make it make sense.

"Martina," I say, but she doesn't respond.

"*Doctor*!" I shout, and that makes her look in my direction.

"This makes no sense." Her features are washed out by the glow from the flashlight, rendering her a picture of fear in black-and-white.

"Listen to me. I understand that you're scared. But there is no harmless explanation for this. We have to get out of here. Because right now, we're sitting ducks." I enunciate every word, hoping she'll be able to take in half of them.

"We can't." The light from her phone is vibrating. Her hand is shaking.

"Yes, we can," I insist. "I know there's a flood warning, but I think that might be a risk we all have to take."

She stares at me. Her eyes are gigantic in her pale face.

"No." Martina shakes her head. "I mean we *can't.* The gates."

"What do you mean?" I ask. "What about the gates?"

"They're electric." She wets her lips.

"The gates . . . are electric," I repeat dumbly, my mind flashing to those cast-iron gates.

So pretty and ornate. Not high enough that you couldn't climb over them if you tried, but . . .

"You can't open them manually?" I ask her, and she shakes her head.

"No," she says. "They can only be opened with the button."

I run my hands through my hair, then down my face, trying to think.

"Fuck," I whisper.

"No," Martina moans. "No, no, no."

"It's okay," I tell her, hoping it's not a lie. "It'll be okay. We'll figure something out."

"It doesn't make any sense," she says, her voice a low whine. "It doesn't . . . because who would . . ."

"That doesn't matter right now," I say, my voice harsh and tight. "We can figure all that out later."

"But it doesn't make any sense," she repeats. "I help people. We help people. No one would want to do this. No one would want to hurt us."

"Jesus *Christ*, of course people would want to hurt you," I shout. "You've hurt them! How many people have you broken here? How many people have you bankrupted? It could be any one of them!"

"You have no idea what you're talking about," Martina says weakly, but I keep going.

"Look at the way you treat your patients!" I spit out. "You drug them, you *steal* from them—"

"I have never stolen from anyone!" Martina protests hotly.

"What about Pernilla's wedding ring?" I throw it in her face.

"I didn't take her goddamned ring!" Martina responds. "I encouraged her to take it off! I'm holding it for her, because there are no safes in the cabins, and she was scared one of the rest of you would take it!"

I'm momentarily thrown off, but then I snap back into focus.

"Okay, fine, but it doesn't matter. Someone is here, and there are countless people it could be. It could be a former partner of one of your patients, out for revenge. It could be an employee you fucked over, like Dr. Nina. It could be a random person who just realized there was a whole group of women isolated in the woods and decided to pounce on the opportunity. It doesn't *matter* who it is, we just need to get everyone together and *leave*!"

"What do you mean, Dr. Nina?" Martina stares at me.

The rain is smattering against the thin wall. The hollows under her eyes have grown cavernous.

"What do you know about her?"

"I know you fired her, and then threatened her. Those little notes you have been sending to her drove her to closing her new practice and moving. That sounds like plenty good enough motivation to want to get back at you."

"I never—what?" Martina asks.

Lightning flashes outside the window, temporarily illuminating the small room in harsh black-and-white.

"Fuck," I breathe. "That scared me. Whatever. Can you please take your phone and call the police? Tell them to send someone. Anyone. Even if the regular cars can't get through the flooding, they must have something. A fire truck. A tank. Anything."

Martina shakes her head slowly, as though it's on a hinge.

"If the electricity is out, that means the landline is down." Her voice sounds strangled. "And the signal booster, too. We won't have any reception."

"So . . ." I don't finish my sentence.

We're stuck.

No one is coming.

"Shit," I whisper.

The wind is making the walls shake. For a second, I feel like the room is beginning to spin.

But then I hear it.

All the way on the other side of the corridor.

The front door, opening slowly.

Chapter 44

I FREEZE.

I feel, more than see, Martina straightening up, sense her about to call out, and I move quicker than I would have thought possible; I push my hand over her mouth, and she makes a small, shocked noise, her breath warm against the palm of my hand.

"No," I whisper.

She tries to protest, move her face away from my hand, but I look around frantically, searching for a way out of the room.

The window is too high up, and too small. It's possible Martina could squeeze through it, but there's no way to get her up there.

The bedrooms. The windows in the staff bedrooms are small, but they might be big enough. It would be a bit of a jump, but not bad enough to hurt either of us, assuming that we stick the landing. And Sandra's bedroom is the closest one to us on the right-hand side; we can sneak in there, wake her up quietly, and get her out with us.

Still keeping my hand over Martina's mouth, I peek out through the door. I don't see anyone in the corridor yet, the long, dark tunnel still empty.

Even as I look down it, I feel the taste of adrenaline on my tongue, the tingling of danger under my skin.

We don't have more than a few seconds. We have to go.

"Turn your flashlight off, and be quiet," I order Martina, hardly more than an exhalation, and then I remove my hand from her mouth and open the door, quickly but silently.

I can hear footsteps from the small foyer. It's a wet sound, and a heavy one.

Any moment now, I'll see them again. That silhouette.

Shadow made flesh, come back to haunt me.

I can't move too quickly, or they'll hear me.

I pull Martina with me, praying with every breath she'll listen, that she won't decide it's gone too far, that she'll recognize what's happening. With every passing microsecond, I expect to hear her voice behind me.

We're over here! Who is it?

I let go of her and push down the door handle to Sandra's room.

It yields.

When the door swings open, I dive in through it, and Martina follows. I turn around and close it behind her. The click sounds like thunder. I can only hope it couldn't be heard from the foyer.

The room is dark, so very dark. Through the window, the outside looks like a biblical punishment, the forest swaying as one, as though in a trance, some dark and horrible ritual, distorted by the rain over the windowpane. The whining from the wind pushing its way through the wood sounds like the crying of an infant.

But that's not what catches my attention.

It's the smell.

It's ammonia, and something else. Something thick, and sweet, and horrible. Outside, it was possible to mistake it for illness; in here, it's everywhere, coating every surface. Unmistakable.

I'd know it even if I hadn't ever smelled it before. I know it the way I know the smell of air, or water.

No.

Martina has put her hand over her nose, and her eyes are bulging out of her head. I can hear footsteps coming down the corridor now. Slow and steady, with all the time in the world.

I hear it as though I'm underwater.

Because it doesn't matter anymore.

Now, looking at the bed, I see what I couldn't see through the window.

The figure under the covers looks so very small. Not a person anymore, but a thing.

The covers are pulled up over her head. Only that little tuft of hair sticking out.

But, oh, the unnatural stillness of it.

The silence of it.

I begin to walk over to the bed, but Martina catches me by the arm, shaking her head. Her eyes are full of tears, her face so pale it looks like a mask, her skin like wax.

The steps stop outside the door. I can feel the other breathing outside, as though in sync with my own, with Martina's.

All of us stuck in this strange unity. The horrible intimacy of expectation.

Then that sound again. They have walked into the storage space.

I tear out of her grip, and Dr. Martina, crying now, tries to shake her head, grab onto me again, but it's no use.

I have to know. I won't believe it until I know. Until I've seen.

The three steps over to the bed feel like crossing an ocean.

I pull the covers back.

Sandra is lying on her side. Her arms are curled up to her chest. Her hair is half pulled out of her ponytail, and it's a blessing; the back of her skull is caved in, a sickening break in the smooth curve that should be there.

Her eyes are open.

One eye is staring into nothingness, still stark, and gray, and perfect; almost as though she might turn to me now and laugh, that oh-so-familiar laugh I've known all my life, the soundtrack to my childhood. Sharp and crass and mocking.

But sweet, underneath it all. So sweet.

The other one is painted obscenely red.

The blood has pooled under the skin on the side of her face resting against the pillow. I can see the bruised horror of it reaching up toward her cheekbone.

When I reach out to touch her cheek, it's cold and stiff.

I feel my lips tugging in a smile. This is funny, really. It's a funny joke. So typical of Sandra. She's always been such a prankster.

Probably trying to teach me a lesson. She and Martina probably set this up together. What fun they must have had.

Sandra has always treated me like a younger sister. She always thought I was too impulsive, too irresponsible.

This'll teach her, she must have thought, laughing to herself. *It'll scare her straight.*

I grip Sandra's shoulder, and I start shaking her. She's such a good actor. I can't believe she's managing to lie this still.

Someone grabs ahold of me from behind, both shoulders, crushingly strong, and turns me around, but I struggle against it. I have to make Sandra move. I have to get her to look at me.

If I can just get her to look at me, it will all be fine.

Martina manages to spin me around.

There's a sound, and it's coming from me. A deep, guttural groaning, like stone grinding against stone. I didn't know I could make a sound like that.

Martina's eyes are huge, and terrified, and deeply, deeply sad.

It's only when I see her cheeks streaked with tears that I realize mine are too.

"We have to go," she whispers to me, so close to my face it feels like our lips might touch. "The window."

"No." I breathe it like a prayer.

"Isobel," Martina says, as the sound of rummaging in the next room becomes clear, a living body with violent intent moving around.

"We have to go."

"But . . ."

I turn to look at my oldest friend, who will surely, any moment now, reveal this all as a ruse of some kind.

"We have to take her with us," I whisper. "We can't leave her here. We have to get her to a hospital. We have to—"

This time, it's Martina who puts her hand over my mouth. But gently, softly.

She shakes her head.

"She's gone, Isobel," she whispers. "And if we don't get out, we will be too."

She removes her hand, and she walks over to the window, sliding it open. The sound of the storm comes rushing in, a maelstrom of wind and chill and water. Then she climbs up onto the ledge.

The noises from the other room stop.

"Isobel," Martina says, no longer bothering to stay quiet, "you have to jump."

And she jumps out.

I can't move. I can't look away from her.

I always thought the dead would look peaceful.

Sandra. Sandra, who's always been so strong. Physically and mentally. Who never let anything faze her.

Who always laughed the loudest at her own jokes.

Who always hugged me like it was a chore.

Who agreed to help me with this, because it was the right thing to do.

The steps are quicker now. One, two, three, and they're outside the door.

I hear the doorknob turning. Feel the wind dusting my face with rain.

I imagine Sandra staring at me with that stern look of hers. I hear her voice in my head, clear as new ice.

It's now or never, babe.

I climb up on the windowsill, and I jump, too, landing painfully on my cut-up feet, my ankle wanting to roll, and the storm wanting to push me over, and instead I run, run after Martina in the rain, and I can't tell if I'm screaming or if it's the wind.

I will never unsee that eye. That red, empty eye.

Her name is pounding in my head like the beating of a heart.

Sandra. Sandra. Sandra.

I don't know where I'm running. I just follow Martina, and I run as fast as I can, despite the wind pushing me back.

There's nowhere to go. No one is coming.

I can see the cabins in the distance, the main building a dark blur, when I feel someone grasp my arm, nearly tugging it out of the socket, and through the storm I hear my name:

"Isobel!"

Chapter 45

Under the scent of plastic, and wind, and sweat, there's something familiar. Something about the way the wet hair is tickling my cheek. Something about the smell.

Eucalyptus.

And the voice in my ear.

"I'm so glad you're okay."

He releases me, and for a second, I think I've finally cracked. There's a peaceful sort of quality to it, for that moment, because maybe none of this is real.

Because he can't be here.

"Get away from her!" I hear someone shouting, and then someone tugs me back, and I am starting to feel like rag doll.

Martina is utterly drenched, wet hair clinging to her cheeks and rage in her eyes.

"No," I try to say, "it's not him, he's—"

"Don't take one step closer," Martina pants, still behind me.

Armin looks from me to the doctor; I see confusion and anger battling on his face.

"Okay." He puts his hands up. "I don't know what's going on here."

I look behind him, over at the staff quarters, and I feel another surge of adrenaline.

"We can't stay here," I tell him.

"Who are you?" Martina asks Armin, her face twisted up. "We've called the police!"

"No." I tear myself loose from her. "It's not him. He's okay. I promise."

Martina doesn't take her eyes off Armin.

"Isobel, what's happening?" Armin asks me.

"I'll explain," I try to say, but my teeth are chattering, my head swimming. My knees feel like jelly.

"But we have to . . . we can't stay here."

"Okay," Armin says, following my line of sight.

"Main building," I manage to get out.

We're close enough that we're in through the door in only a couple of minutes, door shut behind us. It's warmer in here, and for a moment, I feel like I need to collapse; I see Martina falling to the floor on her knees.

But I can't. I look at Armin, and I say:

"We have to block the door."

My voice doesn't sound like my own.

He doesn't ask. I walk over to the couch and grab it by one end.

Armin takes a hold of the other end, and we pull it in front of the door; I see Armin wedging it under the doorknob.

My body seems to decide I've had enough, because I sink down into the couch, water dripping off me onto the fabric, staining it darker.

I rub my fingers over it.

I think of the dark droplets on Sandra's white sheets.

Tears are still running silently, making my eyes sting.

When I feel the couch cushion giving way to Armin beside me, I know I should look up, know I should say something, but I can't find the voice to do so.

"Hey." Armin very gently places his hand on top of mine. "Isobel."

I close my eyes. I see Sandra.

"Can you tell me what's going on?"

I reach for the words. I can't find them. I need to tell him about the person in the woods, outside the window, about the stolen files, about the generator, about everything.

But what comes out, as a whisper, is:

"Sandra is dead."

"What?"

I don't know if he couldn't hear me, or if he just can't understand what I'm saying, but I repeat:

"Sandra is dead."

There's a buzzing in my ears. And in my hands. There are black spots dancing in front of my eyes.

It doesn't sound real. It doesn't feel real, either. I try laughing, to see if maybe that will break the spell; if it might make me wake up, and all of this will have been a terrible dream.

But the sound that comes out of me is nothing like a laugh.

"Who are you?" I hear a voice, as though from far away.

"I'm Isobel's friend," another voice answers. This one is better, calmer; I press my forehead against my knees, and I try to fill my lungs with air, try to remember how it feels, try to listen to that second voice.

"What are you doing here?" the first one asks.

I feel like I'm underwater.

"I was worried about Isobel," the second voice responds. "She wasn't calling me back. I hadn't heard from her in days. So I drove here."

Then a hand on my upper back, and that second voice, the good voice, Armin's voice, closer to my ear:

"Breathe. Just breathe. Come on. In and out."

I gasp for air, and I think:

I can't do this. I can't. I don't know how to do this.

"It's okay," Armin tries to soothe me. "It's going to be okay."

But I know that it's not.

I draw another deep, rattling breath.

"Isobel," I hear, and I look up.

Martina is sitting in front of me. Her face is blotchy with dissolved makeup, her hair a wet, disheveled mess.

But she's looking me in the eyes.

"Name four colors you can see right now," she says.

She doesn't sound like Dr. Martina. She doesn't sound calm, or ethereal, or superior. Her natural voice is slightly higher, a bit nasally.

"Colors?" I repeat, confused.

"Look around the room," she instructs me. "Name four colors you can see."

I still can't breathe. I still feel like I'm about to pass out, like I'm floating above my body.

But I look around.

"Green," I say, and then I look at Armin, who is wearing a deep-teal raincoat.

"Teal."

"Good," Martina encourages me. "Two more."

I look down at my jeans.

"Gray," I say.

I close my eyes and see only red.

"Eyes open, Isobel," Martina tells me. "Come on. One more color. You can do it."

I open my eyes again.

"White," I say, looking at her shirt.

She nods and smiles. "Okay. Good. What was the name of the first school you went to?"

"Gustav Vasa Primary School," I respond.

"And the name of your first pet?"

I have to think back. "Harry the Hamster."

Martina nods slowly. "Very good. Can you breathe?"

I inhale deeply, and find, to my surprise, that I can. "Yes." I'm surprised.

She smiles, and it's, I think, the first real smile I've seen from Dr. Martina. She sinks back down into her heels.

"Very good." She's sounding quite breathless herself.

Armin looks over at me.

"Isobel." The way he says my name is comforting enough to make me want to cry. For a moment, I just take him in; his long, slim face, those spiky eyelashes, the little parenthesis between his eyebrows.

I feel the temptation to just break down, to hope he will take care of it. Of me. Or that someone will. That some unknown authority figure will come by and fix this, get everything back to normal, so that I can fall apart.

But I can't. Not right now.

"What's going on?" he asks me.

I breathe in through my nose; out through my mouth.

"I think someone is trying to kill us." Saying it is painful; it makes it real. But I have to keep going.

"They killed Sandra. They destroyed the backup generator. I don't know why this is happening, but we have to get everyone out of here, and we can't. I don't know what we're going to do, but we have to do something."

Armin stares at me.

Then he looks from me to Martina.

And then he nods.

"Okay."

Only now does some of what he said earlier fall into place in my mind.

"Wait," I say. "Did you say you drove here?"

"Yeah." Armin looks at me warily. "My car is right outside the gate."

Patient Registration Form

Name: Susannah Viola Wallin
Date of Intake: 2023–09–04
Date of Birth: 1995–02–16
Gender: Woman
Pronouns: She/Her
Gender of Romantic or Sexual Partners: I identify as pansexual, but I've mostly dated women.
Dietary Restrictions: I'm allergic to mango. I know, weird. Other than that, I eat everything!
Medical Conditions (any nonpsychiatric medical conditions or medical incidents we may need to be aware of): I broke two of the knuckles on my right hand when I was sixteen. They are fully healed, though, no lingering pains!

Diagnostic History (any psychiatric diagnoses, current or previous): None :)

Previous Experience of Psychological Treatment (any therapy or counseling you have gone through in the past, or are currently undergoing): I've been to therapy a couple of times, but I've never found a therapist I've really liked. They never really seem to listen to my point of view. That's part of why I'm so excited to get to work with Dr. Martina, because I feel like she will really get me and see me for who I am.

Inciting Incident (explain here, in your own words, why you have sought treatment at the Himlafall Clinic): My fiancé broke up with me out of nowhere. It absolutely destroyed me. I did everything for this girl, and I tried so hard, and I loved her so much, and I just don't know what I did wrong. I want to get her back, but I need help figuring out how to explain to her how much she hurt me, and that she can't keep acting the way she does.

I feel like all I do is give and give and give and people just keep letting me down. I feel like Dr. Martina will understand, because she seems like she's the same kind of person I am. I really feel like she will understand me.

People just keep leaving me. It feels like they all disappoint me in the end. My last partner kept trying to put words in my mouth. She would make up these wild stories about how I had done things to her and twisted my words. All I ever wanted was for her to love me and affirm me the way I need. I never asked for much.

I'm still so angry. But I love her. I need Dr. Martina to help me figure out how I can explain this to her.

I know we can be so happy if she just stops all this and takes me back.

Chapter 46

"The roads weren't flooded?" Martina asks Armin.

He shakes his head.

"No," he says. "I mean, not yet, at least. It was wet, sure, but it was draining just fine."

"And your car is on the other side of the gates." The urgency is making Martina's voice high and reedy.

"Yeah," Armin confirms for the third time.

"So we go." Martina gets to her feet, pulling her wet hair back from her face. "We climb the gates and we drive and get help."

She reaches for my hand.

"Come on. Get off the couch, we have to move."

"Wait." I shake my head. "No."

"*No?*" Martina repeats incredulously. "What do you mean, *no*?"

"I mean we can't just go." I stare up at her. "We can't just leave the others here."

Martina throws her hands up in frustration.

"Are you fucking kidding me? This is what you've been asking for this whole time! Don't you see what this is? This *friend* of yours"—she gestures toward Armin without looking at him, her eyes locked on my face—"is our knight in shining fucking armor!"

"You want to just leave the others here? With whoever did that to—to Sandra?" My voice only hitches a little on her name.

She would have been proud of me. Sandra always said I got too caught up in my emotions. Never focused enough on the practicalities of the situation.

I bite back the grief that threatens to overwhelm me and get to my feet.

"We can't do anything right now," Martina says. "We need to get help."

"Yeah," I agree. "And we're taking the others with us. We're not just leaving them here."

I turn to Armin.

"How many people can you fit in your car?" I ask him.

"Five," he responds. "Maybe seven, eight, if it's an emergency. And . . . I mean, yeah. This is definitely an emergency."

"We get the others." I declare to Martina.

"We don't have time." Martina grits her teeth. "We need to leave."

I look at her, refusing to waver.

"Those women are *your patients*, Martina. You have a goddamned responsibility to them."

"Not like this!" Martina shrieks. "Are you insane? I have a responsibility to give them therapy! I have a responsibility not to fuck them and to give them treatment! I don't have a responsibility to stick around and get murdered for them!"

She's panting, drenched and terrified, arms thrown wide and pupils huge and dark. Every trace of Dr. Martina Hastings wiped away.

I wonder how it is I was ever frightened of her. How it is I ever felt she had any power over me.

"Fine," I say. "You might not think you have any responsibility to them. But I do."

I look to Armin.

"We have to go get them," I tell him quietly, in the private voice I use only with him.

Armin locks eyes with me, and then he nods.

Martina looks back and forth between us.

"You can't be serious." Her voice is flat.

"I'm not leaving without Isobel," Armin points out. "And I don't think she's leaving without the other patients."

"Or staff," I add. "Belinda and Anna, too."

"Fuck," Martina groans into her hands.

Then she grows still. Her shoulders slump.

And she nods.

"Okay. Let's go, then, before some psychopath with an axe breaks down the door."

Chapter 47

There's nothing to arm ourselves with in the main building; no convenient knives, or baseball bats, or mallets.

We move the couch, and then I describe the impromptu plan to Armin:

"They should all be in the cabins. The cabins are on the left. We have to run, and get them one by one."

Martina interjects:

"And if someone is standing outside, waiting for us to come out so they can beat us to death?"

There's a thin layer of dry sarcasm, bitter bravado to hide the quaking underneath. It almost works, and I kind of respect her for it.

I've done the same thing myself.

"I don't know, Martina," I say. "Then I guess we run, and whoever gets to the car takes off."

I hear her muttering something; I don't care to hear what it is.

I look at Armin, and he nods. His face is set in a grim mask, his shoulders tense.

"I'm really sorry about this." I don't have the words to apologize for what I've gotten both of us into.

I'm sorry.

You were right.

Thank you.

None of it seems enough. There aren't enough words, nor is there enough time.

I just hope we'll have more.

He manages a tense smile.

"Just like you, Isobel, to get me pulled into some kind of messed-up horror movie." He tries for a joke. I appreciate the effort.

"Okay." I breathe in deep. "Let's go."

I pull the door open.

The storm is still brutalizing the landscape. I'm too scared to feel the cold; I see no one, and so I take off running again, my muscles aching and my feet screaming at me. I hear the others behind me, and I see the cabins as vague, unformed shapes, with dark windows and blurry edges.

I don't allow myself to think that we might be too late.

I can't let myself imagine that we might find them all in there, just like we found Sandra.

I just focus on the cabins, and on the people inside them. The women who didn't deserve this.

Pernilla, and Katarina, and Clara, and Leyla.

I might not like all of them. They might not like me. But I owe this to them. I owe it to try.

When I get closer, I hear, from a distance, a voice, hoarse and shrill:

". . . anyone hear me? Hello! Hello! Come on! COME ON, I KNOW ONE OF YOU FUCKERS MUST BE ABLE TO HEAR ME, JUST COME AND—"

It's Clara's cabin, and when I run up to the door, I see that it's vibrating; someone is pounding on it.

"Clara?" I yell through the door. "Clara, open the door!"

"It's not Clara." I hear Leyla from behind the wood, unmistakable relief in her voice. The pounding stops. "I can't open it. It's locked."

"What do you mean, it's locked?" I ask.

Armin and Martina are only a few steps behind me, and Martina runs past Armin, pushing at the door handle.

The door stays closed.

"I don't know what happened," Leyla shouts from behind the door. "Clara passed out, and she won't wake up, and when I tried to go get help the door wouldn't open."

Martina fumbles with her jacket before pulling out an overfull key chain. She sorts through it with pale-white fingers, her nail polish now chipped and flaking, before pushing a key into the lock.

She turns it. The door swings open.

Leyla is standing behind the door, her short hair wild and messy, her eyes edged with red.

Clara is lying on the bed. Her face is small and slack, the sheets under her messy; one of her arms is wedged under her slumped-over body.

"What's going on?" Leyla asks, grasping at me, as I look past her to the woman on the bed.

"I don't know," I tell her honestly. "Something bad. Something really bad. We're trying to get everyone out of here."

Armin pushes past both me and Martina, and he kneels by the bed, puts two fingers to the side of her neck and his ear to her face.

Leyla turns and asks:

"Who is that? What is he doing?"

"Is she alive?" I ask Armin.

Martina has closed the door behind us and gone over to the window, peering out of it, staring at the dark, brooding eye of the pond.

Armin nods. "She's alive."

The relief makes me feel like I'm choking. Or dreaming.

"Her pulse is slow, but it's steady, and she's breathing," he adds.

I turn back to Leyla and ask:

"What happened to her?"

I see Leyla's eyes filling with tears.

"I came back here with her, and she wasn't feeling well." She wipes the tears away, quickly and roughly, with the back of her hand.

"I got her on the bed, and I got her a glass of water, tried to get her to stay awake. I thought it was just shock. But then she just . . . passed out. And I couldn't wake her up again. And when I went for the door, I couldn't get it open. I've been screaming for help, and trying to wake her up, but no one could hear me. And she . . ." Leyla clamps her mouth shut, squeezes her eyes together, and shakes her head.

"She must have taken some of those pills you gave her." I turn to Martina, and I can't keep the judgment out of my voice.

"Pills?" Leyla asks.

"You can't blame me for this." Martina sounds offended. "They're sleeping aids. I gave her very clear instructions on how to take them. I didn't tell her to dose herself in the middle of the day!"

"You shouldn't be giving out pills at all!" I can't keep from yelling. "You're a psychologist, not a drug dealer!"

"I have a PhD in psychiatry!" Martina yells back. "Those were legal prescriptions!"

"Yeah, sure they were," I say. "I'm sure the board would love to hear that you've been handing out sleeping pills like candy to your vulnerable patients without oversight."

"You've been giving her *pills*?" Leyla shouts.

"They are *legal sleeping aids*! They are *meant* for—"

I interrupt Martina. "Why was the door locked? Did you tell the caretakers to lock us in?"

"Of course not!" Martina sounds shocked. "Why would I do that?"

Armin stands up from beside the bed. "I think she's stable," he says.

"How would you know that?" Martina shoots off at him. "Are you a doctor?"

"I'm a dentist." His face is tight. "So I've worked with patients under anesthesia. And I'm trained in CPR and basic life support."

Some small, buried, petty part of me is thrilled to see the dislike written all over his face.

Martina rolls her eyes, but I ignore her. Instead, I turn to Armin, and ask, in a low voice: "Do you think you can carry her?"

He looks down at Clara, and swallows; I see the muscles in his jaw tensing.

"Carry, maybe," he responds, equally quietly. "But get her over the fence . . . I'm not sure."

"What are you guys talking about?" Leyla interjects. "And who is this guy? What is a dentist doing here?"

"He's my friend," I explain. "He came to check on me. He was worried about me."

For a brief moment, something wiggles in the depths of my mind, some spark trying to light, connection attempting to be made, but then it's gone again. I have no time for brooding.

"I've got a car outside the gates," Armin adds. "We're trying to get everyone in it and get you all away from here."

"Why?" Leyla asks.

She looks around the room, at our grim, silent faces. Martina turns her face away, and she lands on me.

"Something happened. Didn't it? Something worse." It's not a question.

Leyla stares me down.

"We found a . . ." I can't make myself say the word *body*. I can't reduce her to that. "We found *Sandra*."

Leyla doesn't shout, or slap her hand over her mouth; instead, her whole body goes very still.

"Accident?" is all she says.

I shake my head.

There's a beat, a moment of silence.

Then Leyla turns to gaze at Clara.

"I'll help carry her. I think we can get her over the gates together." She rolls her eyes, and adds:

"I'm stronger than I seem."

"I'm not questioning that," Armin hurries to say.

Leyla leans down and pushes the hair out of Clara's face, and a light bulb goes off in my head.

"Oh," I say.

Leyla shoots me a look.

"So *that's* why she was out there last night." I'm speaking mostly to myself. "She was coming back from . . . okay."

The question flies out before I can stop myself:

"Why was her lip bleeding last night?"

Leyla turns to Clara, her face softening infinitesimally.

"She fell on the way back," she says. "Bit her lip. She was trying to be sneaky. Wasn't looking where she was going."

"What?" Martina asks. Then she catches me looking between Leyla and Clara, and she says:

"You've got to be kidding me. Fraternization is *not* allowed between patients!"

"Fuck off, Doctor," Leyla tells her. "I think we've got bigger problems right now."

"Leyla is right," I interject. "We've got to get moving. We have to get to the other cabins."

"I'll stay with Clara. You go round up the others." Leyla's face is grim and determined.

I nod.

"Okay," I say. "Let's go. I don't know how much time we've got, but . . ."

I don't get to finish the sentence.

Instead, the door swings open, and Anna half falls in through it, panting and crying. She slams it shut behind her, and when she scrambles away from it, I see that her pink rain jacket is gone, her hair streaming with water.

"Please." Her voice breaks. "I don't know what's happening. She's gone crazy."

Chapter 48

"WHO?" I FALL TO THE FLOOR BY HER SIDE. "WHO'S GONE crazy?"

When I put my hands on her shoulders, I can feel that she's shaking.

"Belinda," she manages to choke out. "She's gone insane. I don't know what got into her. Did you see her? Did you—did she get to you?"

"No." I shake my head, my heart beating painfully fast in my chest. "What did she do? What did she say?"

"She destroyed the generator." Anna is whispering through cold blue lips. "She tried to—I think she drugged the tea. I feel woozy."

The tea.

My eyes are drawn to Clara, on the bed.

Fuck.

"Anna." I draw her up into a sitting position. "What did she say to you?"

Anna is shaking, sobbing so hard her whole chest is heaving, snot and tears and rain running down her face.

"She wasn't making any sense. I ran away from her. I ran and I was trying to find you, to find—find the doctor. I thought maybe she could talk some sense into her, but . . ." She looks up at Dr. Martina, big blue eyes glistening.

"I think . . . I think she was trying to kill me." Her voice is flat with shock, her cheeks burning red with cold.

"That's . . . no." Martina closes her eyes tightly. "Belinda isn't—you must have misinterpreted things."

Anna is hugging herself. She doesn't seem like she's listening.

"Anna, where is she now?" I ask her, throwing a fleeting glance at the door, my whole body tensing at the thought. "Was she chasing you?"

She shakes her head.

"I hit her." There is both shock and wonder in her voice. "She was behind me, and I hit her. I hit her really hard."

"Where?" I ask her.

"Down by the pond." Anna's voice is faint as falling snow. "By the main building. She . . ." The words die in her mouth.

I swallow. My mouth tastes like ash.

"If she drugged the tea," I say slowly, without looking at the others, "we won't be able to get everyone to the car. Not if they're all passed out."

Anna is swaying gently where she is sitting. When she turns to me, her pupils are pinpricks.

"I left her there. She wasn't . . . she didn't get back up. I just ran. I just turned around and ran away." She sounds barely older than a child, her voice high and lilting.

"That was good, Anna," I try to reassure her. "You did really good, okay?"

Leyla is the one who says it.

"We have to go find her." Her voice is raspy. "If Anna managed to hit her, then maybe we can . . . together, I mean."

She doesn't sound certain, but I hear the truth in what she's saying.

"Find her," I finish her thought. "Incapacitate her, to make sure she can't hurt anyone else. And then someone takes the car and drives to get help."

Leyla is nodding; Martina has turned to the window, looking out through it again.

"I don't think it's a good idea." Armin sounds hesitant. "If she's already killed someone . . ." He turns to Anna.

"Was she armed?"

This is, it seems, the first time Anna has noticed Armin in here, because when she looks at him and frowns she seems back to normal for a moment, and she sounds like herself when she asks:

"Who are you?"

"He's my friend," I explain. "Don't worry about him. He's going to help us."

Anna turns back to me.

"We can't drive away," she insists. "Not with the gates closed and the power down."

"Armin has a car outside the gates," I tell her. "We've got a plan for how to get out."

"Oh" is all Anna says, and she looks down at her lap, at her own pale fingers, threaded together. The big sweater she is wearing is drooping off her shoulders, heavy and darkened with rain.

"This is absurd." Martina turns back around, and her voice is high and tight. "I'm not going to go chasing a murderer through the storm."

"Armin and I will go," I say. "Anna can show us where she left Belinda."

Leyla speaks up.

"What about Clara?"

She's still standing, tense and rigid, by the bed.

"You can stay with her. It's better that way." I look over at Martina. "The good doctor can lock the door, in case . . . well, just to make sure that no one can get in."

"But she is coming with us, right?" Anna interjects, looking from me to Martina.

Martina is shaking her head.

"No." I can hear how dry her mouth is from the way her tongue is clicking. "No. I absolutely will not. I will stay here with Clara. It's my duty to her as my patient."

"Jesus." I'm about to protest that she didn't much care about her patients when she wanted to just take off without them half an hour ago, but to my surprise Anna interrupts me.

She looks up at Martina, standing by the window, and says, eyes brimming with tears:

"Please, Doctor, you have to come. You might be able to—if she's gotten back up, you might be able to talk her down. She might listen to you. You're the only person she might listen to. She looks up to you. She thinks you're a genius, I know she does."

Martina doesn't say anything.

"Please, Doctor," Anna pleads. "You have to come. You *have* to."

Something about the raw desperation in her voice seems to get through to Martina.

"Okay." The sound of her voice is pure defeat. "Okay."

"Let's go, then." I rise to my feet, pulling Anna up with me.

When I open the door, my stomach cramps, and I swallow to keep from throwing up out of sheer fear.

"Show us where she is. Show us where you left her."

Chapter 49

ANNA DOESN'T WANT TO GO FIRST, SO FRIGHTENED THAT SHE starts shaking when I ask her to, but she tells me where to go.

"By the pond. Right under the main building."

She's grabbed onto Armin's arm; hunched over from the rain, she looks smaller, shorter, though I think she's probably got a couple of inches on him were she to stand up straight.

He looks at me and nods, his mouth set in a grim line.

Part of me wants to run. Part of me wants to hide, hide away and pray this will all just dissipate, protect myself and close my eyes against it until it's over, one way or another.

The image of Belinda—tall, slender Belinda, Belinda who got me coffee that one time against orders, Belinda who greeted me with a soft smile on that first day—is impossible to square with the figure in the window. The shadow in the woods.

The murderer who took Sandra's life.

But, then again, I don't really know her. I don't know what was hiding behind that placid smile. And did she not frighten me, on occasion? Did I not suspect there had to be something darker behind all that smooth perfection?

If I'd only realized then just how much darker it could get.

I steel myself, and I set off down to the drowned path.

The pond is overflowing, bubbling at the edges, like some demented witch's cauldron; without the small protection of the cabins by my side, the wind wants to push me into that icy cold water, but I manage to stay upright. I can't check that the others are behind me, can only trust that they are following along.

I can't see more than ten feet ahead; all I can see is rain. It's coming so fast and strong it hurts, and so does the cold, my skin stinging under my soaked jacket. I feel chilled to my very core, my chest so tight it's hard to breathe, and when I open my mouth to inhale, it fills with the taste of the rain.

The main building is a blurry shape to my left, the pond a dark, gaping mouth to my right. I try, desperately, to look for someone on the ground, hoping with all my heart that she's there, that Anna managed to get a good enough hit to keep her down for long enough.

And yet, at the same time, the animal in me is hoping she won't be there.

As long as she's not here, I'm safe.

I don't want to find her; I want her to be gone. I want her to have left, to leave me alone, to leave all of us alone.

At some point, I'm sure I'll wonder why. Why she did all this. But right now, it doesn't seem to matter.

"I don't see her," I shout over my shoulder; I don't know if Anna can hear me.

But when I turn back, I glimpse it.

On the ground. A shape. At first, I might have mistaken it for water, but it's still, where the water is moving.

I feel my stomach turning again, and the cold has me in an iron grip, and I want to turn, want to run, but I don't.

My father would have turned.

He would have taken the car and left.

But I run to her, and I get down by her side, even as I'm shaking with fright, because she's lying with her face down, her legs half-submerged in the roiling pond, her hair a dark sludge of water.

"Belinda?" I yell, and I grab her by the shoulders and turn her over.

Her face is still beautiful. Her eyes are half-open, and for a moment I think she's looking at me. I think she's dazed, and I think, *That's good. Anna hit her hard. She won't be able to hurt us.*

But then I see the gash at the top of her head.

The rain has washed the blood away, leaving the gaping ruin of her skull pristine.

The cut has cleaved the top of her head, stopping an inch away from her hairline. I can see the hair pushed into the split by the force, the white of the bone poking through, and something else under there, something worse, something I can't—I can't—

There's a sound behind me. Like a cry. A name called out.

But I don't turn around, because I can't look away. I'm frozen in the moment of what I'm seeing.

Anna said that she hit her, I think absurdly. *She only said that she hit her.*

And then I feel it. A prick at the base of my neck.

The world starts to swim in front of my eyes, and I feel a strong pair of arms catching me, and it's almost a relief to feel the world slipping away. To let someone catch and carry me.

"It's all right, Isobel," she whispers in my ear. "It's all going to be okay now."

And then it all dissolves around me, and I'm falling.

Report of Missing Person

Name of Missing Person: Susannah Viola Wallin
Date of Birth: 02/16/1995
Name of Person Making Report: Maximilian Lucas Wallin
Relationship to Missing Person: Sibling
Date of Report: 11/13/2023
Last Seen: 09/02/2023
Background: Susannah Viola Wallin is 28 years old, 5'10", and described by her brother as having an athletic build, blond hair, and blue eyes. She was last seen by her family on the evening of September 2, and is described by her brother as having been in a heightened state of emotion ("excited, almost manic").

According to her brother, Susannah had recently been broken up with by her fiancée, Linn Walsjö, and had made plans to get treatment at a therapeutic clinic by the name of Himlafall (located approx. five hours from Stockholm). This treatment was supposed to go on for a week.

According to her brother, Susannah never made contact upon returning home, and he states that he is not certain she ever came back from the clinic. Brother further states that he has made multiple attempts to contact the clinic in question, but that they have refused to answer any questions about his sister.

Maximilian Wallin claims to have made multiple ("dozens") attempts at contacting his sister, and says that he at first thought she might have been avoiding his calls but is now concerned she has gotten hurt or is being held by the clinic in question. As proof he offers that multiple of her bills have gone to collection and that, according to him, none of her friends have heard from her.

Addendum 11/14/2023: The Himlafall Clinic has been reached by phone and has confirmed that Susannah Viola Wallin left the clinic voluntarily on September 8.

Addendum 11/17/2023: Contact has been established with Susannah Viola Wallin upon attempt at speaking to her fiancée, Linn Walsjö. Visual confirmation of identity was made. Susannah expressed that she is in good health and that her brother is attempting to find her against her will, and further expressed her wish that no one is to be made aware of her location. Case is to be considered closed.

Chapter 50

"HEY, SWEETIE."

My body feels very far away. My eyelids are too heavy to lift; I don't want to open my eyes. There's pain there, somewhere far away, and I don't want it to get any closer. I just want there to be quiet. I just want to be left alone.

"Isobel, can you hear me?"

The voice is soft and sweet, but it can't trick me. I know better. Once I open my eyes, they will know I'm awake, and they will make me get up, and I'm so very tired.

So tired.

I try to say *I don't want to go to school, I don't feel well,* but my lips won't move the way I'm used to; instead, the words fracture in my mind, and I try to turn my face away.

"You have to wake up now, sweetheart. It's time."

"I . . . I c-can't . . ."

My lips feel strange. Dry and stretched and numb.

I want to roll over and pull the covers over my head, but I can't. I'm not lying down. I'm sitting.

Why am I not lying down?

There are memories trying to reach me, but when I grasp for them, they scatter. Like they are taunting me.

"Come on, now."

The voice isn't happy anymore.

A loud noise, and a sharp, stinging pain on the side of my face, and I have to open my eyes now.

It's very bright in here. Too bright. I recognize this place, but I can't remember where it is, and that makes me feel like crying.

There is a face in front of mine. It's smiling gently.

I know it, but I can't recall who it is. I only know it's someone who—someone who—

I open my mouth, but my throat is so dry, and I begin to cough.

"Here, honey." She hands me a glass of water, helps me wrap my hands around it. It's cold and smooth in my clumsy hands, but still, I manage to bring it to my lips and drink.

"Isn't that better?" She reaches up to push the hair out of my face. Her touch is very light, and my eyes droop closed again as I lean into the touch.

"I'm tired," I mutter.

"I know, honey," she says. "I know you are. It's the tranquilizer. You'll feel better soon."

"Where am I?" I search for her name, and when it comes back to me I feel a moment of triumph.

Anna.

I remember now.

When I try to say it out loud, it comes out slurred and slow, but she laughs. It's a very nice sound. High and bright.

"Yes!" she says. "Exactly. See, you're going to feel better soon. Drink some more water."

I force my eyes open again, and I see her get up to her feet and walk away, hear her steps receding.

There's someone else sitting there. I can see them, a shadow out of the corner of my eye. There's a sound coming from them. Groaning, or sobbing.

But I can't see them. I can't even turn and look.

God, my head is pounding. There's pain everywhere. In my face, in my feet, in my shoulder. My body doesn't feel like it belongs to me; I'm hunched, and when I try to sit up, I almost slide off the chair.

"Hey, now, Isobel," comes Anna's voice again. "Take it very easy, sweetie, okay? You're going to feel a little woozy for a while. That's normal, it's nothing to be scared of, but try not to move around too much."

"Okay," I whisper, and I try to drink from the glass again. I spill down my shirt, and it should embarrass me, but I am so thirsty, and so tired, that I can't be bothered to care.

Anna—her name is Anna, but who is she?—comes back into my view, pulls a blanket back up around my shoulders.

"There." She smooths it down. "You got very cold out there. I don't want you to get sick."

It dawns on me that I do feel cold. Or, not exactly; it feels like I have been cold, or I used to be cold.

I try to look up and look around, but my head is too heavy, or maybe my neck is too weak. The room is bright and warm. There's a sound, coming from somewhere, a soft pattering of something, but otherwise it's quiet.

Am I sick? Is this a hospital?

Maybe. I can't remember.

When I manage to tilt my head, I see a window to my right. The outside is cloudy and gray, and I see a dark mass of water beyond it.

It makes something stir in my mind.

A flashing image. A pond. Water, cold water everywhere, and fear, and a face. Pale and perfect but . . . wrong.

A word comes to me.

"Himlafall. I'm at . . . Himlafall."

It's no more than a whisper, but it feels right.

I'm at the Himlafall Clinic. Yes. I was going to do something. It was very important.

But I can't remember what it was.

My head rolls over to the other side, and now I can see more: a couch opposite me, and a desk, and someone sitting in a chair. No, she isn't sitting; she's tied to the chair, and her eyes are wide and unblinking, full of tears, and there is a gag in her mouth, white fabric stained with dried blood, and the sight of it makes me start to dry heave.

Something is wrong.

The electricity was out. How did it come back on?

"Hey, hey." Anna comes back to me, quick and swift like an angel. "Just breathe. You're a little nauseous, that's normal, but you're going to be fine."

I feel her hand against my stomach.

"Breathe all the way down into your stomach. There you go, as deep as you can."

My body stills again, and my face feels wet.

"It's okay." Anna laughs again. "It's all okay, sweetie. You don't have to be scared. You're going to feel like yourself very soon, all right? And everything is going to be just fine."

"What happened?" I manage to say. It's slurred, but clearer than it was, and I take some perverse pride in that.

Anna's hand disappears from my stomach. She wipes the tears from my cheeks very softly, like a mother.

Like my mother, when I was very little.

"I'm so sorry I had to lie to you." Her face contorts. "I had to set everything up, you see. I had to make sure nothing would ruin it."

When I look over at the woman in the chair, her name comes back to me, too. And her face, not bloody and terrified like it is now, but calm, and strong, and intimidating.

Martina. That's Dr. Martina.

Where is Armin? Armin was here. Where is he?

Anna straightens up again, and she clasps her hands in front of her, and when she smiles, it lights up her whole face.

"You know, at first I was just going to leave you there with the others," she tells me. "But then I thought better of it. You deserve to be here, too."

"What?" I try to say, but other memories are reappearing now, muddled and confused.

Rain, and cold, and fear.

I was running. We were all running. We were trying to get away, because—because—

Anna's smile grows wider.

So many teeth.

"When I found out about you, I actually thought about just telling you," she muses. "Maybe I should have. I should have trusted you. But I was scared, you see. I was worried it would all go wrong."

"You're . . ." I blink, hard, as she turns double for a second.

She turns and walks away, over to the desk.

The glass of water slips out of my hands and tumbles onto the floor, icy cold water spilling over my feet.

She stands behind Martina and looks down at her.

Her face twists into cruelty.

I hear Martina trying to scream behind the gag. A muffled, pathetic sound.

I have to do something. What is it I'm supposed to do?

Anna looks over at me, and there's a spark in her eyes. Like we're sharing a private laugh, she and I.

"What do you think, Isobel?" Her voice a coquettish joke. "Because I think it's time to start the show."

She doesn't wait for me to respond. Instead, she reaches down and pulls the gag out of Martina's mouth.

"Time for your therapy, Doctor," she spits, and as Martina begins to scream, it all comes back to me in a crushing, all-consuming wave.

Chapter 51

Anna slaps Martina hard in the face, and Martina yelps, an instinctive sound of pain, and begins to cry.

"Stop," I try to say, but it just comes out as a croaking sound.

It feels like a nightmare, running from a monster with the air thick as syrup, screaming without a voice.

Martina's head has fallen forward. Anna is staring at her, unmitigated hatred on her face.

"Come on, Doctor," she says, her voice a parody of the syrupy-sweet tone she's been speaking in so far. "Don't be like that."

She grabs Martina's soaked hair and tugs at it, so hard it brings a groan from my throat, and Martina's head snaps back, her eyes wide in fear.

"Please," I hear Martina try to whisper. "Stop."

"Good girl!" Anna coos. "Look at that. I knew I could get you to pay attention."

She reaches down and tugs at the rope tying Martina to the chair. It's thin twine, and I can see it cutting painfully into her skin, digging welts into her arms.

"All good?" Anna asks her. "Comfortable?" The smile on her face isn't a smile at all. It's what children see in the dark.

"Please, Anna," Martina whispers. Her lips are swollen and bruised.

Anna walks around the desk, slowly, and as she reaches Martina's chair, she shoots me a conspiratorial little glance.

A wink of a smile.

Then she sits down, and she clasps her hands together in front of her, in a pitch-perfect imitation of Martina herself.

"So, Martina," she says. "Are you ready to begin your session?"

"Why are you doing this?" Martina asks, and she begins to cry again.

Anna pauses. Her eyes linger on Martina, lit with a strange, glowing joy; she's drinking her in, this broken vessel of a woman.

Then she sighs, and she shakes her head. Her blond hair, now dry, dances on her shoulders, the movement dizzying to my drunken eyes.

"Where to begin, Martina? You've ruined so many lives. And what's more, you take absolutely no responsibility for it."

She raises her eyebrows.

"Here at the Himlafall Clinic, we take responsibility very seriously. Remember?"

Her voice grows sharp, the last word like the crack of a whip.

"I don't know what you're talking about," Martina whispers. "Please, I'll do anything you want. Just let me go. You can have whatever you want. Just please, stop this."

Anna sighs, her shoulders rising and falling.

"See, this, right here, Martina, is the problem. You won't acknowledge your own fault in things. You prefer to just look away."

She looks over at me.

"Right, Isobel?"

She doesn't wait for me to respond.

I have to get up. I have to stop this. But I can't remember how. My body isn't mine; it won't respond to my commands.

"How about we start with one of your favorite exercises, *Doctor*?" Anna sneers. "How about we start with you telling me what you think you've done wrong."

Martina opens her mouth. Her lips are red with blood, in a horrific parody of the lipstick she usually wears.

"I don't know." Her voice is raw with tears and pain. "I don't know what you want me to say."

Anna studies her, coolly and cruelly, savoring the moment.

"Doctor," she then says, ever so softly. "I want you to understand what you've done. That's all. I want you to acknowledge the damage you've done."

Martina stares helplessly at her. I see her fingers flexing at her sides, swollen and useless; her back bent, her chin quivering.

"I just wanted to help people." Tears and blood are dripping off her face.

"BULLSHIT!" Anna screams at her, making her jump.

Anna has sprung up from her chair, and she's breathing hard, chest pumping, teeth bared.

"Bullshit," she repeats in a lower tone of voice.

A vein is pulsing in her forehead.

"You don't want to help people," she continues. "You just want to help yourself. You want to take people's money, and you want to take their love, and you want to take their lives away from them. You twist them, and you gaslight them, and you distort the truth. You're *poison*, Martina. You poison people. You're a toxic narcissist, and the truly disgusting thing is that you don't even realize it."

By the end, her voice has grown soft and smooth as silk. She's almost purring.

"Ask Isobel." She indicates me with a slight tilt of her head. "I heard her talking on the phone. She understands it. She sees you for what you really are."

She looks over at me, something like pride in her eyes.

"I heard you talking to your friend. Saying all the things I had felt for so long." Her eyes fill with tears.

"I almost gave up and left, you know." She puts her hand over her heart. "Especially when you asked about me. I got scared. Thought you might be a cop, or a private investigator, or something. Come looking for me. That's why I wrote that stupid note. I'm sorry about that, by the way, but I freaked out.

"But then, when I heard you talking to him, saying all that about Dr. Martina . . . I knew I was right. I knew I had to keep going."

"No." I shake my head, "I didn't—"

"You did," Anna insists. "Please, Isobel. You have to learn to receive praise and affection when it's given."

"I swear . . ." Martina's voice wobbles. "I swear I never meant to hurt anyone. I was doing my best. I was just trying to do—I was just trying to help people see themselves and their lives for what they really are. The way I wish someone had helped me." She's sobbing.

"Maybe I did it wrong, maybe I made mistakes, but I never wanted to hurt anyone," she weeps. "I care about my patients. I care about all of them."

"Well." Anna reaches over the desk and grabs ahold of Martina's chin with long, elegant fingers. She tilts it upward, and she does it carefully, so she can look into Martina's eyes.

"In that case," she says, "how come you didn't recognize me when I came back, Doctor?"

Martina is staring back into her eyes, hypnotized.

"I did," she tries to say. "Of course I did. I was so . . . proud of the progress you'd made."

Anna stills. She looks at Martina. Searching.

And then her grip grows stronger, and Martina groans in pain.

"No." Anna's words are barely more than a breath. "No, you didn't. I know you didn't." She smiles.

"Because that other fucking hack of a doctor you had working here told me I'd never be allowed back in here."

Anna lets go of Martina's chin, wrenching her head to the side and making her cry out.

"I didn't really think it would work, you know," she notes, almost as if to herself. "I changed my hair, dyed my eyebrows, but I have to admit there was a part of me that really thought you'd know it was me. I thought you would see right through me. Because you *see people*, right? That's your whole thing. I think a part of me was actually hoping you would. Because at least it would prove that I was someone to you. Even if that someone was not welcome here."

Anna's mouth twists, and I see her eyes filling with tears.

"But I wasn't, was I? I was no one. You didn't even care enough to read my patient file after I left. I just told you I'd been here, gone through your program, and you accepted it. I quoted your stupid fucking books back to you, and you ate it up." She blinks rapidly. "All I ever wanted was for you to help me. I thought you would fix it. You told me you could fix it. You made me feel like you could understand. I wrote you messages, and you told me to come here. You told me you'd help me. And I paid all that money, and I came to your little retreat, and you *weren't even here*! I wrote you on Instagram and told you I was coming, and you didn't even answer it! You didn't *care*!"

I try to get up off the couch, but I fall onto the floor, banging my knees and biting my tongue. When I look up, Anna is staring at me, her eyebrows raised in vague distaste.

"Isobel, you're going to have to wait your turn." She's mocking me, but there is something darker underneath her derisive tone.

Then she opens the desk drawer and pulls something out. She snaps her fingers at Martina.

"Hey. HEY! Look at me!"

Martina looks up.

Anna holds the file up next to her face.

"Recognize this?" She smiles, as though posing for a picture. "It's mine! It's my patient file from last year! Took me a couple of weeks, but I finally found it a few days ago. At first I was just trying to do . . . well, exactly what Isobel over there was doing, actually. I was trying to find proof of what you're doing here. How you're harming people."

Her smile hardens until it's no more than a mask.

"But once I read what was in it, I realized it wouldn't be enough," she says, in a strange, strangled monotone.

She puts the folder down on the desk and opens it.

"Let's read it. Shall we?"

Martina doesn't respond.

Anna licks her finger and picks up the first paper.

"Here we go," she says. "Patient: Susannah Wallin."

Nina Sundin
Willmar Way 14
119 08
Stockholm

I know where you live, you fucking cunt.
You ruined my life.
I will come for you. You won't know when.
You ruined my life and you are going to pay.
I see you through your window sometimes.
I wonder if you can feel me looking?
One day, very soon, you will turn around and I will be there.
I'll be waiting for you.

Chapter 52

"SUSANNAH?" I REPEAT.

Susannah. Anna.

I remember the pictures I found. The teenager, smiling with her mouth full of braces; the young woman with the long, expertly curled lengths of hair, the face plastered in makeup.

She looked like anyone else. Like a thousand girls walking the streets of Stockholm, or London, or New York. Young and blond and beautiful in a way that would never stick with you.

I didn't look for her here. I didn't see her face in Anna. I thought Susannah was long gone, her body buried somewhere deep in the woods. I never expected her to be behind the reception at Himlafall.

Waiting. Watching. Biding her time.

When I asked Anna if she had heard about Susannah, she froze, for just a second.

Not because she didn't recognize the name, but because she did.

Because she thought, for a moment, that I might know her. Recognize her.

That wasn't confusion I saw on her face; it was relief, when it dawned on her that I didn't know.

And I told Belinda that Susannah Wallin had recommended Himlafall; she seemed upset.

Not because Susannah Wallin had gone missing in the woods. Not because she had been told of some grand conspiracy.

It was because she thought it strange that I had named her coworker, seemingly without recognizing her.

She must have asked Anna about it. Asked Susannah. And Susannah told her it was a lie, or a mistake. And so Belinda thought to suspect me; not because Himlafall is a cult, not because there were secrets she didn't want me to find, but because she thought it was a strange lie to tell. That I might have some unhealthy fixation on one of the caretakers.

Tendency to lie for attention. Keep away from Anna.

The taste of bile fills my mouth.

I was wrong. I got it all so wrong.

Anna—Susannah—has begun reading from her file.

"Patient presents as well-mannered and empathetic. She talks about her former fiancée"—Anna chokes up on this word, then clears her throat and continues talking—"with obvious warmth, and says her goal is to get back together with the fiancée in question. Patient needs adjusting of goals, but in general appears well-adjusted, though in obvious distress."

Anna pauses.

"That was your bitch of an employee, by the way," she notes to Dr. Martina. "Dr. Nina." She breathes out hard, through her nostrils.

"Do you know what it feels like to take all your life savings, every penny you've got, and pay them to you, and drive five hours north to go to your stupid fucking treatment clinic, thinking that you're going to be there—thinking the person who's taught me so much, the person who's kept me going through hard times, the person who responded to every DM I wrote, even late at night, when I thought about *killing* myself—is going to be there to help you, only to be met with Dr. *fucking* Nina?!"

Her voice is climbing, but she stops herself, takes a deep breath, and turns to me, in a cutesy little aside.

"I don't know if you've met Dr. Nina, Isobel, but she's a dried-up old bitch. I think she might be a psychopath, honestly. Says something about this one's hiring policies."

She laughs, a high, girlish sound.

"Then again, maybe I should be grateful for that." She turns back, and the smile she gives Martina is almost warm. "If you'd been more diligent about who you hired, I never would have had this opportunity!"

She stops and frowns.

"But, then again, if you'd been better at your goddamned job, I wouldn't have had to do this in the first place. Catch-twenty-two, I guess. Or maybe it's an ouroboros? I'm not sure."

She shrugs.

"Anyway," she says. "Let's jump forward."

She flips a few pages.

I see her eyelid twitching, see her biting down, hard, her jaw tensing.

"This is the good part," she notes, to me. The audience. "You've got to listen to this."

She raises her voice again.

"Patient shows low receptiveness to challenges to her world view." Her voice grows lower, more gritted. "Patient describes previous relationship patterns that are clearly abusive in nature but refuses to acknowledge them as such. When given even mild pushback on her version of events, patient reacts with alternating self-victimization and overt aggression."

She stares down on the page for a few seconds. I can see the paper shaking. Her nostrils are flaring.

But when she turns back to Martina, her voice is calm.

"*Self-victimization*," she says. "I came here to get help. I was in *pain*. The love of my life had just broken my heart. I trusted you. And instead, I got attacked, over and over again, by some fucking *nobody*. Someone who was only here because you were too busy taking cutesy pictures for Instagram and doing interviews down in Stockholm to do your job."

"I'm sorry," Martina whispers, but Anna shakes her head. The paper crumples in her hand.

"That's not good enough, Doctor," she says. "You know what your Dr. Nina told me when I said that I couldn't understand why Linn had left me?"

She waits. She waits until Martina says:

"I don't know."

"She said *Actions have consequences*." Anna smiles, teeth gritted.

"Actions have consequences," she repeats. "Like it was all my fault. Like I had done it to myself."

She slams the folder down onto the desk, and Martina shakes her head.

"I wouldn't have said that to you," she says. "I'm sorry, but I didn't—"

"But you *weren't here*, were you?!" Anna yells at her. "You weren't fucking here! You weren't here when I needed you! *None of it* would have happened if you had just been here like you promised! It's all on you! All of it is your fault!"

I try to get back up on my feet, grab onto the armchair and pull myself up, slowly, because I have to put an end to it. I have to stop it, somehow, have to do something, have to wake up, have to move, have to act, have to, have to.

Anna falls quiet, and she stares down at Martina.

"You made me do this." She is suddenly terrifyingly calm. "You made me do all of it. I never wanted any of this. I just wanted Linn to take me back. I just wanted her to hear me out."

She turns away for a moment, and I see her pressing a hand to her face.

I manage to get up into the armchair, prop myself up, but my knees want to give way, my head swimming.

"Anna," I try to speak. "Susannah. It's okay. I get why you're angry. You have every right to be."

If I can just get through to her, if I can just calm her down . . . she thinks I'm on her side, so let her think I'm on her side.

Anna shakes her head.

"You don't understand, Isobel." When she turns around, her eyes are red. "You don't know what it is to love someone so much you can't live without them. I couldn't live without her. She was my everything. She was my soulmate. I'm not perfect, but she wasn't, either. We fought. But couples fight. I know we could have made it. She overreacted. I knew that if I could just make Linn listen, if I could just make her hear me out . . . I thought *she* would help me." She spits out the *she*.

"It must have been horrible." I'm swaying slightly. "You must have felt . . . so alone."

Anna swallows, and she nods.

"I did. I really did." Her voice breaks. "I never meant to hurt her. She just made me so angry sometimes. But people get angry. Everyone gets angry sometimes. It's normal. I tried to explain it to her, over and over again. I tried to explain to her that if she would just be a little bit careful, if she would just listen to me more, I wouldn't get so mad. I only got mad because I loved her. I'm a passionate person. That's why she loved me."

My knees are shaking.

"Maybe . . ." I try. "Maybe you can tell her that now. Maybe she'll want to talk to you. Martina can help you. We can call her now. Right, Doctor? You can coach Anna on what to say so that . . . Linn . . . will listen."

Martina looks over at me at the sound of her name, gray-faced and terrified, but then she swallows and nods.

"Yes," she croaks. "Yes, of course."

Anna's features contort, rage and sorrow battling on her face.

"No." A sigh, searingly quiet. "No, it's too late now."

She turns away.

"I didn't mean to."

I can barely hear her.

It's working. I'm calming her down. I can still put an end to this. I can get her to let us both go.

"You loved her." I have to get through to her. "Martina hurt you. She abandoned you. She shouldn't have made you think she was your friend. It was wrong. But you don't have to prove anything to her. You can just go. Move on with your life. You don't want to hurt anyone."

It's the wrong thing. I always say the wrong thing in the end.

Anna turns around. Her eyes are blazing.

"You're right. I didn't."

Linn.

Her palms were sweaty, her eyes aching from staring at the screen. The comments rolling in were making her feel simultaneously stronger and weaker.

Strangers, on the other side of the world, giving her advice, as though it were all so easy; as though a whole person, two whole people, could be distilled down to a few easy sentences, a few easy steps to follow.

Some part of her was angry with them, for not knowing her very pain; for not understanding how very scared and lonely she was without Susannah, how utterly unmoored. None of them could know the thousands of lovely little moments, the long, slow mornings in bed they had spent together, the way Susannah used to kiss her eyelids and tap out love *in Morse code on her naked hip.*

Some other part of her, a stronger, better part, probably, knew that they were right. Knew that a thousand good moments couldn't make up for how small and worthless she had felt toward the end. That part was what had led her to post her innermost secrets anonymously on the internet for strangers to see, in the hope that she could make herself listen.

That part knew she had to stay strong. Had to shut Susannah out of her life, once and for all. Had to forget how good Susannah could make her feel, and remember the feeling of a lip splitting under an open palm. The bone-deep shock of staring into her fiancée's eyes and realizing there was nothing there but contempt.

Linn looked at the little Smurf clock by the computer. Susannah had said she'd stop by at 8 PM. The round, bright blue clockface showed that it was three minutes till.

Her stomach clenched.

Linn leaned back in the ergonomic office chair she'd bought herself as a present a few weeks ago and closed her eyes.

After this, it will be over, *she told herself.*

It should have made her feel better. So why did it make her want to cry?

Susannah had asked for a good ending. She'd said that they had loved each other deeply, and that they owed each other closure.

Susannah loved that word. Closure. *During the course of their relationship, Linn had come to learn a lot about what Susannah loved and didn't love.*

She loved what she called good communication, *which meant they had to talk for hours about what Linn had done or not done to upset Susannah, which almost always ended in Linn crying and begging for forgiveness.*

She loved working on herself, and on her trauma. And on Linn, and what she called Linn's trauma. *She always liked to call back to her own trauma, when Linn tried to push back on something, and she liked to refer back to Linn's upbringing to explain why Linn was so* emotionally stunted.

She loved self-help books, especially those written by psychologists. More than anyone, she loved Dr. Martina Hastings, who she called her guru. *A few months before Linn had broken off their engagement, she'd even suggested they go to Dr. Hastings's therapeutic retreat together. To work on their communication. Or, more accurately, Linn's communication.*

She didn't love the way Linn wore her hair. Or the way Linn talked to her. Or to other people. Or the fact that Linn preferred to snack during the workday, rather than eat big, sturdy meals, a habit Susannah insisted would disrupt her body's natural rhythm.

She didn't love Linn's collection of Smurf-themed kitsch, which she called childish, or Linn's job, or the way Linn had decorated her apartment. A few months in, she had made Linn get rid of the teddy bear she'd had since she was a kid. She had called it infantile, and said it was a sign of regressive thinking.

Linn missed that teddy bear now. She missed it every night, as she was trying to go to sleep, trying not to mind the emptiness of the bed. Trying not to cry into the pillow. Trying not to miss Susannah.

The doorbell rang. Linn's eyes flew open.

She felt a surge of excitement. Or maybe fear.

Nausea swirled in her stomach, and for a moment, she was overtaken by an urge to ignore it. To stick her fingers in her ears like a kid and wait until the sound went away.

Knowing Susannah, it might take hours.

The comments were still staring at her from the computer screen.

Surely, she could do this. She had already gathered Susannah's things in a little box, so it would be easy to take with her.

Maybe, just maybe, it could be okay. Maybe Susannah was right.

Maybe just saying goodbye could finally sate that aching loneliness, that feeling of not being quite whole, not being quite enough, that had been haunting her ever since she gave Susannah the ring back.

Linn stood up from the chair. The doorbell rang again, a short, sharp, insistent sound that made her head hurt. She walked out of the office, into the living room, up to the front door.

It was like she could feel Susannah, on the other side of the thick wooden door. The heat of her. Her scent still seemed to invade every corner of the apartment; Linn didn't know if it was really there, or if she was imagining it. Olfactory haunting.

"Baby?"

She could hear Susannah pleading.

Last time she had come, she had been banging on the door. Screaming. Angry.

She didn't sound angry now.

"Please, baby, open the door."

She sounded like herself again; like the woman Linn had fallen in love with. The woman she had seen less and less of, as time had gone on.

"I just want to talk. I'll leave if you ask me to leave. I just want to see you, one last time."

Linn's eyes were stinging.

She had always been able to rely on her brain. When she had fallen short in other areas, her intelligence had been enough to get her through.

A smart girl. That's how people thought of her. Never quite funny enough, never quite charming enough, but sharp.

Why was it, then, that Susannah made her feel so unsure?

Linn stared at the lock. It looked a thousand miles away.

"I love you." Susannah's voice sounded choked, and the pain in it caused Linn to want to weep.

She saw herself reaching out, like in a dream, as though someone else were controlling her hand. Saw her own fingers close around the lock and turn it.

The clicking seemed to stop the world.

Maybe a second passed. Maybe an hour. Linn felt like she couldn't move.

Then she saw the door handle twisting down, and the door slowly opening.

Susannah looked beautiful. She always did. The first time Linn saw her, a thought had struck her, as if not her own: She is like the moon.

Pale, and luminous, and perfect.

Susannah's face broke out in a smile so wide it must hurt.

"Hi, sweetie."

She stepped in through the door, and for a moment, it was like time travel; like they were in the Before, when none of the bad things had yet happened, when Susannah had never looked at her with anything but what felt like pure adoration. When Linn had never been afraid of her.

Susannah reached for her, but a little voice, far back in Linn's mind, whispered:

No.

It almost sounded like her mother's voice, the way she remembered it.

Linn found her voice again.

"I put your things in a box."

She thought that she sounded small, and weak. Why would anyone ever listen to her?

And, indeed, Susannah didn't.

Instead, she closed the door behind her, like she had every right to. Like she belonged there.

"I think you should take your things and go." Linn was whispering, and it hurt to say it, and it frightened her, too. Enough that she looked down on the floor.

"Come on, baby. We're not in a hurry." Susannah was using her affectionate voice, the one that seemed to imply that Linn was being silly, that she was causing trouble, but that Susannah was willing to put up with it.

It would have been so easy to give in. Everything in her body was straining toward Susannah.

But that little voice, the same one that had made her post to that forum, the same one that had made her give the ring back, the same one that kept telling Susannah to go even as Linn's blood was dripping onto the black-and-white tile in the kitchen and Susannah looked as though she might do something far worse than slap her, wouldn't let her give in.

"No," Linn said. "You can take your things, and we can say goodbye. But then I want you to leave."

The silence fell like thunder between them.

"You're not scared of me," Susannah said. Like a question. Like a command. "Jesus, Linn. For fuck's sake."

Linn flinched.

"Come on,*" Susannah said, raising her voice. "What do you think is going to happen? What, you think I'm going to hit you? Is that really the kind of person you think I am?"*

"No." But she couldn't keep herself from shrinking back, the memory of the pain and the shock still vivid in her mind.

Susannah shifted in an instant. She'd always had that ability.

"You hate me," Susannah spit out. "Is that it? You hate me now. I thought you loved me, but I guess you think I'm just fucking trash."

"I don't." Linn didn't want to play this game; didn't want to reassure Susannah, didn't want to keep bending until she broke.

"But you have to go. You said you'd leave if I asked you to leave. And I'm . . . asking you."

When she looked up, Susannah's eyes were huge, brimming with tears, making Linn's whole body ache.

But then her arm shot out, and she pushed Linn in the chest.

It hurt, hurt worse than it should have, and it knocked the air out of her; she almost fell, stumbled backward over the cast-iron shoe stand Susannah had insisted on buying, but managed to catch herself on the door to the closet and stay upright.

She gasped for air as Susannah grabbed her arm and hauled her up. She tried to cry out, but she couldn't breathe, and all that came out was a pathetic gasp.

Susannah shook her by the arm, making it feel like the arm would tear from its socket, and Linn moaned in pain.

"I'm not going anywhere until you talk to me!" Susannah wasn't yelling; she was talking normally, like they were just having a conversation, but her eyes were blazing black, her pupils fully dilated, and this was worse than last time, so much worse.

"Fine," Linn managed to gasp out. "I'm sorry."

She just had to calm her, like she had a thousand times before. All she had to do was buy some time.

This had been a mistake. But this time, she would learn. She wouldn't make this mistake again. She would protect herself.

Susannah let go of her arm, and Linn pulled it to her, massaging it; Susannah's lips twitched as she looked at Linn.

Like she was fighting a smile.

And for the first time, Linn felt a spark of anger.

That little voice again.

This is not right.

I should call the police.

Linn was going to lie. Make up some story. But she had never been a very good liar.

She had never had cause to be, before Susannah.

Susannah saw something in her face. Linn didn't know what. But she saw her own feeling mirrored in Susannah's eyes, saw the rage returning, so Linn turned and ran.

Ran toward the office. Ran toward the phone.

She only made it a step before a hand got ahold of her hair and tugged, tugged backward, so hard she tasted blood, so hard she felt her scalp lifting from her skull.

And she lost her balance, and she fell.

For a moment, she was flying. Floating in the air. A singular eternity.

The knowledge ringing clearly within, finally.

This is not what love feels like.

And then she was flying no longer.

She heard the crunching of her skull as it struck the cast-iron shoe stand before she felt it.

And then she was on the floor, and she couldn't move. She knew she had to move, but she couldn't feel her hands. Or her feet.

Or anything at all.

"Linn? Linn? You're okay, baby, you're okay, I didn't mean to. It wasn't my fault, you shouldn't have run like that, I got startled. I didn't mean to,

it was an accident. You're going to be fine, okay? Can you get up? You have to get up, baby. Please. Come on."

The voice dissolved into a buzzing sound, and then she couldn't hear anything at all anymore.

For a moment, it was a relief.

And then that, too, was nothing.

Chapter 53

"I TRIED TO HELP HER." ANNA IS CRYING, HER EYES WIDE OPEN. "I tried, but it was too late. It was an accident. But I knew no one would believe me. I didn't mean to do it, but no one ever believes me. No one ever listens."

"I can listen." I'm grasping for something to hold on to, something to hold me upright.

Anna turns back to Martina.

"Do you know how long I stayed in that apartment with her?" she asks her. "With her body? Six months. That's how much I loved her. I laid her in the bathtub and covered her with charcoal powder so that she wouldn't smell. I sat there, and I talked to her. Every day. That is love." Her voice is thick.

"You might not have believed me, your little doctor friend might not have believed me, but I loved her." She wipes her upper lip, a ragged sob making her shake.

"I would have stayed there and died with her," she continues, "but I knew I had to put an end to you. To all of this. I knew I couldn't let you hurt any more people, the way you hurt me. The way you hurt Linn. I tried to report you, but those *fuckers* didn't even do anything."

For a moment, she's silent, and then she grabs one of the awards from Martina's desk and throws it at the wall. I let out a scream, and I duck, the world still spinning around me; when I straighten, on unsure feet, Anna is panting, her cheeks blossoming with color.

She stills, and strokes her hair behind both ears. When she speaks again, her voice is calmer. Surer.

"I tried to tell everyone. The ethics board. Journalists. Your loyal fans. But no one would listen. Because that's how it is with manipulative people. You trick everyone, just like you tricked me. I knew no one would believe me without proof."

She smiles, and there's a terrifying pride in her smile, the way her skin is stretching, the way her cheeks are dimpling.

"So I came here to get proof."

Anna turns to me.

"Just like you did, Isobel." True warmth, permeating her words. "And we're going to get it now, together. We're going to tell the whole world what happened here. What she did."

I know I shouldn't. I'm too weak still. I should just go along with it and not provoke her.

But I can't. I have to know. If nothing else, I have to know.

"But what about Sandra?" Her name should be a ravaged wound in my mouth, but instead, even after everything, it is a comfort. As if just by saying it, I can conjure her in here.

Sandra, who would have known what to do.

Anna's face falls for a moment, as though her mask has slipped. Under it is something naked and gaping.

"I didn't . . ." She shakes her head, and her lower lip trembles. She puts a hand up to her sternum.

"It wasn't on purpose. It wasn't supposed to happen." She chews on her lip, looking down, and then asks, in a small voice:

"Did you see her?"

"Yes." And, oh, how it hurts.

"I'm sorry." She sounds almost . . . tetchy. Like a child caught doing something bad. It leaves a sour taste in my mouth.

"She shouldn't have been here. It wasn't . . . No one else recognized me. No one was supposed to recognize me. But she did. She saw me, and she asked me what I was doing here, and she got upset. She said I wasn't supposed to be here."

For a moment, it's like Sandra is standing here, next to me. Clicking her tongue in that annoying way she always used to.

Bullshit, she'd say.

"I wasn't trying to hurt her." Anna's eyes are so round, and so innocent, that I can almost believe her. "She was coming to see you. I just . . . I had to keep her quiet. Until I was done. I tried to tell you, in the woods. I called your name. Didn't you hear me?"

Her voice, out there, in the darkness. *Isobel.*

"It wasn't my fault," Anna pleads. "You have to believe me. I never would have hurt you on purpose. I'm not like that. You know me. You *get* me. We want the same thing. Sandra wasn't my fault. It was . . ."

She looks down at Martina.

"It was your fault." Her face hardens. "None of this would have happened if not for you. You did all this. You did this to us. And you're going to admit to it, finally. You're going to admit to all of it."

Anna tugs at the drawer, and she pulls out a phone. Martina's phone.

She waves it in Martina's face, and then she smiles.

"We're going to take a little video. You're going to tell everyone what you did. I'll upload it to your social media. You're always going on about how honest you are, right? So it's time to live up to that. It's what you promised everyone, ever since the start. You always said honesty is the most important thing. So let's be honest."

Anna puts the phone down on the desk, and comes around to the front of it, a glint of silver in her hand.

It's one of the steak knives from the kitchen. Small, and lean, and sharp.

Martina starts begging: "No, no, no . . ."

"Calm down, for fuck's sake." Anna sounds almost bored now. "I'm going to cut you loose. It can't look like we're making you do something you don't want to do."

She gets down next to Martina, and when she's sitting there, looking up at Martina, there's something akin to tenderness on her face.

She pauses, and she reaches up with the hand holding the knife, Martina still as a statue, and my breath catches in my chest.

With her thumb, she wipes the tears away from under Martina's eyes.

"There." There is a loving smile in the corners of her lips. "All better."

The thin rope around Martina's right arm snaps, then around the left; she gasps in pain as the blood starts flowing back in, her fingers red and swollen, deep gouges in her arms on both sides.

"Perfect." Anna stands up and smooths back Martina's hair. There is greed in her eyes, in the way her fingers linger among the strands.

Like she wants to own her. Or be her.

Still.

Martina makes a slight movement, as though to get up from the chair, and Anna, quick as a snake, yanks ahold of her hair and snaps her head back.

She lingers there, her hold pulling Martina's head at an unnatural angle, gazing down into her eyes.

"I thought you were so much better than the rest of them," Anna mutters, her eyes glazed over. "I thought you understood me. I thought you would see me."

"I'm sorry," Martina says, her voice tight with the strain, her throat bulging. "I'm sorry, Anna. We can talk about it. We can fix this, I promise."

"I know." Anna looks over at the phone, but I can see her arms tensing, her grip on the braid tightening.

"I know you're hurting." Martina's voice is cracking. "I let you down, and I'm so sorry. I let everyone down. It's all my fault, I see that now."

I see Anna's grip loosening, just a little bit.

"You don't have to do this, Anna," Martina says. "You must be so tired. This is such a heavy burden. You've worked so hard. Aren't you tired?"

Despite it all, despite the pain and the drugs and the terror, I hear it there, a trace of that old power.

Anna's hand is still grasping the knife, but her grip is slackening, the knife dangling from her fingers.

"It's never too late, Anna," Martina says. "Not for me. Not for you. You deserve to be happy. Is this going to make you happy?"

Anna opens her mouth, just slightly; no words come over her lips.

"Let me help you," Martina says. "I can help you, Anna. Whatever you want, I'm here for you now. I failed you. I see that. I take responsibility for that. But I'm willing to work with you on that. I'm willing to put the work in and heal our relationship. If you are."

Anna takes a deep, shuddering breath. Her whole focus is on Martina.

I could run, now. While she's distracted. She wouldn't leave Martina to chase after me, I'm almost sure of it. I'm clumsy, but I'm better now than I was a few minutes ago. I might be able to make it out, across the parking lot, climb the fence.

It's what my father would have done.

"You can have everything you want," Martina says. "You can be anyone you want. If you just let us go."

I feel the shift in the room, like an electric charge.

Anna's eyes flash with anger, and she raises the knife, and I don't think. I don't let myself think.

I scream, as loud as I can, and I grab the heavy brass award, and I throw it at the window. It explodes into a million pieces, the crash deafening, and the flying glass and roaring wind shocks Anna into ducking, only for a second.

I don't think. There's no time.

I reach out for Martina, and I find that she's already sprung from her chair, and I grab her hand.

And we run.

Chapter 54

I'M BLEEDING. THE GLASS CUTS THROUGH MY SHOES, PIERCING into the soles of my feet, but I barely feel it.

The rain is beating against my face, the ground slipping under my feet.

I'm slow. Too slow, too clumsy.

But it's my only chance. Our only chance.

She's never going to let us out of here alive. None of us.

Martina's hand is pulling me along now. Somehow, she's gotten ahead of me. She's pulling me up the slope, across the gravel, and in the gray, dusky light, I can see the gates, and the car beyond it.

Freedom. Safety.

Is Armin still here? Or did she kill him, too? Did she kill all of them?

"COME ON!" Martina screams at me, and she tugs at my arm, and I run, run as hard as I can, because I have no other choice.

The rain is lighter now, the ground soft as mud, and I'm slipping, and there's blood in my eyes, blood from somewhere, something, stinging. The air feels like fire in my lungs. I'm gasping, running, and the gates are so very close now, only a few yards away, and we might make it, we might—

I don't see it. I hear the thud, and I see her falling.

Her grasp on my fingers disappears, and she falls, face forward, into the mud and the water and the gravel, her body limp. She doesn't try to catch herself.

I fall to my knees next to her. I try to tug at her, get her to her feet, and I'm screaming:

"Get up, get up, GET UP—"

Then I see the blood.

The rock hit her square in the back of the head. It's lying next to her head. The blood is trickling, oozing down the sides of her head, and she's so very still, and the scream that tears out of me this time is one of rage.

I turn around.

Anna is standing a few steps away, her chest heaving, her eyes blazing. Her hands are claws, her teeth bared.

In terror, and hopelessness, and madness, I laugh. I keep laughing, as I get to my feet, and stand over Martina.

"Still got your aim, I see," I say, because what else is there to say? "You should have gone with that softball scholarship, Susannah."

"Get away from her," Anna screams at me.

"No," I say. "You're not getting her."

Anna screams, wordlessly, in pure fury.

"I thought you were with me," she yells. "I thought you *understood*."

"I don't think anyone can understand you," I say back. "And even if I could, I wouldn't want to."

She lunges at me.

I'm too slow to move aside, and she catches me around the chest, raking her nails down the side of my face. I try to push her away, but she's too strong, and she pulls me to the ground.

I try to kick; I hit, pull, scratch, but she's stronger.

She puts her knee on my arm, her whole weight on it, and I yell as I feel the bone beginning to give. She grabs ahold of my head, lifting it and pounding it into the ground, making my head ring.

I don't know if I feel it cracking. My vision goes white for a moment, and when I come to, her face is very close to mine, her breath hot on my skin.

"You're just like the rest of them," she hisses. "All of you."

I try to wrench her off me, but her grip is too tight. I grasp with my free hand after something, anything, to hold on to, to pull myself away, but all I find is water. Water and gravel.

Her blood and tears are dripping onto my face, more intimate than a kiss.

"Say it's your fault," Anna orders me. "Say it, and I'll let you go. Say you're sorry."

She puts her hand on my throat, and she pushes, hard enough for my body to convulse, and then go limp.

"We can still do this," she whispers, and I think that she means it. "Just say you're sorry. We can take care of it together. I know you know what she is, too."

Her fingers are still resting, featherlight, against my throat, her nails pricking at my skin.

"Just say you understand," she pleads.

I feel something against my fingertips. Being pushed into my hand.

I inhale, and I see hope in her eyes. The beginnings of a trembling smile on her lips.

"You can't go around blaming people and hurting them, hoping you'll feel better, Susannah," I say, coughing. "That's not how it works."

The hope is extinguished and replaced with anger.

Her grip on my neck tightens again.

I close my fingers around the object in my hand, shut my eyes, and swing as hard as I can.

When the rock connects, I feel it all the way down my arm.

Anna slides off me, and I crawl away, releasing the rock and clutching at my throat, sobbing and retching. I grab her and turn her over, and I see the whites of her rolled-back eyes through her half-open eyelids, see the spot where the rock connected.

She's breathing, but it's faint.

Then I turn to Martina.

She's still lying on her stomach, but her face is turned to me. Her hand is stretched toward me, her fingers still flexed from having pushed the rock into my hand.

I lean over, and I pick it up.

It's one of the rocks with the inspirational quotes. Despite the blood covering it, I can still read the inscription.

All you need is within you.

Laughing, sobbing, I pull myself to my feet, and I turn and throw up into the gravel.

I guess, in the end, Dr. Martina really did give me the tools I needed.

Six Months Later

I'm woken by Armin's alarm going off. He's not in bed; I find him in the kitchen, drinking his cup of coffee with a straw, staring out the window at the bright fall day outside.

Most mornings, I make fun of him for that straw, and he responds by quoting countless studies showing it reduces staining; today will not be one such morning.

I sit down on the chair next to him, and he turns to me and smiles.

"Morning," he greets me. His cheeks are covered in stubble; he hasn't had time to shave yet.

I'm tempted to reach out and touch it, but I recognize the shadows under his eyes, the tense tilt to his mouth.

"Bad night?" I ask him.

He doesn't always like to be touched, after the nightmares. I asked him, once, what happens in those dreams; he just shook his head.

I understood. I have dreams too. In some of them, I'm back in that office, drugged and helpless; in some of them, I'm being chased through the woods.

But most of them are about him. About finding him unconscious by the pond, so still I thought he was dead, that Susannah had killed him, too.

In the nightmares, she did.

"Not the best," he admits. "But I've had worse."

I smile, and he reaches out and takes my hand, his fingers cool to the touch.

The sky outside is high and bright blue, the trees below aflame with autumn color. When I go over to the fridge, I see that he's already taken care of last night's dishes, and scrubbed down the counters as well. There's a pod already prepped for me in the Nespresso, and a clean cup waiting to receive the coffee.

"I was going to clean the kitchen," I tell him without turning around.

"Yeah, you always say that. I'll believe it when I see it."

"How am I going to learn if you always do it for me?" I ask him.

He snorts in response.

Once the coffee is done, I fill the rest of the cup with milk and sit back down next to him.

"Do you want to talk about it?" I ask him.

"Nah." Armin stirs his coffee with his straw. "It was the usual. It really wasn't that bad last night."

I know he's lying. I don't push it.

"When are you going into the office?" I ask him.

"Tenish," he responds. "Do you want me to drop you by your apartment?"

"That would be great. I need to pick up something to wear. I've got that lunch."

"You sure you don't just want to grab something from my closet?" Armin asks.

"Yeah, it'd be good for me to stop by home," I say. "Water my plant."

"That plant is plastic," Armin points out.

"Still," I respond. "He gets lonely."

"Mhm." He nods. "Don't want the plastic flower to feel neglected."

"Hey." I laugh. "Don't talk that way about Robert Plant. He's family."

Then I lean over, lingering and drawing in the smell of him before I kiss him softly. He tastes like coffee, and home. His fingers touch gently at the base of my neck, and I feel a quick frisson, my breath shortening and my lower stomach tightening.

When he pulls back, he's smiling. It's a special smile, one I've only gotten to know in the last few months, and I feel the same one on my own face.

"See you after work?" he asks me.

"You've got therapy," I point out.

"Fine," he agrees. "See you after therapy?"

"Sure. I'll cook something. What do you feel like eating?"

Armin gets up from the table, grabbing his own cup to put in the dishwasher.

"Anything, as long as you don't burn the coating off my nice frying pans," he says, and I yell after him:

"That was *one time*!"

As I put yesterday's clothes back on, quickly brushing my teeth while he's in the shower, I'm struck by the thought, as I am sometimes these days, out of nowhere, that we're not the same as we were.

I don't know if we would have gotten here had Himlafall not happened. That doesn't mean it was worth it.

I brought it up with Leyla on the phone the other day. She'd just dropped off Clara at her parents' house, and called me from the car on the way home.

"*Do you ever feel guilty when you feel happy?*" I asked her. I'd asked Katarina the same question a few days earlier over lunch.

"*Why should I feel guilty?*" she asked me back.

"*Because you met Clara at the scene of a massacre,*" I said. "*Because we're still here, and we get to be happy. At least sometimes.*"

"*You think too much,*" Leyla responded. "*That's your problem.*"

"*Yeah,*" I said. "*Maybe I should get treatment for that. Go away to a clinic somewhere.*"

We both laughed at that. A little bit too loudly.

When Armin comes out of the shower, I'm already done, sitting on the bed and taking in the sight of him as he gets dressed.

"Are you objectifying me?" He pulls a sweater-vest over his dress shirt.

"You'd think it would be impossible to objectify a man in a sweater vest," I say. "But yes."

"Good." Armin grabs his briefcase. "Let's go, before you get any ideas."

In the car on the way to my apartment, Armin clears his throat.

"Are you feeling okay about it?" he asks.

He doesn't need to clarify what he means.

I'm struck by the impulse to pretend, to put up a happy front, but instead I swallow it down and say:

"I don't know. Mixed emotions."

Armin nods as he stops for a red light.

"You said everyone really liked the piece, though. Even Pernilla's daughters."

Hearing her name is still difficult, but I nod.

"Yeah." I bite the inside of my cheek. "But still. I don't want it to seem like I'm . . . I don't know. I don't want it to seem like I'm profiting off a tragedy."

Armin remains quiet for a while, driving down the street, the white and terra-cotta facades of Stockholm passing on both sides of the car.

"It happened to you, too," he says finally. "And I think it's a story worth telling. But it's your decision."

He parks in front of my building, and before I get out of the car, I lean over and kiss him again, letting it linger, feeling my pulse slowing, beat by beat.

"Knock 'em dead," he calls after me when I step out onto the street. "Or don't, if you've changed your mind. Either way, I'm proud of you."

I smile. Despite the crisp October day, the sun still feels warm on my face.

My apartment smells empty after a few days away. There's a light coating of dust on the floor, but then again, that was there when I left, too.

I shower, and I put on the nice blazer I prepared for the meeting, and then, taking a deep breath, I open my laptop.

The document with my article is still open where I left it.

I haven't picked a title for it; nothing has felt right. I've tried everything from "Meditations on a Massacre," which was somehow both too pretentious and too callous, to "Irresponsible Therapeutic Practices Lead to Murder," which sounded too flat and impersonal.

My eyes go to the opening paragraph.

> After the events that took place at the now-closed Himlafall Clinic this past spring, it is hard to fathom how something that began with such good intentions could end in such a tragedy.

The Himlafall Clinic began as one woman's dream. Martina Hastings, who had been a practicing psychologist and psychiatrist with a PhD and three bestselling books behind her, wanted to build a place where women could come and heal from past romantic relationships, to give them a better chance at finding love in the future. It was a grand vision, and an attractive one, bolstered by Martina Hastings's millions of followers, something that, along with her professional and academic credentials, secured her the funding she needed almost immediately.

The Himlafall Clinic ran, seemingly successfully, for almost two years, before it all ended in tragedy, with five people dying violently. So what happened?

When news broke, the papers called Susannah Wallin a mentally disturbed woman who went on a killing spree. But that description is not only reductive but also untrue. Susannah Wallin's medical records showed no history of severe mental illness. Telling the story of the Himlafall Clinic as one of a mentally ill woman "snapping" and committing murder is one that is easy for most people to digest, but it distorts the actual truth of what happened by leaning into harmful stereotypes.

Susannah Wallin did not commit any of her violent actions in a psychotic state. While her murders may have been impulsive, the way she went about covering them up was not. Susannah Wallin impersonated her murdered ex-fiancée for nearly six months; she used her credit cards to buy food, bought charcoal powder in order to prevent the neighbors from smelling the decay, and accessed her phone and email account in order to resign, as Linn, from "her" job.

These actions cannot be explained away by calling Susannah Wallin "crazy." These actions were calculated and carried out over the course of many months. Calling Susannah Wallin crazy soothes us, because it is an easy answer to a difficult question.

The story of Susannah Wallin, Himlafall, and Martina Hastings is not one about mental illness. It is a story about mismanagement, abuse, and the things we are willing to overlook. It is the story about a driven woman who wanted to create a place for other women to heal but who failed to account for the people she could not help. It is the story about a woman who could not accept culpability for the violence she had enacted on others. It is the story of how our culture perpetuates the idea of women as harmless, thereby blinding us to the harm that all people are capable of doing.

But most of all, it is a story about the victims.

It's the story about Linn Walsjö, Susannah Wallin's ex-fiancée, who felt like she could tell no one in her life about the abuse she was suffering.

It's the story about Sandra Morel, who tried to stop Susannah and ended up bleeding out in her bed.

It's the story about Belinda Koskinen, who thought she was safe in her place of employment, and who was struck down by someone she considered a friend.

It's the story about Pernilla Boman, who came to Himlafall as a client and died from an accidental overdose of sleeping pills put in her tea by someone she thought was a trusted employee at a well-regarded psychological clinic.

And it's about Dr. Martina Hastings, who died not for her own numerous sins but for someone else's.

So where does it all begin?

It would be easy for me to say it began the day I, personally, walked through the gates of the Himlafall Clinic. That way, I can claim it ended when I climbed back over the gates and drove to get help. But the story didn't begin when I arrived, just as it didn't end when I left; it didn't end when the victims were buried, or when Susannah Wallin received her verdict of life in prison. The people who came through Himlafall, and their loved ones, are still having to live in the aftermath.

It begins, in this writer's opinion, with a vision. As described in Dr. Martina Hastings's bestselling book *Freud's Ex-Girlfriend*, it went something like this: "You should not have to apologize. You should not have to cower, or make yourself smaller. You should get to live unapologetically, without making excuses for who or what you are.

Any person who cannot give you that is denying you the fundamental right of any woman, or any person: self-actualization."

Susannah Wallin wanted to live unapologetically. And in the end, it cost five people their lives.

I stop reading, too consumed by the urge to edit and rewrite—it's too late for that now, and if they hate it, I just have to live with that—and I scroll back up to the top, to where the space for a headline is still empty.

I can't find a way to title it.

Maybe it will just have to stand as it is.

When I look at the time, the clock tells me it's time to go. It'll take twenty minutes to get to the *Stockholm Daily* offices, and my meeting is at noon.

I'm about to close my computer, but then I stop.

I hesitate, but then, at the very top, I write:

by Isobel Lindschold

I look at it. And I smile.

I always imagined that my first big article would be under the name my father ruined for us. The name I walked away from when I was sixteen years old. As a way to reclaim it, and reclaim what he took from me, and from us.

But he doesn't seem to matter so much anymore.

Acknowledgments

The idea for this book came to me when—how else?—I was scrolling on social media.

Before I became an author, I was studying to be a psychologist. I completed three years of university-level studies before my first novel was picked up for publishing, and I ended up taking a sabbatical, which is still, somehow, technically ongoing. (Nine years and counting!)

However, those years of working to be a clinical psychologist mean both that I have quite a bit of academic knowledge about the field of psychology and that most of my friends are working in the mental health profession.

All that to say that when the TikTok and Instagram psychologists suddenly started popping up in my feed, I was in equal parts fascinated and horrified.

Here were people presenting themselves as experts on the human mind, giving advice in the form of numbered lists, guaranteeing you long-lasting change with quick fixes. Here were filtered faces speaking with unearned confidence on how to diagnose the people in your life as psychopaths or narcissists. They were everywhere, hawking vitamins that promised to right your mind, selling ebooks teaching you how to spot so-called toxic people, and offering online courses on how to be happy.

Having both studied the fascinating, intricate, maddening subject of the human brain myself and undergone a total of more than nine years of therapy, I found it both abhorrent and fascinating. Because even with my background, I found myself getting sucked into it.

Don't we all want a quick fix for the maddening experience of being human? Aren't we all secretly wishing there was a pill we could take that would wipe all our sorrows away and make the weight of consciousness suddenly featherlight? I kept scrolling through all the videos promising me that if I only followed this one piece of advice, my life could be easy and free of friction, and I found myself wanting to believe.

Some of these social media psychologists are trying, in earnest, to help; some of them are trying to spread their knowledge in order to make it accessible to those for whom the barriers to accessing in-person therapy are simply too high. And some of them are simply trying to make money off the desperate. The frightening thing is that, from the other side of that screen, it can be impossible to tell the difference.

Dr. Martina Hastings is not real, but she is inspired by all of them. The sad thing is, if were she real, she would be far from the worst of her ilk.

All that being said, an idea is just an idea, and the road from that first spark of inspiration to finished book is a long, very fun, and absolutely infuriating one.

First of all, I want to thank my incredible editors Alexandra Sehulster and Ashley Quintana for believing in the idea when I first presented it and for helping me shape that first draft into a book I hope we can all be truly, wildly proud of. You helped me take a rough idea and turn it into something real and special, and I am so ridiculously grateful. Getting to work with you both is a true privilege.

I also have to extend my sincere thanks to my agent, Anna Frankl, who has been there with me every step of the way. I don't know where I would be without you, Anna—having an agent that both fights for you and believes in you is a gift, and I try to never take it for granted.

Thank you also to the whole team at Minotaur—the designer of the incredible cover, the marketing team, the audiobook team, and everyone who has been involved in taking the Word document on my sad, six-year-old Lenovo and turning it into a book. It always feels a little bit like magic to me, seeing it all come together, and none of it would be possible without all your hard work.

Thank you, also, to the booksellers and to the librarians. It was a school librarian who first introduced me, at the tender age of seven, to the wild and wonderful world of thrillers and horror; and it was a bookseller who suggested to me at age nine that anyone could be a writer if they really wanted to, even me. I am incredibly grateful for all that you do.

To my friends, who've sat with me through my whining and complaining about my objectively incredibly fun job, I owe you all a drink. But special thanks to Katie, my favorite reader, for taking the time out of your remarkably busy schedule to both read my first draft and give me thoughtful feedback. Having a friend who is not only willing to read my work but also an incredibly talented writer herself almost feels like cheating.

My cats, hellish little demons that they are, have done their best to distract me from my writing, and the book is all the better for it. Special thanks to Rizzmatizzle for stepping on my keyboard one August afternoon and deleting half a chapter. You were right, Rizzmatizzle, the writing in that section was quite pedestrian, and the rewrite is much tighter.

None of this would have been possible without my husband. Not only is Mark the person who first told me he thought I might be able to write directly in English, but he is the person who first said the words "break-up retreat." Thank god we're married, or I would have had to pay you royalties.

No one else has ever been as involved with or supportive of my writing. Thank you for believing in me; thank you for listening to me rant about my books; thank you for being with me. Getting to watch you read my new book at the end of the couch is the best feeling I have ever felt.

And, finally, to the mental health professionals, thank you. The work you do is so difficult, and so vitally important. I know firsthand how slow going and frustrating it can be. I know they tell you not to take the work home with you, as though that could ever be possible; I know how much of yourselves you put into the work.

You saved my life—and the lives of so many others I love.

Thank you for that.

About the Author

Elvira Glänte

Camilla Sten has been writing stories since she was a young girl. In 2019, Camilla published the now internationally acclaimed, hair-raising novel, *The Lost Village*. Rights for *The Lost Village* have been sold to nineteen territories around the world, including for film and TV. Her third novel for adults, *The Resting Place*, was one of Goodreads's Most Popular Horror Books of 2022, and the same year, Camilla was longlisted for the prestigious Viktor Crime Award in Germany. An ever-prolific author, Camilla has released the third part in her YA series and continues to write new thrillers.

Find her on Instagram: @AuthorCamillaSten.